The Shadow of Death

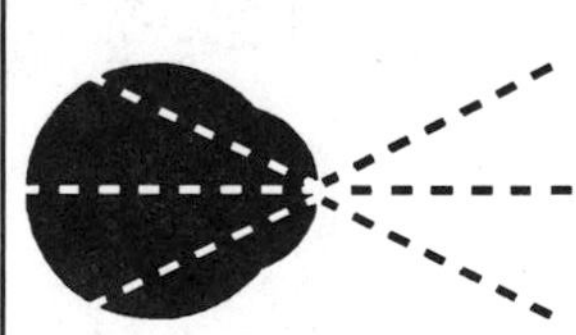

A SISTER AGATHA AND FATHER SELWYN MYSTERY

THE SHADOW OF DEATH

JANE WILLAN

WHEELER PUBLISHING
A part of Gale, a Cengage Company

Farmington Hills, Mich • San Francisco • New York • Waterville, Maine
Meriden, Conn • Mason, Ohio • Chicago

Wheeler Publishing, a part of Gale, a Cengage Company.

This is a work of fiction. All the names, characters, organizations, places, and events portrayed in this novel are either products of the author's imagination or used fictitiously. Any resemblance to real or actual events, locales, or persons, living or dead, is entirely coincidental.

Wheeler Publishing Large Print Cozy Mystery.
The text of this Large Print edition is unabridged.
Other aspects of the book may vary from the original edition.
Set in 16 pt. Plantin.

**LIBRARY OF CONGRESS CIP DATA ON FILE.
CATALOGUING IN PUBLICATION FOR THIS BOOK
IS AVAILABLE FROM THE LIBRARY OF CONGRESS**

ISBN-13: 978-1-4328-6671-6 (softcover alk. paper)

Published in 2019 by arrangement with The Quick Brown Fox & Company LLC

Printed in the United States of America
1 2 3 4 5 6 7 23 22 21 20 19

To Don, for his love and humor and patience and joy. And for always saying "keep writing."

One

Jacob Traherne, sexton at St. Anselm Church in the tiny North Wales village of Pryderi, slung his wet mop across the chancel floor and thought about rugby. First tenor for the North Wales Rugby Choir, he hummed through his solo piece for that night's opening playoff between the Ospreys and the Dragons. Gripping the mop in one hand, he raised his other hand like a priest blessing the congregation and belted out the first lines to the old Welsh hymn Cwm Rhondda.

> Guide me, O my great Redeemer,
> pilgrim through this barren land.

The powerful notes lingered above the empty pews. As he often told Father Selwyn, vicar at St. Anselm, a good game of rugby backed by the voices of a Welsh choir brought him closer to God than the Church in Wales ever could. He wanted tonight's solo to be perfect. His mother would be in the stands and Cwm Rhondda was her favorite hymn. Michael would be there too, which was almost as important.

The bell in the village clock tower chimed four times. Jacob had rolled out of bed while it was still pitch dark and pedaled his bike down the cobblestone streets of the silent village, arriving at St. Anselm well before dawn. You had to be early, he always said, if you worked for church people. He cleaned St. Anselm first, then hurried to Gwenafwy Abbey so he could mop, dust, and polish the chapel in plenty of time for Matins, morning prayer. By the time the sun rose above the tower of Pryderi Castle, the Anglican sisters at Gwenafwy would have already sung the Venite and be heading full blast into the Te Deum. The last thing you wanted to do was show up ready to clean and find the pews filled with nuns.

Sloshing his mop in the bucket of sudsy water, Jacob felt his cell phone vibrate. *A text from Reverend Mother.* A little early even for her. He glanced at the screen and felt his heart pound in his throat. The mop handle clattered onto the flagstones as he grabbed his coat off the front pew and ran down the center aisle of the old church, work boots pounding on the clean floor. It would take ten minutes on his bike to get to the Abbey. He could only pray it wouldn't be too late.

Two

Sister Agatha tried to recall Reverend Mother's homily at Matins that morning. It had really spoken to her at the time, as she sat in the chapel at Gwenafwy Abbey surrounded by the other sisters, so how could she have forgotten so quickly in the space of only two hours? Oh, yes, she thought to herself, Reverend Mother had pointed out that even Jesus took time to stop and smell the roses. That was why he went up into the hills so often to pray. Which begged the question, Sister Agatha thought, were there roses in first-century Palestine? Perhaps some equivalent. Cacti blossoms. Fig tree blooms. Oh, well, Reverend Mother's words at morning prayer might have inspired her two hours ago, but they weren't doing much for her now. She had far too much on her mind.

Striding down the cobblestone path from the Abbey kitchen to the cheese barn, production site of the Abbey's award-winning Heavenly Gouda, she pulled off the long white veil and scapular that all the sisters wore and ran her fingers through her short gray hair. She was determined to find out the meaning of the voice mail she'd overheard in the Abbey office just now. She paused for a moment to collect her thoughts and breathe deeply. The lilacs that bordered the path to the cheese barn were in full bloom. Could it be that Sister Callwen, Agatha's companion and confidant ever since their first days at Gwenafwy Abbey, was about to betray them all? Giving the veil a shake, she fitted it onto her head, smoothing her hair underneath and fastening the little Velcro strip in the back. Although Sister Agatha didn't like change, she had to admit that a bit of Velcro was certainly an improvement over straight pins for securing one's veil and scapular.

She wished she had never heard that voice mail.

She and Sister Callwen had arrived as new postulants on the same spring day four decades ago — each lugging a single suitcase and smiling nervously at the other young women, all of them ready to take vows in the Order of the Sacred Heart at Gwenafwy Abbey in the North Border Country. The eager young postulants had traveled from the far corners of Wales. They had said good-bye to family from bus stops in tiny Welsh villages snug in the shadows of castle ruins, stepped aboard trains pulling out of towns perched precipitously on steep-walled valleys, journeyed in from colliery towns still jagged with the remains of the slate mines.

Sister Agatha, however, had merely carried her suitcase down the winding dirt lane from her family's sheep farm. Unlike the other new sisters, she had lived her entire life not three hundred yards from the front gate of Gwenafwy Abbey. Every day of her childhood, she had walked along the stone wall that bordered the expansive Abbey grounds on her way to and from the village school. She had listened as the sisters sang the morning office, their voices lifting over the meadow blue with cornflowers. She had spied on them in the Abbey gardens as they nurtured neat rows of parsnips, sweet peas, and zucchini. And she had longed to join them when the younger nuns pinned up their habits and played cricket on the green sheep pasture.

And then one day when she was just eleven, her carefree world, filled only with school and games, spun to a halt. Her mother went into hospital and never came home. The day following the funeral in the churchyard of St. Anselm, Agatha answered a knock on the door of the family's cottage. Two sisters from Gwenafwy breezed into the kitchen, arms filled with packages. They placed a basket of food on the table, handed a stuffed bear to her little brother, and slid a box of books across to her. *Nancy Drew, The Chronicles of Narnia, Black Beauty,* and *The Railway Children* tumbled out. The sisters had hoped the books might occupy the little girl's mind as she adjusted to life without her mother. And they did fill her mind — at least a little. Somehow, buried in the adventures of children both fictitious and heroic, she found a path forward. But she found something else as well. She found that there were two things that she truly loved — the cheerful sisters in their long blue habits and the companionship of a good book. Which was probably why, nearly forty years later, she was the official librarian at Gwenafwy Abbey.

Since taking vows at the age of nineteen, Sister Agatha had hardly ever left the Abbey, which was less than a mile from the village of Pryderi and nestled on the northern tip of Branwen County at the edge of the Irish Sea. Rippling green hills, meadows speckled with sheep grazing placidly, limestone cliffs rising out of the sea edge, winding cobblestone and gravel lanes punctuated with stone barns and farmhouses — it had all been her world for as long as she could remember.

And North Wales was a land that had undergone only modest change in the past 750 years — since the first day King Edward had planted the English flag. The crenellated tower of Pryderi castle still cast its long shadow from the edge of the village, and the bells of St. Anselm Church, a newcomer to the region, built in 1544, still chimed the hour. As Sister Agatha was fond of saying, the more the world changed, the more North Wales stayed the same. And in her mind, that was a good thing.

The stone buildings of the Abbey still held an echo of its medieval past. A small cloister, once paced by monks, heads down in prayer, was now an ivy-covered walkway encircling a small courtyard with the two wings of the convent grouped around its perimeter. On the west side, over the gatehouse, Reverend Mother had private rooms, while the rest of the nuns of Gwenafwy shared rooms in a dormitory above the east wing. The first floor below the dormitory housed the kitchen, the long dining room that the sisters called the refectory, and the warming room where the old monks had kept a roaring fire throughout the winter. The sisters now used the warming room to relax during the evening — reading, knitting, and playing the occasional online video game. The attic library, newly remodeled, topped the entire edifice with mullioned windows set into the blue-gray slate of the sloping roof. The outbuildings scattered across the lush, verdant grounds included the cheese barn, a small stable, a stone milking parlor, and a stone shed at the edge of the orchard used to store the Cadwaladr apples that the nuns harvested every autumn. There was even a dovecote at the back of the kitchen where a few wispy feathers still floated. A crumbling tower overlooked the farthest northeast corner of the whole property — once used by the monks as a lookout during the occasional Norman invasion. Gwenafwy Abbey had one neighbor, a potter who had turned his sheep barn into an art studio. The walk to the village for the sisters was all downhill, while the walk back to the Abbey was a steep climb.

Sister Agatha stopped for a moment and sank into one of the Adirondack chairs clustered under the old walnut tree. She needed a moment to think things through.

Sister Callwen was as loyal to the Abbey as anyone could be. And loyal to Sister Agatha as well. She and Sister Callwen had become instant friends that first day at the Abbey. She remembered well how, as young postulants, they had barely dropped their luggage in their tiny rooms when they had been hurried off to evening prayer. She would never forget how Sister Callwen had slid into the pew next to her and squeezed her hand. Or how Sister Callwen had laughed out loud when neither of them could find the right page in the prayer psalter.

Sister Agatha took a deep breath. Birdsong trilled from the lilacs that bordered the path to the nearby prayer garden with its scattered patches of lupines, delphiniums, and foxglove. The scent of baking bread floated from the outdoor brick oven, where six rounded loaves rested on the stone hearth, and two holly blue butterflies hovered over the sweet briar rosebush planted by Father Selwyn's confirmation class. She sighed. Sighing was something she detested in others.

Sister Agatha listened as the village clock tower chimed eight times. Her whole life she had heard the bell marking the hours in this small village. Pryderi was not easy to get to except by train or bus, and its inhabitants were just as glad. The village had never wanted to be a resort town. It was a working town. For centuries, Pryderi had been home to sheep farmers and shopkeepers, teachers and tradesmen. Children played along its cobbled streets, and you could set your watch by the appearance of afternoon tea. The Buttered Crust was the favorite spot for everyday, with its café tables laid out in front when the weather was fine; if you wanted something a little upmarket, there was the faded grandeur of the old Hotel Pryderi, with its starched white tablecloths and fine china.

There had been only a few new members to the Abbey over the years: Bartimaeus, the blind Shetland pony that the sisters had rescued from a questionable petting zoo and named after the blind man in the Gospel story, a small flock of Welsh Mountain sheep, a growing population of chickens, and two pigs. The sheep and the chickens were meant to add to the revenue of the Abbey, which they did faithfully. The chickens were consistent layers, and the sheep were doing fine since there were only three of them — although, if the Abbey expanded the flock, it would have to employ a part-time sheep farmer. The two potbellied pigs,

Luther and Calvin, which the sisters had thought were real pigs when they bought them, were less productive. Instead of providing bacon and sausage for the Abbey's breakfast table, they now starred every Christmas in St. Anselm's live nativity scene.

Looking around, Sister Agatha had to admit that, yes, in one way, little had changed at the Abbey since that day of arrival so long ago. But at the same time, a lot had changed. For one, *she* had changed. She was always surprised — when she bothered to look in a mirror — to see that she wasn't the young woman she had once been with a glowing tan and piercing green eyes. It shocked her sometimes to see that the edges of her face had gone soft and wrinkles spread in tiny wreaths from the corners of her eyes. When she pulled off her veil at night, she half expected long red hair to tumble out, but her hair had been short and gray for years now. Her body, once thin and ready for a game of soccer or a run across the lawn, had also gone soft, like a stack of freshly plumped pillows. Worst of all, when she stood up after kneeling in chapel, her knees creaked like a barn door in need of attention.

The Abbey itself was showing signs of the

passing of time. Over the years, the Abbey had sometimes flourished and sometimes faltered. But now, at the start of the twenty-first century, the Anglican nuns of Gwenafwy were aging, and few newcomers were joining their ranks. Their numbers had dwindled from over one hundred sisters to a mere nineteen. And the average age was no longer thirty-seven but seventy-three.

The sisters of Gwenafwy had just finished their final batch of Gouda for the summer. Three years ago, they had needed a steady revenue stream, and, inspired by the success of a sister convent in France, they had taken a crash course on cheese-making. They had chosen Gouda after doing a survey of all the artisan cheeses sold at markets in North Wales. They'd discovered that almost all cheese was farmstead cheese; Gouda might allow them to create their own niche market. So far, the business had shown moderate success, and the nuns were hopeful that profits would pick up if they could just get some more publicity — like the buzz they'd create if they won an award at the annual Cheese Festival next week at Gwydion Castle, in Gwydion-on-Rhyl. The sisters had signed up for an all-day vendor table and entered Heavenly Gouda in the Cheese-Off that evening.

Sister Winifred, who oversaw the production of Heavenly Gouda, was a woman with a formidable presence and habit of command, even though she was all of four feet eleven and ninety-seven pounds. Thanks to her astute business skills and relentless attention to quality, Heavenly Gouda was starting to turn a profit for the first time since they'd begun the business three years before. Sister Agatha was always saying that Winifred entered every room as though she were the CEO and it was a meeting of the executive board and she was about to fire everyone. This summer, she had pinned her hopes on winning the Cheese-Off. Not only would a vendor tent boost sales, but the winner of the Cheese-Off would also receive a year's worth of free publicity from the Welsh Cheese Makers Association. The entire Abbey wanted to win. Some of the rounds of Gouda that had been stacked on the shelves that morning would be taken to the Cheese Festival.

Suddenly Sister Agatha was back to her present dilemma. Did she really want to confront Sister Callwen? She might learn something she didn't want to know. But then, always a thorough believer in rushing in where angels feared to tread, Sister Agatha stood up, brushed the creases out of her perpetually wrinkled habit, and pulled open the heavy door to the cheese barn. No way out but through, she thought, stepping into the aging room, where a hundred rounds of artisanal cheese lined the floor-to-ceiling stainless steel shelves.

Sister Agatha stopped short. *Good heavens.* Her pulse quickened, and her head felt light. Sister Callwen was nowhere to be seen — but Jacob Traherne lay face down and bleeding on the tile floor, crushed beneath the heavy steel shelving unit. Rounds of Gouda, smashed under the damaged shelves, lay scattered in piles around him; mangled steel supports were jumbled on top of broken plaster, and the floor tiles had cracked under the impact. Blood encircled Jacob's head like a crimson halo. Next to his head lay a Church in Wales hymnbook, *Caneuon Ffydd.* Even as her mind raced with shock and confusion, Sister Agatha noticed that the book was open to hymn number 702, Cwm Rhondda.

Climbing across the debris, she managed to kneel next to the young man and held two fingers against his neck, praying for the steady beat of the carotid artery. Nothing. Just the clammy touch of cold skin. Making the sign of the cross, she whispered a prayer for the dead. Her eyes swept the room. A violent death, to be sure. Murder? Or was her imagination getting the better of her now that she was spending every spare moment writing a mystery novel, listening to detective podcasts, and reading all manner of forensic manuals? She looked around again. Murder. This was no accident.

Taking her cell phone from her apron pocket, she called the police.

Three

"An accident," Constable Barnes said, snapping shut his notebook. "No evidence of foul play."

"But how? What happened?" Sister Agatha asked.

"Blunt force trauma to the head is my guess. Hit by a shelf of that cheese of yours or I'll be a monkey's uncle. Let's let Dr. Beese do her job, and then we'll know for certain."

Dr. Hedin Beese, the newly appointed coroner to the Wrexham County Borough, crouched next to Jacob's body, tapping on the screen of a small tablet with a stylus. Sister Agatha sighed and shook her head. Whatever had happened to good old-fashioned paper and pen? "Look at her," she whispered to Sister Harriet. "She looks younger than some of Father Selwyn's confirmands."

"It's not them that's getting younger,"

Sister Harriet said. "It's us that's getting older. That tablet is probably linked wirelessly to her medical records software at the coroner's office. Very efficient." Tall for a woman of eighty years, though still not as tall as Reverend Mother, Sister Harriet had occupied the back tier of the Abbey choir for nearly six decades, adding her throaty contralto to the hymns in the *Anglican Psalter.* A bit heavyset, she filled out her long blue habit with little room to spare — a blue habit that often displayed a smudge from her charcoal drawing pencil or a spatter from her oil paints. The Abbey's resident artist, she was currently developing her own comic book series — a Sunday school curriculum based on the Old Testament. Her most recent publication, *Into the Lion's Den,* had been a hit with the primary school crowd. She had the broad face of a Yorkshire farmer, and her gray eyes snapped under the white band of her veil.

The sisters of Gwenafwy Abbey huddled in the aging room, some fingering the beads on rosaries, others murmuring soft prayers for the poor soul that lay on the floor in front of them. Sister Agatha had always liked Jacob. In her mind, he was a young person who still exemplified what it meant to be Welsh. Welsh as it had been in the old days — when the people of Wales had understood the importance of hard work, ready hospitality, and good manners. And Jacob, an extraordinary tenor in one of the rugby choirs, had carried on the Welsh tradition of singing.

"My guess," the constable said, "is that your man here was getting something off the top, maybe lost his balance, grabbed the shelf, and pulled everything down. You should have attached those shelves a little better to the wall. See here?" He pointed with the end of a stubby pencil. "The bolts pulled right out of the old plaster."

Sister Agatha stepped forward. "Constable, Jacob is lying face down. Which means he wasn't reaching up *into* the shelves." She waited for him to respond, and when he looked at her blankly, she added, "The shelving unit hit him on the back of the head. He was facing *away* from the shelves when they fell on him."

"Well, yes. Right. I'll make a note of that, Sister," he said. She noticed he didn't do anything of the sort.

"Which begs the question," she continued, "what would he have wanted from the top shelf? Nothing up there but rounds of Gouda."

"Well, like I said, we'll hear from Dr.

Beese. All we know now is the poor man's dead."

Sister Agatha groaned inwardly. *We know a bit more than that.* "And what about the thermostat cover?" she said. "It's been taken off the wall."

The constable shrugged. "It could have been knocked down when the shelves fell."

"Possibly. Though it's not broken or damaged in any way — almost as if it had been removed intentionally."

"Or it fell off," he muttered, turning back to his clipboard.

"And the hymnbook? Open to Cwm Rhondda?" Cwm Rhondda was sung in church, certainly, but it was also belted out with gusto at every rugby game in Wales. Sister Agatha did not believe in coincidence. She made a mental note to research the hymn and then grimaced as the constable casually plucked the hymnbook off the smooth cement floor. *Not even wearing gloves,* she thought, shaking her head. "Why would there be a hymnbook at the crime scene?" she asked aloud.

"Now, Sister. I wouldn't say this is a crime scene. And a hymnbook found in a nuns' abbey doesn't seem that out of place, if you ask me." He flipped the front cover open and read, " 'Property of St. Anselm Parish.'

Now, that is a bit odd, I will admit. It looks like it's from the village church."

"If you want, I can make sure that Father Selwyn gets it back," she said, holding her hand out in the faint hope that the constable would hand it over. He did, with an absent-minded "Thank you" as he stepped away and began to talk quietly with Reverend Mother. "I'll make sure this gets cataloged as evidence," Sister Agatha whispered to Sister Callwen.

"Sister Agatha, seriously," Sister Callwen said in a low voice. "Stop acting like you're Jessica Fletcher on *Murder, She Wrote,* for goodness' sake." Sister Callwen slipped her prayer beads into the pocket of her neatly pressed apron and smoothed a strand of salt-and-pepper hair back under her veil. Sister Callwen's discerning brown eyes missed nothing, and her aquiline nose and high forehead hinted at genteel ancestry. At least she looked more genteel than Sister Agatha, who'd grown up tending sheep and mucking out the pen of the family pig. Even now, with a dead body spread out in front of them, Sister Callwen was perfectly put together. Her blue habit was spotless, and in her apron pocket — which was always at the ready — Sister Agatha was quite certain she would be carrying only three essential items: prayer beads from the Holy Land, *The Anglican Pocket Book of Prayer,* and a fresh, embroidered handkerchief. Sister Agatha couldn't remember the last time she'd had an embroidered handkerchief. Her own apron pockets bulged with her Girl Guides knife, a notebook for jotting down ideas for her mystery novel, her smartphone, and a dog-eared paperback, *The Murder of Roger Ackroyd,* by Agatha Christie.

Sister Agatha took a quiet pride in the fact that she carried her literary hero's name. Although her name had originally been inspired by Saint Agatha of Sicily, a hardy Christian martyr who had shown great courage and downright stubbornness in the face of terrible persecution — as would any saint worth her salt — Sister Agatha was now equally inspired by Agatha Christie, a bit of a saint herself — without all the burning-at-the-stake business, of course.

"And why are you so certain this was an accident?" Sister Agatha whispered back.

"Of course it was an accident. What else would it be?"

Sister Agatha leaned close. "I'm thinking *murder.*"

Sister Callwen rolled her eyes. "You should never have been allowed to take that class on how to write a murder mystery. You've not been the same since. And now you're acting like a wannabe detective." Sister Callwen pulled out her prayer beads.

"Look," Sister Agatha said, gesturing toward the wall where the shelves had been attached. "The plaster isn't broken where the bolts came out. Almost as if the bolts were removed. Deliberately, if you ask me."

"No one asked you, unless I've missed something. And keep your voice down. Everyone is upset enough." Sister Callwen glanced at the wall and frowned. "Those shelves have been an accident waiting to happen." Callwen was chair of the Buildings and Grounds Committee at the Abbey, the group tasked with the endless job of maintaining the aging property — everything from tiles to toilets, old plumbing to even older pews — and with characteristic frugality, Sister Callwen had led the committee in holding the place together with duct tape and prayer. And she was occasionally overheard saying that the only thing that would help the Abbey would be a good earthquake. Or maybe Armageddon.

"Sisters," Reverend Mother said. "Let's gather outside. We need to give Dr. Beese space to work." Reverend Mother ducked her head slightly as she stepped through the door of the aging room. In her sixty-two years, Reverend Mother had never really reconciled herself to her height. Having started center for St. Mary's her freshman year and standing at six feet one in her socks, she had always said that basketball was her first calling All the nuns at Gwenafwy Abbey knew that when Reverend Mother felt the stress of Abbey administration or had a sticky bit of theology to sort out, she could be found making free throws at the hoop outside the Abbey kitchen. Many nights the nuns would awaken gently from their sleep to the thud of a basketball hitting the backboard.

The nuns filed silently outdoors and settled in the Adirondack chairs and picnic table under the ancient walnut tree that stood between the kitchen and the cheese barn. Sister Agatha noticed that Sister Gwenydd, the youngest by thirty years, did not sit with the others but gathered up her postulant's habit and plopped to the ground with her back to the cheese barn; she pulled out her phone and stared at the screen, frowning. It drove some of the younger sisters mad that there wasn't a decent cell signal at the Abbey — unless you climbed to the third-floor library in the newly renovated attic. Sister Agatha took a long look at the young woman. Sister Gwenydd seemed preoccupied, but then murder sometimes did that to people. On the other hand, given that she was the Abbey's newest member, what did they really know about her? And she was from London. Sister Agatha took a dim view of anyone from London.

"Don't you think," Sister Harriet said, "that we need to put in a call to the Health Department in Cardiff? I'm not sure we can sell cheese that has been in an aging room with a dead body."

"Oh, dear. I hadn't even thought of that." Reverend Mother grasped the cross around her neck, hanging on to it as if it were a lifeline. "I know that we shouldn't worry about money at a time like this, but . . ." She stopped, and the nuns looked at her with concern. Sister Callwen guided her to a chair. Reverend Mother was usually steady as a rock — their port in every storm. Now she seemed thoroughly shaken.

"It isn't just sales," Sister Winifred said, turning as she opened the door of the Abbey kitchen. Sister Agatha nearly groaned. No matter how big the crisis, Sister Winifred's first line of defense was to put the kettle on. "I hate to bring this up right now. But the Cheese Festival is in one week. The cheese on those shelves was earmarked for the vendor table."

"We'll be fine," Sister Harriet said, lowering herself into one of the Adirondack chairs. "God did not abandon Moses in the desert. He will not leave us without our cheese." Sister Winifred shook her head as the kitchen door closed behind her. Sister Agatha sighed. *Murder, and we serve tea.*

"The cheese isn't manna," Sister Agatha said. "Although it had better rain down from heaven — because it certainly isn't coming out of that barn anytime soon. And we've been planning for the Cheese Festival at Gwydion Castle for months."

Heads turned at the sound of the barn door shutting, and the nuns fell silent as Constable Barnes joined them.

"I need to dot a few t's and cross a few i's," he said. "And then I'll be out of your way." He looked at his clipboard. "Now, was it often that the deceased went into the . . . what do you call it?"

"The aging room," Reverend Mother replied. "Constable, if I could have just one more moment alone with my sisters."

Heads turned again at the sound of a car coming up the drive. Father Selwyn pulled his 1968 BMC Mini to a stop. Vicar at St. Anselm Church, he had been Sister Agatha's best friend since primary school. At the age of twenty, he'd left for seminary at Trinity Theological — the same year she had taken vows at Gwenafwy Abbey. Crammed into the tiny passenger seat next to Father Selwyn was Gavin Yarborough, St. Anselm's young deacon and candidate for ordination in the Church in Wales. He looked decidedly pale. She wondered if this was Gavin's response to the death of a friend — a young person his own age — or to Father Selwyn's notorious white-knuckle driving.

Sister Agatha liked Gavin. Full of a certain youthful energy and humor, he had jumped into the life of the parish with genuine interest. Although, she had to admit, lately he had seemed to have lost his initial enthusiasm. She couldn't put her finger on it. He had seemed distracted, maybe. Almost disoriented. Perhaps Father Selwyn was working him too hard. There was a lot to be done in a parish, and maybe Gavin wasn't used to hard work. She shook her head. In the old days, when she'd been a girl, Welsh people had known how to work.

"Is it true?" Father Selwyn said, stepping out of the car and hurrying over to Reverend Mother. "Jacob is . . . dead?" He clasped hands with her. Sister Agatha noticed that he still wore his navy-and-silver Girl Guides neckerchief, tied crookedly over his clerical collar. He had recently stepped up as leader of the parish troop in the village. From what she had heard, he was a hit at lanyards, campfires, and billycan damper bread.

She nodded, her eyes filling with tears. "Duw orffwys ei enaid." *God rest his soul.*

"Duw orffwys ei enaid," Father Selwyn repeated.

"If I could just ask a few more questions," Constable Barnes said, nodding to Father Selwyn as he joined the sisters under the walnut tree. Sister Agatha liked it that Father Selwyn stood next to Reverend Mother, holding one of her hands in both of his. As vicar of the village church, he was the Abbey's vicar as well, and she was glad he had come so quickly. She wondered how he had heard. Perhaps Reverend Mother had called St. Anselm. On the other hand, Reverend Mother's phone had been missing for the last few days. Well, someone had called him, anyway.

"How often did the deceased go into that room with the cheese?" the constable asked, not looking up, his pen poised.

"The aging room? Jacob never went into the aging room," Sister Agatha said. "That's the curious thing."

"Not even to sweep or dust or do something that a sexton might take care of?" Constable Barnes gave her a sharp look, eyebrows raised. Sister Agatha resisted rolling her eyes as Sister Winifred placed a tray of tea things on the picnic table and then hovered over it, ready to fill anyone's cup, as if she were bringing fresh water to the troops. And wasn't it just like a group of nuns, she thought, to serve refreshments in the face of murder?

"The aging room was only for those of us who had taken the licensing exam. Jacob wouldn't have just wandered in and then stood around waiting for a rack of Gouda to fall on him."

"Sister." Reverend Mother sighed.

"Was it off limits for him, then?" he asked, accepting a cup of tea from Sister Winifred.

"Oh, no. Nothing like that," Reverend Mother said. "Jacob could go into the aging room if he wanted to — it's just that there was no reason, as Sister Agatha points out, for the sexton to be there."

"Well, now, if he was the sexton, he oversaw all the buildings, right?" Constable Barnes asked.

"Well, yes. Technically." Reverend Mother said. "But the only time I ever had him go in the aging room was to adjust the thermostat. If the temperature is even slightly above fifty-two degrees, the cheese is ruined."

"Had there been problems with the thermostat?"

"No. I mean, not lately. There had been problems at one point, but not for months."

"I'm wondering why he wasn't still at Saint Anselm," Father Selwyn interjected. "He cleans the church at about four o'clock every morning and then gets here to the Abbey around six o'clock. I think so, anyway. I'm seldom up at that time." Father Selwyn was not known to be an early riser and sometimes stumbled into morning Mass looking as if he had rolled out of bed at the rectory just minutes earlier. Which, Sister Agatha knew, was often the case.

"Was it unusual for him to show up during an off hour?" The constable looked up from his notes as the door to the kitchen opened. Sister Winifred pushed backward through the heavy door with a tray of tea sandwiches and carried them over to the picnic table. Unable to sit still, she had returned to the kitchen for more food, even though the breakfast dishes hadn't had time to dry in the rack. To Sister Winifred, tea and sandwiches made everything better. Even murder, thought Sister Agatha.

"He might have. Our Jacob was very much the early-bird-gets-the-worm kind of chap,"

Father Selwyn said. "Johnny-on-the-spot."

Sister Winifred placed the sandwich tray next to the teapot and arranged a pile of silver spoons, linen napkins, and extra cups. Sister Agatha resisted a groan. The group fell silent and watched as Dr. Beese slipped out of the cheese barn and closed the door quietly behind her.

"Tea?" Sister Winifred asked as she walked over.

"No, thank you," Dr. Beese said.

"Sandwich?"

"No, thank you." Dr. Beese opened her tablet and tapped the screen with her finger. Sister Agatha noticed Sister Callwen's frown. Before taking vows, she had received her degree in library science from Aberystwyth University. But that had been decades before — back in the days of the card catalog — and today's technology befuddled her. Sister Agatha knew that even the sight of someone using a tablet made Sister Callwen uncomfortable.

"Can you tell us what happened?" Sister Agatha asked.

"As far as I can tell, the victim was struck by the edge of a steel shelf in the occipital area. I am making a guess that the impact caused a brain bleed, probably in the left occipital lobe. Which killed him. We will know more at autopsy," she said, swiping her finger across the screen. "Time of death would have been early morning. Approximately oh-five-hundred hours."

"Five o'clock this morning? That seems awfully exact," Sister Gwenydd said from under the walnut tree. Sister Agatha thought Sister Gwenydd looked ashen and her voice, a bit shaky.

"Ambient temperature of the body is a fairly good indicator. But also, he was wearing a watch that shattered when he hit the tile floor. Since the blow to his head knocked him down and killed him, it's likely he died at the same moment his watch stopped," Dr. Beese said.

"Did he suffer?" Gavin asked, his voice catching. Father Selwyn put his arm around Gavin's shoulder. "I mean, he died quickly, right?"

"Most likely. Though one can't say for sure."

Sister Agatha couldn't stand it any longer. "Was it murder?" she asked, ignoring the collective groan from her sisters.

"I'm not the constable," Dr. Beese said, snapping shut her bag and looking directly at Sister Agatha. "But I classify the incident as accidental. No evidence of foul play. Although — the left eye is bruised."

"Someone punched him?" Sister Agatha asked. "Perhaps there was a struggle? Jacob fighting for his life?"

"Fighting with what?" Sister Callwen said. "A round of Gouda?"

"It's impossible to tell when the injury to the victim's eye occurred, since he fell onto the tile floor face down," Dr. Beese said. "Although, if I had to guess, I would say that the bruise is nearly a week old."

"It's settled, then," Constable Barnes said, reaching across the table for a tea sandwich. "Accidental death." The nuns watched in silence as he placed the entire creamed egg-and-cress sandwich in his mouth. After a large gulp, he said, "I could use a bit more of that tea, Sisters. If you've got any."

Four

Catching her breath at the top of the balcony steps, Sister Callwen slid into the first pew of the choir loft and looked down over the dark sanctuary of the Gwenafwy Abbey chapel. She had barely slept the night before. Her mind had raced, replaying the horrible events of the day, and whenever she had closed her eyes, all she'd been able to see was poor Jacob stretched out on the floor of the aging room.

The bell in the village clock tower chimed five times, which meant her sisters would soon file in for Matins. *No time to dillydally.* She fished the sticky note out of her apron pocket and read the name and phone number: *Sister Bernice Bolton, Prioress, Sisters of Transfiguration Convent in Los Angeles.* Careful research, many emails, fervent prayer, and some tough conversations had led to this moment. Yesterday's tragedy had made what she was about to do even more urgent. She shivered and wrapped her cardigan tighter, asking herself for the hundredth time, *If this is the right thing to do, why does it feel so wrong?* A beam of light from the rising sun reached the edge of the stained-glass window and, in a burst of daybreak, illuminated the cross on the altar. A sign from above, she thought. She opened her flip phone.

Sister Agatha wished she had taken time for breakfast instead of racing up to her desk in the third-floor attic library the minute Matins had ended. It had been an anguished night at Gwenafwy. Stunned by the death of Jacob, the sisters had stood in shock as the hearse carrying Jacob's body drove out of the Abbey drive. They had all managed to stumble through the day and then fallen into bed after an emotional Compline — night prayer. Reverend Mother, distraught, her voice trembling, could hardly finish leading the evening's final hymn, "Fast Falls the Eventide." It had been one of Jacob's favorites. Sister Agatha had barely slept, and by the looks of everyone at breakfast that morning, no one else had either.

Fumbling for a tissue, she wiped her eyes. Reverend Mother had said that the best thing they could all do today was to pray and work. Each of the sisters had fallen to the tasks that they all had at the Abbey. Sister Callwen had excused herself to the Abbey greenhouse to make a floral arrangement for the altar in memory of Jacob, Sister Matilda had hurried out to her gardens, and Sister Gwenydd had left on foot for the village, no doubt to buy cooking supplies from the village grocer. Sister Agatha planned to do the work she did best — to solve the mystery of who had killed Jacob. He had been dead for twenty-four hours, and no investigation had even been started. Everything she had ever read in forensics had taught her that the first forty-eight hours following a murder was crucial. And yet, an entire day had passed, and nothing had been done at all. She fingered the prayer beads draped around the bust of Sherlock Holmes sitting on her desk and said a short prayer for insight and wisdom.

Like many of the more modern convents, the sisters at Gwenafwy prayed an abbreviated version of the daily office: Matins, noontime prayer, and Compline. Sister Agatha especially liked Matins — rising before the sun to seek God before even seeking one's first cup of tea. As the sisters gathered in the chapel, the stained-glass windows dark and the crested larks nesting in the

Abbey's long row of lilac bushes still silent, she loved hearing their voices join in the ancient words of the *Anglican Psalter.* It was the best moment of the day.

Yet, as much as she loved kneeling in prayer in the chapel, she loved sitting at her desk in the attic library almost as much. The sun was now up and streaming through the east dormer window where she had placed her desk, squares of light warming the thick, coffee-colored carpet, the green valley below awakening to a new day. Her desk, an old teacher's desk rescued from a church jumble, was positioned so that she could look out over the sweeping valley. The desk served two purposes. First, it was her writing desk, a place of refuge where she could be found feverishly writing her mystery novel — a real potboiler with a gumshoe detective named Bates Melanchthon, who tended to shoot first and ask questions later. At least, that was a line she was saving for the dust jacket when she finally sent the manuscript out to a publisher.

When each nun at Gwenafwy Abbey turned sixty years old, the other sisters did whatever was needed to allow that particular sister to realize whatever dream she might have long held. Sister Harriet's dream had been to travel to Rome and immerse herself in a study of modern religious art at the Vatican. Sister Callwen, to everyone's surprise, had chosen to study yoga with a famous yogi. Sister Winifred had spent six weeks weaving native wool on the Shetland Islands. When Sister Agatha had said that she wanted to write a mystery novel, all the sisters had pitched in and paid her tuition at the University of St. David. In the year since graduation, she had been working hammer and tong on a mystery novel complete with murder and mayhem. She spent nearly every free moment researching historical murders, combing through forensic manuals, reading mystery-writer blogs, testing out dialogue on her sisters, and frantically scribbling down every thought and idea the minute it came to her — even if a brilliant thought did hit her in the middle of Easter Vigil at St. Andrew's Cathedral. To Reverend Mother's concern, her protagonist frequented brothels, fought in seedy bars on the East Side of London, and as far as anyone could tell, had never darkened the door of a church. The manuscript was nearly finished, or so Sister Agatha kept telling everyone, and the entire Abbey was a little nervous about its reception.

Her desk in the attic was where she wrote her novel, but it was also her workstation.

Sister Agatha was the Abbey librarian, and it was here in the attic — where the Wi-Fi was best — that she ordered books, cataloged new arrivals, researched interlibrary loan opportunities, and scoured the Internet for the most recent requests of the sisters, which included everything from prayer devotionals and Bible study guides to the latest in cheese production and, she noticed, glancing at a sticky note left on her blotter, a book titled *Automotives for Amateurs.* Sister Harriet had been tasked with maintenance of the convent's aging minivan.

Sister Agatha gazed out the window as the early-morning sun sent its shimmering rays over the village and the ruins of Pryderi castle. She sighed. It was way too early to be without tea. She tried not to think about the traditional Welsh cakes that Sister Gwenydd had made that morning for breakfast. Sister Gwenydd, the newly appointed Abbey chef, made Welsh cake so crammed with currants and so heavy with butter and sugar that they crumbled when you picked one up. Sister Agatha gave herself a shake and read aloud — as she did every morning when she sat down to work — the two note cards she had taped to the wall next to her desk. The first was from the Gospel of Matthew, chapter 6, verse 3: "Seek ye first the

Kingdom of God, and all these things shall be given unto you." She closed her eyes and said a swift prayer. Then, opening her eyes, she read the other card aloud. "The secret of getting ahead is getting started. Agatha Christie." Today she needed to seek and find as well as to simply get started. She faced a real murder with real people — not her beloved fictional characters, but her beloved community of Gwenafwy Abbey. And she would not be distracted by tea and cakes.

Opening the bottom drawer of her desk, Sister Agatha peered thoughtfully at her stash of colorful notebooks. Endlessly pragmatic and no-frills in almost all matters, she had one slightly embarrassing weakness — she absolutely loved a new, fresh notebook. But not just any notebook. Only the expensive, cloth-covered, hand-bound ones that could be found at Smythson of Bond Street in London or the Stamford Notebook Company in Cambridge. She loved how each page was watermarked; every binding, handmade; every spine, carefully stitched; every page, gilt-edged; and how each was covered in elegant cloth or smooth leather. Just opening a new notebook — the slight snap of the binding, the feel of the smooth top page, the gentle aroma of paper and ink — sparked her creativity like nothing else, and, at that moment, when she touched the clean, empty first page, the literary possibilities seemed limitless. The expensive notebooks were somewhat at odds with her vow of poverty, but fortunately for Sister Agatha, Reverend Mother firmly believed that all-poverty-and-no-online-shopping made for a dull life. Even a cloistered life. Consequently, she had quietly approved the notebooks as long as Sister Agatha didn't overdo it. After all, Reverend Mother wore Nike Air Pro V basketball shoes ordered regularly from a store on Oxford Street. And Sister Agatha knew for a fact that they weren't cheap.

The start of a real murder investigation — right on her doorstep — called for a new notebook. Reaching into the drawer, she selected her latest acquisition, which had been waiting for just the right moment — a lizard-print moleskin slimline pocket-sized notebook in splashy orchid blue. The advertisement on the Smythson website had read "minimalist, yet powerful." Perfect. Opening a pack of new Sharpies, she selected one and slipped the cap off. Time to get serious. If only there were tea.

Frowning, she peered at the crisp first page of the new notebook, her Sharpie poised — but only for a moment. She quickly jotted down all the clues she could recall off the top of her head:

Thermostat cover
Aging room
Shelves
Hymnbook open to Cwm Rhondda?

After a moment's thought, she added:

Broken plaster
Bolts
Why was Jacob in the aging room at 5:00 in the morning?

She turned the page and wrote:

Possible reasons:

Cleaning?
Checking on the cheese?
Adjusting/fixing the thermostat?
Lured there by a killer?

Shutting the notebook gently, she tapped her Sharpie against its front cover and thought carefully. Nothing came to her. Maybe the constable was right — maybe Jacob had been in the wrong place at the wrong time.

New notebook, new Sharpie, a murder at

hand — time to consult her mentor, Inspector Rupert McFarland. Retired after a long career at the Strathclyde Police headquarters in Glasgow, Inspector McFarland was now a best-selling mystery writer and the host of the Radio Wales podcast *Write Now.* Sister Agatha never missed the weekly show. Every Sunday evening, Inspector McFarland tackled the toughest crime-writing problems — from smoking guns to dangling participles, from misplaced bodies to misplaced modifiers. Sunday nights found Sister Agatha with earbuds on, furiously taking notes, and then, often as not, she felt so inspired that she stayed up half the night rethinking her plot points, developing new characters, and inventing red herrings. Sometimes she wondered if Inspector McFarland hadn't taught her more than her Master of Fine Arts in Creative Writing from the University of St. David.

Sister Agatha realized that if this murder was to be solved, she would have to conduct her own investigation. Not that Constable Barnes wasn't a decent person and a good constable — he sang in the church choir and was always on hand to help with the needs of the people of Pryderi — but he wasn't a detective. Not in the true sense. Not like Armand Gamache or Hercule

Poirot. If he were, he would have immediately known that there was nothing accidental about Jacob's death.

She would have to be cautious in how she went about her investigation. Reverend Mother would not be thrilled if she interviewed suspects, dusted for fingerprints, made foot impressions out of plaster — all the things a real detective would do without raising the slightest alarm. She would have to be more like Miss Marple in *Mrs. McGinty's Dead.* Miss Marple traveled about the village in disguise, first as a faithful church member, then as an amateur actor, and then as a simple boarding house resident. In the end, she uncovered the murderer before anyone even suspected that she had been hot on the trail all along.

There was something to be said for subtlety, Sister Agatha mused as she pulled out her podcast notebook — an elegant black journal with cream-colored pages and gilt edges from Stamford — and quickly found what she wanted: the very first podcast by Inspector McFarland, a step-by-step instruction on crime writing. She had referenced her notes for this podcast so many times that the exquisite pages were smudged and tattered. Wishing again for a cup of

Welsh Brew, she settled back and began to read.

1. First things first — come up with a credible detective. Your main character could be an ordinary person or a professional such as a medical examiner who finds herself suddenly facing a mystery.

Well, that one is easy, she thought. She made a note in her journal: *Detective — me.* And what about a sidekick? They always had those in murder mysteries. She thought a moment and then wrote, *Father Selwyn.* He wouldn't sign on to helping out with the investigation willingly, of course, but he had been good friends with Jacob and would want to see the murder solved.

2. Figure out where your story takes place. Your setting should be a place you love . . . or hate.

The Abbey, she wrote, and then made a further note: *The aging room.*

3. It doesn't have to be a murder, but murder is always good. Make sure the stakes are high. No one is going

to keep reading if the crime doesn't mean something.

Well, the stakes were obvious. The mysterious death of a sexton. Right in the center of this place of peace and prayer. "Poor Jacob," she said aloud as she began to write quickly. *Killed under falling cheese. DEATH BY GOUDA.* She stared out the window. Three flights below, Sister Harriet was weeding the long rows of kale in the Abbey vegetable garden, and Sister Winifred was deadheading the pansy bed.

All the nuns were hard at work — taking Reverend Mother's advice to focus on the day at hand. She glanced over at the stack of books that needed cataloging. They could wait. Jacob's body, zipped into a long black bag and slid into the undertaker's hearse that morning, had left an image in Sister Agatha's head that she couldn't shake. And he had died alone. Which broke her heart. Lying on the cold floor, bludgeoned by steel shelves — no one had prayed an angel's safe passage for him; no one had held his hand as he crossed over. She swallowed hard and took a deep breath. It was up to her to find out what had actually happened. She turned back to the page of notes.

4. Create a list of suspects — people who might have killed your victim.

She hesitated, then wrote: *Sister Gwenydd.* A small wave of guilt made her fingertips tingle. How could she think so darkly of the young postulant?

On the other hand, Sister Gwenydd was new to the Abbey, and they knew almost nothing about her. Could she have killed Jacob? The heavy steel shelves had fallen on him as he stood with his back to them. Sister Agatha didn't believe for a second that they had just spontaneously removed themselves from the wall and crashed down, no matter what Constable Barnes thought of the old plaster walls. And what had Jacob been doing in the aging room at five in the morning anyway? Had he been lured there by someone who wanted him dead?

Sister Agatha looked out the window as she thought about Sister Gwenydd. The sun had risen above the valley, and the early-morning shadows that gave everything that fresh look of a new day had disappeared. She remembered the day only a few months before that the young woman had shown up at the Abbey, out of the blue really, asking if she could join the community. Sister Agatha had to admit that, on the surface, that did look suspicious. Like that of every religious order in the Church in Wales, the membership at Gwenafwy was dwindling as the nuns aged. No one had joined in more than a decade — a disturbing reality that hung over the Abbey like a dark cloud. Which was probably why they had all embraced Sister Gwenydd with open arms, neglecting to conduct a more careful vetting process. Even though she had looked a bit as if she'd been dragged through the hedge backward — tall and thin, her long curly hair in need of a good cut and wash, and a wardrobe that seemed to consist entirely of skintight jeans and tiny little shirts. Sister Agatha admitted, though, that Sister Gwenydd had cleaned up well. In her blue habit and apron, with a simple headscarf, she fit right in. And, Sister Agatha noted, she seemed happy.

In the end, after some debate among the sisters, Reverend Mother had required Sister Gwenydd to serve for six weeks as an aspirant, a preliminary stage to becoming a postulant. Candidates lived "alongside" the community while the community and the young woman decided the next right step. During those six weeks, the nuns fell in love with her. And with her cooking. A graduate of a prestigious cooking school, Sister Gwenydd combined her two callings — cooking and religious life. She had needed a job at the Abbey, and since they hadn't had a good cook in years — not since Sister Mildred had left for the mission field — Reverend Mother had put the new aspirant to work in the kitchen almost immediately. It had all seemed to come together, and Sister Gwenydd had been granted the official status of postulant two months before, during the Feast of St. John the Baptist. To her credit and the delight of the other sisters, Sister Gwenydd had prepared the entire sumptuous meal, which ended with honey-sweetened grasshopper bars to commemorate the saint.

Sister Agatha picked up her pen and jotted down the things she knew about Sister Gwenydd's past. *Grew up in Manchester. Trained as a chef at a cooking school in London. Both parents deceased. No other family.* Sister Agatha frowned. That wasn't much. Especially now that there had been a murder. She tapped her pen impatiently and wrote, *Find out more about Sister Gwenydd.*

It occurred to her that she also knew very little about Jacob. Turning a page in her notebook, she wrote, *Victim: Jacob Traherne. Sexton at St. Anselm and Gwenafwy Abbey. Lived in the village with his mother. Sang in one of the rugby choirs.* She then made a note to discuss things with Father Selwyn.

Her next suspect to consider was Sister Callwen. She swallowed hard. How could she suspect Sister Callwen of murder? That seemed too outrageous. Yet, there had been suspicious behavior — hadn't she been acting odd lately? And the disturbing voice mail.

No. Ridiculous. Sister Callwen could never murder anyone. She drew a heavy line through Sister Callwen's name.

Then she went back and put a question mark next to it. Too early to eliminate anyone.

But maybe she was looking too close to home. Could Jacob's killer be someone from the village? Sister Agatha tapped her Sharpie on her notebook as she thought about it. Small villages were notorious for producing murder. Look at Armand Gamache and Three Pines. A new murder popped up all the time. Or Father Brown's Kembleford. Another small village rife with murder. She made a note: *Make inquires in the village.* Someone had wanted Jacob dead. And it had to be someone with access to the Abbey and who knew his habits. That made it more likely to be a local job.

She shook her head and, flipping back to

her podcast notes, read Inspector McFarland's final words:

5. Wrap up the story by solving the mystery. Be clever.

Sister Agatha underlined the words *Be clever* and then closed the orchid-blue slimline notebook, sliding it into her apron pocket. Her fingertips touched the hymnbook. In her distress about Jacob, she had forgotten that she held a crucial piece of evidence. *The hymnbook.* Taking it out of her apron pocket, she opened it in the middle with the intent of turning to hymn number 702. Had it been open to Cwm Rhondda by accident or did that mean something? The song was about the harrowing experience of the Israelites in the wilderness as they escaped from slavery in Egypt to finally arrive safe in the land of Canaan. God had saved them time and time again in the journey. *Was Jacob telling us that he needed saving? Was he trying to send a message?* The words to the hymn were well known to any Welshman — church affiliated or not. "Death of death and hell's destruction, the verge of Jordan." Those lyrics could be important. A piece of paper fluttered out of the book as she flipped through the pages looking for number 702. She picked it up and read the scribbled lines:

Jacob,
Don't worry, old chap. She would never do it. You're safe! Ha ha. See you in the beer tent!
— Mordy

She felt her pulse flutter. This was a real clue. A clue worthy of Inspector Rupert McFarland. Someone named Mordy was telling Jacob that he was safe. Safe from whom? Someone referred to as "she." Why did Jacob need the reassurance of being "safe"? And, sadly, he hadn't been safe at all. She slipped the note into her top desk drawer along with the hymnbook.

Pushing her chair back, she stood and stretched. With a murder barely twenty-four hours old, she desperately wanted to throw herself into sleuthing, but her work at the Abbey needed some attention. Sometimes Sister Agatha had to remind herself that although she was a mystery writer and an amateur sleuth, she was an Anglican nun first, and that meant she needed to pull her weight.

As the Abbey librarian, she had a stack of books that wanted cataloging. Shelving books was a good time to think, however. And this case certainly called for some serious thinking. But first, some nourishment. Breakfast would be over by now, but she should be able to find a cup of tea and a bit of Welsh cake. She could bring it up to the library.

As Sister Agatha turned to leave for the Abbey kitchen, she heard the squeal of tires and hurried to the window that overlooked the front drive. A long black car had stopped, and a moment later, the passenger door opened, and a stranger — a young woman — tumbled out. Thin and tall, with that willowy look that seemed all the rage these days, she wore a short black dress, and a mane of thick auburn hair fell across her face as she caught herself before falling onto the gravel. The car peeled away. Just as Sister Agatha was about to open her notebook and add it to her list of strange things happening at the Abbey, she realized that the woman was Sister Gwenydd. She hadn't recognized her in a tiny black dress and heels instead of a blue habit and trainers, her long hair let loose instead of pinned under her headscarf. Why was Sister Gwenydd dressed like a cocktail waitress and getting out of a mysterious car? She watched as Sister Gwenydd looked around and then ran toward the back of the Abbey.

Five

Halfway down, the zipper stuck. Dropping her gym bag on the floor of the public rest room, Sister Gwenydd yanked the postulant tunic over her head, hearing a slight rip as the seam around the zipper gave way. *Damn.*

The sisters had barely filed out of the sanctuary from Matins when Sister Gwenydd snagged a ride into the village with Reverend Mother, making the excuse that she had to get to the greengrocer's early or she would miss all the best produce. It was a relief to get away. The sight of the police car pulling out of the Abbey drive yesterday morning, followed by the undertaker's hearse, had made her stomach churn with anxiety. *That wasn't good. Not at all. And things could very well just get worse.*

Cringing at the sticky cement floor, she slipped out of the white trainers that all the nuns wore and grabbed the black dress from her bag. Pulling it on over her head, she slid her feet into Gucci sandals, her hands shaking as she tried to fasten the clasps. The dress was a bit shorter than she remembered. She jerked at the hemline, trying to make it a little more modest. *Oh, well. It is what it is.*

Trainers, blue habit, and gray headscarf went into the bag — the bag she kept packed and stashed under her bed at the Abbey. She never knew when she would need to take off, slip away in the night. She felt as if every move she made was observed, as if around every corner was a detective or a policeman waiting to arrest her. She tossed her postulant's cross — a silver-cross necklace given to her by the sisters of Gwenafwy on her first tremulous day at the Abbey three months ago — into the bag, but at the last minute, she took it out and slipped it around her neck again, hands shaking as she fastened the clasp. She needed all the help she could get. Glancing in the cloudy mirror, she ran her fingers through her short hair. No blush, no lipstick. There had been a time, not long ago, when that would have mattered. Now, nothing mattered.

At almost the same moment that the sisters at Gwenafwy were clearing up from breakfast and Sister Gwenydd was making her secretive wardrobe change, Reverend Mother was stepping off the elevator at diocesan headquarters in Wrexham. She had raced out of the chapel almost before the last song of morning prayer had been sung, jumped into the minivan, and fairly flown the seven miles to Wrexham. Checking her watch, she was relieved to see that she had arrived at the bishop's office precisely on time. The new bishop had a reputation for starting her day early and apparently had no patience for lateness.

"I have a seven o'clock appointment with the bishop," she said to the receptionist behind the desk.

The young woman, alarmingly thin in Reverend Mother's opinion, her jet-black hair cut severely short, a green-and-blue tattoo crawling up the side of her neck, slowly removed one earbud. "Regarding?"

Reverend Mother noticed that she held the earbud in her fingertips as if ready to slip it back in as soon as possible. The other earbud stayed firmly in place.

"The Diocesan Outreach grant. I received a letter saying that our application was rejected. I'm certain there's a mistake."

"Deadline's passed, you know. Why don't you just apply next year?"

Reverend Mother made an effort to smile. At least the young woman had a pleasant voice, especially for someone who looked like an angel of death. "I have an appointment with the bishop."

The girl refitted the earbud and, picking up her cell phone, tapped the screen. "Should only be a moment."

Taking a seat on the small leather couch, Reverend Mother looked around at the chic decor of the Bishop's office and suddenly felt out of her league — unrefined and unsophisticated. Her long blue habit usually gave her a feeling of purpose, even a certain dignity, but her reflection in the elevator mirror just now had been a bit of a shock. When had her face become so lined and thin? Her shoulders so stooped?

Reaching into her apron pocket, she checked to see that her cell phone was turned off. Nothing rankled her like a phone going off during a meeting. After searching both pockets and finding nothing but her prayer book, rosary, and the list of draft picks from the Rhondda Rebels, the division 1 team from South Wales, she suddenly remembered that her phone had been missing since Saturday. *What an inconvenience,* she thought. *Starting off one's work week — on a Monday morning — without a phone.*

But all she could really think about was poor Jacob. Could it really be murder, as Sister Agatha thought? *Surely not.* Constable Barnes had been quite clear. His death had been an accident — horrible and tragic. But an accident.

The door to the office opened, and Bishop Suzanne Bainton sailed into the waiting area. Tall and striking, Reverend Mother had to admit, Suzanne was absolutely imposing in bishop's clericals. She had not yet seen her since her ordination as bishop of St. Asaph, one of the five dioceses of the Church in Wales. Reverend Mother did remember that her quick rise from parish vicar to the office of bishop had raised more than a few eyebrows.

"Marta, how lovely to see you," the Bishop said. Reverend Mother stood a little too quickly and bumped the coffee table with her knee. A stack of glossy magazines fell to the floor in a slippery cascade.

"Bore da," she said. *Good morning.* "Thank you for finding time to meet with me."

"Bore da. My deepest condolences about your sexton. Father Selwyn called just a moment ago. It sounds like Jacob was a wonderful young man."

"Yes," Reverend Mother said simply. "He was."

"How are the sisters doing with it?"

"We all had a difficult night. It's hard to believe that . . ." Reverend Mother stopped, a sudden rush of emotion tightening her throat. She felt tears about to fill her eyes. She really didn't want to break down. Not now.

"Yes. Of course. Of course. Come in, please," the bishop said, leading the way into her office. She gestured to a large leather couch and then settled into the opposite upholstered chair.

"I like what you've done with the place," Reverend Mother said, looking around, taking a deep breath to compose herself. "Is that an Albrecht Durer woodcut?" Reverend Mother had a sharp eye for German Renaissance art. "It looks original."

"Quite original. Although only one of his minor works. I saw it in London at a private auction and couldn't help myself. Tea?" The bishop picked up the teapot from the table between them.

"Thank you." Reverend Mother waited while the bishop poured two cups of tea, adding cream and sugar to hers.

"How can I be of help today?" Bishop Bainton said, taking a sip.

"It's about the Diocesan Outreach grant. I was hoping you would reconsider the Abbey's application. Our premise is very sound." Reverend Mother felt as if she already sounded defensive and forced herself to slow down. "If we were awarded the grant money, we would use it to supplement our cheese business while at the same time turning it into an outreach to the community."

"No." The bishop lifted a plate and held it out. "Bara brith?" *Welsh fruitcake.*

"What? No, thank you. Why? I would've thought that based on what the Abbey gives back to the diocese, we would be a serious candidate for the grant."

The Bishop broke a tiny piece off her *bara brith* and placed it on the edge of her saucer. "Gives back to the diocese? In what way, exactly?" Reverend Mother watched as the bishop then nibbled the tiny bite. Bishop Bainton was bone thin and looked incredibly fit. Reverend Mother had heard that she swam competitively on a team in Wrexham for the Swim Wales program and that they had even qualified for the final meet in Cardiff. The Bishop's auburn hair was pulled up in a French twist that was both professional and elegant, her skin glowed, and, Reverend Mother couldn't help but notice, her teeth were perfect.

"Well, first, the Abbey is very generous to the parish," Reverend Mother said, taking a breath. She noticed for the first time that the bishop's eyes were each a different color. One blue and one brown. Just like David Bowie, she thought to herself. Reverend Mother had been a David Bowie fan ever since the concert when he'd recited the Lord's Prayer from center stage. "And we're the presence of the Church in the village."

The bishop picked up a file folder from the table. "Fine. Let's review Gwenafwy Abbey's generosity and *presence in the village,* as you say."

Reverend Mother felt her stomach flutter. The atmosphere in the room, which had started as a cordial tea between colleagues, had just morphed into something with the feel of a barrister deposition. She watched as the bishop opened the folder, flipped a few pages, and then stopped. "Gwenafwy Abbey," she said as she scanned the pages, "has ended every year — for the past decade — in a deficit budget. During that time, your membership has declined steadily, and your outreach to the community, although commendable, has remained unchanged."

"What do you mean 'unchanged'?"

"I mean, you're supporting the same three

missions. All of them target low-income people."

"Helping the poor is now a problem?"

"Not a problem as such. But many of our religious orders take a much more contemporary approach to outreach — getting behind environmental issues, lobbying Parliament, participating in local government, crowd-funding for people in need. Your nuns are still organizing Christmas jumbles and having bake sales."

"That's not true. We don't have bake sales!" She set her teacup down, clattering it against the saucer. "And our Christmas jumble is quite a favorite in the village."

"You know what I mean. You're outdated. Some would say that religious orders no longer serve a purpose." The Bishop glanced at the door of her office and then looked back, taking a sip of tea.

"No longer serve a purpose? We are a vital part of village life. Ask anyone in Pryderi!"

"That's your litmus test for vitality? Ask anyone in Pryderi — a tiny village in the North?" The bishop shook her head. "The world has moved on, Marta. And if you haven't noticed, today's women aren't exactly standing in line to become nuns."

Reverend Mother leaned forward, her dark eyes snapping. "Tell that to the sisters of Gwenafwy Abbey. Tell that to the people who depend on us. Tell that to *Jesus.*"

"Oh, come on." The bishop picked up her phone, glanced at the screen, and then set it back down. "Don't bring Jesus into this."

Reverend Mother couldn't tell if the comment was an attempt at humor or an indication of the bishop's true allegiances. "So, this is what we have come to? We don't bring Our Lord into it anymore? I thought service to God and Christ was what it was all about." She tried to hold the bishop's eyes, but the bishop was flipping through the file again.

"Yes, it is," she said without looking up. "But service to God and Christ needs to be efficient service. There is no sin in being cost-effective." She closed the file and tossed it next to the tea tray. "I'll give you until Michaelmas."

"Give us *what* until Michaelmas?" Michaelmas, the feast of St. Michael the Archangel on September 29, was only a month away.

"I will give you until Michaelmas to prove that the Abbey is useful. And financially solvent. If service to God and Christ is so essential to who you are — then surely faith will provide." The bishop glanced at her phone again. "Right?" she said without looking up.

"What would constitute — in your opinion — that the Abbey is useful?"

"Well, for starters — new postulants, increased revenue, a balanced budget, an income that is stable, an up-to-date approach to ministry." The bishop shrugged.

"And if we don't prove ourselves *useful*, what then?" Reverend Mother struggled to keep the anger from her voice.

"Then —"

The Bishop paused as the office intercom buzzed. "Halwyn Griffiths to see you, Reverend Bainton."

"One moment," she said in the direction of the desk. For a split second, Reverend Mother thought she detected a slight break in the Bishop's perfect demeanor, but then the calm self-assurance returned. "Is there more?" the bishop asked her.

"You haven't answered my question. What then? You know, if Gwenafwy Abbey doesn't prove its worth?" Reverend Mother's voice was decidedly laced with sarcasm now. But the bishop didn't seem to notice.

"We will explore other options." The bishop stood.

"Who is we? And what options?"

"Marta. Not everything in the diocese is organic cheese and Sunday school." Walking over to the office door, she opened it and stood to the side. "We have things called budgets — most of them in shortfall. Add to that a Welsh economy that has been dead longer than Lazarus, and you might understand why I'm not so quick to underwrite your aging abbey." Reverend Mother glanced into the waiting area. A man sat on the white leather sofa. Tall and loose-limbed, with black hair and a touch of gray at the temples, he had an aristocratic presence even as he just sat there reading the spring issue of *The Anglican Journal.* Reverend Mother couldn't help but notice, when he turned and smiled at her, his eyes startlingly blue, that the gentleman was inordinately handsome.

"Save your breath to cool your porridge! I'm not having this conversation," Sister Callwen said, selecting a long-stemmed rose from the pile on the cutting table and snipping off a few extraneous leaves. "And I need to finish these flowers before Reverend Mother gets back from the bishop's office. I want to put a vase of zinnias on her desk. She loves the purple ones, and I think she certainly needs a bit of cheering up this morning. Well, not cheering up. But you know what I mean."

Having done a respectable amount of cataloging and shelving in the Abbey library for the morning as well as making notes in her notebook about Jacob, Sister Agatha had come in search of Sister Callwen, who stood arranging flowers and looking perfectly composed — all four feet eleven inches of her. Too composed, thought Sister Agatha. Almost as if someone had not just been murdered in their very midst only the day before.

The greenhouse, on the south end of the Abbey, was filled with light most of the day. The sisters loved it because it was warm and sunny even in the harshest winter. However, in the summer, it was downright steamy. Sister Agatha could feel her habit sticking to her back. She planted her feet and kept Sister Callwen in her steady gaze. *No way out but through.* "I will not save my breath — I want to talk about it. Why was there a message on the office voice mail for you?" Sister Agatha said. No response. "From the Board of Governors. They want to do a follow-up on your meeting with them."

"And?"

"And? Why are you having secret meetings with the Board of Governors?"

"First, anyone can meet with the board."

Sister Callwen hesitated and slowly placed the roses back on the table. She looked at Sister Agatha. "And anyway, the meeting wasn't secret."

"Why wasn't Reverend Mother there?"

"Does she know about it?"

"Aha! So, it was secret — done behind her back. But why? Why would you sneak around? Reverend Mother is our leader, our friend." She had a horrible thought. "Do you want her job that badly?"

"Do I want her job? You think that's what this is all about?" Sister Callwen snorted. "Believe me, the last thing I want is her job." She turned back to the flowers, spinning the vase around and stepping back to take a look at it. "And you think you're the great Abbey detective."

"I do not." Sister Agatha slipped the orchid-blue slimline notebook back in her pocket.

"Step away from this, OK? Why do you care about a voice mail? Go solve the murder of poor Jacob. Duw orffwys ei enaid." *God rest his soul.*

"So, you agree with me — that Jacob was murdered?"

"No! I was just . . . forget it. Forget the board meeting. It'll be better that way."

"It's just that . . . we've been together for

years, you and me and Reverend Mother, and we've never kept secrets from each other."

Sister Callwen looked miserable but stayed silent. Sister Agatha studied her friend for a long moment. "We've given our lives to this place." She struggled to keep her voice steady. "Just tell me that what you're doing isn't going to change things." The silence grew between them as the bell in the clock tower sounded, calling the Abbey to dinner. "Promise me," Sister Agatha pleaded.

"I can't," Sister Callwen said. "I can't promise you that."

Six

Sister Callwen's final words rang in Sister Agatha's head as she walked into the village. Her first stop was the post office to check for her most recent acquisition for the Abbey library — Stearn's *An Encyclopaedia of World History, Ancient, Medieval and Modern.* Sister Agatha had reservations about purchasing such a large, cumbersome hard copy in several volumes when the online version would have been so much easier — no need to shelve, for one thing. But Reverend Mother had tasked her with developing an Abbey library that offered a variety of electronic and hard copy. And Sister Agatha couldn't argue — sometimes it was nice to feel the heft of a book in one's hand, to turn its pages, to breathe deeply of paper and ink.

After checking at the Pryderi post office and finding that the books had not arrived, she turned and headed down Main Street to St. Anselm Church. She really needed to talk with Father Selwyn. The murder was barely a day old, and the clues were stacking up. If she were to sort this all out, she would need help. Inspector Rupert McFarland had emphasized more than once the importance of a good sidekick. Where would Sherlock Holmes have been without Dr. Watson? Or Precious Ramotswe without Grace Makutsi? Or Lord Peter Wimsey without Mervyn Bunter? They would have been *lost,* Inspector McFarland had emphatically answered. *Give your detective a thoughtful, empathetic sidekick if you plan to solve that murder.* Well, Sister Agatha thought, Father Selwyn would be the perfect sidekick — as long as he never realized that's what he was.

Father Selwyn sat hunched over a jumble of fishing lures, feathers, bobbins, and sinkers spread across the coffee table in front of him, his long legs scrunched beneath the edge of the table. His large frame engulfed the tiny love seat. An angling enthusiast, he claimed that since the early disciples had been fishermen, his yearly fishing trips to Scotland were biblically mandated. A tall glass of something green and thick with a straw sticking out of it sat next to the tangle of fishing line.

"Father?" Sister Agatha said, knocking on the frame of the open door. "Got a moment?"

"For you, Sister — always," he said, looking up from the salmon nymph he was attaching to a steelhead sinker. "Just getting a head start on this week's sermon."

"I can see that," she said, surveying the fishing gear. She settled into the overstuffed chair across from him after pushing aside two fishing magazines, a green embroidered stole, and a frayed copy of the *Book of Common Prayer.*

"May I offer you a mango and kale yogurt smoothie?" he asked.

"Since when are you a smoothie fan? What happened to your usual morning glass of scrumpy?" Father Selwyn was known for his love of the hard cider Cloudy Scrumpy.

"Sadly, Dr. Beese has suggested I give it up and replace it with something less, shall we say, good." He held the glass up to the light, eyeing the murky green liquid, and then put it back down with a grimace.

"Right. Well. I'm on my way to The Buttered Crust for a cup of Welsh Brew and an oatcake." The Buttered Crust Tea Shop was one of Sister Agatha's favorite haunts. When she really needed to work on her murder mystery, that's where she went. At the moment, her detective, Bates Melanchthon, was stuck unraveling a gruesome murder that involved both poison and bludgeoning, and if she didn't get away from the sisters at Gwenafwy and all their angst, she would never make any progress. Something about the noisy hustle and bustle of The Buttered Crust stimulated her writing, and a nice cup of Welsh Brew kept her going when all else failed. Welsh Brew was tea at its most perfect. She knew that Father Selwyn preferred Glengettie — which Sister Agatha found a bit highbrow.

"Good enough," he said, tossing the lure and line onto the table. "What's up?" Father Selwyn leaned back on the sofa and, smoothing out his long cassock, looked at his old friend. "You don't usually walk into the village in the middle of the morning. I thought this was your writing time. Or is the muse not on speaking terms with you today?" Father Selwyn's eyes, deep green behind wire spectacles, communicated warmth and a genuine kindness. His gray hair had advanced over the years from thinning to uncontested balding. Having been an avid rugby player before blowing out his knee in a village game, he had a slight paunch that not even a long black cassock could hide. Nice looking — in a comfortable way — Father Selwyn often said that he enjoyed life abundantly and that abundant life included cheese puddings, Glamorgan sausages, and whortleberry tart. Though he was loved and respected throughout the Church in Wales, Sister Agatha considered Father Selwyn to be both her priest and her friend. It barely mattered that his socks seldom matched.

"I'm here to talk about the murder at the Abbey," she said.

"Murder? Constable Barnes *and* Dr. Beese declared Jacob's death accidental."

"Constable Barnes, my foot. He wouldn't recognize a murder if the murderer left a note saying, 'Hey, I just murdered this guy.' " Sister Agatha eyed the green smoothie. Why in the world would someone drink something made of yogurt and kale when a cup of Welsh Brew could solve just about any problem in the world? "The shelves fell on Jacob and killed him. The question is, how? One minute they're securely attached to the wall; the next minute, they're crashing down, bringing along a hundred rounds of Gouda. Neither the constable nor the medical examiner has a clue." Sister Agatha paused. "So to speak." She pulled the orchid-blue slimline notebook from her apron pocket and held it up. "But I have several interesting clues."

"But why? Who would want to murder Jacob?" Father Selwyn took his spectacles off and, leaning forward, selected a plastic worm, neon pink, out of the stash on the coffee table. "Sister Callwen is right — you have been too much immersed in your mystery writing." He tossed the worm back down and looked at her. "You see crime everywhere."

"Shelves don't just jump off walls, Father. That's all I'm saying." The morning light bounced out from the suncatcher hanging in the office window. The octagon crystal splashed cheerful rainbow prisms on the wall across from the window.

Father Selwyn frowned. "As far as I could tell, Jacob didn't have an enemy in the world."

"Funny you should ask," she said, pulling the note from the hymnbook out of her apron pocket. "Take a look at this."

Before she could show him the note, however, there was a knock on the frame of the open door, and Gavin stepped in. "Sorry to bother you, Father."

He nodded to Sister Agatha. She thought the young deacon looked even more disheveled than usual, his blond hair tangled and oily as though he had just rolled out of bed. Gavin seemed young for his age, partly because he had such a baby face, still pudgy and soft, and partly because he had plastered on his baby face the perpetually bored look of younger teens. A look that said he was OK having to talk with you, but wouldn't it be nice if someone more interesting came along? He wore a pair of decent pants, loosely tied sneakers, and a wrinkled button-down shirt. No tie, and the collar was frayed. A bit scruffy for church, she thought, but then she had noticed that everyone his age looked unkempt most of the time. At least in her opinion. Perhaps it was today's style.

"Sit down, Gavin. Finished with the pledge letters?" Father Selwyn said.

"Just about." Gavin ran his hand through his hair, making it worse. He sighed, still standing, and glanced out the window.

"It's your half day off, isn't it?" Father Selwyn asked.

"I was just about to leave. Going to Cardiff for the Ospreys match. With some mates."

"Well, enjoy." Father Selwyn picked up a bright-orange bobber and placed it thoughtfully next to the pink worm. Sister Agatha noticed that he gave Gavin a hard look.

"Are you doing OK, then?" she asked, turning to the young deacon.

"OK? Oh, you mean about Jacob. Kind of. Not really. I've never had anybody die before. You know, my age, that is."

"It's hard to lose someone. Especially someone in the prime of their life. Especially someone as caring and generous as Jacob." Sister Agatha took a breath, and she felt tears sting the corners of her eyes.

"Right. I'm off, then," Gavin said, turning to the door, not seeming to have noticed the heavy silence that followed Sister Agatha's words.

Father Selwyn shook his head at the door as it closed.

"What?" she asked, looking around for a box of tissues. Maybe Sister Callwen had a point about carrying a handkerchief.

"Not to be negative. He's a good kid. It's just that Gavin seemed so promising when I read his application to serve as deacon here at Saint Anselm. The seminary had nothing but glowing remarks to make about him. And now . . ." Father Selwyn's voice trailed off.

"And now, what?"

"And now, he's a hot mess."

"Why?" Sister Agatha located a box of tissues under a stack of baptism certificates.

She plucked out two tissues and blew her nose. She resisted the temptation to open her notebook and write furiously. As Sister Callwen had not so subtly told her, writing everything someone was telling you into a book labeled *MURDER* could be a bit off-putting.

"No idea."

"Youth is wasted on the young."

Father Selwyn put the fishing line down and raised his smoothie. "Hear, hear." He took a sip from the straw and then stared at the glass for a moment. "Not bad, really." He looked up. "If only it weren't so green." They both sat in silence as the church bells rang the hour. "Do you really think someone killed Jacob?" Father Selwyn looked at her directly as he placed the smoothie on the coffee table between them. "You know — sometimes bad things just happen."

"I know that." Sister Agatha dabbed her eyes again. "But sometimes they have a little help. Read this." She handed him the note she had found in the hymnbook.

Jacob,

Don't worry, old chap. She would never do it. You're safe! Ha ha. See you in the beer tent!

— Mordy

Father Selwyn frowned. "You don't suppose it's Mordy Birkby, do you?"

"You're kidding? You know who Mordy is?"

"Well, the only Mordy that I know is Mordwywr Birkby. He goes by Mordy. I know his mother, actually, not really him. It's just that if you know Mrs. Birkby, you know Mordy."

"What do you mean?"

"Because she talks about him all the time. Poor kid. You've heard of helicopter moms?"

"Yes . . ."

"Well, Evelyn Birkby has elevated helicopter mom to drone."

"So why would this Mordy guy want to warn off Jacob? And who is 'she'?" This time Sister Agatha really did open her notebook and, uncapping her Sharpie, begin to write quickly. "Tell me everything you know about Mordy Birkby."

"Well, I don't know much about Mordy. I do know he's about Gavin's age. A little older. More like Jacob's age."

"He obviously knew Jacob. Do you know how?"

"Not sure. Except" — Father Selwyn paused and looked thoughtful — "I think they sang together in Only Boys Aloud. Back when it first started." Father Selwyn was a big supporter of the Welsh choir for young men, established to promote the long tradition of singing in Wales. The night that Only Boys Aloud had appeared on *Britain's Got Talent,* he had canceled Evensong at St. Anselm and put a sign on the chapel door advising everyone to go back home and turn on their telly.

"Yes, I'm sure Jacob was in Only Boys Aloud because he used to talk about it occasionally, and it seems as if Evelyn Birkby mentioned that Mordy was their most-talented-tenor-ever a few hundred times when I served with her on the parish planning board."

"Do the Birkbys go to Saint Anselm?"

"Oh, no, thank God."

Sister Agatha looked up from her notebook in surprise. "Why . . . *thank God*?"

"Well, Evelyn Birkby is at Saint Grenfell Church." Sister Agatha liked the small village of Grenfell with its old church spire, fish market, and miniscule lending library. The small hamlet was just a few miles south of Pryderi and looked like one of those little communities that time had barely touched. "And apparently makes the vicar there crazy," Father Selwyn continued. "She's one of those church ladies that you can't do without — you know, heads up every committee, chairs the pledge drive, keeps the youth program running, but . . ." Father Selwyn grimaced.

"But what?" Sister Agatha made a note. A notorious church lady such as Evelyn Birkby would be a very big fish in a very small pond in a place like St. Grenfell. A feeling of power can lead to anything. Even murder.

"But it's always 'My way or the highway,' and the vicar at Saint Grenfell, Macie Cadwalader, is about to hit the highway. She's young, right out of seminary." He shook his head. "A lamb to slaughter."

"Does Mordy live at home?"

"I wouldn't think so. I heard he's a park ranger over at Snowdonia. You might go to Saint Grenfell and talk to Macie. She's been dealing with Evelyn for the past year. I'm sure she'll be glad to talk with you. In fact . . ." Father Selwyn walked over to his desk and flipped through his calendar, which Bevan Penrose, St. Anselm's office administrator, kept updated. Everyone knew that without Bevan, Father Selwyn would have been lost. "In fact, Macie Cadwalader is going to be in Pryderi tomorrow noon for our Ministerial Association luncheon. Would you like to stop by and talk with her?"

"Of course. Can she meet me for afternoon tea, do you think? Reverend Mother wants all of us on hand to get ready for the Cheese Festival at Gwydion Castle. But I am sure I can get away for tea in the afternoon."

"I'll see if she can." Father Selwyn gave her a long look.

"What?"

"Just tell me — why are you so sure it was murder?"

"Heavy steel shelves don't just suddenly crash to the floor without some sort of encouragement."

"The bookshelves in the rectory library fell over one night. Without encouragement."

"That was because you put them together from a kit, and — you told me yourself — you had four screws and three bolts left over." Father Selwyn wasn't known for being handy with tools.

"Fair enough."

"And why was Jacob in the aging room? So early in the morning?"

"I'll give you that one. I've no idea."

"I know that it all means something." The suncatcher splashed new rainbows across the wall. "I just have no idea what." Sister Agatha looked at her friend. "I need to read more."

"Turn to the scriptures, you mean? That

always helps me."

"I was thinking more like the mystery section of the public library." She ignored Father Selwyn's eye roll. Sliding her notebook back into her apron pocket, she stood to leave and then stopped. "Where did you get this?" she said, picking up a small silver cross from the small table next to the door.

"The cross?" he said, slipping his spectacles on. "Gavin found that and gave it to me. I need to toss it in the 'Seek and Ye Shall Find' box."

"This is a postulant's cross."

"A what?"

"The cross that is given to each postulant at the Abbey — on a chain to wear as a necklace — when they first become postulants. We have them specially made by a silversmith in Cardiff. I'll take it back to the Abbey and see if anyone lost theirs. Most sisters never take it off." Sister Agatha lifted hers up from under her habit collar to show him. "Where did Gavin find it?"

"I assumed here in the church. Now that I think about it, he didn't say exactly."

"Ask him. I'd like to know."

Seven

"I have two books on interlibrary loan," Sister Agatha said, stepping up to the circulation desk at the Pryderi Public Library. She had left Father Selwyn to his green smoothie and walked the two blocks down Church Lane from St. Anselm's to the public library. The library was doing a brisk business this morning, with the toddler class enjoying story time in the far corner and a computer class packed into the tables in the reference section. Sister Agatha remembered when libraries had been quiet sanctums, silent as chapels. Now they were often abuzz with activity and voices. Perhaps a welcome change, she thought. "*The Complete System of 18th-Century Police Medicine,* by Johann Frankie, and *Turbo Twenty-Three,* by Janet Evanovich."

Sister Agatha had always loved libraries, which was why being the Abbey librarian was the perfect job for her. She didn't know what it was exactly — the smell of books, the possible discovery of a new author, or the feeling that the world, contained between the covers of all these pages, was at her fingertips. Her biggest dream was to one day walk into a library and see her own book on a shelf. Better yet, on a display table with her picture next to it.

"Right here, Sister," the older man staffing the circulation desk said, reaching to a shelf behind him and then sliding the books across to her. "Is there going to be a funeral mass said for Jacob?" he asked. "I've looked in the paper, but I haven't seen anything."

"It was just decided," she said. "The funeral will be this Friday. Ten o'clock at Saint Anselm."

"Jacob was a good sort. I'm neighbors with his mother. He did my garden for me one summer — planting, weeding, everything — when I was down-for-the-count with a bad back. He jumped right in."

Sister Agatha realized she should be interviewing people who had known Jacob. Maybe if she could ask a few questions of the right people, she might shed some light on the murder. She would need to brush up on her interview technique. Her mind raced for a moment. She was pretty sure she had a Rupert McFarland podcast on just that subject.

As she collected the two books and turned to go, she caught sight of Sister Callwen sitting at a table in the reference room. She must have finished with the flowers and raced into the village. *That's odd. We could have walked together,* she thought. Along with about ten others, Sister Callwen sat with a tablet in front of her, a stylus in her hand, and seemed to be following along with the instructor. Sister Agatha glanced at the sign by the entrance: STAY IN TOUCH / LEARN TO SKYPE. Why would Sister Callwen want to learn to Skype? She barely used email. She sent letters with stamps and envelopes. She still had a flip phone.

The class would be over in ten minutes, according to the sign, so Sister Agatha pulled a chair up to a nearby table and opened *Turbo Twenty-Three.* Stephanie Plum, hilarious and clever at tracking down the bad guy — in between getting her car blown up and escapades with her boyfriend — might be helpful in figuring out what was going on at the Abbey. Sister Agatha had gotten only a few pages into the first chapter when the Skype class broke up and Sister Callwen emerged from the reference room, stuffing a tablet into her bag.

"Sister Callwen," she said, standing. Much to her surprise, Sister Callwen looked the other way and walked quickly to the front door of the library. Sister Agatha followed her out onto the sidewalk and said her name again, more loudly.

Sister Callwen stopped and, turning slowly, said, "Oh, hello. I didn't see you."

"How could you've not seen me? I was right there. Plain as day. And why didn't you wait for me earlier? We could have walked in together."

"I'm in a hurry. I need to get back to the Abbey."

"Wait. Why're you learning to Skype?" Sister Agatha plopped down on a bench in front of the library. The day had turned humid, and it seemed broiling hot after the cool air of the library. "For heaven's sake, let's sit for a minute."

Sister Callwen shifted her bag to the other shoulder and looked at her watch. "It was just a class on using the Internet for genealogy."

"Then why are they teaching you to Skype? Unless you plan on chatting with the ghosts of dead ancestors, I don't think you need it for genealogy."

Sister Callwen ignored her question. "I'm doing it for Reverend Mother. She wants some of the histories of the early nuns at Gwenafwy researched."

"Reverend Mother is interested in Gwenafwy history?" Sister Agatha rolled her eyes. "Since when?"

"Look. I don't know. I'm just learning how to use some simple technology. I thought you would be pleased. You're always calling me a dinosaur." Sister Callwen shifted her bag again.

"No, it's great. But all you need is Google, and you could have come to me for that."

"I need to go. Enjoy your afternoon." Before Sister Agatha could reply, Sister Callwen had turned and hurried down the street.

Thank God. Nothing new. Just the same article from the *London Times* that she had looked at almost every day for three months. Sister Gwenydd slumped back and sighed with relief. Sister Agatha's desk sat tucked into the alcove created by one of the dormers cut into the sloping roof of the Abbey attic. Sister Gwenydd was glad she had heard Sister Agatha say she was going into the village for the afternoon. It gave her a chance to run up to the library and log on to Sister Agatha's computer.

She read the online article again.

LONDON — MARK JOHNSON, LOCAL SOLICITOR, WAS FOUND DEAD IN HIS APARTMENT ON 541 ST. JOHN STREET. THE CHIEF MEDICAL EXAMINER HAS LISTED THE OFFICIAL CAUSE OF DEATH AS UNDISCLOSED.

Undisclosed? What did that mean? At least it was better than "death by girlfriend" — by the girlfriend who now posed as a nun; the same girlfriend who had accidentally poisoned him, wanting to teach him a lesson with a bad case of hives or a wheezing fit, a day of indigestion, perhaps a vomit or two. She looked up from the computer screen and stared out the window again. Sister Agatha wouldn't be happy about someone using her computer, but the tiny screen on her phone was driving her crazy. She needed to be alone also. The one thing she had not realized about living with a community of nuns was how hard it would be sometimes to just be alone. It wasn't that the sisters didn't respect each other's privacy; they did. It was just that wherever you turned, someone was there. When she heard Sister Agatha remark that she was going to the village to check on books for the Abbey library, she knew she would have an hour of privacy. It was unlikely that any of the other nuns would climb the three flights of stairs to sit and read. And even if they did, she could pretend she was researching recipes online.

Sister Gwenydd reread the *London Times* article. She stared out the window at the green valley unfolding below, not noticing its striking beauty. All she could think about was that horrible morning in Mark's apartment, the day her life had changed forever. It wasn't that she had wanted to kill Mark — certainly not that! She had just wanted him to suffer. A little. A little suffering so he could realize how much she had suffered. She had loved him — and thought he loved her. She had loved him mostly because he was so interested in her and her life. Curious about everything that was important to her — what she had cooked that day, the pâtisserie instructor at Leiths who made her life miserable but taught her more than anyone ever had, the summers she spent in the country with her grandparents, learning the secret of creating the perfect petit fours. And weekends with Mark were wonderful. On Sunday mornings, they would sleep late, walk down the street to the sound of church bells, end up at their favorite coffee shop. And then read the entire *London Times* while sipping steaming lattes.

And, to make her fall in love with him

even more, he was an awesome grandson. His most endearing quality was his love for his grandmother, Gertrude Montgomery, an old woman living in North Wales whom he called "Oma." *Grandmother.* Once every month, without fail, Mark would leave London and go to the village of Pryderi to visit his grandmother in a nursing home there. One time, Sister Gwenydd had gone along with him, and they had spent the night in Pryderi. She remembered being struck by the beauty of the North and by Mark's genuine kindness and almost playful attentiveness to his grandmother, who suffered from dementia. On the train to Pryderi, Mark had kept Gwenydd laughing with hilarious stories about his family. His own parents were in Australia, and since he was an only child, his grandmother depended on him. He was all she had. Sister Gwenydd remembered how Mark had looked when he'd said it, that he was the only one his grandmother had left in the world. That was why he never missed his monthly weekend with her. As Gwenydd listened to him talk about his grandmother, she felt almost giddy with love for him.

At one point during their visit with Gertrude, they had gotten her out of her small room and taken a walk in the pleasant, sunny garden attached to the nursing home, Mark pushing his grandmother in her wheelchair and Gwenydd walking beside, her arm linked with Mark's. She imagined that they were a family. They seemed like a family. Truthfully, it was all she had ever wanted. People to love, who loved her. Her own childhood had been miserable. It wasn't so much that her parents didn't love her — she knew that they did — it was more that they had no way of expressing love. They were just so British. Stiff upper lip and all that. There wasn't a lot of room left for warmth and affection. She had always wanted a family that laughed. She couldn't help but wonder if her parents might have become more loving, more interested in her life, as they grew older. Or as she matured. She had never gotten to find out. They had died tragically some two years earlier on her twentieth birthday.

She and Mark had strolled down the streets of the charming village where the nursing home was. They had sat in a bustling tea shop and put flowers on the grave of his great-grandfather in the churchyard. By the time the short weekend was over, she had fallen in love with Mark and was certain he had fallen in love with her. Which, of course, was wrong. And she had felt like a fool ever after. Within a few weeks of the visit, it was clear that Mark had lost interest. He made excuses for not getting together, and then when he was with her, he spent the whole time on his phone, texting.

Sister Gwenydd cringed, thinking about how hard she had tried to ignore his dismissive attitude, doing everything she could to make him attentive and warm again. The harder she tried to recreate the early days of the relationship, the less interested Mark became. Finally, she had poisoned him.

The night she prepared the stew for him — a stew that theoretically would make him a little sick, mildly uncomfortable — had been the graduation ceremony at the Leiths School of Food and Wine. The Leiths program had involved months of intensive training, grueling fieldwork, and expensive tuition. Graduation meant she had done it — by herself with no help from anyone. And she had big hopes that her degree from Leiths would launch her career as a chef. The whole event was a crowning moment in her life. And all she wanted was to have Mark there, in the audience, sharing that accomplishment with her.

On the day of graduation, guests filled the auditorium — parents and grandparents, siblings and cousins, cheering the graduates on with applause and flowers, snapping photos. Continuously scanning the crowd, she finally realized that Mark wasn't going to show. She walked through the ceremony and the events afterward smiling and laughing and then came back to Mark's empty apartment and let herself cry. And when her tears had finally finished, she simmered a huge pot of lamb stew, stirring in a triple helping of fresh sage. Mark had always claimed to be desperately allergic to sage. The tiniest pinch would send him into a miserable allergic reaction. She left the sage-laden stew with a cheerful note telling him that she would be back the next morning. The last thing she did was prop her Leiths diploma up on the table. Maybe when he saw it, he would be overwhelmed by guilt — as well as hives and wheezing.

Early the next morning, thinking that he had passed a miserable night, she had called him. The call had gone straight to voice mail, and so she assumed he had figured it out and was sulking. By late that afternoon, she had begun to regret her actions, and she went to Mark's apartment to apologize. She found his stiff body, dead at the kitchen table, slumped over a bowl of the lamb stew. Although she grabbed her cell phone to call

999, she stopped. He was dead. No amount of medical help could change that. And she had killed him. Her breath coming in short gasps, her pulse pounding, she had slipped her phone into her jacket pocket and run from the apartment. That horrible moment, three months ago, had been the start of her life on the run.

At first, she hid out in London with some friends; then she went to the Shetland Islands, where she had heard about a job as a sous chef. The job didn't pan out, and the islands were way too wet and wild for her. Not knowing what to do, she considered returning to London when she remembered, with a sudden shock, Gertrude. With a crushing guilt, she remembered Mark saying that he was all Gertrude had. Gwenydd knew what it was like to be alone. It was her fault an old woman was now completely alone in the world. Did she wonder why no one came to visit anymore? Even in her dementia, was she grieving? Gwenydd knew she had to do something. She couldn't stand the thought of what she had taken from the old woman — her only lifeline to the world outside the nursing home. Gwenydd boarded a train to North Wales and the village of Pryderi.

She hadn't planned on staying in Pryderi

— only to stop there just long enough to check on Mark's grandmother. But she had almost no money left to keep running, and Pryderi seemed as good a place as any to stop, at least for a while. When she heard that there was an abbey of Anglican nuns just outside the village, she thought she might hide out there. It would be a place to crash for a few weeks, and she could still do visits to Gertrude. She had once read online about how abbeys and monasteries let people visit with the goal of discerning a "call to religious life." This meant nothing to Gwenydd at the time; her eye had just caught the words "free room and board." She'd done a quick Google of Anglican religious orders and how they differed from Roman Catholic ones, cleaned up as best she could, and knocked on the door of Gwenafwy Abbey. To her surprise, they had taken her in with very few questions asked. Weeks had turned to months, and, without meaning to, she had fallen in love with both the nuns at the Abbey and with the old woman she now thought of as family.

Her weekly visits to the Care Center had become routine — she stopped by for an hour or so every Tuesday when she bought produce at the farmer's market in the village. The staff at the Care Center, friendly in an overworked sort of way, had never questioned her motives. She had even given them her cell phone number in case something ever happened. The sisters at Gwenafwy had no idea she was a murderer on the lam. They thought she was a young woman trying to discern a call to a religious order. And a really good cook. On Reverend Mother's encouragement, Sister Gwenydd had taken over the Abbey kitchen. As it turned out, the nuns were horrible cooks.

I'm not a murderer, she thought to herself. *I simply underestimated a food allergy. He always insisted that sage made him wheeze and vomit. He never mentioned that it made him dead.* She sat up and read again the page in the *Times.* Well, no news was good news. Maybe things would work out after all.

She was about to make her way back down to her room when she saw it:

LANDLORD OF DECEASED TENANT SUES NEW SCOTLAND YARD. JAMES GLAVEN IS SUING NEW SCOTLAND YARD FOR DAMAGES FOLLOWING A SEARCH OF THE APARTMENT OF TENANT, MARK JOHNSON, DECEASED THREE MONTHS AGO. USING EXCESSIVE FORCE, THE MEMBERS OF THE NEW SCOTLAND YARD SWAT TEAM LEFT THE APART-

MENT IN SHAMBLES. NEW SCOTLAND YARD HAS REFUSED COMMENT.

She stood up, her heart slamming in her chest, and stumbled across the room to the dormer window opposite Sister Agatha's desk. From this side of the attic, she could see the sunlit fields, bathed in a blaze of green, dipping and stretching until they all ended in the thinnest edge of silver, the Irish Sea to the north. Normally, she would have been struck by the power of such a view — having lived her whole life in the suburbs of London, she was surprised at how much she loved the Welsh countryside. But this morning, as the clock tower chimed half past ten, all she could see was the image of Mark's dead body slumped over the bowl of lamb stew. Leaning against the cool stone wall, she yanked her long auburn hair out of its ponytail and fought down a rising panic. What if the constable started asking questions about Jacob, and he stumbled across information about her? Worse, what if they found out that she had murdered — albeit accidentally — her boyfriend? Wouldn't she be a natural suspect in Jacob's death? It was as if the dark cloud of that earlier time had followed her and threatened to overshadow her altogether. Her heart began to race again. A quiet inner voice told her exactly what to do — go to Reverend Mother and tell her everything. Maybe the sisters would help her. But what if she told the sisters about Mark, and they kicked her out? Perhaps even worse than going to jail, she would lose the one thing she had always longed for, a place to belong.

She went back to Sister Agatha's computer and, before clicking off, deleted her browser history.

At the same moment that Sister Gwenydd closed the door of the attic library and made her way down the steep stairs, Sister Agatha closed the top drawer of Sister Callwen's desk. She had returned to the Abbey only a few minutes after Sister Callwen. She knew she should have felt a staggering guilt sneaking into another sister's private quarters and rummaging through her dresser and closet, desk, and wardrobe, but things had gotten too weird with Sister Callwen — first the voice mail and then the encounter just now at the library — for her to be bothered with such trivial concerns as privacy and ethics. And anyway, there had been a murder. That changed things. Looking out the window, she could see Sister Callwen, her book bag still slung over her shoulder, two flights below standing next to a long row of zucchinis in the Abbey garden. She and Sister Matilda were engaged in a heated conversation. Sister Agatha shook her head. How could anyone get that worked up over squash?

Turning away from the window, she saw it. The new tablet sat tucked under Sister Callwen's volume of *Psalms for All Seasons* on top of her desk. An iPad Mini 4 with a silver chrome cover. Sister Agatha picked it up reverently. Who would have taken Sister Callwen for an Apple person? She turned it over and tapped the screen. The iPad pinged to life with a photo of Heavenly Gouda with a blue ribbon from last year's Cheese-Off. And it wasn't password-protected. *Just like Sister Callwen.* She tapped the Skype app and then the SENT icon. Nothing. She tapped HISTORY. Still nothing.

Sister Callwen hadn't Skyped with anyone.

EIGHT

"The problem, Father, is that you don't take a Skype class for genealogy." Sister Agatha didn't mention that she had searched Sister Callwen's private room. Father Selwyn could be very particular about things like that.

Wanting some fresh air and time to think, and making the excuse of needing more ink cartridges for the Abbey library printer, she had walked back into the village for the second time that day, hoping to clear her head.

She found herself back in Father Selwyn's study, and this time he really was working on his sermon. Books, Bible, and theological journals had replaced the fishing paraphernalia on his coffee table. *Expository Insights on the Gospel of Mark* sat side by side with *The Complete Book of Clergy Jokes.*

"What was it then?" Father Selwyn poured them each a cup of tea and offered her an oatcake. "I appreciate that you always seem to show up at tea time. Then I don't have to have tea alone."

She poured sugar and cream into her cup, and when she looked around for a spoon, Father Selwyn handed her a pencil, the eraser still wet from stirring his own tea. "I went back to the library and read the class description. It was definitely a class on how to Skype." She swished the pencil around in her teacup and then bit into the oatcake. Crispy, just as an oatcake was meant to be. Stirring your tea with a number-two soft lead pencil was not how it was meant to be.

Father Selwyn leaned back on the slouchy cushions of the couch and brushed crumbs off the front of his cassock. "Well, so what? Maybe Sister Callwen wants to learn something new without everyone knowing about it."

"But why lie and say it's genealogy? I mean, think about it. It's a ridiculous lie. Who cares if she learns to Skype or skydive? Why not just tell the truth? And why the elaborate cover-up about Reverend Mother wanting a genealogy study?"

"It does seem a bit odd."

"And she had a tablet with her. A new tablet."

"So?"

"So, Sister Callwen barely knows how to use a cell phone. She asked me the other day where she could buy a ribbon for her typewriter. She thinks the Cloud has something to do with the weather. That isn't a person who suddenly goes out and buys an iPad Mini 4 in silver chrome."

"Do you think this makes Sister Callwen a suspect in Jacob's murder?"

"I don't know exactly. It seems like a bit of a reach. But as Inspector McFarland says — never dismiss anything, especially early on in an investigation." She paused and looked hard at her old friend. "You just said 'Jacob's murder'? Are you now in agreement that his death was not accidental?"

Instead of answering, Father Selwyn stood up and walked slowly over to the shelves under the window. "I've been thinking since we talked earlier." He picked up a binder that was lying on top of a stack of journals. "This is the work log for Saint Anselm's," he said, handing it to her. "Bevan brought it by for me to check the staff hours this afternoon. I noticed something. You know how conscientious Jacob was. Never took a sick day, never slacked off. In fact, my biggest problem with him was that he worked too hard for what we could pay him." Father Selwyn sat back down on the couch and looked out the window, almost as if he were talking to himself.

"I know," Sister Agatha said, opening the binder. "Same thing at the convent. Always staying late, coming early."

"So, take a look at the third page. He logged in at four o'clock Monday morning. Yet his time of death was approximately five o'clock, according to Dr. Beese. And he never logged out, which is very unusual. Jacob was a stickler for following the rules about things. Then we know he biked over to the Abbey, since you found his bike in front of the cheese barn. Then he must have gone into the aging room immediately — or it would seem so. His dead body was found three hours later. Something made him leave his work, not bother to sign out, and go directly to the aging room. All of which is both puzzling and totally out of character."

"What are you thinking?"

"I think someone or something caused him to go to the aging room. Where he met his death."

"And he went there with a hymnbook from St. Anselm's. Why?" Sister Agatha paused, thinking. "I know that you know Mordy. At least a little. Do you know any of Jacob's other friends? Anyone who knew anything about him and his life?"

"Not really. Jacob was very private."

"Where did he hang out?"

"Well, I know that he sometimes went to the pub in the village, Saints and Sinners."

"Would you go there with me?"

"I'll do one better. I'll buy you a pint."

That night, when evening prayer had ended, a few of the nuns retired to their rooms, but the rest decided that a moonlit walk to the orchard would be restful. It had been barely twenty-four hours since finding Jacob in the aging room, and waves of grief seemed to reverberate throughout the usually cheerful community. Sister Winifred handed out flashlights so that they might look for Reverend Mother's cell phone as they walked. Reverend Mother thought she might have dropped it Saturday afternoon when the St. Anselm confirmands had come with Gavin for a picnic under the apple trees. As her sisters set off, Sister Agatha took the opportunity to slip out and head back to the village for the third time that day, a walk of ten minutes if one set out briskly.

Stepping off Church Lane, the dirt and gravel road that led from the Abbey to the village, she turned onto the footpath from the north end of the bridge over the river and followed as it wound up to the center of the village. She slipped through the narrow alley between The Buttered Crust and the bike shop and followed it up onto the cobbled stones of Main Street. The shops had closed, but the warm summer evening had drawn out the citizens of Pryderi. The streetlights came on one by one as she walked the length of Main Street toward the pub, Saints and Sinners. Sister Agatha noticed a young couple walking hand in hand along the river and several older women strolling through the village center, looking into the windows of the shops as they chatted.

She pushed through the front door of Saints and Sinner at the far end of Main Street and scanned the crowded room for Father Selwyn. She spotted him sitting at the bar, and he waved her over. He had ordered them each a pint of Rhymney pale ale, and when the drinks came, Father Selwyn clinked his glass to hers. "May whatever we might uncover honor Jacob's memory."

Sister Agatha hadn't been in a pub this late at night for at least twenty years, and she was a little shocked at the volume. She and the sisters sometimes stopped by Saints and Sinners for lunch if they were in the village or even for a pint if it was late afternoon. Sunday brunch was an occasional favorite. But late night was a different story. Loud music throbbed over the packed dance floor; two young women who seemed to have had a few pints too many shouted and laughed as they tossed darts at a board; waiters pushed their way between tables, expertly holding trays above their heads. The entire atmosphere was boisterous, smoky, and felt as if it had just the slightest edge of danger to it. Sister Agatha loved it. Her detective, Bates Melanchthon, would have to frequent such a place very soon. Perhaps in the next chapter. She patted her apron pocket to make sure her notebook was at the ready.

Father Selwyn leaned forward and motioned to the barman. He looked about twenty-five years old, a little younger than Jacob, and Sister Agatha wondered if he had known Jacob. He was slender, with an intensity about him. Blond hair fell over his forehead, and, she noted approvingly, his button-down white shirt was neatly pressed, paired up with a tie. *Finally, a young person who doesn't look like an unmade bed.* She noticed that he raised his eyebrows just slightly at the sight of the two of them. She thought that was odd until she realized it probably wasn't often a nun and a vicar walked into the bar. Which sounded like the beginning to a bad joke.

"What can I do for you?" the young barman asked.

"Did you know Jacob Traherne?" Father Selwyn said. He was nearly shouting to be heard over the noise. "He came in here, I think. Pretty often."

The young man hesitated. "I know . . . knew Jacob."

"Could we talk where it's a bit quieter?" Father Selwyn asked.

The young man shrugged. "Cover for me, would you?" he said to an older woman who was pouring drinks next to him. He untied his apron and motioned for them to follow. Opening a small door marked Private at the end of the bar, he led them into a tiny office with a desk and two folding chairs. Crates of wine, a cascading pile of binders, and several boxes of cocktail napkins were stacked along the walls. Two broken barstools had been stashed in a corner. The young man took a seat on the edge of the desk, and Sister Agatha and Father Selwyn each chose a folding chair. "I'm Michael, by the way," he said.

"Father Selwyn and Sister Agatha," Father

Selwyn said, standing again and filling the cramped space with his tall stature. He extended his hand to Michael. "We should have introduced ourselves, but it was so loud out there, I couldn't hear myself think." He sat back down. "You knew Jacob?"

"Isn't that why you're here? Because of Jacob?" Sister Agatha thought he sounded defensive. No, maybe defensive was too strong a word. Guarded, perhaps. That was when she noticed his eyes. They were far too tired for someone his age.

The pulsing music outside the thin office walls seemed to pause for a moment as Michael looked at them. He blew out his breath. "Yes. I knew Jacob." He took a pack of cigarettes out of his shirt pocket and, with trembling fingers, tried to shake one out. He couldn't do it. Father Selwyn reached forward and took the pack from him, Sister Agatha watched with interest as he expertly popped out a cigarette and handed it to Michael. But her eyes went wide as he fished a lighter out of his own coat pocket and held it while Michael lit up. To her knowledge, he hadn't smoked since seminary.

"OK to smoke in here?" Sister Agatha asked, glancing around the small space.

"Nope," Michael said, taking a deep drag.

The cigarette seemed to calm him; his hands stopped shaking, and he looked at Father Selwyn, his eyes even more exhausted. Father Selwyn put a hand on Michael's shoulder before he sat back down. "I'm sorry for your loss. You and Jacob were friends?"

Michael pulled away and, pushing his hair off his forehead, gave a shaky laugh. "What do you want? I know Jacob liked you — he spoke well of you. But I've not got the greatest opinion of priests. No offense. Or nuns either, for that matter," he said, nodding at Sister Agatha.

"We're just trying to tie together some loose ends about Jacob's death. And so we wanted to talk to some of the folks who knew him best."

"And you knew to come to me?"

"Well, we knew Jacob often came to this pub, and we thought you might know something about who he was here with or . . . or anything that might help us understand his death a little better." The puzzled look on Michael's face bothered Sister Agatha. What effect would it have on this young man — obviously a friend of Jacob's — if he was suddenly confronted with the fact that Jacob's death had been murder? Or did he know something about the murder? *Or was he the murderer?* She resisted the urge to pull out her notebook.

Father Selwyn leaned forward. "We aren't here with any agenda, Michael. Just asking a few questions. If you don't mind, tell me about your relationship to Jacob. Were you friends from the choir? Rugby? School chums?"

Michael snorted, took a final long drag on his cigarette, and smashed it out in an ashtray on the desk. "Jacob was my boyfriend. And my best friend. OK? He wanted us to come to you, Father, and see if we could get married. He wanted a church wedding so bad. And I said, 'No way.' I wasn't walking into a church and letting some priest . . . And now . . . and now . . . there's no chance. It's too late." Sister Agatha watched as Michael turned to the window and tears streamed down his face. Father Selwyn went over to him and stood, a hand on Michael's shoulder. The music from the bar kicked in and nearly shook the room, but all she could hear was Michael's ragged sobs.

Sister Agatha clutched the dashboard as Father Selwyn skirted a lorry lumbering slowly up Church Lane. Downshifting for the short but steep climb to the Abbey, he turned to her. "What did you think?"

"Eyes on the road, Father. Please. What do I think? I think there is more to the story."

"So do I." Father Selwyn turned the wheel and, barely slowing down, careened into the Abbey drive, skidding to a halt in front of the lilac bushes. "By the way, Macie Cadwalader said she can meet tomorrow for afternoon tea. Are you still up for it?"

"I am, though it's all-hands-on-deck at the Abbey getting ready for the Cheese-Off."

"Are you letting cheese-making get in the way of sleuthing?"

Sister Agatha found herself too tired to respond with her usual sarcasm. And the pale ale had gone right to her head. "Of course not. But I am a Gwenafwy Abbey sister first — a mystery writer second." But as she climbed the stairs to her room, she wondered.

NINE

"He's talking about his mother. I'm sure of it."

"Mordy's mother?" Sister Agatha said to the Reverend Macie Cadwalader sitting across from her in the back booth of The Buttered Crust Tea Shop. The Buttered Crust was doing a rollicking trade for an afternoon tea midweek. Following Matins, Sister Agatha had spent the rest of the morning working in the cheese barn and then gotten in an hour or two making spine labels for the new shipment of books she had just lugged up to the Abbey library.

"Yep," the young vicar said, looking at the note that sat on the table between them. "Evelyn Birkby. The only woman in Mordy's life that he would warn anyone against. His mother."

"She's that bad?"

"Worse! Have you heard of clergy-killers? You know, parishioners who suck the life out of a pastor? Well, that's Evelyn." Macie Cadwalader shook her head and dug into her buttered scone.

Sister Agatha noticed that she was indeed as young as Father Selwyn had said, but very smart, well-spoken, and made a silk blouse and clerical collar paired up with a dove-gray pencil skirt look quite chic. She had shiny blue-black hair cut in a stylish bob, straight white teeth, and a figure so slim that Sister Agatha could only watch in admiration as she spooned clotted cream over a scone fresh from the ovens of The Buttered Crust. Her green eyes snapped as she described the latest plans for her new church, which she seemed to have taken on by storm. Ordained only a few months before, the young vicar had been sent by the bishop to the tiny parish of St. Grenfell, an aging parish that some had predicted would close its doors soon. But the way she tackled the problems of the struggling church, you would have thought her new parish was St. Asaph's Cathedral. Sister Agatha smiled to herself, thinking of what this youthful enthusiasm and determination might be stirring up over at St. Grenfell. "Do you think she would go too far, though? Would Evelyn Birkby harm someone to get what she wanted?"

"Harm someone?" Reverend Cadwalader frowned, holding a cup of tea in one hand and picking up the note with the other. "Well, I don't know."

Sister Agatha waited. It seemed that the vicar wanted to say more, and as Rupert McFarland was always saying, witnesses had only one speed — their own.

"It's just that Evelyn Birkby is insanely protective of her family — especially Mordy. He's a decent chap, though you seriously want to hate the guy because his mother brags about him constantly. She honestly cannot open her mouth without telling a Mordy story. But he's a good person."

Sister Agatha took a bite of the oatcake the young waiter placed in front of her and picked up her Sharpie.

"Listen to this." Reverend Cadwalader leaned forward, dropping the note onto the table. "The Christmas pageant at Saint Grenfell is a really big deal every year. And the kids progress up the ranks. Like . . . first you're a lamb, then the next year you get to be a shepherd, then the next year one of the kings, et cetera. The really big parts are saved for the oldest kids who have done their time in the manger. So to speak. The most honored character for a boy to play is the angel Gabriel. Everyone wants to be Gabriel because he swoops onto stage with these magnificent wings, has a really dramatic speaking part. It's even better than being Joseph, who really just sits there. Well, anyway, years ago, when Mordy was chosen to play one of the lambs, his mother raised such a protest that he was finally given the role of Gabriel. Can you believe it?" Reverend Cadwalader stared at Sister Agatha. "Gabriel."

"How old was Mordy?"

"Three. The first Gabriel to ever wear diapers." She laughed and took a gulp of tea. "I guess the entire pageant committee threatened to quit, but in the end, Evelyn won out."

"So she's hardcore. But would she kill for her son?"

Reverend Cadwalader looked up, no longer laughing. "I wish I could say she wouldn't. But honestly, she might."

At almost the same moment that Sister Agatha was finishing up tea with St. Grenfell's new vicar, Sister Gwenydd was choosing kohlrabi from the sidewalk stand two doors down. She loved the fresh markets that she found in the village — local produce grown by farmers in the North Country was just so much nicer than anything in London.

Suddenly, she stepped back and ducked behind the display of kohlrabi, her palms sweaty and her breath short. Waiting, she kept her head down until the long black Mercedes disappeared around the corner. The tinted windows of the car made it impossible for her to see in, but she knew the driver could see out. She could only hope the man driving hadn't recognized her standing there perusing the vegetables while dressed in her nun's blue habit. The last time he had seen her — only the day before, but it seemed much longer with everything that had happened — she had been wearing a short black dress and Gucci sandals. She had stayed too long at the nursing home and had raced out without changing back into her habit. She had missed the village bus and had started the walk back to the Abbey. She had thought that if she timed it right, she could arrive just as the sisters were busy working in the gardens, and then she could change quickly and slip into the kitchen to prepare lunch. As she had hurriedly started her walk up the steep climb of Church Lane, a long black Mercedes had pulled up and offered her a ride. In a past life, she would never have gotten into a car with a stranger. But this was Pryderi. Unlike the other sisters, she hated walking back and forth to the village, and she was in a terrible hurry. And anyway, the guy was at least twenty years older, so what was the harm? As she slid into the car, he had smiled. His eyes, startlingly blue, seemed friendly, and he asked where she was headed. When she said the Abbey, he looked at her askance.

"Oh. I'm . . . the new housekeeper," she lied quickly. She pulled her short black skirt down a bit. "The old one isn't there anymore, and I'm filling in." She suddenly felt nervous. *Is this such a great idea?* The guy looked respectable — well-dressed, long-limbed, with an aristocratic nose.

"I didn't get your name," she asked as the car stopped in front of the Abbey. To her shock, instead of answering, he lunged across the seat and pressed his mouth against hers. Grabbing the car handle with one hand, she shoved him back as hard as she could with the other. "Bloody tease!" the man said, his blue eyes turned flinty. Just as she was about to catapult out of the car, he caught her arm and, with a leer, reached over and yanked the silver-cross necklace off her neck, then shoved her out the door.

She knew she needed to report what had happened, but it was all too frightening, and what could she do? She couldn't tell anyone without blowing her own cover.

At least no one from the Abbey had seen her get out of the car.

"New postulants, increased revenue, a balanced budget! Why not walk on water, bring someone back from the dead, ascend to heaven, and sit at the right hand of God?" Sister Agatha said, her face red, voice shaking. Sisters Callwen, Harriet, Winifred, and Agatha had gathered in Reverend Mother's office to discuss Reverend Mother's disastrous meeting with the bishop the day before. Reverend Mother was briefing her leadership team of senior nuns before taking it to the entire community.

Sister Agatha had hurried home from her tea with Macie Cadwalader, her mind racing with plans for investigating Evelyn Birkby as a possible suspect. Before she and Macie had said good-bye, she had asked the young vicar for help in getting more information about Evelyn Birkby. "Of course, I'll do some sleuthing," Macie had said. "It'll be a nice change from planning confirmation and organizing the women's retreat." Perhaps Reverend Cadwalader was just the ticket for finding out what Evelyn Birkby had been up to the night Jacob had been killed. Sister Agatha had just settled into her desk in the attic when Reverend Mother had texted her. An emergency meeting. Sighing, she had closed her notebook and quickly made her way downstairs. Reverend Mother didn't often call meetings this late.

Sister Harriet and Sister Callwen sat on the slouchy leather couch, each holding a glass of Cabernet. Sister Harriet frowned into her wine while Sister Callwen looked thoughtful — as though, thought Sister Agatha, the world wasn't ending. Sitting across from them was Sister Winifred. As usual, she had chosen the most imposing chair in the room — an ancient upholstered wingback left from the Abbey's Victorian days — and she sat with the posture of an Edwardian at dinner with the royal family. Her knitting needles flew, her tiny feet resting an inch above the floor. "Suzanne Bainton is a snake in the grass," she said without dropping a stitch. "She'll be the end of the Church in Wales. I say we inform the Archbishop immediately."

"I agree," Sister Agatha added. "It's time to bring in the big guns." Her hand trembled as she picked up her wine glass. A drop of Cabernet sloshed onto the stack of unopened letters on Reverend Mother's desk.

"Take a deep breath, Sisters. And, please,

stop talking about guns." Reverend Mother sat behind her desk, tossing her basketball from hand to hand. Sister Agatha studied her friend with concern. Ordinarily Reverend Mother was steady in a crisis, the very embodiment of "keep calm and carry on." But today her face was drawn in lines of exhaustion, and she was handling the basketball like a nervous center at the free-throw line preparing for a critical score. The other sisters were picking up her agitation. Sister Harriet had put down her wine glass and opened up her sketch pad. Her charcoal pencil was moving across the page in quick, jagged sweeps. She was always saying that when the going got tough, she prayed, and when the going got really tough, she sketched. The only other sound in the room was Sister Winifred's knitting needles. She worked endlessly on receiving blankets, mittens, and hats for her many nieces and nephews as well as every nun at Gwenafwy. A few Christmases ago, she had knitted a Hogwarts scarf for each sister. The bell in the clock tower chimed eleven times, and still no one spoke.

Finally, Sister Callwen cleared her throat. "Is it possible that the bishop has a point? Should we save the Abbey?"

"What?" Sister Agatha said. "Did you say

should we save the Abbey?"

Reverend Mother held the basketball in front of her and looked over the top at Sister Callwen. "You don't want our life here at Gwenafwy to continue?" Her voice sounded angry and was edged with desperation. "After all that we've done the past few years to revive things? The cheese business is only three years old — it should start bringing in more money in a year or two. We have a vital outreach to the community. We've always been faithful to our calling, to our mission. What more do you want?" Reverend Mother took a shuddering breath and made a visible effort to control herself. She faced Sister Callwen. "What are you thinking? Tell me."

"You may not want to hear it."

"You've never spared my feelings in the past." The caustic tone of her voice sent a chill into the room. Sister Agatha slowly set her wine glass on the coffee table in front of her and, sitting up straight, smoothed the wrinkles in her apron. Sister Harriet stopped sketching, her charcoal pencil poised midmotion, her eyes watching Sister Callwen. Sister Winifred, who hated anything at the Abbey that even hinted of conflict, had gone pale, her knitting needles halted midpurl.

"My apologies," Sister Callwen said. "I'm

only wondering if things have changed beyond our control?" Ignoring the loud snort from Sister Agatha, she continued, "Is it time to admit that the world has gone on without us? Young people don't join religious orders anymore — good heavens, they don't even go to church. The people in the village love us, but do they see us as the hub of their community we once were? And it is no secret that we are aging. Soon there will be none of us left to do the work of the Abbey. Maybe it is time to . . . to . . ." Even Sister Callwen seemed unable to put a voice to everyone's deepest fears.

"Time to give up? Is that what you're saying? Throw in the towel? Roll over and play dead?" Sister Agatha leaned forward, struggling to get up out of the deep chair without spilling her wine. She stood, clutching her glass, her face red, notebook sticking up out of her apron pocket. The other sisters could just see the word *MURDER.* She glared from one to the other. "Did our Lord ever say to the disciples, 'So gentlemen, it's been a nice ride, but I guess we're finished. Go back to your fishing boats'?"

The sisters watched as Agatha took a long sip of her wine and then picked up the Bible sitting on the coffee table as if to read from it; instead, she slammed it down with a thump. Sister Harriet jumped and dropped her pencil. It fell to the carpet, where she left it, untouched, her eyes on Sister Agatha. "No," Sister Agatha said. "Jesus did not give up. And neither did Moses. Or Martin Luther, or . . . or . . ." Sister Agatha paused for one moment and took another rather long drink of Cabernet. "Or Winston Churchill!" She collapsed back into the overstuffed chair, sending a few drops of red wine splashing onto the wingback's floral upholstery.

"Sisters," Reverend Mother said, sitting up straight, the basketball rolling off her desk to the floor, where it bounced twice. "Do you smell smoke?"

They all raced out the door, then stood frozen in shock. Flames shot from the roof of the cheese barn and smoke billowed up against the night sky.

"Someone call the fire department," Reverend Mother yelled, running back into her office. Sister Agatha remembered suddenly that Reverend Mother's cell phone was still lost. "Wake up the other sisters. Get them out of the building." In a flurry of panic, the four sisters flew into action.

Agatha headed out the door and then stopped short in her race toward the milking shed where all the cheese-making equipment was stored, a bolt of fear making her nearly tremble. She had experienced a horrible fire once as a small child on her parents' sheep farm. She had never forgotten the terror of the milk cows kicking and bellowing in their stalls, the sheep piling on top of each other in their desperation to escape the barn. Panicked, she thought of the back of the cheese barn where the animals were kept. Had the fire reached that far back? They had to be released. The chickens. The potbellied pigs, Luther and Calvin. *Good heavens,* she thought, where was Bartimaeus? He would be frantic by now, trapped in his stall.

Picking up her skirts, she sprinted toward the stable.

From what seemed like a long distance away, she heard Sister Winifred screaming her name. But she kept running, straight toward the burning barn, without looking back or slowing down. Suddenly, a heavy blow knocked the air out of her lungs, and she slammed to the ground. Something huge had landed on top of her and covered her face. In a panic, she realized she had been blinded; everything had gone dark. Pushing hard, she shoved whatever it was on top of her off and struggled to sit up, gasping for breath. Flailing in the dark, she realized the veil that had fallen over her eyes was actually a veil. And it belonged to Sister Callwen, who had tackled her, landing them both on the soft grass in front of the lilac bushes. “Good heavens, get off me. You must weigh two hundred pounds.”

“I beg your pardon. I weigh nothing of the sort, and, for the record, I have no doubt saved your life.” Sister Callwen rolled off Agatha and lay on her back on the damp grass. “I could tell you were heading for the stable. You can’t go in there. Are you crazy? The smoke alone would kill you.” Agatha could see that Sister Callwen was breathing in short gasps and remembered how severe her last asthma attack had been. “Don’t just stand there; help me up.” Sister Agatha extended a hand to Sister Callwen and, with a grunt, pulled her friend to her feet. “We’re both far too old for this nonsense.”

Sister Agatha felt a sudden surge of affection for Sister Callwen. The feeling of warmth and affection was quickly replaced by frustration and annoyance. “The animals . . .” Agatha said, her voice rising above the noise. “Bartimaeus!” The fire trucks had arrived from the village and were tearing down the drive. “We can’t do anything now,” Sister Callwen said. “The firemen will get the animals out. But I don’t think the flames have reached the back."

Suddenly, the sound of pounding boots came up behind them. Three volunteer firemen from the village rushed past. "Four chickens, two pigs, and a pony!" Sister Agatha yelled. She waved her arms toward the barn. One of the firefighters raised his hand as he ran past her, dragging a fire hose. He had heard her. Holding hands, the two sisters stood silently for a moment watching as the firemen reached the stable door at the back of the barn.

Sister Callwen was the first to turn away. "Come on," she said. "We need to help the others. They'll get the animals out. Have faith." The two women hurried back to where the other sisters were working frantically. As the firefighters sent arcs of water at the burning roof, the nuns carried items out of the milking shed, attempting to save the cheese equipment. Stainless steel tubs, draining boards, and rind presses lined the edge of the herb garden and spilled onto the walk leading to the kitchen. Sister Agatha and Sister Callwen joined Reverend Mother and Sister Winifred in pushing and tugging at the new homogenizer until they managed to drag it outside and onto the side lawn.

A police cruiser pulled into the drive with

Father Selwyn's BMW Mini right behind it. The firemen continued dousing the roof, and it seemed to Sister Agatha that the flames were starting to dissipate. One by one, the sisters lay down their brooms and buckets and stood, exhausted, next to the fire trucks, watching in silence. Father Selwyn stood beside Reverend Mother, an arm around her shoulder. Just as Sister Agatha heard the village clock chime twice, the firemen called a halt. The fire was out.

"Well," said Sister Harriet, the first to speak. "Look on the bright side. Only the roof is gone; they've saved the rest." No one responded. Moonlight washed the lingering wisps of smoke a ghostly silver and turned the fire trucks a pale gray.

"Come on, everyone," Reverend Mother said. "Tea and cake in the kitchen. Let's refresh ourselves and then try to go back to bed. I wouldn't mind getting at least a little sleep tonight. And remember, we have much for which to thank God." Taking Sister Harriet's hand in hers, she led the way to the Abbey kitchen. Father Selwyn stood, talking with the fire chief.

"It could have been worse," Sister Callwen said, falling in step with Sister Agatha. "And Bartimaeus is unharmed. I guess he was out at the orchard shed instead of in his usual stall."

"Oh, thank God." Sister Agatha said. Her relief at knowing the old pony was safe nearly brought her to tears. She forced herself to hold back a sob that came to her throat. The entire Abbey could have burned to the ground and her biggest concern was an ancient Shetland pony. But all the sisters knew she had a soft spot for Bartimaeus. She brought him an apple or bit of sugar every day, curried his coat until it shined, and considered him a confidant.

"Luther and Calvin and the chickens were turned out by the village firefighters — God bless them — and they all seem quite content passing the night under the porch of the gardening shed," Sister Matilda added. Sister Matilda was the Abbey gardener. Her sleeves perpetually rolled up, a farmer's bib over her habit, and a pair of ancient Wellingtons on her size-ten feet, Sister Matilda had transformed the flower gardens, vegetable beds, and fruit trees of the Abbey into a botanic showpiece. Sister Agatha often watched in awe as Sister Matilda emptied her apron pockets at the end of a long summer day, extracting a cache that could include everything from tulip bulbs to seed packets, kohlrabi to bunches of kale. Sister Matilda's favorite hymn was "In the Garden," and she was always saying she felt closest to God when she was on her knees digging in the dirt. "And the fire didn't spread. I was fearful for my rows of prize zucchini, but all is well."

Sister Callwen nodded to Sister Matilda and then, putting her arm through Agatha's, pulled her along. "The old pony is perfectly fine," she said quietly. Sister Agatha squeezed her arm in wordless thanks. They followed the other sisters into the kitchen.

"And the cheese equipment wasn't damaged either," Sister Harriet said, reaching into the cupboard and pulling out a cake tin. "That's something. The roof is gone, but I'm sure that we have plenty of insurance on the building."

"The problem is the cheese. Most of it had been moved to refrigerated storage. Thank God, we will have enough for the vendor tent and the competition. But all the Gouda that was still in the cheese barn is ruined." Sister Winifred's voice had the slightest tremble, which was so unusual for her that she cleared her voice immediately. "But, it could have been worse. I will not despair."

"Come on, Sister Winifred. Go sit down with Reverend Mother. I'll bring you a cup of tea," Sister Harriet said, slicing cake and putting it on plates. "And some of Sister Gwenydd's almond cake. You'll feel better."

Sister Callwen ran cold water over a tea towel, wrung it out, and handed it to Agatha. "I know you're still angry about what I said about not saving the Abbey," she said in a quiet tone as Agatha wiped her face. "But now . . . with this happening . . . you have to admit, things have changed."

"All that's changed is that now we have an even bigger mystery on our hands," Sister Agatha said. "And I'm not giving up until I get to the bottom of it."

"I am sure you are overreacting," Sister Callwen said. "Just be glad I stopped you from running into a burning barn. What were you thinking?" The two women stood looking at each other for a long moment as the others talked and milled around them, handing out plates of almond cake and pouring tea. Sister Callwen reached up and straightened Sister Agatha's scapular and veil. "You look like a third-former who just ran the fifty-yard dash. Come and sit down and have a cup of your Welsh Brew. It always seems to revive you." Sister Callwen turned and followed the others through the kitchen into the dining room.

Sister Agatha stood still. *A murder, a fire, a*

bishop who threatens to close the convent, a suspicious note sent to Jacob just days before he dies? What was going on here? And suddenly it hit her. Why was Bartimaeus all the way back at the orchard shed? Was that a coincidence or a clue? A rather mundane clue, if it was one. Inspector Rupert McFarland's words came back to her. *Don't look for the fancy clue. Some of the best clues are dressed up as ordinary events.* First thing tomorrow, she and Father Selwyn were planning on meeting with Jacob's mother. That could be valuable in figuring out a few things. She took a deep breath and headed out the door and up the stairs to the library. There seemed to be no time to lose.

TEN

The next morning was a grueling push to clean up from the fire. The cheese-making equipment that was normally stored in the milking shed could go back in, since the fire hadn't touched the shed. But everything from the barn had to find a new home. Sister Winifred had been right — the rounds of Gouda that were on shelves in the barn were ruined and had to be thrown out. There was water damage to the electric range and plaster walls. The shelves that had fallen on Jacob and caused his death had only just been repaired, but during the fire, part of the ceiling had caved in and the aging room was littered with charred beams and shingles. The contractor who had been hired wasn't starting until the following week. Now the task seemed impossible. Looking at the sodden, smoky mess that had once been their beautiful cheese-making barn, the nuns stood in silence. But, Reverend Mother had pointed out, tying on an old apron and pulling a pair of work gloves out of the pocket, previous residents of Gwenafwy Abbey over the centuries had faced worse.

"If she's talking about the Norman invasion — well then, I agree," Sister Agatha said to herself as she fell in with the rest of the nuns, lugging equipment out of the building, sweeping up debris, and salvaging anything that could be salvaged. It was true that only the roof had burned, but the water damage from the fire hoses had been extensive. The sisters were cheered when Father Selwyn and Gavin pulled up followed by several St. Anselm parishioners. By lunchtime, the place was looking respectable, and spirits, if not good, were at least on the rise.

It was late afternoon before Father Selwyn and Sister Agatha were able to leave for their visit to Alice Traherne, Jacob's mother. Both were exhausted and covered with soot, but after a quick cleanup, they resolved to go ahead. Reverend Mother waved Sister Agatha on. "Go," she said. "You might do some good visiting the poor woman."

The quaint charm of Alice Traherne's house — a small but lovely stone-and-brick cottage at the end of a curving lane, surrounded by a cloud of blossoms and entwined with ivy — struck Sister Agatha as something out of a storybook. The idyllic scene felt jarringly at odds with Jacob's shocking death. They made their way up the cobblestone path to the front door and waited after tapping the brass knocker shaped like a mourning dove. She took a deep breath as she prepared to meet with Jacob's grieving mother. No one came to the door, and the only sounds were birdsong from the hedge along the lane and the whir of a Hoover from inside the house.

"Let's try around back," Sister Agatha said. "I think it's pretty clear that someone is home." A bright blue Nissan hatchback sat in the drive and a side door was slightly ajar.

She turned and started toward a small gate in the picket fence that looked as though it led to a backyard. The fence was flanked by a climbing rose vine. Father Selwyn followed and took a moment to breathe in the heady aroma of the rose. "Ah. The Pearly Gates climber. Lovely."

"That's what it's called? Pearly Gates?"

"I know. It's an antique rose. You hardly see them anymore. I learned everything I know about roses from my taid-cu." *Granddad.* Father Selwyn breathed again into the rose blossom. This time he sneezed. "He kept a beautiful rose garden all his life."

Sister Agatha smiled. Not many priests in the Church in Wales could say they enjoyed fly-fishing, practiced yoga, and appreciated the beauty of an old-fashioned rose.

"Come on," she said. "We can't stand around smelling the roses all day."

Stepping through the gate, they rounded the corner of the house and stopped short. Father Selwyn blew out his breath. They had stepped into another world — a genuine English garden. The garden, an intricately designed chaos of late marigolds, crimson fountain grass, snowbells, and reddish-purple Starfire phlox, was bordered at one end by a stone wall and overlooked at the other by a trellis heavy with a cascade of orange blooms. Bees buzzed, and butterflies hovered. The early-morning scent of leaf mold mixed with the aroma of wisteria took Sister Agatha back to a childhood of playing outdoors and running through the meadows of the North Country.

At the far end of the garden, a petite woman wearing a floppy gardening hat, jeans, and a white button-down shirt with the sleeves rolled up, turned and looked at them quizzically. "Hello, Father," she called out after a moment's hesitation. "And

Sister." She came slowly across the garden and, pulling off her gardening gloves, reached for Father Selwyn's hand. "How lovely to see you." Looking at Sister Agatha, she smiled.

Jacob's mother, Alice Traherne, looked much younger than Sister Agatha had imagined. *Expect the unexpected,* Inspector McFarland was always saying. Fit and tan, as though she worked outdoors all summer and at the gym all winter, Alice Traherne had blonde hair pulled back in a ponytail, perfectly manicured nails, and a relaxed elegance about her. An elegance, but also an exhaustion.

"Have you come to discuss the funeral service? I thought we were all set with that?" she said, gesturing to a table and chairs on a small patio.

"We are. This Friday at ten at Saint Anselm." Father Selwyn and Sister Agatha walked over to the patio and sat down. "You know Sister Agatha? From the Abbey?"

"So nice to meet you, Sister. Jacob talked so often of the kindness of the sisters that I feel as if I know all of you."

Sister Agatha smiled. "Jacob never told us you were a master gardener," she said. "There are sisters at the Abbey who would love your garden."

"And they would be very welcome. I only wish we had thought of it when Jacob was . . . here . . . alive." Her voice faltered. "Shall we have tea?" Before they could respond, she called toward the open French doors, "Jonathan, could you bring us tea, please?" To Sister Agatha's surprise, a young man dressed in a white shirt and black pants appeared in the doorway. He had one hand on the handle of the Hoover.

"Be right there, Mrs. Traherne."

A housekeeper who brings tea? Sister Agatha thought. So much for the poor-widow theory.

As if reading her mind, Alice Traherne spoke up. "I originally hired Jonathan to help with the gardening, but after he mowed and carefully raked my entire patch of blue periwinkle, I found he was much more useful cleaning and cooking. Two things I am not the best at. And, I must say, it has been helpful to have another person in the house these past few days. That and the garden's demanding weeds have kept me going."

"This has been very hard," Father Selwyn said.

"To be honest, I'm in shock most of the time. Shock, disbelief, anger. I keep waiting to hear Jacob's voice calling out as he comes in the front door." She paused. Sister Agatha noticed that the butterfly bush that bordered the patio was doing a big business, with three huge holly blues lighting on the orange blossoms, the black edges of their wings catching the sunlight. A wood thrush called from the back garden. She thought it sounded like Sister Matilda's flute at morning prayer. The quiet beauty of the garden contrasted sharply with the chaos and exhaustion at the Abbey right now.

The French doors banged as Jonathan pushed through. He set the tea tray on the glass-topped table and, stepping back, surveyed it. "Shall I pour?"

"No, thank you, Jonathan. I'll pour. You can go back to whatever you were doing."

Jonathan looked from Sister Agatha to Father Selwyn, frowned, and then turned and walked back into the house. In a moment, they could hear the muffled sound of the Hoover.

Sister Agatha began. "I hope you don't mind, but we wanted to ask you a few questions about Jacob. And if in any way it feels painful, then please stop us."

Alice Traherne put down her teacup and looked at Sister Agatha, her eyebrows raised. "What do you want to know?" Sister Agatha noticed that although Alice's voice sounded tired and her eyes were certainly troubled, she had an easy way of carrying herself, a certain poise or dignity. Sister Agatha couldn't put her finger on it. Maybe *grace* was the word.

"I will just ask, then," Father Selwyn said. "Do you think there was anyone who wanted to harm Jacob?"

"Harm Jacob?" She frowned. "Why would you ask that?"

"We don't know for certain, and Constable Barnes absolutely disagrees with us, but there might be a chance that Jacob's death wasn't accidental."

"Are you saying that you think someone killed him?" Alice slowly set her teacup into the saucer. "Do you have some sort of evidence?"

"His manner of death seems unlikely." Sister Agatha hesitated, then added, "Steel shelves just don't spontaneously fall down. And why was he there — at five o'clock in the morning?" She decided not to mention any of her possible suspects.

"You think someone pushed the shelves on him? Who?"

"We are just tracking down any information that we can." Sister Agatha watched her carefully. She didn't seem appropriately shocked. Consumed with grief, certainly.

But not completely stunned by the idea that her son was murdered. Sister Agatha decided to just plunge in. "You seem . . . almost . . . not surprised."

Alice Traherne looked up, startled. "Oh? Really? Well, I suppose it is my background. I used to work in a field where I became accustomed to death and the violence that goes with it."

"Where did you work?" Father Selwyn asked.

"Her Majesty's Navy. I was stationed in Devonport at the naval base there."

Father Selwyn's eyes widened. "You were at Devonport? In what capacity?"

"Deck officer on *HMS Torbay.*"

Father Selwyn's eyebrows shot up. "The nuclear submarine? Jacob never mentioned that you were an officer on a submarine."

"I know. I think that, to Jacob, I was just 'mum,' and he never really saw me as a naval officer. And anyway, I retired when he was only ten and moved to Pryderi. My husband and I were both naval officers."

"Jacob's father?"

"He died in Desert Storm. I was stationed in Devonport at the time. I would have gone to war proudly, but . . ." Her voice trailed off. The sound of the Hoover abruptly stopped and then started again. Sister Agatha reached forward and poured more tea into Alice's empty teacup. "But I was pregnant with Jacob." She stared at the tabletop and then looked up, her eyes bright. "So, you see, I am not entirely shocked by acts of violence. In the military, you see things and hear about things that are shockingly violent. Even without going to war. And they become almost . . . commonplace. In other words, you habituate to the violence. So, later in life, it seems that very little surprises you."

Sister Agatha's respect for Jacob's mother skyrocketed. "Do you think there was anyone who might have wanted Jacob dead?"

"Dead? No. But there is one odd thing."

"What?" Sister Agatha pulled out her notebook.

"Jacob came home with a bruised eye, and he wouldn't tell me anything about it at first. But I kept insisting. He finally admitted that he had gotten into a fight."

"Why? Do you know what the fight was about?"

"I think it had to do with his boyfriend, Michael. But Jacob wasn't a fighter. Never was. Not like a lot of boys his age."

"You think he and Michael got into it?"

She shook her head. "He finally told me

that it was some guy named Aaron. And he wouldn't tell me anything else. I decided to let go of it. Jacob was twenty-six years old. I needed to back off."

"When did it happen?"

Alice shook her head. "Last weekend — Saturday. Two days before he died."

"Hell hath no fury like a . . . gentleman . . . scorned." Sister Agatha clutched the dash of Father Selwyn's BMW Mini as he swerved around a lorry. They had just left Alice Traherne's house and were heading back to the Abbey. Sister Callen had just texted to let her know that there was to be an all-convent meeting in an hour. Tea was always served at Reverend Mother's all-convent meetings, and Sister Agatha was sure she had seen Sister Gwenydd putting together the ingredients for a Monmouth pudding as they were leaving the Abbey.

"What? Do you think there was some romantic rivalry between Jacob and Aaron?"

"Jealousy can lead to violence. So can the need for control in a relationship." She checked her seat belt. "You might slow down a bit, by the way."

"I would like to see this Aaron in person."

"Me too," Sister Agatha said as Father Selwyn braked to a screeching halt. A flock of sheep were crossing the lane in front of them. She waited while he rolled his window down and shouted a cheerful hello to the shepherd. "I'm not sure how we are going to track him down, but if he can be tracked down, I plan to do it," Sister Agatha said, leaning over to make sure that Father Selwyn's foot was indeed firmly on the brake. At that moment, her cell phone pinged. Pulling it out of her apron, she looked at it. "It's from Macie Cadwalader at Saint Grenfell," she said, reading the text.

> TALKED WITH MY CHOIR DIRECTOR. HE'S ON THE MUSIC FESTIVAL COMMITTEE. OPEN THE ATTACHMENT. I THINK YOU'LL FIND IT INTERESTING! HAPPY SLEUTHING! REV MACIE

Sister Agatha clicked on the attachment and then squinted as she read it. A minute later, she looked up. "Pull over. You need to see this." Father Selwyn had peeled off down the road again as soon as the sheep had cleared away. He pulled the little car into a gravel drive leading into a meadow and, putting it in park, took the phone from Sister Agatha and read aloud:

Dear Members of the Music Festival Committee:

I am writing to express my absolute and utter dissatisfaction with your incompetent bumbling of the St. Asaph Music Festival. I will get straight to the point. My son, Mordwywr Mason Birkby, competed in the soloist contest at the festival last year — and he lost! To everyone's complete dismay and shock, he finished second. I cannot express the disappointment he felt. It broke a mother's heart. My son is a young man of extraordinary natural ability and was very clearly the best tenor at the contest — as anyone in attendance that day will attest. The unfortunate reality is, your judges are amateurish, unqualified, and wouldn't recognize true talent were standing in front of them — which it was! The fact that Jacob Traherne was awarded first prize instead of Mordwywr is a travesty. I understand that Mr. Traherne will be competing again this year, as will my son. And I have heard the disturbing rumor that he is the favored soloist!

I am warning your committee — do not repeat your incompetence from last year. If you do not correct the blatant favoritism of your judges towards Mr. Traherne, then I will be forced to take matters into my own hands!

Sincerely,
Mrs. Evelyn Meredith Birkby

Father Selwyn shook his head. "Yes, that certainly sounds like Evelyn Birkby. What do you think she means 'take matters into her own hands'?"

"I think it means that she is now a suspect."

Father Selwyn nodded. "It explains why the note to Jacob in his hymnbook said, 'She would never do it. You're safe.' "

"Do what exactly? Anything it took to make sure Mordy won the contest? Even murder?" They rode in silence as Father Selwyn pulled into the Abbey drive and stopped in front of the kitchen door. "What next?" he said, turning to Sister Agatha.

"I'd like to talk with Mrs. Birkby."

Father Selwyn blew out his breath. "Holy Mother. Better you than me."

ELEVEN

Reverend Mother watched as Sister Agatha, the last to enter, hurried in and slid into her usual spot — the ottoman in front of the bookcase. The entire community had gathered at her request in the warming room, a long, cavernous hall with a huge stone fireplace at one end once used by the monks on cold winter nights. Now the nuns used it as their community room, a place to gather for conversation, meetings, knitting, reading, and the occasional late-night binge on Netflix.

Reverend Mother stood by the fireplace, which was filled with an arrangement of fragrant lilacs, and listened to the cheerful greetings, quiet laughter, and chatter as the sisters settled into the comfortable couches and overstuffed chairs. She was relieved to see that perhaps they were bouncing back — at least a little — from the traumatic week. A death and a fire in the span of four days was too much for any community. Which was why she had decided to wait to tell them about the bishop's mandate. But she couldn't wait any longer. What was Sister Agatha always saying? *No way out but through.* A Monmouth pudding sat at the ready on the center table with a stack of spoons and plates next to it. Reverend Mother smiled. Sister Gwenydd had been busy.

The last rays of the sun slanted through the mullioned windows in such a way that the room took on a golden hue. Would this be her last summer at Gwenafwy? She looked around and felt a tightness in her throat. Sister Harriet seemed older and frailer than she had last noticed, while Sister Gwenydd was young and full of promise, forever staring at her phone — which she was doing at the moment. Sister Agatha, just back from the village, wore that determined look that Reverend Mother had learned to pay attention to — it was a look that usually spelled trouble. Sister Callwen, Sister Winifred — as dependable as the day was long. These women were her friends, her sisters in the truest sense. But more than anything, she realized — they were her responsibility. She couldn't let them down. Not now.

She said a silent prayer, and, as often happened in a moment of prayer, she felt the tiniest glimmer of optimism. Maybe she had been going about this all wrong. Maybe carrying the burden of the Abbey alone was her biggest mistake. Arrogant even. Where was her faith? Where was her trust in the community of believers? A veritable cloud of witnesses surrounded her, and here she was, wallowing in her own fears.

Reverend Mother began to hum the hymn sung at noontime prayer, "Here I Am, Lord." The nuns grew silent as her contralto voice went from humming to singing. Stepping forward, she motioned the nuns to join her. They began slowly, but soon the strength of their voices filled the room. "I, the Lord of Sea and Sky, I have heard my people cry." Reverend Mother continued through all five verses until she saw that each woman was smiling and relaxed as they joined as one, lifting up the inspiring words. Her energy had returned. As the song ended, Reverend Mother did not sit, though she motioned for the sisters to take their seats. All eyes were on her.

"Sisters," she began. "Like David in the Valley of Elah, we face a Goliath, and we have only five smooth stones." She hesitated and took a breath. "But also, like David, we have the God of Abraham and Jacob on our side. Not to mention Sarah and Esther, Miriam and Lydia. And we will slay our Goliath no matter what." Suddenly her glimmer of optimism, her feeling of inspiration, vanished. She suddenly couldn't find the words to tell them that the bishop had threatened the Abbey with closing. The pause was so long that a few sisters leaned forward as if something had been said, and they had just missed it. Others exchanged a worried glance. "Reverend Mother?" Sister Matilda said. "What is it?"

Sister Agatha and Sister Callwen exchanged a glance. They knew what was coming. Reverend Mother had waited to tell the entire Abbey what she had already shared with the senior nuns — the bishop's disturbing news.

Reverend Mother forced herself to speak. "All right, it's this. The bishop wants to close the Abbey." She waited while a shocked gasp registered around the room. "I know. It's a horrible thought. I agree. And I pledge to you right now, I will do everything in my power to keep it from happening. Gwenafwy Abbey has been serving this community for nearly a hundred years. It will not be shut down now."

"But how?" one of the nuns asked. "And

does the bishop have the authority to close Gwenafwy?"

"The diocese can close any of the religious orders if it sees fit. Remember Saint Benedict's in Caernarfon?" Reverend Mother waited, her sisters nodding. "Of course, it's usually after great deliberation. And in agreement with the residents of the order." She paused. "This is hard to say, and I don't agree with it, but the bishop thinks we are . . ." Reverend Mother couldn't bring herself to say to her beloved colleagues in ministry that the diocesan leaders thought they were irrelevant. "That we are . . . old-fashioned."

"Poppycock!" said Sister Agatha. "We are central to the life of this village. If we weren't here, who would run the village food pantry? The soup kitchen? The Hymn Sing at the Senior Center?"

"We are far more than just women who bring food to the poor and plan activities for the elderly; we are a contemplative society centered in prayer and worship," Sister Harriet said from the wing chair, where she was mending one of the large Easter paraments. As resident artist, she designed and repaired all the banners, altar paraments, and vestments used by the Abbey. "The nuns of Gwenafwy have seen the North of Wales through its worst times," she said, poking her needle through the heavy brocade material. "We have prayed and fed and loved this community as God has seen fit to send us. I, for one, shall pray for the bishop. She has apparently given in to her fears and lost sight of the Gospel." Sister Harriet paused her needle and, shaking out the white-and-gold linen across her lap, closed her eyes as if starting immediately on her own personal prayer vigil.

"I'll pray for the bishop too," said Sister Winifred. "I will pray that she comes to her senses!"

"Sisters — please!" Reverend Mother said. "The bishop did spell out several problems that she wants to see resolved and did promise — sort of — that if we turned things around, we could go on as we always have."

"Well, wasn't that good of her," Sister Agatha said. "To let us continue bringing the Gospel of our Lord into the lives of others. How very, very good of her." Sister Agatha snorted and, with a trembling hand, picked up the teapot. She tried to pour tea into her cup, but her hand shook. She had lost all thoughts about pudding. Reaching over, Sister Gwenydd filled Sister Agatha's cup. She added two lumps of sugar and a bit of cream. Sister Agatha nodded, and Sister Gwenydd added more sugar. "What exactly does the bishop want resolved?" Sister Gwenydd asked.

Reverend Mother took a breath and forced her voice to sound at least a little cheerful. "Membership is our problem. Or at least one of our problems. As you know, Sister Gwenydd has been our only recruit in a decade."

"I remember when we had a new flock of young women every year," Sister Callwen said. "It was considered a great honor to join to take orders."

"Well, times have changed," Reverend Mother said. "There's no going back to the old days." She paused. "The bishop also said she wants to see increased income, a stable budget, and a more contemporary outreach."

"A what?" Sister Matilda said.

"Well, instead of the usual food pantry and clothing drive for the poor, we are expected to . . ." Here Reverend Mother was a bit flummoxed. "I guess . . . you know . . . do things like, well, save the planet," she finally said.

"Save the planet! Good heavens. Saving the poor isn't enough? Or saving the lost souls of Wales? How about saving a way of life?" Sister Agatha said, her voice rising. "Now we have to save the planet?"

"Yes. We have to save the planet. You know, be more green. More into — I don't know. Recycling! But first, we need to save ourselves. And that's why I've called you all here. To figure out a game plan. The bishop has given us until Michaelmas — when she comes for Mass at Gwenafwy." The Bishop of Asaph had celebrated the Eucharist at Gwenafwy Abbey every Michaelmas since its founding a century before.

"You're kidding. That's barely four weeks away?" Sister Matilda pulled out her smartphone and, after a click or two, shook her head. "Exactly thirty-two days away. September twenty-ninth is Michaelmas. We have thirty-two days to save the Abbey!"

"And the planet," said Sister Agatha. "Don't forget the planet."

The sisters went quiet. Most had been at Gwenafwy Abbey since they were young postulants. It was home. Not one of them had ever actually considered leaving. And, except for Sister Gwenydd, they were all within ten years of retiring and had fully expected to finish out their lives at Gwenafwy. They had always thought that, somehow, the Abbey would continue serving the village of Pryderi and beyond. And now there had been a death, a fire, and a threat by the church hierarchy to their very existence. Their world, which had always seemed unsinkable, was capsizing.

Sister Agatha rose to her feet. “Sisters. I insist that we stop this melancholy attitude at once. It was not the attitude of our Welsh forebears who founded this Abbey, nor was it the attitude of our Lord. And this moping around is not how Wales beat England in the World Cup!”

“Hear, hear!” said Sister Winifred. “I say we all stand, sing Cwm Rhondda, and then roll up our sleeves and get to work!” There were enthusiastic nods from around the table. Except, Sister Agatha noticed, from Sister Callwen, who frowned into her tea. “You don’t agree, Sister Callwen?” she asked. The entire group turned and looked at Sister Callwen. She was the brain trust of the Abbey, always coming forth with logic and reasoning that no one could argue with.

Sister Callwen looked up and seemed almost surprised that anyone was watching her. “No. No, I agree. We must respond to the bishop’s . . . um . . . challenge . . . with confidence.” She turned to Reverend Mother. “What were you thinking, Reverend Mother?” she asked.

“I was hoping we could come up with a

list of possible ways to both raise money and recruit postulants to our Gwenafwy Abbey."

"How about a bake sale?" Sister Matilda said. "Or a Christmas Bazaar like we used to do?"

"First, we only have until September twenty-ninth, so a Christmas Bazaar is out. And a bake sale?"

"We need serious money — a new income stream. Not another bake sale," Sister Agatha said.

"Now, wait a minute, how about a cookbook? A Nuns of Gwenafwy Abbey cookbook?" another sister added. Reverend Mother noticed that Agatha did one of her legendary eye rolls followed by a heavy sigh.

The ideas from the nuns flew thick and fast — from taking in boarders to a petting zoo — and as Reverend Mother listened, her heart sank. None of the ideas were even close to what was needed. And none of them addressed the real issue — young women simply were not joining abbeys these days. And not even the most welcoming and creative abbey in the world was going to change that. She had started out taking careful notes on all the sisters offered, but after a while, she laid down her pen. For the first time, she felt that maybe it wasn't possible to save the Abbey. Maybe Sister Callwen had been right — it was time to close.

Just as the chapel bell began to chime the hour and Sister Winifred concluded her description of how to get a cell tower in the church steeple, Sister Callwen, silent since the mention of the petting zoo, cleared her throat.

"Sisters," she finally said. "As wonderful as all your ideas sound, you have to admit one thing. We have already tried all this. Tried and failed."

"We haven't tried a cell tower," said Sister Winifred.

"Or a petting zoo," added Sister Harriet. "Or a boarder."

"You know what I mean," Sister Callwen said. "It simply isn't enough. We are all aware of that glaring fact. And you haven't even broached our biggest challenge — we need more sisters."

Their faces said it all. Reverend Mother looked out and could not bear what she saw. Theirs was a community that the world simply did not respect anymore. All of them, except Sister Gwenydd, had become nuns back when taking vows was a respected, honored thing to do. Not anymore. And this knowledge had left them discouraged and questioning. Teacups clinked, and the bell in the village chimed. The sisters sat looking at each other.

"I take issue." As the nuns argued and schemed, Sister Gwenydd had been sitting quietly at the far end of the room, working her way through a favorite dog-eared cookbook. "I take issue," she said again. "Young women do want to join religious orders. Or they would. If they had any idea what it is that you do here. Gwenafwy Abbey is the best-kept secret in the world. You need to go viral. Let the world know what you really are. *Who* you really are. You're not the nuns in some 1940s movie. You're . . . well, you're amazing." Sister Gwenydd looked around; all eyes were on her. "I mean it. Let the world know what happens here — the sense of community, the outreach to the poor, the inclusiveness of your lives, the God-ness of it. Tell the world, and I assure you, young women will join. The problem is, no one knows what joining an order would give them."

"And what is that, Sister?" Sister Callwen said, eyebrows raised. "What would joining an order give them?"

"It would give them what they have always wanted but have never been able to find."

The nuns looked at one another. A few

wiped away tears. Others smiled, and conversation began again. Sister Harriet dished up the Monmouth pudding and tea was poured all around. Reverend Mother began to feel her spirits lift a tiny bit. Maybe it was just an issue of getting the word out, doing a better job of advertising. A new postulant or two, a renewed market for the Gouda, maybe even a nod toward making the Abbey a little more "green." The bishop would see the value of the centuries-old religious community.

Reverend Mother was so caught up in her renewed hope that she barely noticed Sister Winifred had pulled up a chair next to her.

"We need to talk," Sister Winifred said in a whisper.

"Right now?"

"More like, last week."

Reverend Mother looked at her sharply. Sister Winifred's eyes were wide and her face pale. She was carrying a business envelope. Reverend Mother read the return address and her head went light. Winifred placed the envelope next to Reverend Mother's teacup. They both stared at it, Sister Winifred frowning, Reverend Mother trying to control her breathing. "I ran up to your office a moment ago to get the budget report — I thought it could help us tonight

— and I saw this. Reverend Mother, why wasn't this brought to my attention?"

"I know. I know. It's just that I thought we had more time . . ." Reverend Mother couldn't look at Sister Winifred. "Tell me it isn't . . ."

"It is. As of midnight, three nights ago."

Twelve

Just as the nuns of Gwenafwy Abbey were gathering in the warming room, Macie Cadwalader, vicar of St. Grenfell, was hurrying down the hall from her office to the church parlor. The women's knitting circle, St. Grenfell in Stitches, was already in full swing. This industrious group of women could be found every Wednesday night laughing, talking, drinking wine, and knitting prayer shawls. Needles clicked, stitches were dropped, and rows were purled while the problems of the world were solved. The women called a cheerful hello to Macie as she helped herself to a glass of the red wine and grabbed a snickerdoodle bar from the platter on the table. *Wine and snickerdoodle bars. Why can't every church meeting be like this?* Macie took a quick inventory of the room, and her stomach fluttered when she made eye contact with Evelyn Birkby. Evelyn was the only woman in the room not imbibing or munching down on chocolate and coconut. She also noticed that Evelyn had chosen the only piece of furniture in the room that was entirely uncomfortable — a straight-backed chair that looked as though it had been donated by one of St. Grenfell's Victorian ancestors. The rest of the parlor was an assortment of comfortable, if shabby, sofas and overstuffed chairs accumulated throughout the years as different church women redecorated at home and then donated their cast-off furniture to the church. Macie sighed. She had tried to convince the council that a church building that looked like her grandmother's living room wasn't going to attract young families. It had been like talking to a group of cheerful statues. The board members, not one of them under the age of seventy, had smiled and nodded and reminded her that there wasn't money to replace furniture that still had a lot of wear left in it.

She looked across the room at Evelyn, who sat ramrod straight, knitting needles clicking, stopping only for a moment as if to brush an imaginary spot off the narrow lapel of her summer pantsuit. Evelyn wore pantsuits themed for the season. Just now, in the heat of August's end, she sported a pale-pink pantsuit with a white stretch top.

The top strained tight across her bosom — a bosom that stood at attention thanks to equal amounts spandex and perfect posture — displaying a design of embroidered seashells. Her earrings matched the summer theme — tiny starfish tinted pink. Her slender but dependable legs — which hit the elliptical full blast every morning during the seven o'clock class at the Pryderi gym — ended in spotless white pumps crossed at the ankle. Evelyn's hair, cast into the last Dorothy Hamill cut left on the planet, also stood at attention. It didn't dare move. Coral-pink lipstick and a dab of blush finished her off. Inwardly, Macie groaned. A battle-ax in pastel. But, at the same time, the backbone of St. Grenfell. Macie knew that most of the church programs, dinners, and fund raisers wouldn't happen if it weren't for the take-no-prisoners attitude and effort of Evelyn Birkby.

Macie also knew that Evelyn's real focus was her son, Mordy. And although she talked about Mordy as though he were still in the fourth form, he was actually a hulking lad some twenty-five years old, six feet seven, who tipped in at twenty stone. A junior ranger at Snowdonia National Park, Mordy could wrestle even the most obstreperous tourist — or feral goat — into obeying the rules of the park. But when it came to his mother, he did whatever she wanted.

Macie looked around the room and found herself smiling. Other than Evelyn, she enjoyed these women. They were funny, no-nonsense, and supportive of her, at least for the most part. She didn't knit and had been a little shocked that there were church ladies who still did. Seminary had given her the impression that all church women were active leaders, heading up boards and finance committees, and that these small women's groups had gone out with the 1970s. She had been surprised when she realized that women still gathered in knitting circles, staffed the church nursery school, and spent inordinate amounts of time planning the Christmas Bazaar. Of course, they also ran the governing boards and finance committees. She occasionally asked herself if there would be a church if it weren't for women.

"So," Macie piped up as each woman looked expectantly at her, needles continuing to click. "Anyone watch *The Great British Bake Off* Sunday night?" She looked straight at Evelyn as the other women began to chime in. She knew that the St. Grenfell in Stitches ladies were as addicted to *The Great British Bake Off* as she was. She kept an eye on Evelyn as the group expressed dismay over the favorite character losing the technical challenge. She listened as Paul Hollywood was raked over the coals for his insensitivity to the young woman whose strawberry marmalade cake had fallen at the last moment. Macie noticed that Evelyn remained quiet.

"Evelyn," Macie said, taking a gulp of wine. "I know you never miss a show. What did you think?" Everyone turned to Evelyn and waited for her response. Evelyn was the chair of the Women's Institute in St. Grenfell village and was known as a star baker herself. At least in her own mind. She had hinted more than once that if there were ever a *Great Welsh Bake Off,* she would probably sweep the tent. "Well, I thought it was interesting. I'm not sure I would have let a savory flan with a soggy bottom win for signature bake." She cast off and started a new row without looking up and therefore missed the nearly synchronized eye roll of the other women in the room. "And I do think those two young women, Mel and Sue, could be a bit more careful with their language."

"So . . . you watched it then . . . on Sunday night?" Macie knew she needed to be a little more subtle, but she needed to nail down Evelyn's whereabouts so she could report back to Sister Agatha.

Evelyn looked up from her needles. "Yes. Why? When else would I have watched it?"

"No . . . no. I'm just glad you didn't have any competing church meetings or something." Macie stuttered a bit and took another gulp of wine. Fortunately, just before things could get weird, Evelyn's phone rang. As she dug it out of her knitting bag, her eyes lit up. "It's my Mordy! Excuse me, ladies, I must take this." Hurrying from the room with her cell phone pressed to her ear, she missed the second synchronized eye roll of the evening.

Macie stood and excused herself, saying that she needed to do some work on her sermon. What she really needed was to call Sister Agatha immediately. Evelyn couldn't have been home watching *The Great British Bake Off.* The soggy-bottomed savory flan had been two weeks ago.

Early the next morning, only four days after she'd found Jacob's body on the floor of the aging room, Sister Agatha climbed the steep steps to her desk in the library attic. She sat at her desk, brow furrowed, and wondered what Armand Gamache might do right now. Interrogate a suspect? Conduct a piercing examination of the case with his crackerjack detectives? Take a walk through Three Pines and enjoy a licorice pipe followed by a café au lait? It was then that she saw it — the three-by-five index card on the floor at her feet. She picked it up off the carpet. *Welsh Laverbread* was printed at the top, followed by a list of ingredients and cooking instructions. The handwriting was spidery, and the card, wrinkled and yellow. *Sister Gwenydd.* All the sisters enjoyed Sister Gwenydd's laverbread, and Sister Agatha had seen her use just this kind of card for her many recipes. Although young, she shunned online sources for the Abbey kitchen and instead used her grandmother's cookbooks and old tin recipe box filled with yellowed recipe cards.

Gwenydd was often seen organizing recipes and menu plans. She seemed to thrive in her job as the resident chef. It had certainly improved life at the Abbey. For nearly a decade, they had limped along sharing the cooking responsibilities, and the quality of the food had ranged from adequate to culinary disaster. But now, with Sister Gwenydd in charge of the kitchen, the sisters gathered around the long oak table for every meal, eagerly eyeing dishes of steaming cassoulet, baskets of fragrant baguettes, lentil and carrot salad with goat cheese and mint from the Abbey herb garden. The sisters waited in more anticipation than they liked to admit for the meals and snacks that their young postulant prepared for them. They could hardly believe their luck that a talented chef had landed on their steps wanting to join the Abbey.

But what would she have been doing in the attic? And sitting at Sister Agatha's desk?

Sister Agatha placed the recipe card front and center on her desk. She tapped her Sharpie on the top of her orchid-blue notebook. Her phone vibrated. *A text from Macie Cadwalader.* She read it quickly. Why would Evelyn say she had watched *The Great British Bake Off* when she clearly hadn't? Had she been home and just not watching the show? Or had she been out? *Out waiting in the shadows for Jacob to go into the aging room so she could shove the shelves on him?* It was a little hard to imagine, but then, a suspect who lied regarding her whereabouts was always of particular concern. Sister Agatha had texted Macie back, giving her the further task of determining for certain if Evelyn had been home or not the night Jacob died.

By midmorning, Sister Agatha could stand it no longer. She needed to get away from the Abbey where she could think. She made the excuse that she had some library business to do in the village and slipped out to The Buttered Crust Tea Shop. She chose her favorite booth and sat making notes about Alice Traherne and Evelyn Birkby. Rupert McFarland had warned against keeping sloppy notes. *A good detective is an organized detective,* he was always saying. Well, her notebook was crying out for some neatening, and she needed to get to it while she could. She waved absently to the young man behind the counter, hoping he would come over and take her order. She recognized him as either Keenan or Kent Bowan, one of the twins from St. Anselm's youth group.

Suddenly, an agitated voice rang out above the pleasant chatter. Looking up, she saw that it was Daniel Fychans, proprietor of The Rogue Creamery, a dairy just down the road from Gwenafwy Abbey. Daniel and his wife, Elizabeth, had remodeled a century-old milking parlor into a hip, upscale store. They sold everything from fresh kale grown by local farmers to honey made from local bees, organic butter and hand-woven tea towels, wheels of cheese, loaves of freshly baked bread, and jars of almond butter. The farm had been in the Fychans family for generations; by comparison, the nuns at Gwenafwy Abbey were newcomers, having arrived a mere hundred years before. Bigger and more corporate, their production of cheese had at first outsold the Abbey every time. But Heavenly Gouda was catching on as a niche market and was starting to compete even with multiproduct farm stands like The Rogue.

Daniel stood in front of the cash register. "Run it again. I'm sure it's fine," he said. Sister Agatha noticed that his face was red, and he seemed to be breathing hard. She wondered for a moment if he was going to have some sort of cardiac episode. Sister Agatha had a theory that dog owners often looked like their dogs, so, when she'd seen Daniel out walking his dog up Church Lane one afternoon, she hadn't been surprised that little Sparky was a bulldog. Short, squat, and with a military-style crew cut, Daniel had a very in-your-face approach, even when all he was doing was selling organic honey. He truly looked like a bulldog about to defend his place in the pack.

"I've run your card three times, and it's not working," the young man behind the counter said. "Try another card." Sister Agatha had to admit that the kid didn't seem too concerned, considering that Daniel's red face and bulging neck muscles made him look as if he were ready to implode.

Daniel grabbed the card and shoved it back in his wallet. "I'll give you cash. What's the cost?'

"One pound thirty. Same as when it was on the card." The boy yawned and looked over Daniel's shoulder.

"Don't be a jerk." Daniel carefully counted out the cash and dropped it on the counter. Grabbing his tea and scone, he pushed past the woman behind him, forcing her to take a step back.

"Good gracious," the woman exclaimed, clutching her pocketbook.

Sister Agatha opened her laptop and breathed a sigh of contentment. She would finish with email, work through her notes on Jacob, and then put in an hour's work on her mystery novel before hurrying back to the Abbey. She had horribly neglected her novel. Poor Bates Melanchthon. She could barely remember what he had been up to last. Oh, yes. Poison and bludgeoning. Reverend Mother cut her a wide path to do her writing, but she didn't want to push it, especially now, with things so topsy-turvy at the Abbey.

She continued her quick scroll through

her email — Bates Melanchthon would have to wait. She expected an email from the main-branch library in Cardiff concerning some interlibrary loan books that she would need to reply to, then she could get back to solving murder, both real and fictional. Almost everyone in the village knew she was writing a detective story and gave her a wide berth when they saw her hunkered down over her keyboard.

"What can I bring you, Sister?" the young waiter asked, finally appearing at the end of the booth. He stood tapping his pencil against a tablet.

"Kent, is it?" she asked.

"Keenan. What would you like, Sister?"

"Tea, then, Keenan. You were in Father's confirmation class last year, weren't you?"

"That was my brother, Kent." Keenan looked over her head out the window, where a gaggle of teenage girls stood laughing on the sidewalk. They didn't seem to notice that it was pouring. "Mum didn't want us in the same year because we fight."

"I see. Welsh Brew, please."

"I'm sorry?" Keenan was still looking out the window.

"Welsh Brew."

"Got it." He stumbled into a chair as he walked away, not taking his eyes off the girls.

Sister Agatha sighed and shook her head. "I weep for our future," she said under her breath.

"What was that, Sister? Did you want a scone too?" Keenan said, turning.

"No, thank you — just the tea, please." Sister Agatha clicked back into her email account and, scrolling down, opened an email from the bishop's office. It was an email blast to the entire parish concerning a proposed missions trip to Haiti.

Sister Agatha was about to delete it — she really wasn't in the mood to read anything coming out of the bishop's office, especially after yesterday's conversation with Reverend Mother. Then she saw that other emails were attached and quickly scrolled down. Sister Callwen had replied to the bishop on this email. It took only a moment for her to realize that Sister Callwen's note had been attached unknowingly. The folly of hitting REPLY ALL to an email was something Sister Agatha had learned about the hard way. It looked as though Sister Callwen had thought she was having a private communication when she was actually sending to a group. Sister Agatha hesitated. This was clearly supposed to be private. But was it her fault Sister Callwen was so ignorant about the Internet? Sister Agatha clicked on the email. The first line made her catch her breath.

"Welsh Brew, Sister," Keenan said, placing the steaming cup in front of her. "You don't want an oatcake? Right out of the oven. Well, yesterday, anyway."

"No, thank you," she said, without looking up. "Just tea." She didn't notice when he walked away. Sister Callwen's email started with the subject line CONFIDENTIAL, which was enough to catch anyone's attention. Sister Agatha knew she shouldn't continue reading. She scrolled down. There was a one-line email message:

SUZANNE,
MOVING FORWARD. I THINK YOU'LL BE PLEASED.

Pleased? Pleased by what? And why was she calling the bishop by her first name? When had they become such good friends?

"Bwrw hen wragedd a ffyn," Father Selwyn said, plopping down across from her. *It's raining old wives and walking sticks.* He plucked two paper napkins out of the dispenser on the table and wiped raindrops off his face. "Sister, you look like you've seen a ghost. The Holy Ghost, I hope." He leaned out of the booth. "Glengettie, if you please, Keenan. And put an oatcake next to it, if you will."

"What do you think of Sister Callwen?" she asked, still looking at her computer screen.

"Well" — he frowned — "a bit starchy at times, if you know what I mean. But a heart of gold. You're not still stuck on that Skype business, are you?"

"Up until now, she's been a good friend." Sister Agatha was dismayed at the catch in her throat.

"Up until now? What do you mean? Sister Callwen is as loyal and good a friend as anyone could want."

"I found an email from her to the bishop. And it doesn't sound at all on the up and up." Sister Agatha turned her laptop around so that the screen faced Father Selwyn. "Read that." Father Selwyn accepted the cup of tea from Keenan with a nod of thanks and a smile. "Diolch, Keenan." *Thank you.* He took a hesitant sip and then, setting his cup down, looked at Sister Agatha. "Reading private emails from others in our faith community, are we now?" He pulled out his reading glasses and leaned toward the screen.

"I don't notice you hesitating, Father."

He cleared his voice and read aloud.

"Moving forward. I think you'll be pleased." Father Selwyn sat back. "So, what's the crisis? Sounds like nothing."

"What do you think she's talking about?"

He shrugged. "I don't know. Final plans for the Saint Asaph's annual rummage sale. The potluck at the shelter. The annual garden party at Pryderi castle. Why? What are you thinking?"

"I find you maddeningly obtuse sometimes, Father."

"Worse has been said." He picked up the scone that Keenan had slid in front of him. "You know what I like? A scone with plenty of cranberries. Look at this." He held it out to Sister Agatha. "Chock-full." He leaned out of the booth and shouted in the direction of the counter, "Well done, Keenan!" Sister Agatha noticed that he sprayed the table next to them with crumbs.

"You don't think it's even a little suspicious?"

"Of what?"

"Of the problems at the Abbey. What I think . . ." She could barely say it. "What I think it means is that Sister Callwen is involved in the bishop wanting to close us down. Could be involved. Somehow." Sister Agatha felt as if her entire world had grown dark.

"Sister, all you have is one email." He gave her a hard look. "Don't jump to conclusions. Doesn't your Rupert whatever-his-name-is have something to say about that?"

"McFarland. Inspector Rupert McFarland. He would say look for changes in behavior. Like the fact that Sister Callwen is learning to Skype, has a voice mail from the bishop's office about 'following up,' has openly said that we should think twice about supporting the Abbey, and now this. Why is Sister Callwen even emailing the bishop? She doesn't like Suzanne Bainton. None of us do. She's no friend of the Abbey — that's common knowledge. Nor to the small village parish. Admit it — she cares much more for the big suburban churches. Ones that bring in revenue."

"Well," he said, staring into his teacup and then picking it up and taking a sip. "I hate to say it, but it does seem that way. At least some of the time." Father Selwyn looked at Sister Agatha. "But Callwen has been your friend forever. Didn't she save you from the fire?"

"Well, yes. I think she threw my back out."

"It's just such a leap to make. Sister Callwen . . . sabotaging the Abbey? In cahoots with the bishop?"

They both sat in silence a moment, the

noisy bustle of the Buttered Crust morning crowd going on around them. Father Selwyn cleared his throat. He looked at his friend over his teacup. "Sister Callwen aside — maybe you need to stop speaking so openly about the bishop."

"Why?"

"No reason, really. I just would. Suzanne is the bishop, after all. And an influential person in the Church in Wales." Father Selwyn glanced around the crowded shop. He picked up his teacup, swirled it, and then set it back down. "I have a confession to make," he said. "I haven't been entirely honest with you about something. And I feel very bad about it. It was just that . . . it seemed trivial at first." Father Selwyn stopped and looked at the door of the coffee shop as the bell jingled, then back again to Sister Agatha. "I understand that a meeting of the Board of Governors was called at the diocesan office and Sister Callwen made a presentation."

"What kind of presentation?"

"Well, that's the frustrating part. It was a closed meeting, which means everything that happened is confidential."

"I thought you had a sort of, you know, diocesan mole? Father Andrew. Did you ask him?"

"Father Andrew is *not* my mole — I wish you wouldn't phrase it that way. And, yes, I did ask him. But no, for some reason, he drew the line at telling me what exactly went on."

"So, she is up to something."

"It seems that way." He paused. "But turning against the Abbey? Sister Callwen?" Father Selwyn shook his head. "I don't know. It seems a stretch. But I need to get back to the church — Gavin is waiting for me to go over the funeral liturgy with him. Jacob's funeral will be his first ever as an officiant. I think he's nervous." Father stood and picked up his umbrella. "Don't forget our workout at the gym tomorrow morning. You promised you would do the Couch to 5K with me."

"Don't worry — I can do both. Investigate murder and walk around the track with you."

THIRTEEN

"Enter into the gates of the Lord with thanksgiving, and into his courts with praise: be thankful unto him, and bless his name," the nuns on the Gospel side of the chapel prayed, singing from the *Anglican Psalter,* joining their voices together. Sister Agatha enjoyed prayer at noon, although she was sometimes engaged in library business and missed the midday gathering in the chapel. Reverend Mother was tolerant of the sisters sometimes missing the midday prayer service if they were truly doing the work of the Abbey. Sister Agatha hesitated to find out for certain if tracking down a murderer was included in Reverend Mother's understanding of "the work of the Abbey."

Keeping her eyes on her psalter, she reached into her apron pocket and her fingertips touched the recipe card, stashed between her Girl Guides knife that she had carried since receiving her Queen's Award at the age of sixteen and a battered copy of *Death on the Nile.* She pulled the card out, slipped it inside her open psalter, and read it carefully again. A recipe for laverbread. Laverbread, pureed seaweed rolled in oatmeal and fried to a crisp, was an acquired taste, and only those who had grown up along the Welsh coast were terribly partial to it. When Sister Gwenydd had learned that the sisters at the Abbey loved laverbread for their breakfast, she had set about learning how to make it. The young woman had certainly risen in Sister Agatha's estimation the morning she had placed a platter of freshly made laverbread on the breakfast table.

Flipping the recipe card over, Sister Agatha saw a very different handwriting. *Buy tinned laverbread if short on time, fair enough substitute if heated slowly in the oven.* It was written in purple ink. Sister Agatha was sure she had seen Sister Gwenydd using a whole set of colored pens — purple, pink, green — as she jotted on recipe cards. The next sentence, in florescent green ink, read *Investigation pending/Scotland Yard.* Sister Agatha slipped the card back into her pocket and looked across the chancel at Sister Gwenydd. The young woman, eyes trained on the psalter, belted out the prayer response in a clear voice that had a barroom sing-along feel to it, a little out of key with the chanting of the ancient prayers but appealing nonetheless. *Investigation pending/ Scotland Yard.* Why would Sister Gwenydd have written such a note on the back of a recipe card? Investigation pending? What investigation? Did it have a connection to Jacob? Or to the person who had killed Jacob? That was when she noticed that Sister Gwenydd wasn't wearing the silver postulant's cross. Was it *her* cross in the "Seek and Ye Shall Find" box? And if it was, how had it gotten there? Father Selwyn had said it was Gavin who'd found it. Found it where?

"For the Lord is good; his mercy is everlasting; and his truth endureth to all generations," came the response from the nuns on the Epistle side.

The liturgy of midday prayer lifted around her as she thought hard. What would Inspector McFarland say? On last Sunday's broadcast, the Inspector had tackled the sticky issue of red herrings versus good, solid clues. She tried to recall his lecture. *Red herrings look like clues but could function as disastrous interruptions to solving the mystery. Don't let your detective be taken in! A good red herring could derail the unsuspecting and send your story down the proverbial rabbit hole.*

"Amen," the sisters sang as one.

Was the recipe card simply a red herring? A distraction? It might have nothing to do with Jacob's death. Or was it a solid clue that she couldn't ignore? In the same way, was Michael just a distraction? Last night it had seemed imperative to interview him again, but in the light of morning, Sister Agatha wasn't as confident. She wanted desperately to pull out her phone and click on her Radio Wales app to listen again. But even with the note card burning a hole in her apron pocket, she resisted. Reverend Mother was so particular about listening to YouTube during chapel.

The tension in Reverend Mother's office nearly knocked Sister Agatha over.

The rest of the day following tea with Father Selwyn at The Buttered Crust and midday prayer in the chapel had been a whirlwind of activity. She had given a class to the sisters on how to use several of the databases she had set the Abbey up with. The nuns were interested in everything from the Religion and Philosophy Atlas to PubMed. It was challenging to keep up with them. Then, after dinner, she had gone back to the library to organize and shelve the set of new theological reference books that had just arrived from Canterbury Press. While she worked, her conversation that morning with Father Selwyn swam in her head. She became so engrossed in thinking through everything that had happened that when her phone vibrated in her apron pocket, she was tempted to ignore it. She really only glanced at the text because she thought it might be Macie with some news about Evelyn. Unfortunately, it wasn't Macie at all. It was Sister Callwen. AN EMERGENCY MEETING OF ALL THE SENIOR LEADERSHIP TEAM. Again? Pulling out her earbuds and leaving the journals on the floor, she had quickly made her way downstairs for the second emergency meeting of the week. This wasn't good.

Sister Agatha glanced around the room. Reverend Mother stood at the window, her back to the sisters, her basketball gripped in both hands. Sister Winifred sat on the leather couch staring straight ahead, motionless. She wasn't knitting. Not a good sign. Sister Callwen sat next to her, with her lips pressed in a thin line and her eyes closed in what Sister Agatha hoped was prayer. Sister Harriet perched on the ottoman with a manila folder on her knees, flipping rapidly through its pages. Whatever she was looking for, it was clear she wasn't finding it. Sister Agatha noticed that not a single glass of wine had been poured. Nor was there a pot of tea steaming with Welsh Brew. And there was not a cookie in sight.

"What's going on?" she said, sitting on the edge of a wingback chair near the door.

"Reverend Mother has given us some disturbing news," Sister Callwen said, her eyes still closed.

"Tell me, for crying out loud." Sister Agatha was not one for drama. Unless it was of her own making, of course.

"Our insurance company. They've canceled our building insurance. There's no money to replace the barn roof," Sister Harriet said, not looking up from the file on her lap.

"What?" Sister Agatha said. "Why?"

"Because we didn't pay the bill," Sister Winifred said. "The policy lapsed and the company canceled us."

"Can they do that?" Sister Agatha said. "Don't they have to send us lots of notices and final warnings? I say we call the diocesan solicitor. They can't get away with just canceling us for a single late payment!" Sister Agatha looked around the silent room. "That's outrageous."

"No, Sister, it isn't *outrageous*. What is *outrageous* is that they have been sending us notices and final warnings and . . . well . . ." Sister Callwen was cut off by Reverend Mother.

"The truth is . . ." She paused and took a breath, placing the basketball she had been holding on the desk. "I allowed the policy to lapse. The notices came and I . . . I ignored them. I have no excuse except fear — I knew that each envelope carried an invoice — and our insurance bill is the biggest payment we make every year. It made me so anxious that I kept putting off opening it . . ." Reverend Mother's voice broke. She stopped, and no one moved. She cleared her throat and said, "I have let you down. All of you. Terribly. I will offer my resignation tonight without hesitation."

Sister Agatha felt as if everything that had been right and good in the world had spun to a crashing halt. Still, no one spoke. She looked around the room wildly.

"All right, that's it," Sister Harriet said, tossing the file folder to the floor. She locked eyes with Reverend Mother. "I have something to say. First, you are not resigning. Yes, it was amazingly irresponsible of you to ignore a bill — especially one so important as the insurance policy. But more important — we all have played a part in this disaster. We've not supported you or helped you shoulder the burden of running the Abbey." Sister Harriet looked around the room. "We are each completely self-absorbed with our own concerns and cares." She turned back to Reverend Mother. "*We* have let *you* down."

Sister Winifred jumped in. "Here we are — teetering on the brink of financial disaster every year for the past decade. No wonder anxiety overcame you." Sister Winifred reached into her knitting bag and whipped out what looked like the longest scarf Sister Agatha had ever seen. She began to knit ferociously.

"And we all just merrily go along, wrapped up in our own little worlds," Sister Harriet said. "I know that all I have thought about for weeks is my latest submission to *Dark Horse Comics.* As if that were anywhere near as important as the Abbey or supporting Reverend Mother or . . . or . . . following Jesus! We just assume the Lord will provide, and we don't have to do anything."

"And He has!" Sister Agatha interjected.

"Yes, indeed. But that doesn't mean Reverend Mother should be left alone with the burden of waiting on the Lord. By herself. We should have all been there with her," Sister Harriet said.

"And then the bishop putting this extra burden on her," Sister Winifred said, speaking almost as if Reverend Mother were not in the room with them. "And the death of Jacob. And the fire. It's simply too much for one person." She turned to Reverend Mother. "We are all here for you. We stand behind you and will do whatever is needed to get us out of this mess. If you promise to please, please not ignore any more bills."

Sister Agatha thought Reverend Mother looked a little less pale than she had a few minutes earlier. "Absolutely," Sister Agatha said. "We're here for you. One hundred percent."

Sister Callwen cleared her throat. They all turned and looked at her. "Sisters," she said. "I do not mean to condemn Reverend Mother — I agree, we all could have been more supportive, and I commit to being so in future. But the crisis is still before us. How do we carry on without the cheese business, and what is to be done about replacing a roof for which we have no money?" She looked around at each sister.

"What about a diocesan loan or perhaps donations from the villagers?" Sister Harriet offered.

"Let's get an estimate from a roofer first, and then we can go from there," Sister Winifred said. "It might not be as bad as we think."

"That's the spirit," Sister Agatha said. "This Abbey has indeed faced bigger crises than needing a new roof. We must have more faith."

The mood in the room had lifted at least a little, and everyone except Sister Callwen joined in a cautious discussion about next steps. Together they decided to get an estimate on the cost of repairing the roof. In the meantime, they could move much of the Gouda production into the Abbey kitchen and dining room. A little ingenuity and hard work and things could go back to the way they had always been. And just in time for Christmas sales.

Just as Reverend Mother was declaring it late and time for everyone to retire to their rooms, the phone on her desk rang. The sisters listened as she nodded and agreed. She said good-bye and slowly replaced the receiver, staring at the top of her desk.

"What is it?" Sister Callwen asked. "You look like you've seen a ghost."

"That was the fire marshal in the village," she said, looking at Sister Agatha. "The fire wasn't an accident. It was arson. Someone set fire to the barn. Someone deliberately tried to burn down our barn."

The meeting in Reverend Mother's office had ended badly, and Sister Agatha was relieved to be able to excuse herself early and come out in the clear night air, even if it meant stumbling across the rutted ground to the orchard. She pulled out her notebook and, in the bright moonlight, wrote the word *ARSON* in all caps. She really needed to call Father Selwyn, but he had politely put a gag order on her from midnight to breakfast. Capping her Sharpie, she slipped the notebook back into her apron pocket. She had been unable to resist saying "I told you so" to Sister Callwen about the barn, which had upset everyone and made the whole meeting erupt in discord. Things had only calmed down when Sister Harriet looked out the window of Reverend Mother's office and saw that the barn door had been left open, which meant that Bartimaeus had probably wandered off again. Although being out and about late at night had saved him the night of the fire, they were afraid he would stumble in the dark and break a leg or maybe fall into the irrigation ditch as he once had.

Sister Agatha had offered to look for him

as a chance to get away from her sisters, who, frankly, were getting on her nerves. Also, she needed time to think. Everything that had happened in the past few days had pointed to foul play, and although no one had believed her, the call from the fire marshal had affirmed it. Although, in all honesty, she knew she might have resisted gloating.

Murder *and* arson. Her mind raced as she picked her way along the rutted path. Had the person who had killed Jacob set fire to the barn to destroy evidence? That didn't make sense, since there wasn't any evidence left from the investigation. But the killer might not have known that. Or perhaps there was evidence left that the killer knew about but the constable did not. Well, that wouldn't be too hard to imagine — Constable Barnes had hardly given a thought to Jacob's death. Or was someone out to destroy the Abbey? To shut it down? Murder in the cheese room would certainly stop production — even permanently ruin the sale of Heavenly Gouda. You wouldn't need to burn it down to make that happen — a dead body would be sufficient for the health inspector. So why burn down the barn? To finish off the job? To make sure there wasn't even a remote chance that cheese production could start up? And did the arsonist somehow know there was no insurance?

Sister Agatha stopped in her tracks. Clouds scudded across the moon, making her path dark and then quickly eerily light again. Moonlight had always fascinated Sister Agatha. It felt mysterious yet friendly, like a good P. D. James novel. She pulled out her notebook out and wrote, *Did anyone else know about the lapsed insurance policy?*

She found Bartimaeus munching an apple. "Careful eating apples, old boy," she said. "A few others have had their downfall by taking a bite of an apple." She ran her hands over his thick coat and was comforted by his gentle nicker. "What do you think, Bart? Did the same person who killed Jacob set fire to the barn?"

"Oh, I hardly think you can jump to that conclusion," a voice from the shadows said.

Sister Agatha screamed just as Gavin stepped out from behind a tree. "Gavin! Holy Mother!" She leaned against the pony, trying to catch her breath.

"Sorry, Sister."

"It's nearly midnight. What are you doing here?" She realized she was shaking. She took a deep breath. *Take it easy,* she told herself. *It's only Gavin.*

He held up his phone. She could see little

figures dancing across the small screen, and it chimed a bouncy tune. "I'm playing Pokémon."

"You're what?"

"Pokémon."

"In the orchard at midnight?"

"Did you know that the statue of Saint Andrew in front of the Abbey is a PokéStop?"

"A what?"

"A PokéStop. It means you can catch Pokémons there. And I'm a level eight, which means one more level and I can go to battle. And the village green is a Gym. That's where you do battle."

Sister Agatha snapped the rope onto Bartimaeus's halter and began to lead him back to the barn. Gavin followed, stumbling a little as he walked, since he never took his eyes off his cell phone. "You don't think you're a bit old for this business? This pokie-whatever-it-is?"

"Pokémon. Everyone's playing it right now."

"Father Selwyn's OK with you just wandering off in the middle of the night to play . . . your game?" Sister Agatha still hadn't entirely recovered from being scared out of her wits, and then the whole mess with the murder and arson just made the immature behavior of the St. Anselm's deacon even more annoying. "Aren't you supposed to be studying for ordination or something?"

"Sister, all work and no play, you know what they say. It's important to have downtime. They taught us all about self-care in seminary."

"Really? In my day, it wasn't about self-care. It was about care for others." Wales had changed. No doubt about that. They continued walking in silence, mainly because Gavin had his eyes glued to his phone. Sister Agatha would never have admitted it, but the little tune coming from his phone was catchy. When they reached the barn, he stopped playing long enough to open the door for her to lead in Bartimaeus.

"Does he have water?" he said. "I can get him some."

"No, he's OK. There's plenty of water in the trough. Though you might pull down a bit of hay." Perhaps Gavin wanted to make amends for scaring her, but Sister Agatha wasn't in a forgiving mood. She ran a currycomb over the old pony, who tossed his head with contentment while Gavin forked hay into the manger. They left the barn and walked up the path to the Abbey kitchen.

"Are you heading back to the rectory?" Sister Agatha asked, pulling open the heavy kitchen door.

"Yeah."

"Oh, quick question. Father Selwyn said you found a postulant's necklace at Saint Anselm. Where exactly?"

"A what?"

"Sorry. A silver cross. You gave it to Father for the 'Seek and Ye Shall Find' box?"

"Oh, right. Um . . . in the church somewhere. I think."

"Where in the church?"

"On the sidewalk, actually. Out front."

"Where was it? Out front or in the church?"

"Um . . . out front. Definitely out front on the sidewalk." He stared at his phone for a moment and then looked up, flashing a cheerful grin. "Just caught a Squirtle!"

Sister Agatha shook her head. "I weep for our future," she said for the second time that day, stepping into the kitchen, the door shutting behind her.

"What was that, Sister?"

And for the second time that night, Sister Agatha screamed. Sister Gwenydd sat on the floor with the contents of a kitchen cabinet spread out in front of her. Surrounded by pots and pans, it looked like she was either about to embark on a cooking spree or preparing for a midnight yard sale. "Does no one sleep around here?" Sister Agatha said as she collapsed into a kitchen chair. Sister Gwenydd stood up and brushed off her habit.

"Sorry. I was just doing a little inventory, and then I started cleaning, and before I knew it, I had taken apart all the lower cabinets. Which, by the way, haven't been cleaned and organized since about 1950, from the looks of things."

"Between you and Gavin just now, I'm surprised I haven't had a heart attack."

"Gavin? What was Gavin doing here at this hour?" Sister Gwenydd sat down across from Sister Agatha.

"Playing some game called Pokémon. Did you know we're a PokéStop?"

"No, we're not."

"We are. Gavin said he comes here to catch his little pokie-whatevers. In fact, he just caught a Squirtle."

"No. We are *not* a PokéStop. Believe me; I would know. The closest PokéStop is the village green. There's nothing out in this direction. If Gavin is coming out here to play Pokémon, then it's no wonder that all he has ever caught is one sad little Squirtle."

"What makes you the expert?"

"I'm a level twenty-nine. And I have three Egg Incubators, two Lure Modules, and twenty Ultra Balls. If the Abbey were a PokéStop, I'd be all over it."

"I see. By the way, Sister, what happened to your postulant's cross?"

"My cross?" Sister Gwenydd reached up to her throat as though the cross were there.

"Yes. Usually you wear it."

"Oh. Right. I took it off when I went running yesterday. I guess I forgot to put it back on." Sister Gwenydd stood and stretched. "Turn out the lights and lock up, would you? I'm going to bed."

FOURTEEN

As soon as Matins ended the next morning, Sister Agatha and Father Selwyn met up in front of St. Anselm. It was the first day of the Couch to 5K program at the Pryderi gym, and they were going to walk to the gym together. Reverend Mother had encouraged all the sisters at Gwenafwy to participate in the program. She thought it would be good if everyone at the Abbey made fitness a priority. So far, only Sister Agatha and Sister Matilda had signed up. And Sister Agatha had only signed up because Father Selwyn had pushed her into it.

"The pamphlet says regular exercise can increase bone density in some people," Father Selwyn read aloud, catching his toe on the sidewalk and nearly falling headlong into a bin of tomatoes in front of the Lettuce Eat Vegan grocery store. The village was quiet so early in the morning, although

Sister Agatha was sure The Buttered Crust was doing a fair business.

"I'm quite happy with my bone density just as it is," she said, skirting a corgi and its owner out for an early morning walk. Sister Agatha had her trainers in a bread sack, and Father Selwyn had his tied together at the shoelaces and slung over his shoulder. Sister Callwen had been very clear — no street shoes on the indoor track. Neither Sister Agatha nor Father Selwyn was terribly fond of exercise. Father Selwyn had his yoga class but admitted to liking it because he got to periodically lie down on the mat.

"There are also mental benefits of running," he read on. "Taking on the challenge of the Couch to 5K can help boost your self-confidence." He took a long look at Sister Agatha. She strode beside him, her head held high, notebook in one hand, bread sack in the other. "Although I don't know if your self-confidence really needs boosting." He turned back to his reading. "According to the pamphlet, you need to walk a certain amount every day until you can run or walk a 5K. And supposedly you progress at your own speed."

"What we need to do is find Aaron. He had a fight with Jacob. I would say that makes him a person of interest."

"I agree." Father Selwyn waved to Millicent Pritchard, the young woman who worked at the Just for You Florist Shop.

Only a few more blocks to the gym, and Sister Agatha found herself a bit winded. When they passed The Buttered Crust, she noticed that Father Selwyn looked longingly in the window. She slowed. "No way," he said. "We said we would get some exercise. And the Pryderi gym is just the ticket. We are *not* stopping for tea. Anyway, I heard they had tea available after you did your walk."

"With cake?"

"Sister."

Father Selwyn and Sister Agatha reached the front doors of the gym and turned in. A small crowd milled around the front desk, many of whom Sister Agatha recognized from the parish. The Couch to 5K was more popular than she would have thought. Signing in, she and Father Selwyn changed into their trainers and hit the walking track. She waved to Sister Matilda as she jogged past them. She had traded her Wellingtons for trainers and was tackling the jog around the track as if it were a stubborn garden weed that needed pulling out. Looking around, she realized that Father Selwyn's cassock and her blue habit were not at all the latest in exercise fashion. Both young and old breezed past them wearing what she thought were the most ridiculous outfits — they looked ready for a marathon run along the beach, not a thirty-minute walk at the Pryderi gym. "Good heavens, Father. Is this what people wear now, just to go for a walk?"

"It appears it is. Sadly, you and I are behind the times for the modern gym."

"We would fit right in at The Buttered Crust."

"The Buttered Crust is specifically why we are doing the Couch to 5K. Too many scones and oatcakes."

"Agreed." Sister Agatha smiled at two young women as they glided past. She recognized them as tellers from the village bank. She noticed that they worked their arms like pistons as they jogged, and each carried a tiny dumbbell in each hand. "Before I forget, where did Gavin tell you he found the silver cross that was in your office?"

"He just said 'in the church.' Why?"

"He told me last night that he found it on the sidewalk in front of the church."

"Do you want me to ask him?"

"No. Don't worry about it. Are you ready for the funeral tomorrow?"

"I think so. As sad as it makes me, it should be a beautiful celebration of Jacob's life. The rugby choir is singing, and his mother has filled the sanctuary with flowers from her gardens."

Sister Agatha nodded. Sometimes it was hard to believe Jacob was dead. She took a breath and looked around. The walking track at the gym was no time to get emotional. "Are we doing this right? I mean, everyone seems to be passing us. And they seem so happy. Do you think that's what they mean by endorphins?"

"Maybe." Father Selwyn looked around. "Or they heard there was tea once you finished."

"This tea is terrible." Sister Agatha stood next to the table set up outside the walking track. Tall glasses with drinking straws were lined up on the table. A sign read TRY A BEET SMOOTHIE! Sister Agatha grimaced. Sister Matilda stood at the tea table discussing times and upcoming races with the postmaster at the Pryderi post office. Sister Agatha noticed that he wore a bright-orange spandex shirt with black knee-length shorts of the same stretchy material. Sister Matilda's sneakers lit up, flashing neon pink every time she took a step. Sister Agatha shook her head. This was not the old Wales.

"That's because there's no sugar for the tea," Father Selwyn said. "And I think there's not likely to be any. Maybe tea without sugar is the thing at the gym." They stood and watched Sister Matilda as she accepted a tall purple smoothie from the table. "I'm trying one of those. How bad could they be?" he said.

"Based on their color, I would say awful," Sister Agatha replied.

Suddenly a loud voice came from the front desk. A tall young man with bulging muscles covered with tattoos and a pair of boxing gloves slung over his shoulder seemed to be shouting at the young receptionist. Sister Agatha looked at Father Selwyn, and they instinctively began to move toward her. The young man put both hands on the counter and leaned in, his face red and contorted, then swept his arm along the length of the desk, knocking to the floor clipboards, pens, pamphlets, and the tower of water bottles that the gym sold. The clatter brought the office manager running in. A shouting match ensued, which Sister Matilda later recounted at the Abbey as having language that she hadn't heard since her days on

London's East Side, with the manager finally convincing the young man to leave upon threat of calling the constable. He stomped out, kicking the tumbled water bottles on his way. The office manager came over to the tea table and began to apologize to the stunned Couch to 5K participants. Sister Agatha hurried to the counter where the shaken receptionist stood. "Are you OK?" she asked.

"Yeah," she said. "I'm OK. I'm just sick of that guy. Someday he's going to hurt someone."

"What's his problem?"

"He gets all crazy when he has to wait his turn to use the exercise equipment. Thinks he's better than everyone. A major temper." The woman began to put things to rights on her desk. "Probably on steroids."

Father Selwyn walked over carrying several of the water bottles. "Who is the young man, if I may ask?" He began to restack the bottles for her.

"His name's Aaron Hughes. Unfortunately, he's here all the time." She reattached the pen to the clipboard and set it back on the counter.

"Aaron Hughes?" Sister Agatha said, opening her notebook.

"Yeah. He comes in with this really nice

guy — Michael." She shook her head. "I don't know what he sees in him."

Sister Agatha's back ached. She stood at the long draining table pressing fermented curds into cheese molds. All she wanted to do was hole up in the library and see what she could figure out about the relationship between Michael, Jacob, and Aaron. Especially after the angry outburst she and Father Selwyn had witnessed at the gym. But Sister Winifred had needed help, and there seemed to be no one else available — even Sister Gwenydd, who could usually be found in the kitchen, had disappeared into the village — so here she was, up to her elbows in cheese curds. The health board had given the Abbey temporary clearance to set up cheese-making inside the main building of the Abbey. Several of the nuns had spent hours the day before — while Sister Agatha and Sister Matilda had been at the gym — moving tables, tubs, curd rakes, frames, hoops, and molds into the kitchen and dining room. They had hoped that with all the moving and cleaning that went with it, someone would come across Reverend Mother's lost cell phone. But it never showed up. The antique sideboard had been pressed into service to hold recipes, manuals, packages of rennet, and extra muslin. The stainless steel homogenizer, jockeyed into position with great effort, now sat cheek by jowl with the dining room table and the statue of St. Asaph. The old saint wore a hairnet that Sister Gwenydd had placed on him to lighten everyone's mood.

What Sister Agatha really wanted was time to think and to consult her notes from Rupert McFarland's podcast on suspects, and she also needed time to finish organizing the journal section of the library — even a tiny library like the one at the Abbey could fall apart if neglected. But since she had not helped move all the equipment yesterday, the least she could do was step up with the curding.

"We need a good sale this summer," Sister Winifred said simply.

"Are you worried?" Sister Agatha said.

"Cautious, not worried." Sister Winifred peeled off her latex gloves and snapped on a new pair, then slid two cheese molds across the draining table. "The stakes are high this year. Reverend Mother's anxiety is rubbing off on me. I want us to be successful, and I don't want to feel desperate."

"Desperate?"

"You know, like Daniel Fychans at The

Rogue Creamery. He came by the other night and grilled me on our finances — even wanted to see my fund balance sheet."

"Your what?" Sister Agatha prided herself on knowing nothing about finance. She squeezed her way to the other side of the crowded room and, leaning across the curding vat, used a long rake to move the cheese through the dense liquid. She felt mesmerized watching the curds glide and bob. She shook her head to clear it. "Why would Daniel Fychans be interested in us?"

"I have no idea," Sister Winifred said, taking the rake away from Sister Agatha. "Let me do this. It takes concentration." Sister Winifred liked things done right.

"What did Daniel want to know?"

"At first, just about this year's Heavenly Gouda sales, but then he let on that The Rogue Creamery wasn't doing that well. And when I asked him directly what was going on, he stormed off. Without finishing his tea." To Sister Winifred, leaving your tea was a great breach of social etiquette.

"So you think he's desperate? About money?"

"I don't know for sure, but it sounds like it. Making a success of a small business is harder than it looks, and the entire Fychans family depends on the profits from The

Rogue Creamery. It would be enough to stress out anyone." Sister Winifred put the rake down and tossed her gloves in the trash. She stretched her back and lifted her arms above her head. Sister Agatha watched as she bent over, putting the palms of her hands on the floor, and then arched her head up and closed her eyes. "What on earth are you doing?"

"The sun salutation, of course. You should take Father's class — Yoga for Seniors. We start every session with the sun salutation. And we end with this." Sister Winifred knelt on the tile floor of the kitchen, dropped back on her heels, and stretched down, her fingertips inching forward until her arms were entirely stretched out and her forehead touched the floor. Sister Agatha thought she looked like a monk at prayer. "Try it," Sister Winifred said into the tiles, her voice muffled. "It's called child's pose."

Sister Agatha tossed her notebook and pencil onto the table and let out an exasperated sigh. Would no one at the Abbey take her investigation seriously?

Sister Winifred stood up and, raising her hands above her head, bounced on her toes. "Would you like to see my warrior pose?"

At the same time that Sister Winifred and

Sister Agatha were cleaning up from the curding, Sister Gwenydd was stepping through the front entrance of the Pryderi Care Center. "Sign in, please," the woman at the front desk said, without moving her eyes from her computer screen. Signing one's name in the guest book seemed to be the nursing home's one nod to security. Sister Gwenydd scratched her name illegibly on a line halfway down the page. If anyone bothered to read the guest book, they would never figure out who had visited Gertrude Montgomery, the late Mark Johnson's grandmother, at 4:20 on Thursday afternoon. She hurried down the hall to Room 17, Gucci sandals clicking on the tiles. She had felt guilty leaving the Abbey — Sister Winifred had needed help with curding, and she had slipped away instead, before anyone could notice that she was gone.

The chair scraped the floor as she pulled up next to the old woman. "Beautiful day, isn't it?" Sister Gwenydd said. "We could go outside if you want. Take a spin around the garden?" The old woman smiled, humming tunelessly as she sat in her wheelchair, staring out the window. "Or not." She took one of Gertrude's hands in both of hers. "We can stay right here. How about if I do your hair and nails?" She reached behind her chair and retrieved her bag. Digging through it, she pulled out a hairbrush, a couple of nail files, moisturizing cream, and several bottles of nail polish. "I'll put these right here, and you can choose your color," she said, setting the nail polish on the tray table in front of Gertrude.

Gertrude picked up the first bottle and held it to the light and handed it to Gwenydd.

"Neon green it is, then." Sister Gwenydd smoothed moisturizer into the old woman's hands and then, after gently filing each nail, applied the polish. Next, she slowly brushed the thin gray hair, smoothing it back with her fingers and tying it into a soft scarf. "You're beautiful," she said holding up a mirror. "What do you think?"

Dementia clouded Gertrude's short-term memory, which meant she would never know that the young woman who visited wasn't really her granddaughter. She certainly wouldn't know that she was the one who had murdered her grandson. And, hopefully, no one else would know either.

After visiting for another few minutes and then sitting quietly, she made a quick goodbye to Gertrude and stepped into the hallway, narrowly missing a collision with

Sister Harriet, who hurried by talking a mile a minute with the director of nursing. Both women were engaged in such an animated conversation that neither noticed the young woman in the short black dress standing in the doorway of Room 17. She jumped back and pulled the door shut. Her mind raced. Had Sister Harriet seen her? How would she ever escape undetected?

She glanced at the clock. The Cardiff farmer's market closed in an hour. She needed to shop and fill the minivan with produce. She couldn't exactly return to the Abbey empty-handed, but then she couldn't risk running into Sister Harriet dressed like this, either. She had always changed in the back seat of the van at the far end of the farmer's market parking lot — not ideal, but she pulled her habit on over her clothes, and it seemed to work. Now, if she ran into Sister Harriet dressed in jeans and a T-shirt, what explanation could she offer? She had already had one disastrous event dressed like this with the man in the car — she didn't want to risk anything else that might ruin her cover.

Grabbing the gym bag, she shut herself into Gertrude's tiny bathroom. She pulled her habit on over her clothes and traded her Gucci sandals for the black trainers that all the nuns wore. Glancing into the mirror to adjust her veil, she felt startled, as she always felt now when she caught her reflection in a mirror. How had she gone from carefree graduate student at one of London's most prestigious cooking schools to postulant at Gwenafwy Abbey in rural North Wales — and murderer on the lam — almost overnight? She ran her fingers through her hair and took a deep breath. What was it that Sister Agatha always said? *No way out but through.* She hurried down the hall, scribbled a sign-out time in the notebook, and sprinted to the minivan.

"When it comes to breakfast, there is nothing better than Welsh laverbread still warm from the oven," Sister Harriet declared, lifting a slice of the pureed seaweed off the serving platter. "It's especially nice to have a good breakfast on a day like today." The nuns were planning on walking into the village after breakfast and gathering at St. Anselm's for Jacob's funeral. For a moment the table was silent, heavy with renewed grief.

Sister Gwenydd, after visiting Gertrude the day before, had woken up the next morning inspired to make a bigger-than-usual breakfast for the sisters. Sitting there with Gertrude, it had hit her how lucky she was to be at the Abbey. Although Reverend Mother would have said "blessed," not lucky. She realized that the unconditional welcome of the sisters at the Abbey had made it possible for her to get to know Gertrude. Gertrude seemed like family now. And, she realized with a start, so were the sisters at Gwenafwy. And they were family in the very best sense. The kind that cared about you, noticed you, paid attention. And that was all she had ever really wanted. Which was why, when Mark had skipped out on her graduation at Leiths, she had felt so devastated. Of course, she thought, poisoning him was probably going a bit too far.

She had loaded the breakfast table with her best offerings: laverbread, cockles, sausages, bacon, scones, fresh marmalade. She had also thought that throwing herself into cooking might help take her mind off the disturbing development she had found on Google. As good as she felt about Gertrude and the sisters, the words *Scotland Yard* kept going through her head. She instinctively reached up and felt for her postulant's cross. She shuddered. And who had been that awful man in the black town car?

The only blight on the table was the laverbread. Sister Gwenydd prided herself in preparing only homemade food with fresh, local ingredients. But this morning's laverbread was right out of a tin from the Tesco's in Wrexham. She seemed to have misplaced the recipe card from her box, not that she really needed a recipe for laverbread. Her grandmother had taught her the recipe years ago, during the summer of her tenth year when she had lived with her grandparents. The best summer of her childhood. In truth, the only time as a child she could claim to have been happy. She had never seen her grandmother again after that summer. Her grandmother had fallen ill and died before the family could make it back again. *Gertrude isn't dying,* she reminded herself. Other than her dementia, she seemed healthy. Sister Gwenydd shook out her napkin and spread it across her lap. On the other hand, Gertrude was eighty-nine. *She very well could die.* Why did the world have to be perpetually topsy-turvy? She decided to focus on her cooking and stop worrying about who was coming into her life and who was leaving.

"I don't know how you manage to do it all — it must be your youth," Sister Winifred said, looking at Sister Gwenydd.

"Do it all?" Sister Gwenydd said.

"You know — cook for us, shop at the farmer's market, visit the residents at the Care Center. You're a model postulant."

"Excuse me?" Sister Gwenydd said. She dropped her fork, and it clattered against her plate. "The Care Center?"

"In the village." Sister Winifred looked up from her plate of sausages. "Wasn't that the minivan I saw parked out in the lot yesterday afternoon?"

"Oh, right. Yes." Sister Gwenydd took a quick drink of tea. "Yes. I was visiting . . ." Sister Gwenydd tried to think of any possible way to finish her sentence but couldn't. *I was visiting the remaining family member of the man I murdered in cold blood.* No, that wouldn't work at all.

Sister Agatha noticed that Sister Gwenydd looked anxious and gave a weak smile as she busied herself with rearranging the steamed cockles on the serving platter. She also wasn't wearing the silver cross — the piece of jewelry that both she and Gavin had lied about. *Why had they lied?* Inspector McFarland would have said that the lies suspects told were sometimes more important than the truth they told. Evelyn was lying as well. *Who else?* Sister Agatha wondered. She slipped her notebook out of her apron pocket and, uncapping her Sharpie, wrote rapidly.

"How wonderful," Sister Harriet said. "I wish all of us were so quick to jump into outreach to the community." Sister Harriet stabbed a piece of Welsh bacon off the large serving platter. "You cook, you visit the elderly. Thank God the Holy Spirit blew you in here!" She beamed in Sister Gwenydd's direction. "I only wish we could attract another ten young women like you, and this Abbey would have a new start on life."

"We will all be more often at the Care Center, I hope," Reverend Mother said. She sat at her usual place at the head of the long table. Sister Agatha thought she looked more tired than she had seen her in years. She jotted a few more thoughts in her notebook. Her head suddenly felt light, and she stopped writing. "The diocesan office called," Reverend Mother continued. "And asked that we make a special effort to look in on Bishop Lewis. His family has very recently moved him to the Care Center. At the age of ninety, he's quite frail. I would like us all to visit."

Sister Gwenydd felt her stomach drop. This was a disaster.

"Why don't we all go together?" Sister Harriet said. "Wouldn't that be better, Sister

Gwenydd? Instead of you going alone? I propose that we start a visiting ministry — and shame on us for not doing it sooner."

"Sister Gwenydd, since you have inspired us, you should be in charge. Organize a visiting group, and we shall all go with you next time," Reverend Mother said. "Everyone in?" All nineteen sisters turned and looked at Sister Gwenydd, who managed a weak smile. "It's settled, then," Reverend Mother said. "And a visiting ministry will help us get our focus off our troubles here at the Abbey. It's always good to look outward when you find yourself looking inward. Especially today."

Sister Agatha wished Reverend Mother would say something, anything, that might reassure or encourage them. They had faced murder, arson, the bishop's threat to the convent. And now they would confront the loss of Jacob. She wished for a bit of scripture, a prayer, a scrap of homily or poetry. Usually Reverend Mother was so good at saying just the right thing. Today she just sat there. No words came. Perhaps there was nothing to say.

FIFTEEN

From her seat in the choir loft, Sister Agatha had a bird's-eye view of the entire congregation as it gathered at St. Anselm for Jacob's funeral.

Most of the village and every member of the Abbey had crowded into the church; the pews filled slowly back to front as people quietly entered — men with loosened ties and unbuttoned jackets, the women fanning themselves gently with the funeral bulletin. The sisters of Gwenafwy who had opted to sing with the St. Anselm choir were seated up in the choir loft. The other sisters sat together in the pews below.

Sister Agatha scanned the crowd. She was convinced that Jacob's murder had been a local job. Whoever had snuck into the aging room that night and shoved the shelves down on him had had to have been familiar with Jacob's routine and had to have known their way around the Abbey. In fact, it was reasonable to assume that Jacob's killer was right under her nose at this very moment. As Inspector McFarland was always saying, murderers had a way of showing up at their victims' funerals. More than anything, she wanted to trade the psalter for her notebook and make some quick notes. But with Reverend Mother in the same pew, she resisted. Instead, she decided to systematically work through each person of whom she had suspicions and commit her thoughts to memory. When she got back to the Abbey, she could write it all down.

She began with Constable Barnes, in full dress uniform, sitting at the back of the church. The constable was a big man. His wife was famous throughout the parish for her baking, especially her Welsh honey cakes. And it appeared that the constable had had one honey cake too many. His dress uniform jacket stretched tight across his shoulders, and he kept trying to run a finger under a very constricted collar. He looked uncomfortable, but not necessarily suspicious. She knew Constable Barnes to be a good sort; his only fault was refusing to see the death as a murder. Once Sister Agatha had asked him if he had ever read Hercule Poirot, and his reply had been that he only ever read Westerns and that the bad guy always got gunned down in the street at noon. She mentally checked Constable Barnes off her list. He wasn't covering up a murder, just burying his head in the sand. *Westerns, indeed.*

Father Selwyn's rich voice resonated from the pulpit and brought her back to the liturgy of the funeral. "The spirit of the Lord God is upon me, because the Lord has anointed me to comfort all who mourn."

She thought that Father Selwyn, in his black cassock and white surplice, offered a reassuring presence in the midst of heartache. And he had a good pulpit voice — commanding, yet heartening — not an easy combination to pull off. Gavin was less impressive. The young deacon stared sullenly from his seat to the right of the pulpit, his baby face framed by his usual tangle of dirty hair. And his white surplice was slightly wrinkled.

Moving her line of vision to the row of pews to the front, Sister Agatha stopped at Daniel Fychans, who sat next to his wife, Elizabeth. Even in church, Daniel looked like a bulldog about to lunge. Sister Agatha wondered what Daniel was so pent up about. He clutched the hymnbook, white-knuckling it, staring straight ahead with his lips not even moving. When the hymn ended, he snapped the book shut and shoved it into the rack in front of him. His wife, on the other hand, sat poised, at home in the church, her eyes closing during prayer and her soprano voice lifting a little above the harmony of the rest of the congregation. Her black linen jacket over a simple white silk blouse had the elegant cut that said expensive. Sister Agatha thought back to when she had seen Daniel in The Buttered Crust Tea Shop, when he had tried to pay for his tea with a maxed-out credit card. Daniel had had the same enraged, frustrated look on his face then that he did today. And according to Sister Winifred, the profits at the Rogue could be precarious right now. Did Daniel see Heavenly Gouda as competition? If Gwenafwy Abbey cheese sales took a nose dive, then the Rogue would get all the cheese profits to be had in North Wales. Would Daniel be desperate enough to want to shut down the competition? A dead body in the aging room, a fire in the cheese barn? Had it all been Daniel's handiwork in an effort to ruin their business? Murder and arson seemed a long shot, but money had driven better people to worse things.

Alice Traherne sat in the front pew with Michael next to her. Sister Agatha had eliminated both the mother and the boyfriend from her suspect list because they each seemed genuinely devastated by Jacob's death. And they had no discernible motive. *Of course, that's what Miss Marple initially thought about Letitia Blacklock in A Murder Is Announced.* Sister Agatha couldn't stand it. She had to make a few notes. She grabbed a pledge card from the rack in the pew in front of her and scribbled, *Reread* A Murder Is Announced, and then shoved it in her habit pocket. She ignored Sister Callwen's puff of disapproval.

On the other side of Alice sat her brother. Older and heavyset with salt-and-pepper hair, he held Alice's hand, his jaw set and his eyes bloodshot and puffy, as if he were recovering from a hangover. A drinker? she wondered. Or just jet-lagged? He had flown in from Melbourne the evening before, his long flight being the reason the funeral had been delayed a few extra days. He couldn't be a suspect — he hadn't even been in the country the night Jacob was killed. Probably the only truly airtight alibi in the room.

The side door to the sanctuary opened, and Sister Agatha watched as Aaron Hughes strode into the sanctuary. Latecomers to any church service usually slipped in the back door and slid as inconspicuously as possible into the nearest pew. Aaron surveyed the room as if he were at the cinema, scouting out the best seat in the house. Moving casually down the center aisle, he chose a seat in a pew near the front. If Aaron had killed Jacob, would he walk into the funeral with so much self-assurance? Or maybe that was exactly what a brazen murderer would do. *Never judge a book by its cover,* Inspector Rupert McFarland would say. *Or a murderer by his smile.* She could only hope Michael wouldn't see him. She thought back to Aaron at the gym, the way the muscles in his neck bulged, his voice biting and angry as he swept the water bottles off the counter. All because he had to wait his turn to use the equipment. What would he do if he thought another man was sleeping with his boyfriend — after his boyfriend had dumped him? Sister Agatha shuddered and mentally moved him to the top of her suspect list.

Sister Agatha shifted her gaze to the other side of the church. Sister Gwenydd sat in a middle pew. Sister Agatha took a long look at the young postulant. How was it that she had just happened to want to join the Abbey? Sister Agatha wondered if she even had a religious background. Most postulants had been immersed in church all their lives. But Sister Gwenydd didn't even know her way around the *Book of Common Prayer*. And what about the recipe card referencing Scotland Yard and an investigation? Did Sister Gwenydd have some sort of connection to the police, and if so, why? Had she committed a crime? And if she had committed one crime, could she not commit another?

She scanned the pews again and wondered if the imposing woman with flawless hair, perfect posture, and black pantsuit was Evelyn Birkby. Sister Agatha didn't recognize her from the village, which meant that she could be from St. Grenfell. And the woman certainly matched Macie's description. Why would Evelyn come to the funeral? To make sure she had done the job properly? Or just to hear Mordy's solo? Her son was singing "Amazing Grace" as a tribute to Jacob. Mordy was certainly a strapping lad. He sat in the tenor section of the choir loft, his voice rising above the rest during the opening hymn.

There didn't seem to be anyone else to investigate. In truth, she knew every single person in the room other than the young people from the pub and the rugby team. Would one of them have it in for Jacob? Rugby players could be a rough lot, impulsive and hotheaded. But what would any of them have against Jacob? He didn't even play rugby — he sang in the choir.

Sister Agatha knew that she had one more suspect, but she cringed inwardly even thinking about it. *Sister Callwen.* She just couldn't imagine Sister Callwen killing someone. Once Sister Agatha had watched her refuse to kill a spider, insisting they were part of God's creation as she gently coaxed the spider onto a sheet of paper and deposited it outside. But Sister Callwen had been acting so strangely and so out of character that no self-respecting detective would exclude her from a suspect list. Especially since the start of her strange behavior corresponded with Jacob's death.

Father Selwyn finished the reading from the Old Testament and the pallbearers came forward to lift the black casket to their shoulders. The raw memory of that awful morning in the aging room came flooding back to Sister Agatha — how the coroner had zipped shut the black vinyl body bag, Jacob's body lifeless inside. How the nuns had stood in shock, blood and broken plaster on the floor around their feet. How Sister Winifred had stepped up, one of her knitted prayer shawls in hand, which she silently presented to the coroner. How he had taken it from her and, shaking out its snowy folds, carefully laid the prayer shawl across the black bag.

Sister Agatha breathed deeply and looked around St. Anselm's sanctuary again and realized what was different — the church was filled with young people. The rugby choir occupied every spot in the choir loft, while the players of the Osprey Rugby League filled the front three pews. The church was crowded with young people — and all with the stunned appearance of those in shock. They were too young to have experienced much death, she thought. Perhaps they were genuinely surprised that mortality itself could invade their lives. She couldn't put her finger on it, but their grief had fierceness. Interesting, she thought. A fierce grief. She would ask Father Selwyn. He had seen so many in the parish through the experience of mourning that he might have an insight to offer.

Sister Agatha felt her eyes fill with tears, and she tried to focus on Father Selwyn's voice as he spoke the familiar prayers. Sister Matilda, sitting on one side of Agatha, blew her nose; Sister Callwen, on the other side, closed her eyes in prayer. Then, as the casket moved forward, the voices of the North Wales Rugby Choir were joined by the sisters of Gwenafwy Abbey, filling the nave with the old Anglican hymn:

> Guide me, O thou great Redeemer,
> Pilgrim through this barren land;
> I am weak, but thou art mighty;
> Hold me with thy powerful hand.

Alice Traherne walked directly behind the casket, her face stoic, her brother's arm around her shoulders; Michael followed several steps behind them, his face a mask of pain. The recessional made its way down the center aisle toward the wide front doors of the church. Sister Agatha watched, holding her breath, as Michael moved toward the aisle seat where Aaron sat. Sister Agatha held her breath as their eyes met. Michael's neck above his tie went blotchy and red. Aaron looked coolly at Michael, the hint of a smirk on his face. To Sister Agatha's horror, Aaron stood in the pew and grabbed Michael by the front of his shirt, shoved him a step or two backward, and then just as quickly let go. Gasps went up from the congregation. As the casket and procession continued down the aisle, the two young men locked eyes, and for one moment it looked as if a fight would break out. Two of the rugby players rose to their feet and moved quickly down the aisle. One stood in front of Aaron, staring him down, as the other player straightened Michael's coat and tie for him and then shoved him none too gently back in line with the recessional.

Jacob's mother was several steps ahead and so wrapped in her own grief that she didn't notice the disturbance. Her brother, however, cast a worried glance back at Michael. Sister Agatha watched as Constable Barnes stood and slowly made his way into the side aisle. She stood as well and slipped out of the pew, ignoring Sister Callwen's wide eyes and Reverend Mother's questioning glance. Stumbling over those in the choir loft and whispering her apologies, she made her way out of the pew and then hurried down the back stairs of the loft.

Sister Agatha stood at the entrance to the church and watched as Aaron turned abruptly and headed back up the empty center aisle toward the altar and then out the side door. She hurried out as well and stepped out onto the sidewalk just as Aaron crossed the street. She walked over to Constable Barnes as he stood looking across the street watching Aaron. Their eyes met, and he shook his head.

"What do you think now, Constable?" she asked.

"I think that I don't like the looks of him." He nodded across the street where Aaron stood next to a small red sports car.

The big front doors to the church opened. Father Selwyn led the casket out. Sister Agatha and the constable stepped to the side as the pallbearers slowly brought the casket down the front steps of the church.

"Do you still believe that Jacob's death was just an accident?" Sister Agatha asked him quietly.

He shrugged and, taking her arm, guided her a few steps back from the crowd now surging out the church doors. "It's not the first kerfuffle I've witnessed at a funeral, Sister. It doesn't mean anything more than two hotheaded young men unable to act decently." But she noticed that his voice betrayed uncertainty. They watched in silence as the pallbearers slid the casket into the back of the hearse and shut the wide back doors. Although the hymn had ended, the organist continued to play, the powerful notes reverberating out the open windows of the choir loft. Tears filled Sister Agatha's eyes as Constable Barnes, whose family had long sung in the colliery choirs of Wales, quietly added his rumbling bass:

When I tread the verge of Jordan,

Bid my anxious fears subside;
Death of death, and hell's destruction,
Land me safe on Canaan's side.

Sixteen

The morning's funeral was heavy on her mind as Sister Gwenydd walked to the Llewellyn church to deliver a round of Gouda for their weekly soup kitchen. She had hoped a walk in the late afternoon sun would help her calm down, but she had covered the two miles and back, and she was as distraught as ever. Sitting in the church for Jacob's funeral that morning had made her realize how dangerous it was for her to stay at the Abbey. It was only a matter of time until someone, most likely, Sister Agatha, discovered that she, Sister Gwenydd, was running from her own act of murder — accidental though it was. And then wouldn't that make her a prime suspect for Jacob's murder?

She stopped and, taking a deep breath, looked around. The dramatic beauty of North Wales always astounded her. Clouds skidded across a blue sky, and a slight breeze lifted small puffs of dust on the road. The valley below was resplendent in billowing green, dotted with grazing sheep, crisscrossed by stone fences, punctuated by St. Anselm's spire. Just when she had found a family, she was going to be forced to leave.

She had always known that the time would come when she would leave, slip away some dark night. The Abbey had never been a permanent plan. At the end of the day, she was nothing more than a young woman on the lam, not a postulant. And if Sister Agatha didn't blow her cover, Scotland Yard certainly would. An image of the police standing in Reverend Mother's office flashed through her mind. She trembled at the thought. Tomorrow all the sisters from the Abbey were accompanying her to visit the residents at the Pryderi Care Center. They had the clear purpose of seeing to the aging bishop and then visiting anyone else who wanted the company of a few nuns. What could she do? Gertrude never remembered Sister Gwenydd's name or seemed even to recognize her; yet if Gertrude suddenly saw her dressed as a nun, what would that do to the elderly woman? And what if the staff at the Care Center recognized her and asked why she was wearing a habit? The time had come, perhaps, to leave and go under cover somewhere else. The problem was, she couldn't imagine leaving.

On an impulse, she turned off the lane leading back to the Abbey, climbed through a meandering hedge of wild gorse, and sat down on the warm grass of a meadow. A small flock of sheep grazed about a hundred yards away, uninterested in the young woman trespassing on their green pastures. Before coming to Wales, she would never have sat on the ground and gazed at the sky. But the sun-drenched valleys, flower-filled fields, and winding country roads of the North were beginning to change her. Although she sometimes longed for the feel of a sidewalk under her feet or the pounding beat of a London nightclub, she just as often found herself stopping to listen to birdsong, or breathe in the heady scent of lilac, or wonder how the late-summer vegetables were faring.

A bird circled overhead; the grass smelled warm and fresh, and the sky seemed impossibly blue. The world around her pulsated with tranquility, but her inner world churned with anxiety. Her reasons for living at the Abbey had always been pure survival — a roof over her head, a meal ticket. And a convenient location to Mark's grandmother. Then, after being at the Abbey for a few weeks, she had begun cooking for the sisters — they were pretty much awful cooks. They had fallen in love with her culinary skills and had immediately offered her a genuine gratitude that she had never experienced in her previous life. At the Leiths School in London, things had been cutthroat — and certainly no one praised you for making an awesome Welsh rarebit. But now, it felt as if her existence at the Abbey was at risk. If Jacob had been murdered and the barn set on fire, then the police were going to be around asking questions, looking into things. She could easily be revealed as a criminal on the lam. No matter how much she had begun to think of herself as a nun.

She lay back on the grass and watched the clouds cross the sky. The Abbey itself had been a surprise to her. She had arrived at Gwenafwy thinking that it would be something out of an old movie — silence and chanting, barren cells and long cold hours kneeling in prayer. A crucifix on every wall. She hadn't been prepared for the humor, the strong opinions, the social justice work, or the quirky personalities. She especially hadn't been prepared for the immediate hospitality and authentic welcome the nuns offered her. She had been taken completely aback by how quickly she was embraced and brought into the life of the Abbey community.

She stood up, brushed off her skirt, and made her way back to the road. She knew one thing — she couldn't keep going to the nursing home dressed as Aubrey Matteson, great-granddaughter of Gertrude Montgomery. And she also couldn't go dressed as Sister Gwenydd, postulant at Gwenafwy Abbey

She looked up at the sky and began to walk as fast as she could toward the Abbey. Thick dark clouds had suddenly blown up on the horizon, and a sharp wind tossed her hair. She wished she had grabbed a jacket. Her cell phone vibrated. *The Pryderi Care Center.* They had never called her before. Panicked, she answered with a frightened "Hello" just as the rain came down in torrents.

"I'm sorry, Sister, but you cannot have the minivan. Tomorrow's fish pie will just have to happen without fresh haddock and mackerel." Reverend Mother barely glanced at the young postulant. She sorted frantically through a pile of papers on her desk, hardly noticing the rain and wind pelting the windows of her office. "You can't make something else? Everything you make is so good. I'm sure we'll love it, whatever it is."

Sister Gwenydd had followed Reverend Mother back to her office nearly begging for the keys to the minivan with the excuse of needing leeks. When she had talked to the Care Center, all the nurse would tell her was that Gertrude was in distress, and the physician on duty was considering sending her to hospital. They wouldn't tell her anything more over the phone but said that she should probably try to come immediately. A heavy rainstorm with wind and thunder had blown up, and she couldn't imagine making the mile-long walk to the Care Center in it. Walking to the village in fair weather was pleasant, but not in lightening, thunder, and a downpour.

Reverend Mother swept a stack of files off her desk and shoved them into an already bulging canvas bag. Sister Gwenydd noticed a pair of basketball shoes sticking out the top.

Reverend Mother looked at Sister Gwenydd for the first time. "You seem distracted, Sister. Everything OK?"

"I'm fine. I just really need to go shopping in the village."

Reverend Mother grabbed an umbrella off the hook next to the door and heaved the bag over her shoulder. "Sister Callwen and I are on our way to talk with the insurance agent. There is a slight chance they will reinstate our policy. We need the van." She hurried out the door while Sister Gwenydd stood helplessly, her hope fading with the sound of Reverend Mother's footsteps.

The minivan hit a bump and Sister Gwenydd felt her entire body jolt. Sister Callwen seemed to hit every pothole on the gravel lane between the Abbey and the village. The heavy wind rocked the van, and thunder boomed overhead. Lying on the floor behind the back seat, her feet under a bag of soccer balls and her head crammed into a box of clean socks for the homeless shelter, she couldn't believe that she had fallen this far — hiding in the back of a minivan driven by nuns.

In the dark, she felt around and found a quilt bunched up in the corner and fashioned a kind of pillow out of it. The quilt smelled like cheese rind. She remembered that they had wrapped a case of Gouda with it about a month before. Whose job was it to clean out the minivan, anyway? Sister Callwen and Reverend Mother were talking rapidly in the front seat, but she couldn't entirely hear what they were saying. She caught snatches of the conversation, and it seemed to have something to do with the barn fire. She wondered how far the insurance office was from the Care Center. She thought it was within walking distance, but she wasn't sure. Though desperate for more information about Gertrude, she had put her cell on silent. The Care Center hadn't said exactly that Gertrude was dying. She couldn't even let herself think about that. Certainly, the Care Center would have told her if that was the case. Or would they? She had never dealt with a nursing home before and knew nothing about how they worked. A soccer ball had come free of the bag and now bounced into her head. Would they never get there?

The van slowed and then lurched to a stop. She held her breath as Reverend Mother and Sister Callwen got out. As soon as the doors to the van slammed shut, she shrugged off the quilt and took a deep breath. Fumbling in the dark, she found the latch, popped open the back door, and tumbled out with the soccer balls, which bounced across the parking lot. The rain had let up a little, and the thunder was now just a distant rumble. Looking around, she realized she was in a small parking lot behind the town hall. St. Anselm's spire rose against the early evening sky. Pulling out her phone, she punched in the Care Center address and then waited while the satellite figured out her location. She was less than half a mile away. If she hurried, she could get to the Care Center, find out what was going on with Gertrude, and get back to the minivan before Sister Callwen and Reverend Mother. It was a gamble, but she had done far riskier things since the day she'd found Mark's dead body slumped over a bowl of lamb stew.

"I'm here to see Gertrude Montgomery. You called me?" Sister Gwenydd said, her heart fluttering. The walk to the Care Center had been longer than Google Maps had indicated, and her anxiety had risen with every hurried step. Sister Gwenydd didn't recognize the young woman behind the desk. "Gertrude Montgomery?" she said again. "You called me?"

"Who called you?" the young woman said. "A nurse? Or someone at the desk?"

"I don't know. That's all right. I'll find her myself." Sister Gwenydd turned and ran down the hall toward Room 17. What if Gertrude was gone, her bed made up, her things in a box ready for removal? Her mind racing, she burst through the door. The old woman lay on the bed, eyes closed. A nurse stood next to her. "Oh, thank God." Sister Gwenydd let out a sigh of relief. "I got a call, and then it took forever to get here." She took Gertrude's hand. "What's happened?"

"Your grandmother is going to be OK. Mrs. Montgomery had what seemed like a stroke — extreme confusion, trembling, sweating. But it was just a drop in blood sugar. Dr. Sharaf happened to be here, and he gave her a quick injection of glucose, and she's doing pretty well." The nurse made a note on her clipboard and then looked up with a quizzical expression. "We'll know more tomorrow."

"Thank goodness. I mean, low blood sugar isn't good, right? But it can be fixed. Treated. Can't it?"

"Of course. In the elderly, it's more serious, but with proper precautions, she'll be just fine."

"What is it? You're not telling me something?" The nurse seemed to be staring at her.

"I'm sorry. It isn't that. It's just that I didn't know you were a nun."

Sister Gwenydd suddenly realized that in her frantic efforts to get to the Care Center, she had forgotten all about changing out of her habit. She stood there in Gertrude's room in her blue postulant's veil and habit. "Oh, right," she said. "I'm a nun. At Gwenafwy Abbey. Well, a postulant. Not quite the same as a nun."

"I've always assumed you were a shop girl or worked in an office or something. Not a nun."

"Well . . . we don't always have to wear our habits. Or at least, not as postulants." Sister Gwenydd flushed with her lie. Oh well, in for a penny, in for a pound, as Sister Agatha would have said. "And from now on, I'll be in a habit because I'm advancing in the stages to being a nun." Wow. Lying was way too easy. Maybe she wasn't becoming more nunlike after all.

"And what do I call you? Do you still go by Aubrey?"

"Sister Gwenydd."

"All right then, Sister Gwenydd it is." The nurse seemed to lose interest as she turned back to her patient. "I am glad to see Mrs. Montgomery's resting comfortably."

"And she's going to be OK, right?" Sister Gwenydd suddenly remembered that she needed to get back to the parking lot before the minivan left. "I was told I needed to sign something?"

"I wouldn't think so now. Not if it is as

simple as low blood sugar. Call tomorrow and see where things are. Dr. Sharaf comes around in the morning." The nurse looked at her. "It's all right, dear. Go home."

If only it were as simple as that, she thought to herself as she ran down the hall and out the front door.

Sister Gwenydd slammed shut the door of the dairy truck and waved as it drove down the moonlit gravel lane. She had left the Care Center and run most of the way back to the minivan — only to find it gone. Sister Callwen and Reverend Mother had apparently finished at the insurance office and then left for the Abbey. Sister Gwenydd had stood in the empty parking space as if, by trying hard enough, she could conjure up the minivan. No minivan appeared. She had turned to walk down the street in the direction of the Abbey — she really didn't feel like walking — when she saw the delivery truck for The Rogue Creamery parked across from Saints and Sinners. The Rogue Creamery wasn't too far past the Abbey. Surely Ned, the delivery guy, would give her a ride. She waited for a few minutes outside the pub and was about to give up and start walking when he came out.

"Nos da, Sister," he said. *Good evening.*

"Going in for a pint?"

"Not tonight. I was hoping for a lift back to the Abbey," she said.

"Miss the bus?" Ned grinned and fished the keys out of his pocket. There wasn't a bus between Pryderi and Gwenafwy.

"Something like that. Can you give me a ride?" She tried to sound casual.

"Sure thing. Hop in. Just don't mention to the boss that I was at the Saints, will you? He isn't keen on me having a pint when I'm driving his truck."

"My lips are sealed." Sister Gwenydd climbed into the passenger side of the delivery truck. Suddenly she jumped and let out a small squeal. A very fat hedgehog, curled in a ball, was riding shotgun on the passenger seat.

"Don't mind Cedric there," Ned said, scooping up the hedgehog and putting it in a cardboard box on the console. "He likes to go for a spin every now and again. So I take him on my rounds with me." As if he knew he was being talked about, Cedric raised his head and gave Sister Gwenydd a disparaging look.

"I didn't know hedgehogs could be pets."

"Oh, aye. Cedric's been with me ever since I found him on the side of the road. Just a wee thing. His mother in the ditch, dead as a doornail." Ned palmed the steering wheel with one hand and gave the hedgehog an affectionate scratch with the other. "He's a good lad. A bit fat at the moment."

Sister Gwenydd thought that if hedgehogs could be classified as obese, this one would qualify. "What do hedgehogs eat?" she asked. Cedric's box, lined with a fleece cloth, was scattered with lettuce leaves, pieces of cucumber, and what looked like a bit of goat cheese. Ned launched into a detailed discussion of the care and feeding of hedgehogs, which then morphed into a lengthy play-by-play description of the latest win by the Ospreys, his favorite team. Sister Gwenydd cared little for rugby and possibly less for hedgehogs, although she had to admit, Cedric did have a lot of personality. She tried her best to act interested. As long as Ned kept talking about hedgehogs and rugby, she wouldn't have to fill in any silences with what she had been doing that had left her stranded in the village. Ned seemed uninterested in her story anyway. Which would not be the case, she thought, with anyone she might run into at the Abbey.

She assured Ned that he didn't need to drive all the way up to the Abbey and that dropping her at the gate by the road was just fine. Bone tired, she hoped to slip in the kitchen door and get up to her room without anyone noticing. But as soon as she slammed shut the door of Ned's truck, wishing him and Cedric a good evening, she could hear the thud of a basketball against the backboard. Reverend Mother was shooting baskets.

The hoop was just outside the kitchen door, the only door at the convent for which Sister Gwenydd had a key. Happy that there was no moonlight that night, she approached as quietly as she could and then stood hidden in the shadows of the lilac bushes. Was this the moment that she would slip silently away? Never to return? She felt too tired to even consider it. The stable was off to her right. She could spend the night there. Once, when she had been on the run, she had curled up in a horse barn on what seemed to be a fresh pile of straw; it had been a low point that she didn't want to revisit. She watched as Reverend Mother arced the ball from center court. It swished through the net. Jogging forward, she caught it, dribbled back, and, facing the net, launched the ball into the air again. "Good evening, my sister," Reverend Mother said, as the ball again swished the net. This time,

Reverend Mother let it bounce and roll under the lilacs. She looked directly into the shadows where Sister Gwenydd stood. "I must say, you look like you could do with a cup of tea."

SEVENTEEN

"And why do you think you killed him?" Reverend Mother asked, setting out a plate of oatcakes and giving a glance around the kitchen. Her cell phone had been lost for several days and she kept thinking she was going to spot it lying somewhere. She often left it in the oddest places. The last time it disappeared, Sister Matilda had found it in the bottom of a box of zucchini ready to be sold at the farmer's market. "Sister, your *bara ceirch* are quite good. Thin and crispy like this is really the best way to make them." She broke off a piece of the oatcake Sister Gwenydd had baked the day before and sat at the kitchen table, crunching quietly. "A blessed day for us, when you stumbled upon our little community."

Sister Gwenydd didn't know which to respond to first, the question about killing Mark or the affirmation that the Abbey was blessed to have her with them — crispy oatcakes, subterfuge, deception, potential homicide, and all.

"When I got to his apartment, he was sitting at the table, but kind of fallen over. You know, over the bowl of lamb stew. I touched his shoulder and . . . he was . . . stiff — rigor mortis. Like you see in movies."

"But how do you know that *you* killed him?"

Sister Gwenydd crumbled her oatcake into pieces. The batch really had crisped up nicely. "He'd obviously eaten the stew and then had the big allergic reaction that he was always so afraid of, and then he . . . you know . . . died. Never even got up from the table." Sister Gwenydd couldn't get that last horrible image of Mark out of her head — his head face down, hands reaching out, flies buzzing around the table. She shivered.

"What did you think would happen when he ate the stew?" Reverend Mother took a slow sip of tea.

"Well, I didn't think he would die. An itchy rash, hives. That's all. But usually he just has a little sage. Most dishes call for a pinch of sage. I put in . . ." Sister Gwenydd paused. "I put in at least a cup of fresh sage. You know, I minced it quite well."

"That's what I don't understand. It doesn't seem enough to kill someone —

even a heaping dose of sage. Especially if one's reaction was normally hives and itching."

"I think it was so powerful that his throat closed. Or maybe the trauma to his system gave him a heart attack or something."

"And you say you've followed the case on the Internet?"

"Yes. And for a long time, there was almost nothing except the obituary and one reference in a police log — absolutely nothing on cause of death. But now the case has been reopened." Reverend Mother looked thoughtful and poured more tea. The dark night sky had started to turn gray, and, through the kitchen window, a pink streak appeared on the horizon. "I think they're on to me."

"Who is 'they'?" Reverend Mother bit into another oatcake.

"Scotland Yard. The authorities." Sister Gwenydd tried to stop her voice from breaking, but she couldn't. "The police."

Reverend Mother sat back, sipping her tea, her brow furrowed. The only sound was the clock ticking on the wall. Sister Gwenydd wondered if she should offer to pack up and be out the door before the sisters rose for morning prayer. It would be horrible not to say good-bye. But a life on the run excluded the luxury of emotional goodbyes. "I don't know what to do."

"Nonsense. The path ahead couldn't be clearer." Reverend Mother took a final sip of tea. She stood, stretched, and began to stack the tea things in the sink.

"Yes, right. Of course, I'll leave right away. I can't thank you enough. For . . . well, for everything." Sister Gwenydd tried to stand and found that she couldn't.

"Leave?" Reverend Mother dried her hands on a tea towel. "Why would you leave? After breakfast, you will tell the sisters everything. The entire truth." Reverend Mother must have noticed Sister Gwenydd's sharp intake of breath. "Don't worry. I will stand right beside you. And then — with their help — because we are a community of faith and not just a group of people who happen to live together — we will get to the bottom of this. We will find out if indeed your sage overdose killed your young man, and, if it did, you will turn yourself in." Reverend Mother seemed far too cheerful for Sister Gwenydd.

"What do you mean — turn myself in? Like . . . do you mean . . . to the police?" Sister Gwenydd felt her skin tighten, and her hands shook. "I'll be arrested."

Reverend Mother smiled. "Most likely.

However, I don't think you killed him. It just doesn't make sense. And even if you did, you didn't *mean* to murder anyone. No malice aforethought, at least not beyond making someone miserably itchy. Quite different. I'm sure any jury in Wales would take that into consideration."

"I could do jail time." Sister Gwenydd stared at Reverend Mother.

"Yes, absolutely. But not forever. And when you get out, you could come back to being a nun. But if you keep running, how will you ever finish your postulancy and take orders?" Reverend Mother looked at Sister Gwenydd as though Sister Gwenydd were a fourth-form schoolgirl who was not quite paying attention.

"But I'm not really a nun." Sister Gwenydd paused. "Am I?"

"You tell me." Reverend Mother stood still, tea towel in hand.

"I do feel as if this is where I'm supposed to be. But I don't entirely know why."

"Because you have been called. Called by God. Just as Sister Agatha was called. And Sister Harriet was called. And I was called. I don't say this lightly, but ever since you came through our doors, I have known you were responding to God's call."

"Even though I was running from something?"

"Good heavens." Reverend Mother tossed the tea towel onto the counter. "We're all running from something. Now then, it is nearly time for morning prayer. Right after breakfast — which I believe you are cooking — I will summon all the sisters, and you will tell your story in its entirety. And then we will get busy putting it all to rights."

Sister Gwenydd thought that if a person could live without taking a breath, she was medical proof. She had finished her account of murdering Mark, running from the police, and ending up on the doorstep of Gwenafwy pretending to want to join the religious order when all she wanted was a place to hide and a good meal. She was a fraud, and now everyone knew it. She looked at her plate of untouched food and willed herself not to cry. A bird called outside the window, and the faint sound of the village clock tower chimed the early hour. Finally, a voice spoke up. It was Sister Harriet.

"Well, I, for one, don't think you killed him," she said, picking up her teacup and giving it a swirl as if it were a glass of Cabernet, then taking a sip. There was a murmur of assent around the long table. "I mean, how could sage kill a grown man?"

"Don't be so sure," Sister Agatha said. "In *A Pocket Full of Rye,* the murderer put yew leaves in the victim's breakfast marmalade." The sisters watched as she reached for the tub of marmalade and spooned a generous helping onto a scone. "Dead as a doornail within the hour."

"That was fiction," Sister Matilda said. "I hardly think it applies."

"Fiction based on real life. Agatha Christie did meticulous research."

"Agatha Christie aside," Reverend Mother said, "what is everyone thinking? How do we proceed?"

Sister June pushed her chair back and stood. Before joining Gwenafwy, she had been a solicitor in Cardiff. When Reverend Mother saw her rise to her feet at the breakfast table, she knew Sister Junc had her litigator hat on. "Reverend Mother, may I address the community?"

"This is not a courtroom. Everyone is free to speak."

Sister June cleared her throat. "I notice that some of you seemed a bit surprised and, perhaps, angered when you heard that we had been duped for these three months by our postulant." She paused and looked around the table. Sister Gwenydd concentrated on her breathing. She noticed that several nuns nodded, a few looked down at their empty plates, and absolutely no one protested. "And even though Sister Gwenydd is the first postulant this convent has had in twelve years and she has brought to us a certain youthful energy very much lacking, we may feel particularly betrayed and discouraged by her news." More nods. "You may think that Sister Gwenydd should indeed discontinue her path to religious orders." Sister June paused and Sister Gwenydd held her breath. Radio silence. "Lying," she continued, "is destructive to community, while murder is nothing less than a felony."

"But what if she didn't mean to kill him? She said herself that she only wanted to make him miserable," Sister Harriet said.

"Doesn't matter. If the intent is to cause grievous bodily harm to the victim rather than specific intent to kill, the effect is the same as that of the felony murder rule."

"In other words, she killed him, and no jury in the world would think otherwise," Sister Agatha said, in response to the befuddled look on Sister Winifred's face.

Still standing, Sister June looked around the table, and Sister Gwenydd felt tears at the edges of her eyes. She blinked hard to keep them back. Sister June took a deep breath, and before she could continue, Sister Callwen blurted out, "Oh, please. Get to the point! What is it you want to say?"

"I want to say that we need to put aside personal feelings and support our sister. She's young, she's impulsive, and she's magic in the kitchen."

And with that, Sister June sat down.

Sister Gwenydd started to breathe again.

"Agreed," said Sister Harriet. "And who is to say that God didn't send her to us? Who is to say that it is not our duty as Christians to embrace her?"

Sister Matilda spoke up. "I think it's a little like the old days when churches offered sanctuary to people being hunted down by . . . oh, I don't know what . . . tyrants. She's like Martin Luther when he hid out in Wartburg Castle and the Pope declared him an outlaw!"

Sister Callwen nearly choked on her tea. "Good heavens, it's nothing like that! You can't compare a young woman who wants to teach her boyfriend a lesson, possibly kills him, who hides out pretending to be a postulant so she can have free room and board, *to Martin Luther*?"

"And what would you do? Send her

straight to jail?" Sister Agatha said. "Let's keep in mind there is no empirical evidence that the sage killed him. Innocent 'till proven a cold-blooded murderer' is what Rupert McFarland would say. We are a long way from proving anything here."

Sister Callwen frowned at Sister Agatha, and then turned to Sister Gwenydd. "How in the world did you survive before you arrived here? You know, while you were on the lam?"

"Well, I slept on the train a bunch. In a barn once. All-night launderettes. Places like that. It was . . . not easy." Sister Gwenydd twisted her napkin in her lap. "I came here when I realized that Mark's grandmother was alone. He was all she had left, and I had . . . Well, I had taken him away from her."

"Tell us more about this grandmother," Sister Harriet said, pouring a cup of tea for Reverend Mother and holding up the teapot for anyone else. "I'm the most interested in her. Not so much the deception or even that Sister Gwenydd is a murderer — which I don't think you are, dear." She smiled at Sister Gwenydd. Sister Gwenydd dared to look at the roomful of nuns and saw that they were looking back at her with open expressions.

"Well, her name is Gertrude Montgomery. She's eighty-nine and has advanced dementia. Sometimes she thinks I'm her daughter. Other times, she doesn't know who I am at all." Sister Gwenydd tried to pick up her cup of tea, but her hand trembled so much she put it back down. "But she always seems happy to see me."

"You say you visit every week?" Sister Matilda said.

Sister Gwenydd nodded. "At least once. Sometimes twice, if I can. When I go to the farmer's market."

"What were you going to do when the weather turned cold, and the farmer's market was no longer open?"

Sister Gwenydd shrugged. "I hadn't thought that far ahead."

"Could we move forward with this?" Sister Callwen pushed her plate away. "We have cheese, prayers, and a convent to save." She looked around the table. "Do we have a plan?"

"At the very least, I think we should find out whether it was the sage that killed the boyfriend — I can't quite believe that it did. And, maybe even more important, since she is still living, let's set up a schedule for visiting Mrs. Montgomery," Reverend Mother said.

"And as much as no one wants to say it, are we calling the police?" Sister Callwen asked. A murmur went around the table. Sister Gwenydd wasn't sure if it was a murmur of agreement or dissent. She sensed it was both.

Sister Harriet must have sensed it also. "Sisters," she said, waiting until everyone was quiet and listening to her. "Something very egregious has happened here. And I don't mean the poisoning of an errant boyfriend — that sounds more to me like a stupid prank gone bad — very bad, indeed. But what I am really talking about is the betrayal of this community. We understood Sister Gwenydd to be a serious candidate for taking orders. And she simply wasn't. Isn't. We were lied to and that is no small matter."

"What do you suggest then, Sister Harriet? Trust is not easily restored, once broken." Sister Matilda spoke with a tinge of ice in her voice.

"Agreed." Sister Harriet looked out at the sisters. "Have any of you ever found yourselves on the run, so to speak?" She waited. At first the sisters looked skeptical, but then a flicker of light seemed to break in. A few sisters nodded, and some offered rueful smiles. "We have not perhaps fled from the police — a literal run. But are we not all on the run, one way or another? Haven't we all fallen short and wished for grace?" More nods around the table.

"Well, I for one, like to do things by the book," Sister Winifred said. "But in this case, the book we must turn to is the Gospel. We need to all remember that a life of faith is indeed a life on the run. We are running from our past selves to our better selves — new in the light of God's love." Sister Winifred smiled at Sister Gwenydd, and then turned back to Sister Harriet. "In other words, you make a good point."

"All right then," Reverend Mother said. She looked around the long table. "Before we move on, I want to make sure everyone has said what they want to say. If you are holding back feelings about the choices that Sister Gwenydd has made, please speak now." Reverend Mother paused. "I will wait." Sister Harriet poured tea all around, and Sister June helped herself to the last of the scones. "Well, then. What I want to do next is unprecedented. But I must be certain that our way forward, through this most unusual situation, is clear. I typically do not ask for a formal vote, since I believe that a community of faith should always come to consensus, but this one time, under these extreme circumstances, I want a show of hands." Reverend Mother looked at Sister Gwenydd. "I will go with the feeling of the convent." Turning back to the other nuns, she said, "All for supporting Sister Gwenydd and keeping her on as a postulant here at Gwenafwy, please raise your hand." Sister Gwenydd could barely look up, but one by one each nun raised her hand. Several smiled warmly, and only one or two avoided eye contact. "All opposed?" No hands raised. "Then, I declare us in agreement. Sister Gwenydd stays, and we support her wholeheartedly." And, to Sister Gwenydd's great surprise, the nuns broke out in applause, and, pushing their chairs back, everyone stood, smiling and clapping.

Eighteen

"What do you mean, this is your table?" Sister Winifred said, thumping a wooden crate onto a table at the front of the vendor tent. She and Sister Matilda had arrived at the Gwydion Cheese Festival just as the sun peeked over the Gwydion Castle tower. On the drive there, they had talked of nothing but Sister Gwenydd's shocking confession the day before. They had both agreed that, although they were stunned by her revelation, to do anything other than support her would be unchristian. Especially since she hadn't intended to poison anyone. Sister Matilda dropped Winifred off at the vendor tent and left to park the minivan.

Sister Winifred recognized the man in front of her as James Collins, manager at Blackthorne Farms. She looked him up and down, giving his wellies a disparaging glance; she could have sworn they had a trace of sheep manure on them. All around them, the annual Cheese Festival was coming to life. Workmen raised tents; trucks beeped, backing up to unload cartons of cheese; goats bleated from the goat farm displays; and the two wine dealers in a nearby tent seemed to have skipped morning tea and gone straight to wine tasting. Held in the shadow of the medieval castle, in the village of Gwydion-on-Rhyl about twenty-five miles south of Pryderi, the Cheese Festival was hugely important to the success of Heavenly Gouda.

"You've got the wrong table," she told him, fixing him with a stern look. "This is the vendor table for Gwenafwy Abbey. We registered for it ten weeks ago — the day registration opened." Sister Winifred reached into her tub of supplies and pulled out a tablecloth. Giving it a shake, she smoothed it across the long table. To make her point, she placed the sign HEAVENLY GOUDA, GWENAFWY ABBEY firmly in the center of the table. Everyone knew that the ticket to a successful sales day was a good table.

"Now, Sister, it isn't your table at all," he said. "I'm sorry, but this table belongs to Blackthorne Farms. I registered it myself."

"Then I'm sure a convention official will have confirmation of your registration. In the meantime, if you will move, I have work to do." She continued to unload supplies. All she wanted now was to set up the table and then have a cup of tea — not an argument with a cheese rival. He crossed his arms. "This table belongs to Blackthorne Farms."

Sister Winifred pulled out a stack of pamphlets advertising Heavenly Gouda, arranging them in a fan on the table. "I expressly reserved this spot three months ago, when I paid our registration. Now if you will excuse me, I have a great deal to do before the tent opens." Sister Winifred began setting out cutting boards, cheese knives, handmade candles, and tins of crackers.

Sister Matilda, clutching a file box in one hand and balancing a jam split on top of a cup of tea with the other, pushed her way through the tent door. "I am so glad to be out of the van," she said, dropping the file onto the table and dabbing a bit of jam from the corner of her mouth. "Did you notice that every time I hit the accelerator, the thing lost power like a Dominican at the end of Easter Vigil?" Sister Matilda smiled. "Good morning, James," she said. "How are things at Blackthorne?" Not noticing his frown, she turned back to Sister Winifred.

"Honestly, if the bishop can't see clear to get us a new van, I'm calling her the next time we break down on the A4."

Sister Winifred opened the wooden crate she had placed on the table and lifted out a perfect round of Heavenly Gouda. She continued to set up the various items in the display. Careful thought had gone into this year's table presentation. The sisters had planned late into the night, and they knew exactly how they wanted their table to look. Sister Winifred had reserved the Gwenafwy table as soon as registration opened. She'd wanted to secure the best location for sales and visibility, which meant the table just inside the opening on the central aisle. Not only did Sister Winifred plan on big sales from the vendor tent, but she also wanted to collect information for building up an email list of customers. Heavenly Gouda was gaining popularity throughout the region, and they expected big things at this year's Cheese Festival — both in sales at the vendor tent and at the competition that evening, the annual Cheese-Off.

"I've already checked with the convention official," the Blackthorne Farms manager said. "She says you are not registered for a table. But there is one last table that's still open." He paused. "Over there."

Sister Winifred and Sister Matilda peered across the large tent. At the very far end of the tent was a large red arrow and, under it, the word PORT-A-LOO. And just to the left of the sign and arrow was indeed an empty table. Her heart sank. Surely they wouldn't be next to the public restrooms.

"Here," he said. "Look at the registration sticker on this table." He pushed aside the tablecloth. "See here — it says BLACKTHORNE FARMS." And with that, he picked up the round of Gouda and handed it back to Sister Winifred.

Sister Agatha checked her phone for an update on how things were going at the Gwydion Cheese Festival. *Nothing yet.* Well, she thought, the sisters were no doubt doing a record sale in the vendor tent by now. The door to The Buttered Crust jingled, and, looking up, she waved to Gavin from the back booth. She had been at the village library using the WorldCat database — the Online Computer Library Center — to borrow books for the Abbey when she'd spotted Gavin working at Between the Covers, the used bookstore in the library's basement. Father Selwyn had thought it might be good for Gavin to volunteer his time in the community. She had invited the young deacon to meet her for tea when his shift was over.

She was certain that Father Selwyn had information on Daniel Fychans that he wasn't sharing. She also knew not to push him on anything that might be confidential. Father Selwyn was a priest first, a sidekick second. But something wasn't adding up about Daniel, and she needed information if she was going to get to the bottom of it. The young deacon might not be so cautious about confidentiality of a parishioner, and perhaps, if encouraged, he might inadvertently reveal something about Daniel. She felt a twinge of guilt. It wasn't entirely ethical to pry information out of the unsuspecting Gavin, although if he volunteered it on his own, she wasn't going to complain. And, anyway, a man was dead, and the future of the Abbey was at stake. Bending the rules was certainly justified.

"Thanks, Sister," Gavin said as he slid into the booth. "I would've been stuck sorting books all day with Mrs. Clyde if you hadn't come along." He rolled his eyes. As usual, he looked as if he'd been dragged through a hedge backward.

"May I buy you a bite to eat?" she asked. She waited while Gavin ordered a blackberry scone, a toasted tea cake, and, after a moment's hesitation, a hot bacon sandwich. "You don't mind I'm ordering so much, Sister?" he asked. "I'm out of groceries at the rectory, and I've not had lunch."

"Of course not. But why are you out of groceries?"

"It's my own fault. I just really hate to shop, so I've been living off Yorkie chocolate bars and orange Tango."

"Sounds healthy. How are things at Saint Anselm's?" She was hoping for anything that might lead to a discussion about Daniel Fychans.

"Oh, you know," Gavin said, taking a gulp of tea. "Youth group, preaching, doing Bible study. I do a lot of visiting the elderly." He wiped his forehead with a paper napkin, then balled it up and tossed it onto the table. "That's the worst."

"The worst? The elderly?"

"Driving around to their houses or wherever, and then I have to sit and talk with them — you know how old people are. If you don't stay a full hour, they complain. I guess they're lonely." Sister Agatha thought he said it as if loneliness were due to some failing of the elderly. "At least, that's what Father Selwyn says." Keenan brought their food, and Gavin dove in. Sister Agatha watched while he took a huge bite of the hot bacon sandwich, then chewed and swallowed. "He thinks visiting is the best way to connect with the people of the parish." More chewing, more swallowing.

"You don't agree?"

Gavin shook his head and took a long drink of tea. "In seminary, we didn't learn anything about visiting. In fact, I don't remember it even being mentioned." Gavin started in on the oatcake. Another long drink of tea.

"What did you study in seminary?"

"Justice stuff. You know, like LGBT rights or lobbying Parliament about immigration. Or the environment. But here I am, finally in the parish — almost a real priest — and all I do is drive around talking with old people and sorting books for the book fair. I haven't done any social justice at all." He drank the last of the tea. "I guess I thought being a priest would be more . . . you know . . . exciting."

Sister Agatha realized why the ordination committee might be stalling a bit on him. "When you were out visiting, did you stop by The Rogue Creamery? And talk with Daniel Fychans or his family?"

Gavin nodded and wiped his mouth with the balled-up paper napkin. Sister Agatha handed him another. "Mrs. Fychans is on the Saint Anselm homebound list. So, yeah, I visited her." Sister Agatha watched aghast as he looked at his phone, laughed as he read something, and then spent a minute texting before looking up again. No wonder Reverend Mother had outlawed all phone use during meals.

"How are the Fychanses, by the way?" She could feel Father Selwyn's glaring look as though he were there in the back booth with her.

"The Fychanses?"

"Yes." Sister Agatha tried to look casual as she took a sip of tea. "The Fychanses. How are they?"

"Well, I don't know if I should talk about it, because I think it qualifies as confidentiality." Gavin hesitated. "On the other hand, you're a nun, and I'm a priest. Or I will be. I mean, I'm doing the work of a priest, and I'm a deacon and everything. So, if I tell you what Mrs. Fychans told me, it would be a professional confidentiality. We learned that in seminary — I had to do this two-day seminar on confidentiality — and if it's a professional confidentiality, then I can tell you what she said. It's not a big breach of anything." Gavin looked at his empty teacup, as though staring at it might make tea appear. He finally looked up. "Right?"

Sister Agatha couldn't speak for the guilt sweeping through her. She nodded, saying a silent prayer for forgiveness.

"Well, here's the thing. The old woman told me that her great-nephew stole all this money from them. He does it by, like, going into Daniel's online accounts and taking his password, which was his birthday — you almost feel like he deserved it, you know, if he was so dumb as to make his password his birthday — don't tell Father I said that, about deserving it. Then, turns out, the nephew hacked into all kinds of accounts — credit cards, a checking account. He stole a checkbook from a money market account and wrote checks on it."

"That's terrible." Sister Agatha sat back in the booth. No wonder Daniel had sounded desperate when he had talked with Sister Winifred.

Gavin popped the last of the scone in his mouth. "They're, like, totally devastated. The whole family. And he's completely getting away with it. Mr. Fychans's mother — the old lady — won't let anyone in the family go after the nephew. Can't call the constable or anything. The whole place is basically owned by her. She told me a couple of days ago, when I was visiting."

Gavin frowned. "I doubt Daniel would like it if he knew that I knew."

Or that I knew. Sister Agatha took a quick sip of tea. "Did she mention Gwenafwy? You know, something that maybe the Abbey could help with?" She hoped she sounded casual.

Gavin shrugged. "Nope. The really bad thing is that the Fychanses' yearly pledge to the church is the biggest in the parish. So you can bet Father is in a panic." Gavin sat back and looked at Sister Agatha and then at the remaining piece of oatcake on her plate. "Are you going to eat that?"

Nineteen

"I agree that the vendor tent was awful, but let's regroup and throw ourselves into tonight's competition, the Cheese-Off," said Sister Matilda. "Perhaps a bite to eat will refresh us." She reached across the café table for a soda cracker spread with pâté. The Cheese Festival offered tempting goodies at every turn. The Cheese Festival offered it all — from charcuterie to cheese, delicate pâtés, crispbread and crackers from Welsh bakers, honey from the Rhyl Bee Company. The wine tent had stacked bottles of prizewinning wine five racks high. With two hours to kill before the Cheese-Off, the sisters had claimed a table outside the music tent. Sister Matilda offered a dish of Welsh rarebit, a paper parcel with three jam splits, and a loaf of sourdough bread. Sister Winifred opened her knitting bag and pulled out a bottle of Chardonnay, two plastic wine glasses, and a corkscrew. She opened the wine and poured two glasses. "I admit, sales were nothing like what we wanted, but tonight's competition is more important than the vendor tent." She held her glass up. "Cheers. The competition is really the whole reason we come to the Gwydion Cheese Festival. Especially if we can advertise that we won the Gouda competition." Sister Winifred didn't feel the optimism she was trying to inject into her words; the day at the vendor tent had been dismal. Apparently, no one headed for the port-a-loo was also interested in purchasing a nice wedge of Gouda.

"How many people are competing in the Cheese-Off?" Sister Matilda asked, biting into a Welsh rarebit that oozed with heavy cream and melted Cheshire cheese.

"There are seven categories with a total of twenty-seven subcategories," Sister Winifred replied. She picked up a booklet and read aloud. " 'This year's categories include fresh unripened cheeses, Welsh and Scottish originals, international-style cheeses, flavored cheeses, cultured milk products, and rind cheeses.' Our category is rind cheese, aged Gouda subcategory."

"I still think we should have entered a flavored Gouda; if you'll recall, I was voted down by our less adventurous sisters," Sister

Matilda said. Taking another sip of wine, she looked over at Sister Winifred. "You look rather pensive. Are you OK? I know today was a terrible disappointment. But we must move on. Imagine what Sister Agatha would say right now. Never, never, never give up."

"That's Winston Churchill, not Sister Agatha, and I'm not giving up. I'm just tired," Sister Winifred said. "I'm frustrated. And puzzled. How in the world did we lose our good table to Blackthorne Farms? I'm confident I registered for the table just inside the front opening of the tent, in the middle aisle." She frowned into her wine glass. A local fiddler started an old Welsh ballad, and the sisters sat for a moment listening. "OK. We need to perk up a bit. I have high hopes for the competition. Let's talk through our checklist and then head over to the judging tent," Sister Winifred said. "The cheese is already in the refrigerator at our table, so I'm not worried about it. It needs to be in the fridge for three hours to place it at the exact temperature for judging. It has been in there since one o'clock this afternoon, which is four hours. It should be perfect." Sister Winifred pulled out a yellow legal pad and a pen. "You go through our file while I check each item off my list. I want our ducks in a row."

Sister Matilda reached into her bag and pulled out a thick file. "The copy of the pledge we signed stating that our cheese was made in Wales and from a Welsh milk source. It was part of our entry form, but I thought I would bring along a copy just in case. Signed by Reverend Mother."

"Check." Sister Winifred made a mark on her yellow legal pad.

"Cheeses must be entered as whole wheels, loaves, rounds, or blocks."

"We're entering a round," Sister Winifred said, making a check on her page. "A perfect round — nicely shaped and an exquisite color. Pride may go before a fall, but I like this year's cheese."

"Which is what makes our port-a-loo table all the more disappointing," Sister Matilda said, scooping up the last bit of Welsh rarebit.

"Sister Matilda, please. We're regrouping. Play the game forward, as Reverend Mother says."

Sister Matilda flipped a page and continued. "All entries must clearly state the name of the cheese, the dairy where the cheese was made, the wholesale value of the cheese."

"Check, check, and check," said Sister

Winifred, boldly marking her page.

"One more thing," Sister Matilda said, putting the list down and turning to the file in her bag. "We will need to show our copy of the County Health Department permit to operate a dairy-processing plant. I suppose 'cheese-making Abbey' falls in that category. I have it right here." She continued to flip through the file. "Sister . . ." she said. "It's not . . . the Health Department permit . . . I can't find . . ." After several moments, she looked up, her face decidedly pale. "I don't have it. And there is no entering the competition without it."

At the same moment that Sister Winifred and Sister Matilda were sitting down to their Welsh rarebit and chardonnay, Sister Agatha was pushing open the door of St. Anselm's parish hall. She and Father Selwyn had planned to walk over to the Saints and Sinners Pub — they wanted to talk with Michael again, and walking to the pub and back would fulfil their Couch to 5K workout for the day. Or most of it anyway. The parish hall was set up with rows of folding chairs, a large coffee urn on the back table, and a podium in front. Father Selwyn was putting the last chair into place as she walked in. "What's this?" she asked. "A late afternoon congregational meeting?" She noticed that he wore running shoes with his long black cassock.

"No, Gamblers Anonymous," he said. "They use the parish hall."

"A good use of church space then. How often do they meet?" Sister Agatha eyed the plate of sweets that sat next to the coffee urn and resisted taking one. The Couch to 5K was only nine weeks away.

"Every Thursday. Ready for our walk? And we need to pick up the pace this time." Sister Matilda had gently suggested that their workouts resembled pleasant strolls in the countryside and that they might not be burning nearly as many calories as they thought. They hadn't told her that most of their walks ended at The Buttered Crust Tea Shop.

Sister Agatha looked around. At least fifty chairs filled the room. "This many people are addicted to gambling in Pryderi?"

"Well, I always set up extra, but you'd be surprised. Gambling addiction is more common than you think. But we need to get out of here before people arrive. I like to respect everyone's privacy."

"Of course, but before we leave for the pub, I need to give Gavin a message. Reverend Mother wants him on hand at the

Abbey the day we have the children from the village school. They always have an end-of-summer picnic at the Abbey. Reverend Mother thinks it would be helpful to have a more youthful presence. We were hoping Gavin might lead games and help out."

"I'm sure he would be glad to do it. His strength seems to be kids." Father Selwyn glanced around. "Although, I believe he's not available just now. Why doesn't Reverend Mother just text him? That's the best way to get Gavin's attention."

"Her cell phone's missing. Or lost for good."

"Well . . ." He turned as Gavin and several others came through the door, talking and laughing. Father Selwyn motioned for Sister Agatha to follow him, and they slipped out the side door into the hallway.

"Gavin goes to Gamblers Anonymous?"

"He does. But it's confidential — at least in general — who goes to these meetings." Father Selwyn motioned for them to walk down the hall away from the door. "I wouldn't want the parish to find out. There are plenty of people who wouldn't be OK with the idea that our deacon and candidate for ordination is going to GA. And then there's the fact that it's no one's business."

"Is the diocesan council concerned that

he's in recovery?"

"No. Not particularly. Perfection is not a requirement for anyone entering the priesthood in the Church in Wales." Father Selwyn and Sister Agatha stepped outside and stood on the sidewalk in front of St. Anselm's. The sun had come out from behind the clouds, and the air was crisp. Autumn seemed right around the corner suddenly. Which reminded her, so was the bishop's deadline of Michaelmas. "And being in recovery is a positive sign."

"What if he were to start gambling again?"

"Why do you ask that?" Father Selwyn reached up and started pulling dead blossoms off the geraniums that grew in the hanging basket outside the church door.

"No reason. I've just never entirely understood that whole ordination process for vicars. It's so much more complicated than joining a religious order."

He brushed his hands on the front of his cassock, leaving a yellow smudge of pollen. "If Gavin doesn't go back to actively gambling, the council is in full support of his ordination. But if he went back," Father Selwyn paused as though he'd had a thought. A sudden thought that brought him a moment of discomfort, and then he moved on just as quickly as it had gone through his mind. "If he did start gambling again, it would change everything."

"I've heard back from Sister Harriet," Sister Matilda said, staring at her phone. "She's tracking down the certificate in the Abbey files. I'm sure I put the original in the file to bring today. I'm positive I did."

"I believe you, but it doesn't matter now. We need a fax machine, and we need it fast," Sister Winifred said. The sisters had gathered their habits above their knees and were running toward the far end of the festival grounds — where they were pretty sure the festival headquarters were housed.

"Wait a moment," Sister Winifred said, stopping. "We need to figure out if we are going in the right direction." She managed to catch her breath. "I should have joined the Couch to 5K with you." She consulted her map of the castle grounds. According to the information packet, the festival headquarters were in the old stables of the castle, which had been made over into a gift shop and administrative offices. "Don't beat yourself up, Sister. We left in an awful hurry, and I should have been better about going over everything with you. This is your first Cheese Festival, after all." Sister Winifred flipped the map over and stared at it. "I have no idea where that office is relative to where we are. We have less than forty-five minutes to get the fax from Sister Harriet and get back to the judging tent. If we don't display that certificate on our table, the judges won't even look at our cheese."

"Follow me!" Sister Matilda said, looking up from her phone. "I have it on my navigation app." She took off at a sprint. Sister Winifred followed as they dodged festival-goers, skirted the goat pens, and, after barging through a tea tent, found themselves in front of a quaint building made of native red sandstone with a sign that read FESTIVAL OFFICE/CLOSED.

Sister Matilda rattled the door handle, and Sister Winifred thought she was about to throw herself against it. "Holy Mother! We must get in. If we don't get that fax, we are disqualified, and I have let down the entire Abbey." Sister Winifred's voice took on a desperate wail, which attracted, as Sister Matilda described it later, the closest thing to a guardian angel she had ever known. A dignified, older gentleman came around the corner. He wore riding pants and a tweed jacket, and he held a leash with a golden retriever at the end. "May I help somehow, sisters?" he said, while the dog pounced the length of his lead and landed on a paper cone of discarded fish and chips.

"We are desperate to receive a fax, and we were hoping the festival office might allow us use of their fax machine," Sister Winifred said. "But the office is closed — for the day, no doubt."

"Perhaps if Sister Harriet took a photo of the certificate and emailed it to me, and we showed it to the judges — you know — on my phone. An electronic certificate." Sister Matilda paused. "What do you think?"

"No, it has to be a hard copy — it said so in the papers we were sent."

"I just got another text from Sister Harriet. She says she's waiting for the fax number so she can send it."

"May I inquire into what exactly is the problem, if I may be so nosy?" the old gentleman asked. He looked so interested and so kind that Sister Winifred said later that she couldn't ignore him, although she really didn't feel as if she had the time to stop and explain to a perfect stranger that they were about to be disqualified from the Gwydion Cheese Festival Cheese-Off, one of the most important and crucial moments for marketing the Abbey's cheese, and that the Abbey depended almost entirely on the sale of Heavenly Gouda to survive. Nor could she possibly explain how horribly disappointed she was over the terrible day in the vendor tent. Instead, she took a breath and said, "We are from Gwenafwy Abbey, and we . . ."

"Oh, my, the wonderful Abbey in the North Country that produces that incredible cheese, Heavenly Gouda? We just love your Gouda here at the castle." And with that, he took out a set of keys from the pocket of his tweed jacket and unlocked the door to the office. "I cannot pretend to know how to use the fax machine, but they do let me have a key to most buildings."

"Are you one of the festival officials?" asked Sister Winifred, brushing past him. Without the slightest hesitation, she entered the small office and switched on the overhead light.

"Oh, no, no. Nothing as important as that," he said. The old gentleman followed the sisters into the office.

"Oh? Excuse me, but who are you, then?" Sister Winifred said, not even looking at him. "Sister Matilda, do you think we can just barge in and turn on office equipment?"

"With all due respect, we have twenty-seven minutes to get this fax and get ourselves over to the judging tent. I am barging in." Sister Matilda clicked on the copy machine sitting against the wall of the tiny office.

"Barge away!" the old gentleman said. "I assure you — it's perfectly fine."

Both nuns stopped and looked at him. He made a slight bow in the way that only his generation still knew how to do. "Lord Gwydion," he said. "At your disposal. If I can't give two sisters permission to use the fax machine, what good am I?"

"I just know that he wouldn't kill someone," Michael said. He set two cups of tea in front of Father Selwyn and Sister Agatha. "Aaron's a bit of a prat. Everyone who knows him knows that." He frowned and took a swipe at the top of the bar with a cloth. "But he wouldn't kill anyone." Saints and Sinners pub was quiet — the evening crowd hadn't arrived. Three employees seemed to be preparing for the onslaught, however — setting up chairs, cleaning cutlery; two waitresses that Sister Agatha recognized from last year's book group at The Buttered Crust were occupied filling salt and pepper shakers. Michael had been polishing the brass railings along the bar when Father Selwyn and Sister Agatha walked in.

Father Selwyn took a sip of his tea. "I'm

not sure of the last time I sat at a bar and had tea."

"What caused the fight between Jacob and Aaron?" Sister Agatha thought that tea while sitting at a bar was really the way to go. When Michael hesitated, she added, "The coroner reported that Jacob had a black eye, and his mother said he got into a fight with Aaron."

Michael balled up the cloth that he had been polishing with, then unfolded it, smoothed it out across the bar, and, without looking up, carefully folded it again. "Well, OK," he said. "Aaron and I used to be together. We went out for a year at least. We met at Off the Ropes."

"Is that a pub?" Sister Agatha asked, opening her orchid-blue notebook and uncapping her Sharpie.

"It's a boxing club in Wrexham. Anyway, so we were together about a year when I met Jacob."

"Where did you meet Jacob?"

"Well, not at the gym. He wasn't into working out or anything. We met at an Ospreys game. He was in the choir and did a solo." Michael smiled. "It was sort of love at first sight. Which was a problem, because I was sitting next to Aaron at the time." Michael pulled a rack of glasses up onto the bar and started polishing them one at a time. "I hate to say it, especially to you two, but I started cheating on Aaron. You know, seeing Jacob on the side? We lived together at the time — me and Aaron. Long story short, Aaron found out — he saw a text that I had sent to Jacob — he kicked me out, and it's been me and Jacob ever since." Michael paused. "Till now."

Father Selwyn frowned at his pint of Guinness. "So that explains Aaron's behavior at the funeral?"

Michael nodded.

"When did the breakup happen? You know, when Aaron kicked you out."

"About ten months ago or so, I guess."

"So why the recent flare-up with Aaron and Jacob? If it was all over ten months ago?" Father Selwyn asked.

"We ran into Aaron and some of his mates at a club in Cardiff, and both he and Jacob had probably had one too many and got into it. Me and some other guys dragged Aaron off, but not before he punched Jacob."

"So, Aaron went after Jacob?" Sister Agatha said, Sharpie at the ready.

Michael was silent for so long that Sister Agatha worried the evening crowd would arrive before he answered. She closed her notebook and put her pen down. *Interviewing a suspect is like making a soufflé. Patience is a virtue, and never slam the oven door.* She would wait Michael out.

Michael blew out his breath. "No, Jacob went after Aaron."

"Why? If you were with Jacob and the relationship with Aaron was over?"

Michael stared at the bar top and then looked out the window. "Because I went back to Aaron. Just for one night. I don't know why — I had argued with Jacob about the wedding thing. He was so set on a church wedding. I stormed out and ended up at the pub, and there was Aaron. And, well, one thing led to another." Michael looked back at them, his blue eyes bright with tears. "I felt a prat the next morning, so I went to Jacob and apologized. It seemed like we might be OK, but then the next night, we ran into Aaron and some of his mates. Jacob saw him and went a little crazy."

"So, you and some guys pulled Jacob and Aaron apart?" Sister Agatha said.

"Yes." Michael took a deep breath.

"Then what?" Father Selwyn took another long sip and looked at Michael.

"Then Aaron started screaming at Jacob while his mates held him back. I got Jacob

into my car and got him out of there."
"What was Aaron screaming?"
"That he was going to kill Jacob."

Twenty

"I say we are damn lucky to have made it," Sister Matilda said as she put the finishing touches on the judging table. The round of Gouda sat front and center with the copy of the Board of Health certificate next to it. Sister Winifred had taken the Gouda out of the small refrigerator as soon as they had raced up to the tent. The three nuns stood behind the table looking as composed as possible — not at all as if they had sprinted across the grounds only minutes earlier. The judging team, four tables away, was moving in their direction.

"Luck had nothing to do with it," Sister Winifred said, smoothing her habit and taking a breath. "Lord Gwydion was sent from above. We would still be standing outside that office door if he hadn't come along." Sister Winifred's face was flushed, but for the first time since the discovery of the port-a-loo table, as the nuns had started calling it, she felt a glimmer of hope.

"Well, we're lucky the office staff keeps their fax number taped to the wall above the copy machine. And we are very lucky that Sister Harriet was ready and waiting to send the fax once I texted her the number. Even luckier that it was Sister Harriet and not Sister Callwen. She could no more fax a document than fly to the moon." Sister Matilda was a woman of faith with a healthy belief in luck. "And we are extremely lucky that none other than Lord Gwydion was standing there — as if he were waiting for us. I'm counting on our good luck to hold as those judges taste our Heavenly Gouda."

"We won't need luck. We have the best cheese in Wales," Sister Matilda said. "Maybe in the entire UK."

"Well, the best aged Gouda, anyway." Sister Winifred tried to stop her grin; she wasn't going to jinx their luck by getting overly confident. Both nuns felt the tension of the day lift. The failure of the port-a-loo table and the mad rush to get the health certificate faded into the background as they gazed at the wheel of Gouda on the judging table. They did indeed have the best cheese at the festival. Heavenly Gouda was a work of art, labor, prayer, and love.

The tent was hushed and the tension high

as the judging team went from table to table, talking for a few moments with each cheesemaker, cutting out a piece of wax, inserting the cheese trier, twisting and pulling out a plug of cheese. The judges would sniff, examine, taste, chew, and spit, silently making notes and ending with a few apple slices to cleanse their palates. The day had turned hot. Fans had been turned on throughout the tent, and, as the sun sank, the humidity rose.

Finally, the team of judges stood in front of the Gwenafwy Abbey table. Removing a triangle of red wax, the judge plunged the cheese trier into the round of Gouda. Sister Winifred said a silent prayer. This was the moment when all would be made right in the middle of a day where everything had gone wrong. The judge looked up and called out sharply, "We need a red hat!"

Sister Winifred froze. With poker faces, the judges stood silently, avoiding eye contact with the sisters. "A red hat? Why?" she spluttered, her eyes wide. Red hats were chief judges, and their word ruled. They only came into the picture when something was terribly amiss.

The judge held up one finger. "No talking, please." The sisters watched in shocked silence as a new judge, sporting a red badge on his lapel, arrived at the table. He conferred with the other judges, then pulled the cheese trier out of the wheel. He very slowly pushed it into a new spot. "I agree," he said, nodding. "This cheese is too soft to be in the Gouda category. A real Gouda must be slightly harder. This entry is disqualified." The judging team moved on to the next table.

"Impossible!" Sister Winifred picked up a knife from the table and, removing a piece of the red wax, pushed the knife into the wheel. Her hand gripping the knife froze, and her eyes closed.

"What is it?" Sister Matilda asked. "Is it truly too soft? Sister Winifred, tell me." Sister Matilda reached forward and took the knife out of Sister Winifred's hand. She slid it into the piece of cheese.

"Holy Mother. This Gouda might as well be *Brie.* What in the world?"

"Let's go home, Sister. I'm finished." Sister Winifred picked up the round of Gouda to pack up when she paused, holding it in midair. "Good heavens," she said. "Feel this. It's . . . warm. No wonder it's so soft. But how? We had it refrigerated for six hours at exactly twenty-three degrees." The two nuns turned and, at the same moment, looked at the small fridge on the floor next to their table. It was plugged into a surge protector and hooked up to the main power line of the tent. Sister Matilda reached down and pressed a small button on the surge protector, which immediately glowed red. "Turned off," she said.

"In our rush to get set up," Sister Winifred said, "we didn't bother to check if the thing was turned on."

"No," said Sister Matilda, shaking her head. "I did check. I know I did. It was on."

Neither of them said anything. They just stood there looking at each other.

"I say we go to Saint Andrew's," Sister Winifred finally said. "If we hurry, we can join the monks in evening prayer. I should have started the day with prayer. But no — all I could think about was selling and winning and . . . oh, I don't know. The last thing Reverend Mother said to me was, 'We need this festival.' " Sister Winifred dropped her eyes to the wheel of Gouda in her hands. "Face it, Sister. I've let her down."

"I can't do it," Sister Winifred said. The thought of driving away from the Cheese Festival with a van full of unsold Gouda and no medal or blue ribbon to show for all their hard work seemed unbearable. The two sisters stood in the parking lot next to the minivan, the noisy excitement of the festival ramping up around them.

"It does seem too bad to just drive home, our tails between our legs," Sister Matilda said. "We did pay for a full registration. I might at least have tea and something to eat before we get on the road."

"And I did think I might attend one of the educational break-out sessions, the Evening Cheese Chats," Sister Winifred said. "Bring home some new ideas for running the cheese business."

"If we're really staying, then I'm drowning my sorrows in tea and cakes. Throw in a tub of clotted cream and the world might start to look good again. Which workshop were you thinking of?"

"Well, either *Beyond the Rind* or *A Better Whey.*" Sister Winifred gathered her bag and straightened her habit. "I'll decide when I get there. Let's meet back here in two hours. And then, Sister, ready or not, we go home."

Sister Winifred saw the bishop before the bishop saw her. She watched as Suzanne Bainton swept along through the Cheese Festival crowd, one hand holding a glass of wine and her other hand holding the arm of a tall, handsome man. As always, she looked stunning in her clericals. Suzanne Bainton was so thin and fashionable that Sister Agatha had once said that the bishop looked like a runway model who had gotten lost on her way to Paris and ended up in seminary. Sister Agatha had not intended it as a compliment. Sister Winifred wished she could have just made it back to the minivan without running into anyone, especially the bishop. The Cheese Chat had been depressing enough; she had gone in hopes of getting her mind off the disastrous day, maybe learning a few pointers on making the Abbey's Gouda production more efficient, or their bookkeeping more concise, or their sales more vigorous. But instead, all she got was more doom and gloom. The instructor had kept reminding everyone that if they were still doing it all "the old-fashioned way," they would never be a successful small business in today's world. She had almost told him that the old-fashioned way was precisely how the sisters at Gwenafwy made cheese.

"Sister Winifred," said the bishop. "How good to see you. How was the competition? Heavenly Gouda sweep awards?"

"Not exactly," she said. She couldn't bring herself to recount the long, miserable day.

"Oh?" The bishop took a sip from her

wine glass and then raised it in greeting to an elderly gentleman in a clerical collar. "I thought Heavenly Gouda cleaned up at the festival last year?"

"Well, we have certainly been blessed in the past," Sister Winifred said. She turned to the man standing with Bishop Bainton. "I don't believe we've met. I'm Sister Winifred Martindale from Gwenafwy Abbey."

"Lovely to meet you, Sister," he said. "You are one of the cheese contestants?" He seemed genuinely interested. The man was well-dressed and long-limbed, with an aristocratic nose and eyes that were startlingly blue. In the wake of his warm demeanor, Sister Winifred felt a tiny bit of the day's tension lift.

"Yes, we produce a semisoft cheese we call Heavenly Gouda."

"Ha! I love it. Heavenly Gouda." He took Sister Winifred's hand in a strong clasp. "My name is Halwyn Griffiths. I'm a local developer."

"And what do you develop?"

"Oh, this and that."

Bishop Bainton cut in. "Has my office called you about the Annual Ecumenical Wine and Cheese event? We are in Aberystwyth this year. At Saint Mary's." The bishop turned to Halwyn Griffiths. "A gathering of Catholic and Anglican church leaders. All the biggest names. There is some talk that Justin might be there."

"Justin? On a first-name basis with the Archbishop of Canterbury, are we? Well done, you! I'm impressed." Halwyn took a step back as though admiring the bishop. Sister Winifred noticed that his warm smile did not reach his expressive blue eyes.

"Justin and I were at Cranmer Hall together. School loyalty, you know."

"Wasn't Reverend Mother at Cranmer Hall?" Sister Winifred asked.

"Fascinating," Halwyn said. "I didn't know that nuns took degrees from our Anglican seminaries. But it makes perfect sense, doesn't it? Today's nun needs a theological background, I would think."

"Reverend Mother certainly did not take a degree from Saint John's," the bishop said. "I don't recall exactly, but I believe she dropped out after first year."

"So instead of ordination, she followed the path to a religious order? Refreshing." Halwyn looked thoughtfully at Sister Winifred. "And what is your background, Sister? Have you always wanted to be a nun?" He smiled. Perfect teeth. Sister Winifred noticed things like that. "A nun who makes cheese?"

In another circumstance, she would have asked Halwyn Griffiths to get a cup of tea with her or even a glass of wine. And although she was not one to brag, she felt the sudden urge to let him know that she had studied seriously before she took orders. "I've a degree in paleontology from the University of Glasgow. In fact, I worked on the Qumran site in the West Bank as a postgraduate. The experience led me to join a religious order."

"Now that is a story I would like to hear," he said.

"Sister," the bishop cut in. "About the Ecumenical event."

"No worries. The Abbey will supply the Gouda. We're happy to do so and appreciate the sale. The large diocesan events are a good way to promote our cheese." Sister Winifred didn't want to reveal just how desperately the Abbey needed the revenue.

"That's just it. We're going with a different cheese vendor this year. The committee said they wanted something a bit fancier. Not that we don't love that delightfully old-fashioned cheese you sisters make." The bishop waved across the cobbled street to an acquaintance. "We must go, Halwyn," she said. "The Bishop's Gala awaits." And with that, they swept off. Sister Winifred stared after them, wondering if things could get worse.

Twenty-One

"Sister Agatha, you're pulling up begonias, not weeds," Sister Callwen said. The sun was just rising above the chapel spire as the two sisters tackled the raised flower beds along the pebble drive that led from Church Lane to the Abbey's main buildings. Sister Winifred and Sister Matilda had stumbled bleary-eyed into breakfast, and their news had not been good. In fact, it had come as a crushing disappointment. Reverend Mother had felt as if some fresh air and gardening might help everyone to refocus.

Sister Agatha stood up, stretched her back and gazed across the spacious gardens of Gwenafwy, where all the sisters were busy pulling weeds, raking leaves, and planting fall annuals. Though the morning was bright and cheerful, anxiety pervaded the atmosphere at the Abbey. Jacob's death, the bishop's criticism, arson, and now the festival misadventures weighed heavily on the sisters and seemed to infiltrate everything they said or did.

Sister Agatha was gardening with Sister Callwen, partly so she could observe Sister Callwen and see if she was acting normally. She had to admit, Sister Callwen was looking disappointingly normal, with no overt signs of suspectlike behavior. Sister Agatha also had her cell phone in her pocket hoping to hear from Macie Cadwalader, who was doing some observing of her own. Tonight was a Women's Institute meeting at St. Grenfell, and president of the WI was none other than Evelyn Birkby. Macie had told Sister Agatha that she was determined to get some information out of her. She stopped for a moment and made a note in her notebook. *Sister Callwen shows no signs of having murdered anyone.*

"Maybe you want to go back to your computer or your library books or see if Sister Gwenydd might use you in the kitchen garden."

"Nonsense. Reverend Mother has asked that everyone pitch in, and that includes me. And anyway, I like the fresh air," Sister Agatha said. "It helps me think."

"Well, see if you can leave a few flowers in the ground."

"I am aware of the difference between a

flower and a weed." Sister Agatha paused, a plant gripped in her gardening glove, clods of dirt clinging to its bundle of roots. She held it up. "Weed, right?" Sister Callwen gently took the blue begonia out of her hand and began to replant it. "Oh. Well, some flowers are tricky." Sister Agatha turned as a large panel truck with THE ROGUE CREAMERY painted on the side pulled into the Abbey drive. "I'll be back," she said.

"Don't hurry." Sister Callwen said quietly as she packed soil around the roots of the begonia. "Please."

Sister Agatha waited as the truck came to a gravelly stop. The driver side opened, and Daniel Fychans stepped out. "Bore da, Sister," he said. *Good morning.*

"Bore da, Daniel. What brings you to the Abbey?"

"Nothing important. Is Reverend Mother available?"

Sister Agatha gestured for him to follow her in the side door of the Abbey. She led him down the long hallway and then up a short set of stairs to Reverend Mother's office. Sister Agatha knocked, and then pushed the door open. Reverend Mother was sitting at her desk, surrounded by several files and a stack of forms. Her basketball held down a pile of papers on one corner of the desk, and her autographed and framed picture of Barack Obama, a pile on the other corner. "Daniel Fychans, Reverend Mother."

"How good to see you, Mr. Fychans," Reverend Mother said, as she rose from her chair and gestured for Daniel to sit down. "How are things at the Rogue?"

"Just fine," he said.

"Tea?" Reverend Mother asked.

"No, thank you." They both looked at Sister Agatha.

"Sister?" Reverend Mother said. "Did you need something?"

"I thought maybe I could be of use?" Her voice trailed off. Reverend Mother had only recently started to encourage her investigation into the death of Jacob. But Sister Agatha knew that she would never get the hint that she needed to stay in the room to hear whatever it was that brought Daniel to the Abbey.

"She can stay," Daniel said. "I was just wondering if the Abbey could use a homogenizer. We're selling off a bit of our equipment, and I thought you might be interested. We'll give you a decent price."

"Why are you selling equipment?" Sister Agatha once again fought her desire to whip out her notebook and Sharpie.

"We're downsizing. That's all. Not a big deal."

"I'm not certain that we need a new homogenizer at the moment, but Sister Winifred, our business manager, might be the better person to talk with." Reverend Mother leaned back in her chair. "It seems that we are all facing hard times in this economy." She gestured to the papers strewn across her desk.

"We're not facing hard times. Like I said, we're downsizing. Perhaps I could speak with this business manager of yours on the off chance she might be interested?"

"Of course. Sister Agatha, take Mr. Fychans to Sister Winifred, if you will."

Daniel stood. "My wife and I send our condolences. We both liked Jacob very much."

Reverend Mother smiled and then frowned. "Yes. He was much loved." Sister Agatha thought she looked suddenly old. Reverend Mother had never looked old. They all stood in silence for a moment; the voices of the nuns working in the garden below came through the open window. Reverend Mother seemed to rouse herself, and she stopped frowning. "The Rogue did well at the Cheese-Off."

"We did, thank you. Though we barely

made it back in time. We went straight from London to Gwydion. Visiting our nephew, Brian. He's in hospital there."

"I'm sorry to hear that. I will add him to the Abbey prayer list."

Sister Agatha cut in. "Did you say you were in London?"

"Yes. Saint Thomas's on Whitebridge. Why?"

"When did you leave for London?"

"When did I leave? Friday night, I guess." He nodded to both women. "I'll be on my way, then." The door closed behind him. They listened to his boots click down the hall on the tile floor.

"He was lying," Sister Agatha said after a moment. "I know for a fact that he was in the village on Friday. At The Buttered Crust. So he was definitely not in London."

"Why would he lie?"

"Why indeed? Guilty people lie."

"Are you sure you saw Daniel? It wasn't someone else?"

"It was Daniel." Sister Agatha pulled out her notebook, finally able to write the notes she was desperate to jot down. "No question about that." Sister Agatha turned to leave, but when she got to the door, she remembered the question she kept forgetting to ask Reverend Mother. "Remember the day Jacob was killed — how we all stood under the walnut tree and Father Selwyn came with Gavin?"

Reverend Mother nodded.

"Well, how did he know to come? We had only just called the constable at that point. Did you call Father?"

"No . . ." Reverend Mother looked thoughtful. "I didn't."

"Do you think one of the other sisters did?"

"It would be unlikely. Why?"

"I don't know. Just curious."

When Sister Agatha left Reverend Mother's office, she wandered to the back of the Abbey, where Sister Matilda was digging in her favorite garden, an experimental plot she had recently started — a biblical herb garden. Lemongrass and mint, sweet myrtle and oregano, marched in straight rows. At the head of each row, Sister Matilda had placed a small sign citing chapter and verse, letting the interested gardener know exactly where in the Bible that particular herb could be found. Sister Agatha convinced Sister Matilda to take a break and tell her more about the Cheese Festival. When she heard Sister Winifred refer to a missing document, her detective radar went on. She knew she might be overreacting, but it sounded a little suspicious to her.

"Why do you think the document wasn't in the file?" Sister Agatha asked. She and Sister Matilda sat side by side on the stone wall that overlooked the meadow.

A patchwork of fields dotted with barns spread out before them, the valley burnt green and gold with the end of summer.

"I guess I simply forgot it. We were rushing around; it was very early in the morning. I don't know," Sister Matilda said. Sister Agatha noticed that she bit one of her nails and looked off into the distance, not making eye contact. Behaviors uncharacteristic of Sister Matilda.

"And when you called the office to have it faxed, where was it?"

"In the file cabinet where I left it." Sister Agatha watched as she untied and retied her left shoe. "I guess."

"That doesn't seem like you. I mean, you're usually so organized and put together."

"Anyone can make a mistake, Sister. I am certainly not above such error."

Sister Agatha hesitated. Sister Matilda was known in the Abbey for her ultrasensitivity to criticism. Last Easter, she had volunteered to bake unleavened bread for Sunday

Mass, unaware that if you simply leave out the yeast, the unrisen dough will turn a loaf of bread hard as a brick. Instead of breaking the bread to serve for communion, Father Selwyn chipped tiny bits off with his pocket knife. Sister Agatha had then made a quiet joke about the Bread of Life turning into the Rock of Ages, to which several other sisters chortled behind their prayer books, and Sister Matilda didn't speak to a single nun for three days. Sister Agatha certainly did not want another communion bread incident. "I'm sure you were very careful. Tell me about the morning before you left for the festival."

"We loaded the van," Sister Matilda replied, an edge to her voice. "Several big crates of Gouda. Decorations for the vendor table, the file box with all the necessary paperwork in it."

"Where was the file box stored? In the van?"

"I don't know." Sister Matilda's face had flushed.

Sister Agatha looked up from her note-taking. "You don't know? How many places in the van could the box be? Was it in the front, the back, the console, strapped to the roof?"

Sister Matilda let out her breath and, pulling off her headscarf, ran her fingers through her short hair. "All right. Fine. After we had loaded everything into the van, we went inside for a cup of tea. I wanted to get going, but you know how Sister Winifred is about her tea. So, we sat down at the kitchen table, and she poured tea as if it's Sunday afternoon and not four hours before the vendor tables open. I got impatient, and so I left her and went out to the van. Well, anyway, I went out the kitchen door, and from where I was standing, I could see that the front passenger door was open, and someone was there. She was leaning into the van. Into the front seat. Then she stood up and looked right at me."

"She? Who? Who did you see?"

"Well. Reverend Mother."

"What did she say when she saw you?" Sister Agatha felt her pulse flutter.

"Nothing. That's the weird part. I said her name because I was so surprised to see her — you know, so early. But she waved me off. And walked away."

"Where?"

"Toward the orchard."

"The orchard? At four in the morning? Are you sure it was Reverend Mother?

Sister Matilda shrugged. "It looked like her — tall and with that kind of loping walk.

You know how she walks slightly stooped?" Sister Matilda paused. "I just figured it was her. No one else in the Abbey is that tall."

Sister Agatha nodded. Reverend Mother walked as though she were always approaching the basket for a two-point layup. "So, you saw someone. And, in the dark at least, she looked like Reverend Mother, walked like her, and had her posture?"

"And was wearing a habit." Sister Matilda took a shuddering breath "There's one more thing. She . . . they . . . the person had something in their hand."

"What was it?"

"Well, it was flat and square." Sister Matilda sighed and looked away. "Now that you mention it, it was the size and shape of the envelope I had put the Health Department document in." The sisters sat on the stone wall watching the sheep as they grazed in the meadow. The clouds scudded above, and a lorry rumbled past. Finally Sister Matilda spoke. "Why would Reverend Mother take the certificate out of the van? She had to have known it would ruin everything."

Sister Agatha sighed. "I'm questioning if it really was her or someone who looked like her."

"Who else would be at the convent at that

time of the morning?"

Sister Agatha looked directly at Sister Matilda. "When was the last time someone was at the Abbey at four in the morning?"

Sister Matilda turned pale. "The night Jacob died."

Sister Agatha slid off the stone wall. "I'll see you back at the Abbey. I have some work to do."

"Are you OK?" Sister Agatha said. She had never seen Sister Winifred as subdued as she was that afternoon. Her conversation that morning with Sister Matilda had left her worried — was it possible that the disaster at the Cheese Festival yesterday was linked to Jacob's murder? The two sisters stood side by side in the Abbey kitchen doing what Sister Gwenydd referred to as "salting the cheese." They removed the cheese curds from the hoops where they had been packed and then immersed them in a salt solution. Working with the cheese wasn't really Sister Agatha's favorite activity. Sister Winifred, on the other hand, was passionate about Heavenly Gouda. She had developed the cheese business from a half-baked idea to a growing source of revenue. Compulsive about quality control, she kept a meticulous eye on the entire process, from the first pan of warm milk to the final sales at the village farmer's market. This morning, Sister Agatha watched as she slopped the curds into the brine and then didn't even bother to wipe the counter clean. Grabbing a fistful of paper towels, Sister Agatha gave the stainless steel a quick swipe.

"What? Oh. I'm fine," Sister Winifred said, squeezing between the long kitchen table and the farmhouse sink. She stopped and stared across the brine vat out the window. "It's just that I feel sick about losing the sales and everything for the Abbey. And tomorrow is the All Churches Together Conference." Church members throughout the parish attended the day-long event at St. Anselm. "I'm supposed to give a seminar on starting a small business in your church, and I had really been looking forward to it. But now I'm dreading it. To be honest, I feel like a fraud. My own small business isn't exactly a role model."

Sister Agatha frowned. It wasn't like Sister Winifred to be so dejected. She wondered if the Cheese Festival had been just one more catastrophe in the series of catastrophes that had befallen the Abbey — unexplained misfortunes ever since Jacob's death. Or, perhaps, his death was the biggest unexplained misfortune of all. She watched as

Sister Winifred pulled out a kitchen chair and, sitting down, peeled off her gloves and tossed them in the trash. She drummed her fingers on the tabletop and stared past Sister Agatha out the window. Sister Agatha hesitated. She had information that wasn't going to make Sister Winifred feel any better. Oh, well. *No way out but through.*

"I called the festival office to ask about your registration at the vendor tent," she said. "According to the office, someone called and canceled your table the day before the festival. That's why, when you arrived, Blackthorne Farms had it. And why you were given the last open table — by the port-a-loo."

"What? Canceled? Who would do that?"

Sister Agatha took a deep breath and peeled off her own gloves. She sat down across from Sister Winifred. "Reverend Mother," she said. "Reverend Mother canceled your table."

Sister Winifred gasped, her eyes wide, as Sister Agatha shook her head. "You can't tell anyone. Promise me."

"I won't. I promise. But why? Did she tell you?"

"I haven't talked to her yet. I need to get some more information first."

The two stared at each other. A song

thrush trilled from outside the open window, and the old kitchen range gently hummed. But they couldn't notice any of it. It was as if the world had stopped turning and gone dark all at once.

Twenty-Two

St. Anselm's parish hall buzzed with activity. Church people from the four different parishes of North Wales crowded into every available space — classrooms, hallways, kitchen; one group even carried their folding chairs up to the bell tower. Sister Agatha always enjoyed the annual All Churches Together Conference — a full day of workshops: "Church Planting: There's More to Church Growth Than Tulips and Marigolds," "Kitchen Ministry: Starting a Food Pantry in Your Fellowship Hall," "Stewardship: Living Abundantly in an Age of Scarcity." Most of the nuns from Gwenafwy came to the conference. Reverend Mother had thought it would be good for them to get away from the Abbey for a day. Not only were they dealing with their grief as well as the uncertainty of the future, but they were all still reeling from the Cheese Festival results only two days earlier. On top of all that, with the entire cheese production crowded into the Abbey kitchen and dining hall, there had been a notable rise of short tempers. Sister Agatha could hardly wait until the cheese barn was back in operation. Apparently, it took a long time to get your license reinstated after a dead body was found in your aging room and your roof was torched.

Sister Agatha wandered out of St. Anselm's parish hall in search of a cup of tea and some conversation. Her next workshop, "Writing for Worship," didn't start for another twenty minutes. She would have been more interested in "Writing for Murder," but worship was the closest she was going to get at a church conference. She just hoped there would be at least something about murder. She started down the hall when a sign caught her eye: CONSERVING CHURCH BUILDINGS: TO SAVE OR TO SELL? THAT IS THE QUESTION. *How dreadful,* she thought. *The idea of selling off the historic buildings of Wales.* She picked up an information flyer from the stack by the door and, slipping in, took a seat in the back row. The leader of the workshop was someone named Dennis Sanville, who was, according to the pamphlet, the head of property services for the Church in Wales. Sister Agatha caught only the tail end of his lecture, but it made her shiver. "The sale of the rectory at All Saints Parish in Blaenpenal is part of the Church in Wales rejuvenation project," he said in a cheerful voice — too cheerful for Sister Agatha, considering that his words were a death knell for all that she held dear. "The old buildings we have now just aren't viable." He then pointed to a complex graph on his PowerPoint. "We need to tear them down and start construction on new, green buildings as soon as possible."

She did not join in the applause but sat stoically wishing she had not stumbled upon the workshop. That the Church would even consider destroying the old churches and rectories was unthinkable. She looked around. Even worse than the applause of the audience was the fact that in the front row, perhaps applauding most enthusiastically of all, was Bishop Suzanne Bainton herself.

"She sat there plain as day applauding the idea of destroying Welsh history," Sister Agatha said, clutching the dash as Father Selwyn pulled the BMC Mini into the passing lane and zipped around a lorry. "Tear down the rectory of All Saints! What's next?

Saint Anselm?"

They were heading over to St. Grenfell to talk with Macie Cadwalader. The young vicar had texted Sister Agatha at the end of the day, just as the All Churches Together Conference was ending, saying she had interesting information about Evelyn Birkby but didn't want to give details on her phone. Father Selwyn suggested they drive over to St. Grenfell and hear it together. Sister Agatha agreed as long as she could combine the trip with a quick stop at the St. Grenfell Public Library. The library society there was redecorating and getting rid of some old bookshelves. She wanted to take a look at them for the Abbey library.

"I'm not saying it doesn't disturb me," he said. "But you have to admit it makes sense to consolidate and update these old buildings."

"I'll admit nothing of the sort!" Sister Agatha glared at him, clutching the dashboard with both hands. "You're not on her side, are you?"

"No, of course not. I'm all for the conservation of old buildings — you know that. It's just that I've struggled with the heating bills of an eighteenth-century church and rectory for ten years. There are nights when I actually dream of central heating, a boiler that doesn't rumble like a freight train, a shower that actually shoots out hot water."

"You're getting soft, Father. You can bet our Welsh ancestors didn't worry about hot water or central heating."

Father Selwyn pulled the Mini over to the side of the road and, accelerating through a narrow shoulder of gravel, peeled past a farm truck. "I get the feeling there's more going on for you than anger over the rectory at All Saints." He turned and gave her a long look.

"Father, please. Eyes on the road. Don't you think that the real reason the bishop wants to shut down Gwenafwy has something to do with building newer, greener buildings?"

"How could those things even be connected?"

Sister Agatha looked at Father Selwyn as if he had three heads. "First, she has already threatened Reverend Mother with closing us down — demanding huge improvement by Michaelmas or else. That fact alone makes it pretty clear she wants us gone. Then she blatantly attends a seminar on closing old church buildings. *Gwenafwy is one big old church building.*"

"You don't think you're jumping to conclusions? Maybe she was just taking that seminar to educate herself?"

"If I know Suzanne Bainton, she has something up her sleeve."

"Like what?"

"I don't know. Yet. But something. And I think it's connected to Jacob's murder and all the strange things happening at the Abbey. Perhaps having us 'closed' is somehow connected to this interest in rebuilding new and green church property."

Father Selwyn braked just in time to avoid plowing into a flock of sheep crossing the road. He resisted blowing his horn. Blaring your horn at a flock of sheep was about as effective as blowing your horn at a brick wall. Foot on the brake, he turned and looked directly at her. "But that doesn't make sense. If she wanted to rebuild the Abbey, wouldn't she have said that?"

"I don't think so. I just think that for some reason, she wants us out of the Abbey. And think about it — a murder in the aging room would be just the ticket to closing us for good. A death at the Abbey means no cheese. No cheese, no revenue. No revenue, no future. Therefore, she wins." Sister Agatha sat back and gazed across the road. "Welsh Mountain sheep. My grandfather raised Welsh Mountain. Beautiful animals."

"Sister, you honestly believe that the Right

Reverend Suzanne Bainton, Bishop of Saint Asaph, plotted to kill a man so she could close the Abbey, and all because she believes in efficient, environmentally sound buildings?" He pulled the Mini back onto the road as the last sheep crossed, waving to the young woman herding the sheep. "And all this is based on seeing her at a workshop?"

"I do. And I'm going to ask her about it too."

"How? Call her up and say, 'By the way, Bishop, did you bludgeon Jacob Traherne with a shelf full of Gouda so you could decommission an Abbey of old buildings?' "

"Well, of course, I'll be more discreet, but yes, I am going to say that — basically anyway. I'll see her on Sunday. When she comes to Saint Anselm's for confirmation."

Macie Cadwalader's office was nothing like Father Selwyn's, Sister Agatha thought, as she took a seat on the bone-white velvet love seat. All the furniture looked French. Or maybe English. She wasn't sure. Whereas Father Selwyn's office was warm and cozy, if not a bit shabby and cluttered, Macie's study was elegant and airy, filled with light and accented with simple clean lines. Perfectly coordinated in chic colors and fabrics, the spacious room looked as if a designer had spent hours expertly selecting fabric and furniture, paint and prints. "I love your office," Sister Agatha said, looking around.

"Thanks. I like a room with a certain energy. You know what I mean?" she replied, pouring a cup of tea for Sister Agatha and then one for Father Selwyn.

"I do. What color would you call that?" Sister Agatha gestured to the accent wall at one end of the room.

"Radiant orchid. I thought it really pulled the room together."

Sister Agatha nodded. "And your desk is interesting. I don't think I've seen anything quite like it."

"I made it from a pallet, and then, instead of painting it, I covered it with wallpaper."

"A pallet? Wallpaper?" Sister Agatha took a sip of her tea. "Very clever."

"I like to upcycle."

"I don't think there is a vicar's study this modern and upbeat in all of North Wales," Father Selwyn said, perching on the edge of an antique hand-painted chair. "It's just so . . . so . . ."

"Midcentury modern," Macie said, plopping down on a puce ottoman. "How was the All Churches Together Conference? I couldn't attend this year, but I've heard it's always very good." She took a sip of tea, then looked up and, without waiting for an answer, said with a grin, "Want to hear what I learned about Evelyn Birkby?"

"Tell us." Sister Agatha put her tea on the small pink table next to the end of the love seat and uncapped her pen, holding it poised above a fresh new page of her notebook.

"Well, according to my source — a church member who jogs every morning through Pryderi and up Church Lane; he's training for the North Wales Half Marathon in Conwy — anyway, he told me he saw Evelyn Birkby driving down Church Lane at five AM on Monday morning."

"Driving down Church Lane?"

"Yes, right in front of the Abbey. And not driving either — *careening.* Flying. Nearly ran him over. He ended up jumping into a gorse bush."

"And he was sure it was her?"

"Positive. He said she had a hat sort of pulled down over her eyes nearly, but everyone knows her car. She drives a powder-blue Range Rover Sport." Macie took a sip of tea while Sister Agatha wrote furiously. "And she buys a new one every two years. Latest model. Never a spot of mud or a scratch on it. Always powder blue. Mordy's dad has been gone for a good ten years, and he left Mordy and Evelyn well set up. Which is good, of course." Macie put her cup on the edge of her pallet desk and sat back looking — Sister Agatha thought — rather happy with herself.

"Well done," Sister Agatha said, her Sharpie moving rapidly across the page.

"How did you find all this out?" Father Selwyn asked.

Sister Agatha thought Macie's face plummeted from self-congratulatory to abashed in a matter of seconds. "Well, you see . . ." she said slowly. "I didn't *actually* hear it from my church member directly. I mean, he said it. But he wasn't talking to me. Exactly."

"So how did you hear it, then?" Father Selwyn asked. "Exactly."

"I actually overheard it. At coffee hour. Following Evensong last night. I wasn't entirely eavesdropping. I was standing there, and my church member was talking — rather loudly — and . . ."

"And you were in the right place at the right time! It's as simple as that," Sister Agatha said, giving Father Selwyn a sharp look. "Inspector Rupert McFarland says that good sleuthing is like real estate. Location, location, location." She made a quick scribble in her notebook. "And your location was perfect." She snapped her notebook shut. "Good job, Reverend. A threatening letter, a false alibi, and now very nearly at the scene of the crime. Evelyn Birkby has made it to the top of my suspect list."

Sister Agatha leaned on her elbows and looked out the library window. Three flights below, an ethereal light from a full moon illuminated the rolling hills of the valley. It was both beautiful and a little spooky. Like a Louise Penny novel. Sister Agatha was far too practical and down-to-earth to get unnerved by a dark night and a creaky old building. But then, sitting around thinking about murder was enough to make anyone a little nervous. She pondered her suspect list again. *Evelyn Birkby, Daniel Fychans, Sister Callwen, Suzanne Bainton, Reverend Mother, Aaron.* It just seemed impossible that either Sister Callwen or Reverend Mother would turn against the Abbey. Or would they? What about Dr. Sheppard in *The Murder of Roger Aykroyd?* Hercule Poirot had been convinced that Sheppard was a well-meaning doctor until nearly the end of the book, when he discovered that he was a cold-blooded murderer.

She shook her head as though to clear it.

Never dismiss a suspect until you have a solid reason. She could just hear Inspector McFarland's rumbling voice on his podcast. She opened the blue notebook and, turning to a new page, wrote, *Dr. Sheppard/Reverend Mother/Sister Callwen. Unlikely, but possible.*

She ran through a quick checklist in her head: dead body, arson, threat of being closed, disastrous Cheese-Off, possible sabotage within the ranks. She had feared from the beginning that Jacob's murder was an inside job. Opening the notebook again, she turned to her most updated list of suspects. Maybe by looking at the list of names, she could make sense of it all — especially the baffling discovery concerning Reverend Mother.

Evelyn Birkby. Father Selwyn and she had agreed, as they drove home from St. Grenfell earlier that evening, that Evelyn had all the right ingredients as a very strong suspect. But could there have been some other reason for her to be driving past the Abbey so early in the morning? It needed some looking into, but, for now, she was under suspicion.

Daniel Fychans. She closed her eyes and pictured Daniel. All she could see in her mind's eye was Daniel standing at the cash register when his credit card hadn't worked

— face red, voice raised, bulldog personality coming through. Was he desperate over dairy finances? Desperate enough to kill? A dead body in the aging room and a ruined Cheese Festival would certainly go a long way toward helping to destroy the success of Heavenly Gouda sales. She sat back and looked out the window. He had lied about being in London. What would Rupert McFarland say? *All good detectives have one fundamental line of inquiry: means and motive.* She thought for a moment and made some quick notes. Daniel had motive — shut down the Abbey's cheese sales to save his own profit margin. But did he have means? He could have somehow lured Jacob to the aging room at four in the morning and then shoved the shelves down on him, leaving before anyone discovered him. But it was a little hard to imagine. She sighed and moved down the list.

Sister Callwen. Sister Callwen was only on the suspect list because of her unprecedented rise in suspicious behavior: sneaking around, secret meetings, a sudden interest in technology. But Sister Agatha could not imagine Sister Callwen shoving the shelves down on Jacob. And why would she want to kill him? Sister Agatha shook her head. *She wouldn't.* No means, no motive. She started to cross Sister Callwen off the list and then stopped. Too soon to take anyone off the suspect list. Jacob's murder was a long way from solved.

Suzanne Bainton. Well, the bishop seemed more likely to be a murderer than Reverend Mother, but Sister Agatha did lack hard evidence. And, although a dead body might go a long way toward discrediting the Abbey, Father Selwyn had a point — it was a long shot. Bishop Bainton was a powerful person, though, and had the means to get just about anything she wanted — at least in the small world of North Wales. The bishop had means, but her motive was still a bit murky. Sister Agatha put a question mark next to the bishop's name.

Reverend Mother. Absurd. Sister Agatha could hear Inspector McFarland's voice in her head. *Means and motive. What were they?* Well, Reverend Mother did have means. If anyone could have lured Jacob into the aging room, it would have been Reverend Mother. She was his direct supervisor, and everyone knew that he would have done anything for her. Shoving shelves on top of him? It was unthinkable, and yet only a person with access to the Abbey, a key to the aging room, and knowledge of Jacob's schedule could pull it off. An in-house job was the most likely conclusion. And there was no one more "in house" at the Abbey than Reverend Mother. But motive? Sister Agatha forced herself to consider what motive Reverend Mother might have. It was hard to think so harshly of anyone she loved as much as Reverend Mother, but there was a murderer afoot, and no one could be excluded without careful scrutiny.

Did Jacob have some sort of incriminating, insider knowledge on Reverend Mother? Something that she would rather keep hidden? As sexton, Jacob would have had keys to all cabinets, closets, and rooms. Jacob carried a huge ring of keys, while Reverend Mother had a near obsession about not handing out keys to members of the Abbey. Did she have something to hide? And if she did, had Jacob somehow stumbled across it?

And then, what about sabotaging the festival? Why would Reverend Mother want to ruin the Abbey's chance to better its sales? Perhaps Reverend Mother wanted to create a diversion — to deflect suspicion away from her? Sneaky criminals sometimes did just that. But so did good people — if desperate enough. As Inspector Rupert McFarland had been known to say, "Good people can do bad things when caught between the devil and the deep blue sea."

Aaron. A love triangle. A convoluted relationship. A cheating boyfriend. Was it enough to make him commit murder? Jealousy could drive even the kindest person to rage. As anyone would realize if they had only read Agatha Christie's *Five Little Pigs.*

She stared out the window. Her head ached and her stomach churned. She thought back to her phone call with the festival director. He had been very clear — the person who had canceled the registration had identified herself as the Reverend Mother of Gwenafwy Abbey. She looked back at her notebook. The director had said that the Reverend Mother had told him that the Abbey had decided not to have a vendor table this year, citing a lack of cheese ready to sell. *OK.* But what about the botched judging at the Cheese-Off? The contest had also been ruined for them. A missing document, a refrigerator turned off. Sister Agatha sat up — if the culprit was Reverend Mother, why hadn't she also just canceled the contest? Why go to all the lengths to steal a document and turn off the refrigerator? And wouldn't Reverend Mother have had to be at Gwydion Castle to accomplish at least some of the mischief? Sister Agatha knew for a fact that Reverend Mother had not once left the Abbey that day — she had seen Reverend Mother throughout the day, even had a long conversation with her about Sister Gwenydd. And Reverend Mother had worked all afternoon with Sister Matilda in the wildflower meadow. They had been sowing the autumn wildflowers, and at dinner that night couldn't stop talking about their new plan to turn the meadow into a wildlife area, complete with a small pond and bluebird houses. At the time, Sister Agatha had found their new obsession a bit annoying — to her mind, the Abbey needed to focus on solving a murder, not solving the habitat needs of amphibians. On the other hand, it was an airtight alibi for Reverend Mother.

Sister Agatha jumped to her feet. Anyone could have called the festival office and canceled the vendor table — pretending to be Reverend Mother. How could she have been so quick to accuse her good friend? And whoever it was that had called the festival office had most likely masterminded the theft of the document and shutting off the refrigerator. But why? And who? Was Evelyn Birkby involved? It seemed a bit like something she would do. Sister tossed her notebook into the top desk drawer.

She needed to get to the bottom of this.

And the best place to start was where every self-respecting detective started — with a good old-fashioned hunt for clues. First thing tomorrow, she would get started. For now, a cup of tea and bed.

Twenty-Three

Sister Agatha set off for The Rogue Creamery as soon as her conference call with the North Wales Library Association ended. She usually enjoyed the monthly call. Being a librarian in an Abbey was fun, but lonely. It wasn't as if she had lots of colleagues and other library staff to pal around with. And the conference call gave her time to connect with other librarians. But this morning she was preoccupied with clues, suspects, means, and motive. She kept replaying yesterday's conversations with Father Selwyn and Macie. As she walked to The Rogue Creamery, she resisted flipping through her notebook. The last time she had tried to read and walk, she had fallen into a lilac bush.

She reviewed in her head everything concerning the fiasco at the Cheese-Off. A mysterious nun who looked remarkably like Reverend Mother had removed the health certificate from the van in the early morning, and another person who sounded remarkably like Reverend Mother had canceled the vendor table. Had the same person — if it was the same person — also turned off the surge protector in the judging tent? The one ray of hope was Reverend Mother's alibi — she'd been nowhere near Gwydion during the time of the Cheese Festival.

Stepping inside the old stone building of the creamery, Sister Agatha welcomed the cool air. As she walked down the aisle toward the counter, she noticed that nothing seemed to indicate a drop in sales or financial hardship. Maybe her suspicions of the Fychanses were off base. But then, people could be good at keeping up appearances.

Daniel stood behind the counter, sleeves rolled up and brow furrowed as he scanned a ledger. Sister Agatha was once again reminded of a bulldog.

"Bore da," she said. *Good morning.* Even with Daniel's prickly personality, Sister Agatha liked the Fychanses. They were an old Welsh family, people who still remembered what it meant to be Welsh.

"Bore da, Sister."

"I see you did well at the Cheese Festival."

She nodded to the blue ribbon — BEST OF SHOW, GWYDION CHEESE FESTIVAL — pinned to the shelf behind him.

"Thank you," Daniel said shutting the ledger and placing it out of sight under the counter. "Bad luck for the Abbey. When I saw the red hat show up, I knew it wasn't good."

"Yes, well. Our refrigerator wasn't working, and the cheese got warm and too soft for judging."

Daniel shook his head and, tapping his fingers on the counter, looked past Sister Agatha at the front entrance.

"How is your nephew doing?"

"Better, thank you."

"Good. He has been on our prayer list at the Abbey." Sister Agatha placed a jar of pistachio butter on the counter. "When you were at your table at the Cheese-Off, I wondered if you saw anyone hanging around our table?"

"Can't say that I did."

"So you didn't see anyone?"

"No. Just that lad from the church. Young Gavin."

"You saw Gavin in the judging tent?"

"Not exactly in the tent. He was running the fund-raising booth for the parish right next door. He wandered by."

"Oh, right." She would have to talk with Gavin. Find out if he had seen anyone suspicious, although if he had been at the parish booth most of the day, she doubted he would be much help.

"Sorry, Sister. I didn't see anyone even near your table. Of course, I was in and out a bit." He pulled up a barstool and sat down. Balancing a clipboard on his knee, he took a pencil stub from behind his ear.

"Thanks, Daniel," she said. "Now, I need this jar of pistachio butter for Sister Harriet. She says it's the only thing that keeps her going when she's trying to meet a deadline for her comic book."

Sister Agatha had just crossed the small parking lot of The Rogue Creamery to begin her walk back to the Abbey when she heard a child's voice. "Hey, Sister. Wait up." Sister Agatha turned and saw a young girl about nine years old running across the garden toward her. Her mind raced for a moment, and then she remembered the girl's name — Carys Fychans. Daniel and Elizabeth had a granddaughter who lived with them; she attended the parish school, and last spring had spent the day at the Abbey with the third form learning about cheese production. Sister Agatha remembered Carys as particularly interested in everything at the Abbey.

"Hello, Carys. How are you?"

"Good. Are you buying cheese from Grandfather? I thought you made your own cheese."

"We do. But we like your pistachio butter." Sister Agatha held up the sack.

"I had fun that day we were at your Abbey. Remember the pigs and how they got out when Kyra left the gate open?" Carys laughed. "Grandfather never lets me make the cheese, but you guys did."

"Glad you enjoyed yourself. Were you at the cheese judging last week? I mean — in the tent where the judges were?"

"Yep. I was with Grandfather all day. I love the Cheese Festival. I climbed the rock wall. Have you ever climbed a rock wall?"

"Can't say that I have. So, Carys, when you were in the judging tent, did you happen to see anyone around the Gwenafwy table? Our table was three down from your Grandfather's."

"Well, the other sisters were there."

"Before that. Even before the other sisters, did you see anyone?"

"Just him." Sister Agatha's eyes followed Carys's outstretched arm as she pointed. Daniel stood on the front step of the store, talking with a customer. They seemed to be in a heated conversation. Daniel turned and went back inside; the man followed. Sister Agatha noticed that he was tall with a slight stoop. And even from across the parking lot, he was handsome. She stood a few more minutes listening with only half an ear to the ramblings of Carys, who wanted to inform Sister Agatha of every detail of the latest Girl Guides camping trip. Sister Agatha nodded, staring at the door. Neither Daniel nor the handsome man came back out. "Carys, if you'll excuse me, I need to get back to the Abbey." She watched as the girl ran off. Still no movement from inside the building, and no other customers had driven up.

She opened her notebook and quickly skimmed her conversation with Sister Matilda. The tall man did fit Sister Matilda's description of the nun she'd seen the morning of the Cheese Festival. She imagined him dressed in a habit. It was a stretch, but she could see it in her mind's eye. It was true that the woman in the registration office reported that Reverend Mother had canceled their vendor table. But couldn't anyone disguise their voice and claim to be Reverend Mother on the phone? If someone would go to the trouble of disguising their voice, would they also go to the trouble of disguising themselves and dress up as a nun? It was a little far-fetched to think that anyone, especially this perfect stranger, would actually care if the nuns at Gwenafwy Abbey lost the Cheese Festival. But then, it was too early to rule out anything. "An open mind leads to a closed case." Inspector McFarland had said exactly that in last Sunday's podcast.

Sister Agatha walked as casually as she could toward the only other car in the drive. She sidled up next to a large display of kale, hoping that to any passerby, she looked like a nun from the abbey down the road who couldn't decide between the curly kale or the Red Russian. Glancing sideways while keeping one eye on the kale, she took a look at the car's license plate and jotted down the number. Satisfied, she slipped her notebook back in her pocket and, gripping the bag with Sister Harriet's pistachio butter, headed down the lane toward the Abbey.

"And he was the same person that Carys said was hanging around our table at the judging tent. Sister Matilda described the person as a tall, thin nun who walked with a stoop. This guy is tall and thin and has a slight stoop," Sister Agatha said as she and

Sister Winifred walked into the village. Following lunch every day, the nuns all took an hour or two to walk or exercise. Both Sister Agatha and Sister Winifred had wanted time to talk alone, and so they had headed into the village together. Sister Agatha wanted to get Winifred's opinion on what had happened that morning at The Rogue Creamery. She also wanted to stop by St. Anselm for a visit with Father Selwyn.

"But the person you saw is a man. Not a nun."

"Anyone can dress up like a nun."

Sister Winifred picked up the pace — she needed more steps on her exercise tracker. "Look. There is nothing I would like more than to discover that it wasn't Reverend Mother — and for the record, I am clinging to the belief that it wasn't. But even so, isn't that a bit of a stretch?" She stopped for a moment and checked the device on her wrist. "I can't believe I've only walked four hundred fifty-six steps. How is that possible?" Sister Agatha rolled her eyes so hard it hurt. Sister Winifred and her new exercise tracker were driving everyone crazy. Whatever had happened to the old-fashioned idea of just taking a walk? "I mean, think about it," Winifred continued. "You see a tall man at The Rogue Creamery, and suddenly he's the one who stole the certificate, tampered with our refrigerator — all to ruin our chances to win the Cheese-Off?"

"She saw him at our vendor table." Sister Agatha stepped over a puddle in the middle of the lane. "Why would he hang out at our table before you even arrived if he wasn't up to no good?"

"Could he have just been walking by?"

"I suppose, but don't you think it is a huge coincidence?"

"The truth is, if the culprit is this tall, stooped stranger, then Reverend Mother is cleared of any suspicion. Not that we ever thought it was she. I mean, not deep down. And I really want to believe she was not involved. But my wanting it doesn't make it true." Sister Winifred stopped to admire the patch of blue harebells at the side of the road. "I wish we could get our wildflower garden to come alive like this ditch. How can harebell, yarrow, and foxglove simply flourish along a roadside, but then languish in our own garden?"

Sister Agatha rolled her eyes again. She had little interest in wildflowers. "Look at the evidence. We have a witness placing him at the scene of the crime."

"I wouldn't call it crime, would you? More like mischief. And your witness is a nine-year-old girl." She paused to pluck several stalks of a bright yellow flower. "Butter-and-eggs toadflax. Isn't that a great name for a flower?" Sister Winifred paused. "However, I have always liked Carys Fychans — a sensible girl. Like her grandmother."

"Theft of an official document and tampering with equipment to cause harm is not mischief. I would call that a crime. And a witness is a witness. The tall, stooped man is seen at the cheese table when no one else is around; he fits the description of the person Sister Matilda saw at the van — if he was wearing a nun's habit."

"So according to your theory, a tall man — a complete stranger — dressed up as a nun and stole a certificate out of our minivan during the wee hours of the morning, all to ruin our day at the Cheese Festival?" Sister Winifred stopped and looked directly at Sister Agatha. "Seriously? That's not just a little beyond the pale?"

Think with the guile of a criminal, not with the sense a law-abiding citizen. Inspector Rupert McFarland. Sister Agatha snapped her notebook shut. "Reverend Mother is innocent, and we have found our saboteur."

"Which raises more questions than it answers. Why would a perfect stranger want to sabotage our Cheese Festival? And aren't you worried that someone saw you snooping around his car and writing down his license number?"

"I'm sure no one saw me. In fact, neither the suspect nor Daniel even knew I was still hanging about."

"But Daniel knew you had been there. And Carys might have seen you writing down the car's license plate and told him."

"She had run off by then." For the first time, Sister Agatha's bravado was a tiny bit shaken. "I think." To change the subject, she said, "I had my friend at the Wrexham police station run a check on his license plate. The tall man's name is Halwyn Griffiths. Lives in London and Cardiff."

"Did you say 'Halwyn Griffiths'?" Sister Winifred stopped and stared at Sister Agatha.

"Yes. Why?"

"I know him. Well, I've met him." Sister Winifred put her hand to her throat. "At the Cheese Festival. He was with the bishop. And they seemed to be quite good friends."

TWENTY-FOUR

Sister Agatha stepped into the dimly lit sanctuary of St. Anselm and stood for a long moment relishing the pleasant mix of incense, candle wax, flowers, and furniture polish. Having left Sister Winifred at The Buttered Crust, she had come over to the church in search of Father Selwyn, who wasn't in his office, so she had wandered up the stairs to the sanctuary. She had hoped to get his thoughts on Halwyn Griffiths. The news that the bishop was friends with the same man who had impersonated Reverend Mother and quite possibly sabotaged the Cheese Festival had left her nearly speechless. She needed her sidekick now more than ever.

A gentle light filtered through the stained-glass windows, splashing the deep colors across the polished wood of the pews. As she walked down the center aisle, her trainers made a squishing sound on the tile floor.

Stopping in front of the cross that stood over the communion table, she closed her eyes for a moment of prayer. She opened her eyes as the hair on the back of her neck stood up. The audacity of the Gospel always struck her at moments like this — to live out one's life in obedience to the words of Christ was a shattering and shuddering thing to contemplate.

Father's rumbling voice came up from the fellowship hall directly below. "Imagine your spine pressing into the floor. Try to hold this position for ten deep breaths." *Yoga for Seniors.* Father led the class every Saturday morning. Her reverie shattered, she decided not to wait for him. Sister Harriet never missed the class, and if she saw Sister Agatha hanging around, the next thing Sister Agatha knew, she would be stretched out on a yoga mat in some contorted shape.

She reluctantly left the peaceful sanctuary and, heading out the side door, walked around the corner of the church. She stopped short, nearly tripping over Gavin. The young deacon sat on the curb at the edge of the church's tiny parking lot staring at the dismembered parts of a bicycle scattered on the pavement. "Good heavens," Sister Agatha said. "What's this?"

"This," said Gavin, tossing some loose

bolts into a toolbox, "is the result of telling the kids in confirmation that I used to work in a bicycle repair shop." He took a long drink from a bottle of orange Tango and then set it back down next to a half-eaten chocolate Yorkie.

"Really? You repair bikes?" Sister Agatha had always seen Gavin as the purely academic type, not so much the roll-up-your-sleeves-and-mess-around-with-a-bunch-of-tools type. He also seemed more animated than when she had seen him last, although now, in addition to scruffy clothes and greasy hair, he had motor oil on his hands.

"My dad owned a garage and taught all of us kids how to fix anything. My brothers still work there. I'm the anomaly in the family who went off to university."

"It must be nice, though, to know a trade." Sister Agatha hiked her skirts up and lowered herself to the curb, grimacing as her knees creaked — maybe Sister Matilda had a point about the limbering effects of yoga.

"I was the only one in seminary with my own toolbox. Mum gave me a Bible, and dad gave me a set of spanners." He gestured at the tools on the pavement. "Nice ones, too."

"I see." Sister Agatha had an appreciation

for good tools, having grown up on a sheep farm. She noticed that there was a set of five spanners of varying sizes. Some were still in their proper slots in the toolbox; a few were scattered on the pavement. "So, you're fixing bicycles for the confirmation class now?"

"Just this once. For Eres Evans. She's got no dad nor brothers, and she needs her bike to get around. I told her I'd give it a go." He gestured a little hopelessly at the extracted chain and brakes.

"I've noticed that you're good with the young people. Are you considering youth ministry once you're ordained?"

"Maybe. I've got to get ordained first. It's not going so great. Father Selwyn says to keep the faith, but . . ." Gavin sighed and carefully placed the screwdriver in its proper slot in the toolbox.

"But what?"

"Nothing. It's a slog, that's all."

"Speaking of Father Selwyn, when does yoga end?"

"Pretty soon, I think. It's not my thing, so I never go."

Sister Agatha watched as Gavin selected a spanner in the set and then struggled to loosen the bolt that held the rear tire. "By the way, were you at the Gwydion Cheese

Festival?"

Without looking up, Gavin nodded. "I did the booth this year for Llandaff Parish."

"Were you anywhere near the judging tent?'

"No. Why?" Gavin didn't look up and began to worry a bolt with one of the small spanners.

"No reason. If you weren't there, you wouldn't know. I was just wondering if you saw anyone hanging around our table." The spanner clattered to the ground, and Gavin scraped his knuckles on the edge of the chain.

He shook out his hand, grimacing. "I was swamped at the parish booth. So, sorry. Didn't even notice the judging tent."

"Your hand OK?"

"Yeah, fine. There's tea in the church kitchen," he said.

Sister Agatha wondered if he was wanting her to leave. Was Gavin suddenly uncomfortable for some reason? Or was he just being Gavin? Self-absorbed, with little time for others. "Will you be at the confirmation luncheon tomorrow?"

"Yeah, I have to do part of the liturgy."

"Good, then. I'll see you tomorrow." Sister Agatha stood to leave. "I don't know much about mechanics, but I think you need to use the big spanner for that bolt." She looked at his tool set. He was missing the largest spanner of his set of five.

"Right. Thanks. Like I said, there's tea in the kitchen."

"Why did I attend the 'Conserving Church Buildings' seminar?" Suzanne Bainton said, looking directly at Sister Agatha. Sister Agatha thought the bishop as imposing as ever. Tall and slender, her dark hair pulled back in a simple French twist, everything about her flawless, from her clergy dress with its pencil skirt to the low-heeled pumps on her feet. Her smile flashed at Father Selwyn as he approached. *And perfect teeth, of course.*

A noisy but happy group of confirmands and their parents crowded into the parish hall at St. Anselm, having just finished the confirmation luncheon provided by the parish events committee. Last year, most of the families of the confirmands had each had their own celebratory luncheon following church, and Sister Agatha remembered that Father Selwyn had managed to stop in at almost every single one, happily consuming food and drink at each house, which had landed him in the emergency room of the Pryderi Cottage Hospital. Bevan had suggested to the Parish Events Committee that this year the church might host a dinner after church. Father Selwyn could then move among the families of the parish, stopping to talk and congratulate, but without consuming a separate full-course dinner with each one. The sisters of Gwenafwy Abbey were special guests this year, since they had hosted a confirmation picnic at the Abbey. Unfortunately, it was at this year's picnic that Reverend Mother had lost her smartphone. Which seemed to be gone for good.

Suzanne Bainton also attended Confirmation Sunday, since, traditionally, the Bishop of St. Asaph served the Eucharist and did a special blessing of the confirmands. Sister Agatha had noticed that she wasn't as quick to attend parish events as her predecessor. Bishop Gregory had loved to show up at parish soccer games, church jumbles, potluck dinners — even good-naturedly sitting in the dunk tank at one of St. Anselm's fund raisers. Sister Agatha had made a beeline toward Bishop Bainton when she spotted her standing next to Father Selwyn.

"I went to the workshop for one simple reason, Sister Agatha," the bishop said, taking a tiny bite of cake from the small plate she held in front of her. Bevan had made three lemon drizzle cakes for the occasion.

"The Archbishop asked me too. And frankly, I felt like telling Barry that I just wasn't up to it. But one doesn't say no to the Archbishop of Wales." She took a sip of tea. "Am I right, Father Selwyn?"

"I'm sure the bishop is interested in the best use of our buildings, and that's why she attended," he said, widening his eyes at Sister Agatha.

She ignored him and smiled at the bishop. "Why did the Archbishop want you there? In that particular seminar?" she asked.

"The Archbishop is very aware that the closing of the rectory at All Saints is still painful for the entire village — and his heart breaks for the good people of Blaenpenal. Perhaps he hoped that the presence of a bishop might make it easier." She frowned into her cake plate, and when she looked back up, Sister Agatha was sure that she saw the slightest trace of tears in her eyes. "Let's face it. I hate the destruction of our historic buildings. And my hope is that I will not have to witness it again for a very long time. If my presence can make the process any less painful for the parish of All Saints, then I want be there."

The bishop's heartfelt response caught Sister Agatha off guard. She quickly recovered herself, though. This was a murder suspect she was talking to. She needed to remember that. "Were you able to do anything to oppose tearing down the rectory?" Sister Agatha asked, giving what she hoped was a neutral look.

"I did everything I could, including fighting for grant money, talking with the Archbishop, meeting personally with the parish council through the whole process. But in the end, it wasn't my decision. If it had been, we would have put diocesan money into a restoration project, not the development of a new building. Though I did advocate using local builders for the new project."

Sister Agatha had begun forming an argument in her head when Ben Penry, chair of the parish council at St. Anselm's, stepped up. "I couldn't help overhearing your conversation, Bishop," he said. "But my brother-in-law lives in Blaenpenal. He said the new construction wasn't offered for bid to local contractors. He said it was given to a group outside of Wales. Something like HG Construction. I've never heard them, and I know every crew around here."

"I don't know anything about that," the bishop said. "I advised the committee to look locally, but I didn't make the final decision."

"But don't you think it would have been better to bring in local workers?" Ben asked. "Don't we owe that to the people of North Wales who are trying to make a living?"

Sister Agatha thought she saw a tiny flicker of anger cross the bishop's face, which was just as quickly gone.

"I do believe in hiring locally. But, like I said, it was out of my hands." The bishop flashed her perfect smile. "Now. I must get the recipe for this wonderful cake."

Twenty-Five

"She's lying," Sister Agatha said as she slid into the back booth at The Buttered Crust early the next morning. She had just left her library meeting, Coffee-in-the-Stacks — a Monday morning coffee klatch at the Pryderi library with the staff. Today's topic had been "Are DVDs replacing books?" Sister Agatha thought they were, though not necessarily among the sisters of Gwenafwy. Father Selwyn raised his eyebrows as he peered over the top of a copy of *Trout and Salmon.* A pile of papers covered the table; the remains of a hot bacon sandwich held down St. Anselm's budget report. Sister Agatha noticed that he seemed to have made it through yesterday's confirmation luncheon without any gastronomical disaster.

"Who's lying?" he said, taking one last look at the magazine and then closing it.

"Who do you think? The Right Reverend

Suzanne Bainton, our esteemed bishop. And she's my fourth suspect to lie. Daniel is lying about being in London; Sister Gwenydd is lying about her silver necklace. Evelyn Birkby is lying about watching *The Great British Bake Off.* Oh . . . and Gavin is lying about Pokémon GO, but that hardly makes him a suspect. More like an overgrown adolescent." Keenan started toward them, and when Sister Agatha called out, "My usual, please," he stopped short and returned to the counter.

"You have a usual?" Father Selwyn said.

"Don't you?"

"Not really. I've always wanted to have a usual. What makes you so sure Bishop Bainton's lying? And lying when? About what?" Keenan came over and put Sister's cup of Welsh Brew tea and two oatcakes on the table in front of her. "I'll have my usual," Father Selwyn said confidently. Keenan looked at him unblinking, tapping his pen on his tablet. Father Selwyn sighed. "Glengettie tea with a cranberry scone."

"Got it." Keenan turned and walked back to the counter.

"See, now you have a usual."

Just at that moment, loud voices came from the two tables in the far corner. "Is that Evelyn Birkby?" Sister Agatha asked in a whisper.

Father Selwyn squinted, looking across the room. "Oh, God, it is." Father Selwyn seemed to shudder slightly. "I didn't notice she was here."

"She's sitting with our neighbor, Joseph Conwy. He has that old farmhouse across the meadow from the Abbey. He's turned the barn into an art studio. Does beautiful pottery." She took a sip of tea, not taking her eyes off Evelyn. "What's he doing with Evelyn Birkby?"

"We shouldn't eavesdrop," Father Selwyn said, watching the couple over his teacup.

"It looks like they are arguing." Just at that moment, Evelyn, resplendent in a pale-green pantsuit with matching earrings and handbag, hair perfectly molded, stood up abruptly, knocking over her tea in her haste. Joe pushed his chair back to escape the tea now running across the table. Evelyn turned and stomped across the crowded tea shop to the door.

Joe stood also, threw his napkin down on the table, and glared at the door.

A laugh came from the table next to Sister Agatha and Father Selwyn's booth. Sister Agatha looked over and saw two old men enjoying their morning tea. "Well, I knew that wasn't going to last," one man said to the other.

"Poor old Joe. He didn't know what he was in for. I could have told him. Stick to your pottery. Leave the ladies alone."

"Now, you're not calling Evelyn a lady, are you? Battle-ax, more like!" Both men erupted in laughter.

Sister Agatha and Father Selwyn stared at each other across the table. "Was that why Evelyn was driving down Church Lane at five in the morning?"

Father Selwyn nodded. "Perhaps she spent the night at your neighbor's."

"And she didn't want anyone to know that such a morally perfect creature as herself was spending nights with a lowly artist."

Father Selwyn shook his head. "I've always liked Joe. He seems such a gentle, kind soul."

"Opposites attract."

"True. And maybe there's a really wonderful side to Evelyn that we're not seeing."

Sister Agatha looked up. "You really think so?"

"No."

Sister Agatha looked back at Joe, who sat staring at the tea puddle on his table. "Do you think I should ask him? Just to clarify?"

"I wouldn't. I think you can pretty much take Evelyn off your suspect list, though.

The letter she wrote was suspicious, maybe even a little threatening, but she was at Joe's — most likely — when Jacob was killed."

"Agreed." Sister Agatha flipped through her notebook and wrote quickly.

"To get back to our original conversation, why do you think the bishop's lying?"

"Obvious as the nose on your face. Remember how Ben Penry said his brother-in-law wanted to bid on the reconstruction of the rectory at St. David's? And the bishop went on about how she wished they could have saved the building and how she tried to get them to hire local builders for the new construction?"

"I remember." Keenan slid a cranberry scone in front of him. He bit into the scone and gave Keenan the thumbs-up. Sister Agatha watched as Keenan went over to Joe and began to mop up his table.

"So, I talked with Ben, and he said that according to his brother-in-law, it wasn't like that at all. The bishop totally pushed the destruction of the old rectory. In fact, the village and the church had launched a campaign to renovate the building. According to Ben, the bishop was very vocal about *not* renovating." Sister Agatha took a sip of tea. "And that's not even the worst part." She paused, looking at Father Selwyn. When he didn't respond, she continued. "It was the bishop's office that recommended that new construction group. HG Construction. From outside Wales."

"How do you know?"

"I'm school chums with the admin at All Saints. She cut the check for HG Construction, and she had to call the bishop's office for information. The admin there said she would get back to her because she had to talk to the bishop — but not to worry, the bishop would have all the necessary information on the construction team."

"But that doesn't mean she hired them. It just means it went through her office."

"Exactly. *It went through her office.* That means she knew all about them. Wouldn't you think from what she said yesterday at the confirmation luncheon that she knew *nothing* about HG Construction?"

"Well, yes." Father Selwyn picked up his tea and then took a sip. "She did give that impression."

"Give that impression? She lied, is what she did."

Father Selwyn sat back in the booth as if the information was too much for him. "The bishop lied," he said slowly.

"And don't you think it is too much of a coincidence that all of this is happening just as a murder is committed at the Abbey?"

Father Selwyn slowly nodded. "Can you find out why the bishop is lying?"

"I think it has to do with HG construction. And I plan to find out first thing in the morning. As soon as the town clerk is at her desk."

"Name again?" The young woman looked at her computer screen, fingers poised over the keyboard.

Sister Agatha had waited outside the office of the Pryderi clerk of courts until the janitor unlocked the door and let her in. She was anxious to find out any information she could, and she had to get over to the town square before any of the sisters missed her — it was her turn to help with the farmer's market. "HG Construction. You should be able to tell by looking at the applications for planning permission." The clerk tapped at her keyboard. Sister Agatha couldn't tell if she was looking up information or playing Candy Crush. "It's not private information, right? It should be public knowledge who owns a construction company that has pulled permits for a public building in Wales."

"Give me a minute." The clerk stared at her computer screen, then resumed typing.

"OK. Here. It's a firm out of London. Private owner. Looks like they've just applied for planning permission for commercial construction." The clerk clicked her mouse and sat back, eyes on the screen. "Lots of stuff here. HG Construction has applied for planning permission all over the North of Wales." She turned to Sister Agatha. "Most of this is public information. You could probably get all of this yourself on Google."

"I prefer talking to real people."

The clerk rolled her eyes. "All right, then. Owned by a guy named Halwyn A. Griffiths."

Sister Agatha caught her breath. *Good heavens.* Halwyn Griffiths owned the car that had been at The Rogue Creamery and was the man Carys had pointed out as hanging around their table at the Cheese Festival. He was the guy Sister Winifred had seen with the bishop at the Cheese Festival. She opened her Sharpie and began to write frantically. "What's the project?" she asked, without looking up.

"Well, it looks like . . ." The clerk clicked her mouse again. "The most recent permit that HG Construction has applied for . . . is building rights to a large piece of property in the northern tip of Wrexham County."

Sister Agatha felt her head grow light. The Abbey sat squarely in the northern tip of Wrexham County. "What do they want to build?"

"A luxury resort and spa." The clerk looked up from the computer screen. "That would be nice for the North, now, wouldn't it?"

Sister Agatha left the clerk's office and made her way to the Abbey's very popular cheese and produce stand set up on the town common. She found Sister Matilda doing a fast trade in Gouda, spinach, and purple cabbages. She was glad to see that everything from the Abbey had sold like hotcakes. All except zucchini. Enough zucchini was grown in the gardens of the private citizens of Pryderi to feed the entire county, and no one was rushing to the farmer's market to buy more. She and Sister Matilda would have to cart it back to the Abbey and offer it to Sister Gwenydd for her *tatws popty* — traditional Welsh stew. She turned to Father Selwyn, who had come to buy a basket of apples and a bag of baby spinach. No one grew baby spinach like the Abbey. Bevan and Father Selwyn ate piles of the stuff, especially now that Bevan had Father hooked on green smoothies. "Got a minute,

Father?" Sister Agatha said, gesturing toward one of the café tables that The Buttered Crust had set up at the edge of the town common. "We need to talk." She looked to Sister Matilda, who waved her on.

"What's up? Did you get in to see the town clerk this morning?" he asked, biting into a Cadwaladr apple. They pulled up chairs as she gave him a recap on the discovery. About halfway through, he tossed the remains of his apple into a nearby bin as if the news were ruining his appetite. When she finished, he stared at her. "So, the bishop is in hip deep?"

Sister Agatha nodded.

"I can't believe it."

"You don't *want* to believe it. There's a difference."

They sat and watched the bustle of the farmer's market and the people going in and out of the village stores. It was a busy afternoon in Pryderi. Father Selwyn leaned forward and said in a low tone, "You know that you're accusing the Bishop of St. Asaph of murder." He sat back quickly when Keenan approached their table. Sister Agatha broke from her usual oatcake and ordered a scone. It had been a rough day. A day that called for something with a lot of butter and sugar. Father Selwyn waved Keenan off without ordering. "Honestly, I don't know what to say about Suzanne. I truly don't. I can only hope she is somehow cleared of this."

They both sat in silence watching the villagers as they moved from one vendor stand to the other on the town common. Sister Agatha usually enjoyed market day. But not today. The news about the bishop had disturbed her — even though it wasn't entirely unexpected news. Father Selwyn, though, seemed in shock.

"But what about your other suspects? There have to be more people involved in this than just the bishop. What about Daniel Fychans?"

"He seems like a strong possibility, but I can't seem to put it all together."

"I agree that he seems to have a motive. Desperate need of money and fear about one's future could certainly lead one to act out of character. But Daniel is a good person. I've known him for years."

"Good people can do bad things."

"Well, it's just that Daniel's on the parish council and has been such a help in the capital campaign. He was a confirmation mentor."

Sister Agatha felt a little guilty. Her

investigation was making Father Selwyn's world crash down. "Well, the stakes are high for The Rogue Creamery. The family has suffered an enormous financial loss and needs money."

"What do you know about that?" Father Selwyn gave her a sharp look.

"I know that the nephew cleaned out the Fychanses. He broke into their accounts, stole Daniel's identity, and spent thousands."

"I don't where you got all that information, but I was just at the Rogue. It looked like it was doing a steady business."

"Well, appearances can be deceiving. I think they are putting a good face on things. If the Rogue is truly going down, then I'm wondering if Daniel has gotten desperate."

"Desperate enough to sabotage the Abbey by killing someone? By setting fire to a barn?" He frowned.

Sister Agatha shrugged. "Maybe." They sat in silence again. The whole thing was getting exhausting. She had been wrong about Evelyn Birkby and Reverend Mother. *What if I am just as wrong about Daniel? Or the bishop?* She gave herself a shake. This was no time for second-guessing. What would Rupert McFarland do in the face of momentary failure? Or Hercule Poirot?

They would most certainly not give in to discouragement. "By the way," she said. "I keep forgetting to ask you. That day that Jacob was killed, how did you find out? I mean, you came out to the Abbey so quickly. I know Reverend Mother didn't call you, unless she borrowed someone's phone. Did one of the sisters call you?"

Father Selwyn frowned into his tea. "Let me think. I was at Girl Guides getting the kids and moms organized for the cookie sales, and Gavin came in. Yes, it was Gavin who told me. As I recall, he came into fellowship hall with the news that something had happened at the Abbey. That he heard that the constable was there. But he didn't have any details. He thought Jacob had been hurt."

"How would he have heard that?"

"I don't know, now that you ask. Maybe he heard it in the village? You know how news travels. Especially if Newell Gelman at the post office was listening to his police scanner. Why?"

"No reason, exactly. But don't you think it's a little weird that he had that information so quickly?"

Before Father Selwyn could answer, Bevan walked up. "Sorry to interrupt," he said, looking at Father Selwyn, "but the Chancel

Arts Committee is setting up for First Communion this Sunday. They want your input."

"Just have them set up as usual. Kneeler next to the baptismal font, front pews for the families. Not much else is different from a regular Sunday." Father Selwyn's voice took on an impatience that was unusual for him. If Bevan noticed, he didn't let on.

"Well, they're going to ask about the silver communion set." Bevan and Father Selwyn looked at each other, and neither spoke.

"What? What about it?" Sister Agatha asked.

"Still missing," Bevan said. "And we've taken the church apart looking for it." Bevan pulled up a chair and sat down. "I would hate to have certain of your councilmembers find out that it's disappeared into thin air. And that no one has reported it."

Sister Agatha watched as Bevan pulled a piece of spinach out of the basket and munched on it. How could anyone who made lemon drizzle the way he did treat a leafy green as though it were the most delicious thing ever?

"Why haven't you reported it missing?" she said, turning to Father Selwyn.

"Because I think we'll find it. I really don't

think it was stolen."

Sister Agatha opened her notebook and picked up her pen. "Describe it, please." She ignored Father Selwyn's groan.

"It's a set of silver communion ware dating back to 1882," Bevan said. "Given to the church by a wealthy family after they returned from a trip to the Holy Land. All three pieces are gone: the chalice, the paten, and the ciborium which is probably the most valuable piece because it has an engraving of the Temple in Jerusalem. With the date, 1882. Solid sterling silver, not silver plate."

Keenan appeared with her tea and scone. "Here's a bowl of clotted cream for you also, Sister."

"Thank you, Keenan," she said. "If I have ever needed clotted cream and a scone, it's today."

Bevan stuffed another piece of baby spinach into his mouth, chewed, and swallowed. Sister Agatha spooned clotted cream onto her scone and took a large bite. "Was it insured?" she asked, dabbing her lips. She almost wished she had stuck with her usual, an oatcake. You really couldn't beat good Welsh oatcakes. Not even with scones and cream.

Father Selwyn rolled his eyes, and Bevan

snorted. "No, the church council decided *not* to put it on the insurance policy."

"And you haven't reported it?," Sister Agatha arched an eyebrow at Father Selwyn. "It could be in any pawn shop from here to Liverpool by now."

Twenty-Six

Sister Gwenydd sat back in her seat by the window, glad for once that The Buttered Crust was crowded, and she could sit unnoticed. She had left Sister Matilda alone at the farm stand and come over here to think. She felt a little guilty, but business had slowed a bit, and Sister Matilda loved talking about vegetables to anyone who stopped by. From her spot by the window, she could see Sister Agatha sitting at a café table with Father Selwyn and Bevan.

She went over her plan in her mind. She would buy a ticket in the village, go back to the Abbey for one last night, and then slip away before morning prayer. She would be on the bus and gone before anyone noticed. The only question was, a bus to where? Tears stung the corners of her eyes. As much as she wanted to stay, she knew she couldn't. She dabbed at her eyes with a crumpled paper napkin and took a shuddering breath. *I got along just fine before the Abbey; I will get along just fine without it.* She smoothed her hair back into her headscarf and, brushing the crumbs of scone off the front of her habit, stood up and found herself face to face with two of the village police officers.

"Are you Aubrey Matteson?" one of them asked. The other officer stood a little bit behind him, between Sister Gwenydd and the door, his arms crossed.

Sister Gwenydd gasped and stepped back quickly, tipping her chair into the tea shop's bookcase lined with rows of used paperback novels. This was the moment she had feared and run from for the past three months, and it was happening here amid the cheerful noise and fragrant smells of The Buttered Crust Tea Shop on the quaint cobblestone streets of Pryderi. Why had she felt so safe? There was nothing safe here. This gentle and ancient village was no more tranquil than the east side of London.

"Yes," she said. "I'm Aubrey Matteson."

At that moment, Reverend Mother, Sister Callwen, and Sister Agatha crowded through the door and pushed their way in. She could see Father Selwyn and Bevan standing on the sidewalk peering in, anxious looks on their faces. Everything faded into a blur and the roar in her head made it almost impossible to hear the next words of the officer. But she didn't need to hear them. She had heard those very words over and over in her nightmares, in her early-morning waking hours, in her darkest moments. She had heard those very words of the officer a hundred times since the afternoon that she had raced down the steps from Mark's apartment and out the door onto the street in London.

"Aubrey Matteson, it is my duty to inform you that anything which you may say will be used against you. I arrest you in the Queen's name as being suspected in connection to organized crime." The other officer pulled her arms behind her back, and she could feel the cutting bite of handcuffs on her wrists.

"Suspicion of what?" she asked. The cheerful din of the tea shop had fallen silent.

"Sister, I suggest you say nothing. They came to the Abbey first, and we have called the bishop's office. Suzanne has promised a lawyer from the diocese." Reverend Mother stepped toward the officers. "Honestly, gentleman, handcuffs? Afraid of being overpowered by a nun in a tea shop?"

"She's not a nun, and you know it, Reverend Mother," he said. "And I could arrest you for aiding and abetting. We got a call from Scotland Yard this morning."

"Did you say connection to organized crime?" Sister Gwenydd asked. She tried not to move. The slightest change in the position of her hands made the plastic handcuffs bite mercilessly into her wrists.

"Antonio Luciano, mob boss in London."

"Who?" Sister Callwen asked. "I thought she murdered her boyfriend. Now we find out it's organized crime? Seriously, we have to start running better checks on the postulants when they first apply and not wait until everyone falls in love with them."

Sister Gwenydd was amazed that even in the middle of the worst moment of her life, she felt a slight trill of happiness at Sister Callwen's words. *Everyone falls in love with them.* "I'm not connected to organized crime. I don't know what you're talking about."

"You weren't the girlfriend of Antonio Luciano?"

"No. Mark Johnson." Sister Gwenydd looked at Reverend Mother, who seemed as perplexed as she was.

"His alias. Or one of them, anyway," the officer said. "Let's go." He steered Sister Gwenydd toward the door, which was blocked by the two sisters and Reverend

Mother. "We'll sort it out at the station. Excuse us, sisters," he said. "Could you please let us through?" The nuns stood unmoving. Sister Agatha crossed her arms and cocked her head to one side.

"Don't I know you from somewhere, officer?" she asked. "You look familiar."

"Well, yes. From Saint Anselm's."

"You were in the catechism class I helped with, weren't you?"

"I might have been," the officer replied.

"Might have been? You most certainly were! You were the little bugger that Father almost didn't confirm because you wouldn't learn the catechism."

"Now, Sister, that was a long time ago." The officer looked pained. Sister Gwenydd would have felt sorry for him had he not just put her in handcuffs. "And I did learn the catechism. Some of it, anyway."

"You obviously missed the important parts, because here you are showing no compassion to one of the Abbey's most devoted sisters. Arresting her like a common criminal in the middle of her tea!" Sister Agatha pulled out her notebook and, uncapping her Sharpie as dramatically as possible, began to write rapidly.

"Now, please. Ladies. Sisters. I have a job to do. Let me do it." He tried to take a step forward but found his way still blocked. "You can follow us to the station if you wish."

Sister Gwenydd watched almost in a dream as Sister Callwen reached into her apron pocket to answer her cell phone. "Yes. I'll tell her," she said. She looked at Sister Gwenydd. "It's the Abbey. Pryderi Care Center has been calling. It's about Mrs. Montgomery. She's taken a turn for the worse. She's . . . she's dying."

Sister Gwenydd paced the jail cell. She had lived in terror of this moment for so long. Arrested, handcuffed, shoved into a police car, fingerprinted. But now that it had finally happened, when she realized that she was living her worst nightmare, it wasn't as bad as her imaginings. The worst of it was not being able to be with Gertrude. When the officer said that she couldn't go to the Care Center, the sisters raised such a protest that they almost got arrested themselves. Finally, Sister Agatha and Sister Callwen agreed to go on ahead with Father Selwyn to be with Gertrude, while Reverend Mother accompanied her to the police station.

She sat on a narrow bench and leaned against the cold cement wall, watching the opening in the door. She had always imagined a jail cell with bars and in a long hallway with lots of other cells, doors clanging as they slammed, guards yelling. Her cell in the village police station was as quiet as a chapel. The room was small and stark, its yellow paint scuffed and peeling. But it did have a small window, which let in a beam of late afternoon sun, and the door was just an ordinary door, not iron bars. A buzzer sounded and two men she didn't recognize walked in.

"Aubrey Matteson?" the first one asked.

"Yes," she said, standing up so quickly she felt light-headed.

"I am Detective George Garrison, and this is my partner Detective Roy Curtiss. We're investigating the murder of Antonio Luciano. Your boyfriend, right?" Without waiting for an answer, he handed her a photo. "Do you recognize this person?" It was an attractive woman about ten years older than Sister Gwenydd. She had that sophisticated, urbane look that Sister Gwenydd's mother always seemed to have so naturally and that Sister Gwenydd could never quite achieve.

"No," she said, handing it back. "Should I?"

"It's Antonio's . . . Mark's . . . wife."

"Wife? He wasn't married. Oh, God. *He*

was married. Did he have children?" Now Sister Gwenydd really did feel lightheaded, as guilt and horror at what she had done rolled over her. Had she taken a child's father away? She sat down quickly and considered putting her head between her knees.

The detective looked down at his notes. "Five," he said. "Three boys, two girls. Good Catholic family."

"Oh, God," Sister Gwenydd said again. She shuddered and stared up at the officers. "I murdered their father," she said, almost to herself, as if she were alone in the room.

The detectives looked at each other. "OK. Slow down," one of them said. "Take a deep breath and tell us what happened."

"He had been ignoring me for weeks. Mark. Antonio. Oh God . . . anyway, making excuses, not showing up when he said he would. It almost seemed like he had somebody else — well, he did, didn't he?" She swiped at her eyes and went on. "The last straw was my graduation from cooking school. I wanted him to come to the ceremony. But he wouldn't. He thought it was ridiculous that it was so important to me. I was the only person in my class without anyone there. You know, family." Sister

Gwenydd felt her throat tighten with an old sadness.

"So, you put a bullet in a guy's head because he wouldn't come to your graduation?"

"What? A bullet?" Sister Gwenydd stood up, looking from one detective to the other. "No! I poisoned him. Killed him with an overdose of sage. In lamb stew. It gave him terrible hives. But I think I overdid it, because when I came back to the apartment to check on him, he was dead." It was out. She had admitted the whole thing to the police. The moment she had run from for months had just happened. "I'll plead guilty at the trial."

The two detectives stared at each other. Finally, one spoke. "You didn't notice there was a bullet in the back of his head?"

"No . . . I . . . I totally freaked out that he was dead, and so I ran. I only stayed a minute in the apartment."

"You didn't notice the blood?"

"Well, there were a lot of flies."

One of the detective closed the file that he was holding and let out his breath. "And you didn't know he was Mafia?"

"He said he was a barrister."

"Oh, Jesus."

Sister Gwenydd felt her breathing return.

"Are you telling me that I didn't kill him? That I didn't poison him with lamb stew made with sage? I'm not a murderer?"

"No. You did not kill your boyfriend. Someone else did that for you. Although I am not entirely sure who at this point." He opened the file and read aloud. " 'The victim was covered in red blotches resembling hives. Cause of death: Gunshot.' " The detective looked up. "I don't know what they taught you at that cooking school, but it sure wasn't homicide."

Sister Gwenydd ran down the hall toward Room 17 with Reverend Mother following on her heels. Even though her confession about the sage had cleared her of all charges, it had still taken three hours to get released. Reverend Mother, waiting to hear back from the bail bondsman, was relieved to find out that none would be needed — and to hear that her young postulant wasn't going to prison for murder. Sister Gwenydd swung into Gertrude's room and was caught short by the sight of Father Selwyn. She stopped cold.

"Into your hands, O merciful Savior, we commend your servant Gertrude. Acknowledge, we humbly beseech you, a sheep of your own fold, a lamb of your own flock, a sinner of your own redeeming. Receive her into the arms of your mercy, into the blessed rest of everlasting peace, and into the glorious company of the saints in light. Amen."

Father Selwyn turned from Gertrude's bedside and looked at Sister Gwenydd. "I'm sorry," he said. He turned back to Gertrude and gently closed her eyes and then moved aside as Sister Gwenydd came next to the bed. She took Gertrude's hand in her own and tried to speak but found that she couldn't. Finally, she said, "She was all I had. Of family, I mean. Not that she was actually family. She felt like family, and sometimes she thought I was her daughter."

"Of course, she was family. And in the eyes of our Lord, you are her daughter," Father Selwyn said.

"And she's not all you have," said Sister Callwen in her quiet firm voice. "You have us. All of us. Gwenafwy Abbey is your family."

Sister Gwenydd gently let go of Gertrude's hand and smoothed the blanket. "I always thought that when people died, they would look like they were sleeping. But she doesn't look asleep. She looks . . . well, she looks . . ."

"Dead," Sister Agatha said.

"Sister! Honestly," Sister Callwen sputtered. "Do you always have to be so blunt?"

"Dead to this world means alive in the next. She has left us and awoken in the arms of our Lord. Nothing can be more comforting than that." Sister Agatha refused to be maudlin.

"By the way," Sister Gwenydd said, looking up. "I'm no longer on the lam. I didn't murder Mark after all. Well, his name wasn't Mark, but that doesn't really matter now." She looked around and waited for dramatic effect. All the nuns and Father Selwyn stared at her. The nurse attending to the body of Gertrude stopped what she was doing and looked up. "He died of a gunshot wound to the head," Sister Gwenydd said, letting out a long breath. "Isn't that wonderful?"

"And you call me blunt," Sister Agatha said.

Twenty-Seven

"Let me see if I have this straight," Reverend Mother said, locking eyes with Sister Agatha, who was suddenly beyond tired.

It had been a long day, starting with the visit to the clerk of courts, then the farmer's market, and then a long evening with Sister Gwenydd at the jail and nursing home. Although she knew everyone just wanted to collapse in bed, immediately following evening prayer she had asked Reverend Mother to call an emergency meeting of senior nuns — Reverend Mother, Sister Callwen, Sister Harriet, and Sister Winifred. "That's what the clerk said. A private contractor who owns a company called HG Construction has filed for planning permission to build a resort and spa on Abbey property."

Reverend Mother shook her head. "Are you sure? You're not mistaken or the clerk gave you wrong information?"

"I'm sure. The clerk said the northernmost tip of Wrexham County. Gwenafwy Abbey is the northernmost tip of Wrexham County. That's us, The Rogue Creamery, Joe Conwy, and Blackthorne Farms. And I have reason to believe that Daniel Fychans has been approached by Griffiths as well. I don't know about the others." Sister Agatha couldn't bring herself to recount spying on Halwyn Griffiths at The Rogue Creamery or copying down his license number or thinking that he had dressed up as a nun and impersonated Reverend Mother. It really was too late in the evening for all that.

"But how?" asked Sister Harriet. "How could anyone build on our property when we haven't sold our land to anyone?"

"We don't own this property," Sister Callwen asked. "We feel as if it's ours, but it isn't. It belongs to the Church in Wales. Well, to the St. Asaph diocese, to be exact."

"But how could the diocese sell it? Without even telling us?" asked Sister Harriet.

"Reverend Mother, you look pale. Are you OK?" Sister Callwen said. They all turned and looked at Reverend Mother. She sat perfectly still in her chair, not even holding a basketball, her most effective stress reliever second only to prayer. "Reverend Mother." Sister Callwen rose and came over to her.

"What is it?"

"That name, Halwyn Griffiths. I've heard it before."

"When? Where?" Sister Agatha slowly pulled out her notebook and Sharpie, not taking her eyes off Reverend Mother.

"Last week. Two days after Jacob died. I was at the bishop's office, remember? And as I was leaving, she had a visitor. And I remember his name. I didn't meet him. I must have seen him in the waiting area, but I was so distraught . . ." Reverend Mother stood. "Halwyn Griffiths. I remember it now. He was meeting with the bishop." She looked around wildly. "This means that the bishop has planned to sell the Abbey all along. That it was her idea or at least she supports it or, at the very, very least, she has full knowledge of it. And the whole time she was telling me about how we aren't productive enough or modern enough . . ."

Reverend Mother turned and walked over to the window. She stood ramrod straight, her back to the nuns, staring out at the dark clouds that raced in front of the bright moon. "All her talk about us being back on our feet by Michaelmas . . ." Reverend Mother said slowly, almost to herself. She turned around. "All she wanted to do was shut us down so she could build a spa." The nuns sat, stunned. Even Sister Agatha put down her notebook. The clock in the bell tower chimed ten times. Finally, Sister Harriet broke the silence. "But why? Why would the bishop build a luxury resort in the parish?"

"Revenue," Sister Callwen said. "Spas are big money these days."

"And making money for the diocese would be a feather in her cap. A cap that's set on being Archbishop of Wales," said Sister Agatha.

"And who knows what kind of a kickback the bishop will get. Not only will she be credited with bringing a windfall of money, but for all we know, she's also lining her own pockets," Sister Harriet said. Everyone was a little surprised to hear Sister Harriet, usually the first to offer compassion in any situation, speak so harshly.

"I think there's even more to it," Sister Agatha said.

"Of course you do," Sister Callwen said under her breath.

"What did you say?" Sister Agatha looked at her longtime friend.

"I said, 'Of course you do,' because the situation isn't dire enough. You'll have to bring mayhem and mystery into it as well."

"Not so much mayhem and mystery,"

Sister Agatha said.

"What then?" Sister Callwen turned to her.

"Murder. I think the bishop and this Griffiths fellow are involved in the murder of Jacob."

Three zucchini fell out of Sister Agatha's arms and rolled under the rhododendron bush next to the kitchen door. Sister Winifred had once called the rhododendron the black hole of Gwenafwy Abbey, since it seemed to be the spot where anything that was dropped was immediately swallowed up — keys, prayer books, once, in the case of Sister Matilda, a prebaked ham. Dropping something usually occurred when one tried to fit their keys into the heavy kitchen door and then attempted to push it open.

The day before had been so hectic, with trips to the jail, the nursing home, and then the distressing meeting in Reverend Mother's office, that the sisters had not even finished emptying the minivan from the farmer's market the day before. Reverend Mother and the other sisters had looked so exhausted at breakfast that Sister Agatha had insisted on dealing with it. She gathered up the mountain of leftover zucchini from the back of the van to lug into the kitchen.

She wedged open the kitchen door with one foot and then, using her shoulder, nudged it all the way open. As she shifted the zucchini in her arms, one rather large specimen rolled under the rhododendron. *Oh well,* she thought, grabbing her keys and leaving the zucchini. *It'll make a nice dinner for some deserving hedgehog.*

"Sister Gwenydd," she said, stepping into the kitchen. "What in the world are you doing?" Sister Gwenydd knelt on the tile floor surrounded by pots and pans, mixing bowls, various large spoons, and a pile of dish clothes. The cabinet doors all stood open, and a bucket of sudsy water sat next to her.

Even with all the cheese-making equipment crammed in, the Abbey kitchen brought Sister Agatha a sense of contentment — a feeling she found only in her favorite libraries and the chapel. Maybe that was because the kitchen, like the chapel and favorite libraries, had not been updated in decades: the creaky wooden cabinets, worn flagstone floor, and yellowed Formica counters spoke of the past and the many nuns who had crowded into this kitchen as they did the work of the Gospel. The microwave and new Keurig coffee maker looked startlingly out of place next to the butter churn and porcelain sink with a pump handle.

Crowded and cramped though it was, Sister Agatha loved the old kitchen. Some of the best conversations between the sisters had taken place sitting around the long farmhouse table.

"I am finally cleaning out these miserable cabinets," Sister Gwenydd said, tucking a strand of hair under her headscarf.

"I thought you would be celebrating." Sister Agatha thought the young woman looked relaxed — happy even. More so than she ever had since coming to the Abbey. Of course, being cleared of a murder charge can do that for you.

"I *am* celebrating. By cleaning. Do you know what I just found inside an old mixing bowl?"

"I couldn't even guess." Sister Agatha hated guessing. Although she loved to make others guess.

"A copy of the 1984 *Book of Common Prayer.*" Sister Gwenydd sat back against the cabinet and looked up at Sister Agatha. "Covered in flour. Who would leave their prayer book in a mixing bowl in the back of a cupboard?"

"Best place for the 1984, if you ask me." Sister Agatha had never warmed up to the new translation and would have preferred the 1614 if possible.

"There's all sorts of junk in this bottom cupboard. One of those big wrench things, a box of latex gloves, a hymnbook. I guess to go with the prayer book." Sister Gwenydd wiped her hands on her apron. "Why would anyone think it's OK just to stash junk in every available space in the Abbey? I found two choir robes rolled up in a ball and stuffed in the crawl space beneath the stairs. Why can't people just throw things away?"

"No one throws anything away in this Abbey. The answer is always, 'We might need that someday.' " Sister Agatha pulled out a kitchen chair and sat down. "I brought you some zucchini."

"I can see that. I'm starting to run out of zucchini recipes." Sister Gwenydd stood up. "I've got something else to show you. Other than the prayer book."

She squeezed her way between the curding vats and the stainless-steel homogenizer to a set of wooden double doors. "It's right here in the canning cupboard." Sister Gwenydd pulled a large box off a shelf and thumped it onto the table. "It's heavier than you would think," she said, pulling out three objects wrapped in felt. Unwrapping them each, she placed a silver chalice, paten, and ciborium in front of Sister Agatha. "Aren't these beautiful?" Sister Gwenydd said. "And look at the engraving on the bowl. I'm not sure, but I think it's the Temple in Jerusalem."

"I thought you would be happy to have your silver communion set back," Sister Agatha said to Father Selwyn early that afternoon. He had waved to her from the door of The Buttered Crust as she left the post office. She was returning the interlibrary loan books from last month's order. She was glad that Father Selwyn had staked out the back booth where they might have a little privacy — she really needed to talk through this whole new development with HG Construction and the bishop with Father Selwyn. It was more baffling than she liked to admit.

"I'm certainly glad the communion set has been found. But how it ended up at the Abbey is puzzling. Disturbing, even."

"I know. Bevan is badgering me to report it. But I hate involving the constable. It'll hit the parish gossip circuit like wildfire, and I'm just not up to it." Father Selwyn took a sip of tea. "I hate to admit it, but I'm sort of hiding out from him. By the way, I've ordered your usual. I'm halfway through my own."

"Diolch." *Thank you.* "I could use a good

cup of Welsh brew about now." Keenan slid an oatcake in front of her. "And an oatcake," she said breaking off a piece and popping it in her mouth. "As concerned as I am about the communion set being at the Abbey — it's just one more weird thing happening there — I am much more concerned about the HG Construction discovery."

"I know. I'm at a loss. Actually, I'm devastated. Well, that's being dramatic." Father Selwyn gave a rueful smile. "But I am flummoxed enough to hole up at The Buttered Crust and drown my sorrows in Glengettie and a cranberry scone. Even though I should be getting ready for tomorrow's event at the castle." The annual garden party at Pryderi Castle was a fund raiser for the parish that the congregation at St. Anselm participated in along with the sisters at Gwenafwy.

"The garden party will take care of itself. We need to focus. Agatha Christie would do a thorough review of the evidence at this point, and I think we should too." She took a sip of tea and opened her notebook. "First, we know that the bishop seems to be in some sort of partnership with HG Construction, which is owned by her friend, Halwyn Griffiths. Or at least they act like friends. We also know that the bishop lied about her involvement with the company — which means she doesn't want anyone to know about it — which could mean that she is up to no good. They seem to have plans for the Abbey property which would hinge on the Abbey 'selling' it to them. Gwenafwy has been there more than a century, and people in the parish are not going to like it. However, if the argument is convincing — that the Abbey is failing — then it would be much easier to convince everyone. Just like the argument for tearing down All Saints rectory. An old building too costly to renovate."

"Which is not entirely untrue," Father Selwyn said. "It was a beautiful structure that the priest lived in for two centuries, but it cost a mint to keep going."

"I'm not arguing that; I'm just saying that there is a pattern here. Especially when you add in the fact that the new construction at All Saints Parish is definitely HG Griffiths."

Father Selwyn let out a low whistle. "Our bishop seems to have gotten in with a bad crowd."

"That's one way to put it." Sister Agatha glanced back at her notes. "Next, we have the bishop practically threatening Gwenafwy with closing if we don't prove ourselves financially worthy. And giving us a whopping three weeks to do it in." Sister Agatha flipped a page. "Per public record, the permits filed for Abbey land estimate the start of construction as November first. No wonder we had until Michaelmas — September twenty-ninth. A month for demolition and then start construction on the resort and spa."

Father Selwyn took a sip of tea and broke off a bit of his cranberry scone. Sister Agatha noticed that he didn't eat but only crumbled it on his plate. "Are you saying you think that Halwyn Griffiths and Suzanne Bainton snuck into the cheese room, loosened the bolts on the shelving unit, lured Jacob into a room he never went in, and, at the exact moment he stood there, shoved the shelves down on him?"

"Maybe. But we need more hard evidence."

"Well." Father Selwyn leaned back and looked thoughtful. "Seek and you shall find."

"Hercule Poirot?"

"Sister." He shook his head. *"Jesus."*

"Sister Gwenydd, you said that you found the silver chalice and paten in the old canning cupboard?" Sister Agatha asked the young postulant. Sister Agatha had left The

Buttered Crust and on the way home had decided that she needed to talk with Sister Gwenydd again. She came straight back to the kitchen to find her.

"I did. Along with a bunch of other junk." Sister Agatha watched as Sister Gwenydd put the kettle on the range and then pulled a cake tin off a shelf above the counter. The sisters gathered every afternoon at four o'clock in the big kitchen for tea, and she liked to have things ready for them. Sister Agatha also knew that Sister Gwenydd was baking several of her specialties for tomorrow's garden party, which was probably why the table was covered with baking pans, a carton of eggs, three pounds of butter, and a cookbook open to "Iced Lemon and Strawberry Sandwich Cake." Sister Gwenydd opened her arms wide, gesturing at the newly organized kitchen. "Doesn't it look great in here?"

Sister Agatha glanced around. The old kitchen looked the same to her. "Yes. Lovely. By the way, I never asked you what else you found in the canning cupboard — I was too focused on the communion set."

Sister Gwenydd opened the tin and revealed an orange pound cake covered in white frosting and almonds. She set it on the one open spot on the table. "Hang on a sec; I have to check this." She picked up her cell phone, which was plugged into a wall socket.

Sister Agatha thought the phone looked as if it had been through the wringer; it was dirty and slightly dented, and the screen was a murky green.

Sister Gwenydd set it back down. "OK. In the canning cupboard, I found the prayer book — like I told you — and the silver stuff. Some old newspapers — why in the world would anyone keep old newspapers? Mostly it was junk that I threw out." She paused. "A couple of tools."

"What kind of tools?"

"A crowbar and two of those wrench things."

"Wrench things? Spanners?"

"I think. Does a spanner have a funny-shaped hole at each end?"

"Don't you know what a spanner looks like?"

"I went to cooking school, so, no, I don't know what a spanner looks like. Can you tell an asparagus server from a jelly spoon?" Sister Gwenydd turned back to her beat-up cell phone and tapped on the cloudy screen. "I bet you can't."

"What did you do with the spanners and crowbar? Tell me you didn't throw them out with the prayer book."

"Of course not. And I didn't throw out the prayer book. I dusted it and then put it in the chancel with all the other prayer books. I put the tools in the sexton's closet."

Sister Agatha pulled out her own cell. Was it finally time to get the constable involved? She had a terrible thought. "You didn't clean them off, did you? The crowbar and the spanners?"

Sister Gwenydd shrugged. "I did — ran the dust rag over them. Why?"

Sister Agatha shook her head as though to clear it. She needed to leave and go find Father Selwyn. The only person she knew with a set of spanners was Gavin. But then, anyone might have a set of spanners. If only she could check his toolbox and see what might be missing.

"When you cleaned them, did they have anything on them?"

"What do you mean?"

"I mean, like white powder. Like from plaster."

"Maybe. White powdery stuff. It could have been plaster. Why?"

Sister Agatha ignored her question. "Anything else in the canning cupboard?"

"Just a plastic bag from the Megaserv. You know, the big grocery on the A12. The stuff was wrapped up in it. The tools, I mean."

"I don't suppose that you kept the bag?"

"Sorry. No."

Sister Agatha sighed. "OK. I've got to be going." She heaved herself up from the table.

"But I did save the receipt that was in the bottom of the bag."

"You're kidding. You threw out the bag but saved a random receipt?"

"Sister Callwen has trained me well. I have to turn in receipts for everything." She opened a drawer next to the door and rummaged around for a minute. "Here," she said, pulling out a slip of paper. "Whoever used that bag buys a lot of orange Tango and Yorkie chocolate bars." She watched as Sister Agatha read the receipt and carefully folded it, almost reverently, and then slid it between the covers of her notebook. "Are you OK?" Sister Gwenydd asked.

"I am. Yes, of course." She looked back at Sister Gwenydd. "What happened to your phone, by the way?"

"It's not mine. It's Reverend Mother's. You know how Sister Matilda has been wanting to categorize the wildflowers that grow along the road leading into the village? Well, she finally got around to doing it, and she found Reverend Mother's cell.

She said it was lying right there, between a scarlet pimpernel and a common speedwell." Sister Gwenydd pressed the button on the side of the phone. "Tell her I've got it charged, and it actually works, although the screen is cracked and hard to read." Sister Gwenydd frowned and then looked up, her eyes wide.

"What?"

"There's a text to Jacob." She handed the phone to Sister Agatha. "At 4:13 AM last Monday. Isn't that . . . the morning he died?"

Twenty-Eight

"Have you seen Gavin, Father? I need to talk with him," Sister Agatha stood next to the 1968 BMC Mini as Father Selwyn attempted to stuff a bag of newly knitted prayer shawls for the Care Center into the boot.

"You might get yourself a proper vehicle, you know," she said. "We find our van quite serviceable."

"Get rid of the Mini?" he said. "Buy a van? Get thee behind me, Satan." He came around to the front of the car and, opening the driver's side, squeezed in. "Haven't seen Gavin since morning prayer, but I'm sure he's around somewhere. Why? What's up?"

"I have reason to believe he's the one who stashed all the stolen property in the canning cupboard at the Abbey." Sister Agatha wedged herself into the passenger side. "Good heavens, it's a tight fit in here." She scrunched her legs up under the dashboard.

Father Selwyn turned and held her in his gaze. "Gavin? Why?" Fatigue hovered in his eyes — something she had not noticed before. She looked out the windshield across the lawn of the castle. The sun had dropped behind the tower, and everything was awash with gold and red. The air had turned cool. Autumn was on its way.

"What are you thinking? Tell me that you're not thinking that Gavin had something to do with Jacob's death." Father Selwyn twisted around in the tiny driver's seat and looked at her directly.

"That's a big leap. Did you ever notice him drinking orange Tango or eating Yorkies?"

"All the time. Why?"

"In the bag with the silver communion set was a receipt from the Megaserv. For orange Tango and Yorkies. I know he practically lives on the stuff." She jumped at the sound of Father Selwyn's ringtone — Max Boyce singing the Welsh national anthem, "Hen Wlad Fy Nhadau." *Land of My Fathers.* He talked quickly and clicked off, then tossed the phone into the tiny back seat and turned the key in the ignition. "Gavin." The engine sputtered to life, and Father Selwyn put the car in gear. "He's in the emergency room."

"Why? Where?"

"Put your seat belt on. Dolgellau Hospital." Father Selwyn turned the wheel and drove across the grass and onto a gravel drive. "Someone beat him up."

Father Selwyn nearly skidded off the A12 twice before he veered into the emergency room parking lot. Hurrying in through the double doors, they saw Gavin sitting up on a gurney in the hall of the Emergency Unit.

"Gavin! Byddwch yn edrych yn ofnadwy," Father Selwyn said. *You look horrible.* The young deacon's eyes were black and swollen, his lips cut, and it looked as if his nose might have been broken. The floor sister came over to them. "Father Selwyn. Good. We can't release him until someone is here to take him."

"You're releasing him?" Sister Agatha said. "But he looks . . ." She hesitated. She didn't want to say how bad he looked or how standing next to him made her feel slightly queasy.

"Who did this to you?" Father Selwyn took one of Gavin's hands in both of his. "Tell me."

"I can't," he said.

"What do you mean, you can't?" Father Selwyn said, in a voice he seldom used and that few people ignored. He turned to the nurse. “Have the police been called?”

“The police brought him in,” the nurse said. “Mr. Yarborough, do you feel well enough to sign out?”

“I want to get out of here.” Gavin swung his legs over the side of the gurney.

“Are you sure he is ready to go home?” Father Selwyn said, turning to the nurse. “Has he seen a doctor?”

“The doctor said there is no sign of head trauma or internal injury.” The nurse checked the bandage across Gavin’s nose. “What you see is what you get.”

Father Selwyn left with the charge nurse to sign paperwork while Sister Agatha stayed with Gavin. “Why don’t you want to tell us who did this to you? Or at least what happened — if you don’t want to name names.”

Gavin shrugged, grimacing in pain. “It doesn’t matter.”

“Somebody puts you in the emergency room, and it doesn’t matter?” Sister Agatha frowned. “How many guys jumped you? And where — at the castle?”

“I don’t know. In the parking lot. I don’t feel like talking. I just want to go home.”

“We’ll take you home, Gavin,” Father Selwyn said, walking up, a sheaf of discharge papers in his hand. "And when we get there, you can tell us exactly what happened."

"He finally opened up. Last night, after I got him back to the rectory. But I can tell you only under the strictest of confidentiality," Father Selwyn said, as he fell into step with Sister Agatha. They walked down the lane toward the Abbey orchards. The early sun slanted across the meadow, and a mourning dove cooed. Bartimaeus saw them coming and trotted over, tossing his head. Sister Gwenydd needed a dozen of the new Cadwaladr apples for a batch of *dinca fala* — apple cake. Father Selwyn had come into the Abbey to see if Reverend Mother would lend Sister Agatha to him — he needed her help, he had said. Reverend Mother had readily agreed and pointed him in the direction of the orchard where Sister Agatha was headed.

"This is a very serious thing for Gavin because he will lose his ordination status. But I'm caught in a bind — I have to follow protocol, which means bringing in the diocese and certainly the police."

"I take it he wasn't just randomly jumped by a couple of mates?"

Father Selwyn snorted. "No. I'm afraid not." He sat on the bench under one of the apple trees. "Gavin's gambling problem has reared its ugly head."

"I thought he was in recovery?"

Father Selwyn stood up abruptly and walked toward one of the trees heavy with fruit. He plucked an apple and placed it into the basket Sister Agatha held. "He was. But he's fallen off the wagon, so to speak. He said that it started about six weeks ago, when he entered a high-stakes game in Cardiff. He borrowed money from a dealer to enter the game. Then he lost his shirt and couldn't pay the dealer back. So, he borrowed from a payday lender. And that's when the big trouble began."

"Payday lenders are legal, though, right? They can't beat you up when you don't pay." Sister Agatha offered Bartimaeus an apple, which he happily took.

"No, but they raise the interest rates by nearly thirty percent. Which they did to Gavin. Pretty soon his original loan had quadrupled."

"It can go up that fast?"

"Faster. Payday loans are a horrible racket. Anyway, so he borrowed from a guy on the street — a loan shark — to pay off the payday loan and stop the interest. The loan shark beat him up when he didn't pay him back."

"So, he paid off the dealer by borrowing from a payday lender, then got into interest so high that he borrowed from a loan shark, who assaulted him when he didn't pay." Sister Agatha felt depressed just thinking about it.

"What a tangled web we weave . . ." They both stood in silence a moment, looking at each other. Bartimaeus shook out his mane and wandered off.

"How much does he owe?" Sister Agatha asked.

"Well, the sad part is that when he borrowed from the dealer, the debt was only five hundred dollars, but that quickly skyrocketed to five thousand in two months of not making payments on the payday loan."

"You're kidding." Sister Agatha was aghast.

"No. The UK needs to outlaw payday loans. It's a gruesome practice."

"I don't really understand it. But I had only just gotten my own credit card when I started ordering online."

"Well, say that you want to borrow five hundred from a payday lender. The loan can eventually translate into a five hundred twenty-percent annual percentage rate. You can't get out from under it — which Gavin quickly learned."

"He must have been desperate."

"Yes, but not as desperate as he was when he couldn't pay back the loan shark." Father Selwyn shook his head. "Like any addicted gambler, Gavin's plan was to pay back the loan by gambling and winning."

"Good heavens," Sister Agatha whispered.

"Good heavens, indeed. Now he owes the payday loan people the three thousand dollars plus interest and a loan shark another two thousand plus interest. And this is a person who is not opposed to beating him up for the money." Father Selwyn blew out his breath. "Obviously."

"What's to be done? We can't just leave him to be . . ." Sister could hardly say it.

"We're not. The first order of business is to get him to a safe place and in treatment. The second is to pay off the people he owes."

"Can't they be prosecuted?"

"Not really; payday loans are perfectly legal, and since he refuses to reveal the name of the guy who assaulted him, there is nothing to do there. He's meeting with Constable Barnes. I had to insist on a police report." Father Selwyn placed a final apple into the full basket and took it from Sister Agatha. They started back toward the Abbey, walking slowly, Bartimaeus trailing behind. The bright sky and birdsong seemed horribly out of place, considering everything.

"What's to happen now?"

"Gavin's parents are coming in from Manchester. They are going to pay off the loans — possibly even the illegal one — and then take Gavin home with them. His career as a priest is most likely over."

"Even if he successfully recovers?"

"Well, I suppose he could reenter discernment for ordination at a much later date. But stewardship of church funds is paramount for anyone in the priesthood. Would you feel comfortable hiring someone as your parish priest if he had a record of gambling and illegally obtaining money?"

"Father . . ." Sister Agatha stopped walking and stood looking at her friend. "When did the silver communion set disappear from St. Anselm's?"

Father Selwyn stopped short. "Two weeks ago." He closed his eyes. *Gavin.*

"Where is he?"

"The rectory. Packing."

"We need to talk with him. And I'd check his luggage before he leaves, if I were you."

"Gavin, take a break for a moment and talk with Sister and me."

Father Selwyn stood outside Gavin's bedroom door. He stepped back, and Gavin came out, wearing a stained sweatshirt and jeans. Sister Agatha, who had followed Father Selwyn down the hall to the deacon's quarters at the old rectory, thought Gavin looked about as miserable as any human being could look. His face was bruised and cut; he moved stiffly, probably due to his three broken ribs. He looked as if he hadn't showered or shaved in a few days. "Come down to my study and rest for a moment. We want to ask you some questions."

"I need to keep packing," he said. "My parents are on their way. And I want to get out of here."

Sister Agatha was a little surprised to hear the edge in his voice. He presented as vulnerable and pathetic. He had lost everything he had worked for, and so the anger seemed out of place. But then, maybe a tinge of anger was not entirely unexpected.

"Come on," Father Selwyn said, placing a hand on Gavin's shoulder. "You'll have time to pack. Aren't they coming tomorrow?"

"They said they might leave earlier."

"This won't take long. Sister has some questions for you. And I would like to clear up a few things myself."

They settled into Father Selwyn's cluttered study. The mullioned windows looked out over the valley, and, from where she was sitting, Sister Agatha could see the tip of the Gwenafwy chapel spire. Gavin slouched into the overstuffed chair and stared at the carpet. The three sat in silence for a moment. Sister Agatha wanted to wait Gavin out and see where he would start the conversation. Finally, he sat up. "What do you want?"

"What was your relationship with Jacob like?" Sister Agatha asked.

"Jacob? Nothing. I don't know. Why?"

"Did you guys get along?"

Gavin stared back out the window. "Not really," he said, looking at Father Selwyn, then Sister Agatha. "Look, I know the guy is dead and all, but he could be a pain in the you-know-what. He was always on me for something. And let's face it — he was the sexton. He wasn't my boss. I'm a deacon. That means I'm farther up the food chain than him, right?"

Father Selwyn's eyebrows shot up, but he said nothing.

"What do you mean, he was always on you? About what?" Sister Agatha said.

"Like always busting my chops for something or other. Sorry, Father. But he was. Always complaining that I didn't make the youth group clean up after their meetings. Or I left the rectory kitchen a mess. Like a dish in the sink is a crime." Gavin looked back at Father Selwyn. "Tell her."

Father Selwyn nodded. "Jacob took great pride in keeping the rectory and church looking its best. Sometimes his sense of the particular was a bit . . . shall we say . . . over the top."

"He was the same at the Abbey," she said. "Always fussing about. Of course, we're nuns. Compulsive cleaning works for us." She smiled, remembering Jacob's careful attention to detail. "OK. He got on you about keeping things neat. What else?"

"Nothing else. I didn't have anything to do with him, really."

"Do you know how the silver communion set ended up at the Abbey?"

"What? No. Why would I know?"

Sister Agatha reached into her pocket and pulled out the Megaserv receipts. She handed them to Gavin. "Are these yours?"

He glanced at the receipt. "Maybe. I go there. But so do a lot of people."

"They were found in the bag with the stolen silver."

Gavin snorted. But, for one moment, Sister Agatha thought his disinterested demeanor wavered. "And?" he said pulling out his cell phone and tapping the screen. "My parents are texting me. I need to answer them."

"And you eat chocolate Yorkies and drink orange Tango." Even Sister Agatha had to admit it sounded lame.

"I didn't know that was a crime."

Sister Agatha paused. "How do you think Jacob died?"

"Why're you asking me? Those shelves fell on him." Gavin glanced at Father Selwyn. "Right?" Father Selwyn nodded, not taking his eyes off Gavin.

"Do you have any idea why he was in the aging room at five AM on Monday — when he was logged in to work Saint Anselm?"

Gavin sighed and leaned his head back on the chair, his eyes closed. "I don't know, Sister. I have no idea why or how Jacob ended up at the Abbey that morning."

"Where were you the morning Jacob died?"

Gavin opened his eyes and sat up. "Seriously?" He looked at Father Selwyn and then back at Sister Agatha. "I make a couple of bad choices, and now you think I killed someone?"

Father Selwyn leaned forward. "First of all, you didn't make *a couple of bad choices*. You made a series of dangerous, out-of-control choices — not the least of which were gambling and then deceiving all us — me, your friends in the GA group, your ordination committee, the parish. I understand the slippery slope of addiction, but your anger right now is puzzling me. You have hit rock bottom. You have nothing about which to be arrogant. Those of us who have nurtured and loved you through your time here as a deacon still love you and will do what we can to continue to help you. But seriously — *lose the attitude.*" Father Selwyn paused as Gavin stared at the square of carpet between them and added more quietly, "No one has said that you killed Jacob. But it is not inappropriate for us to ask your whereabouts. Frankly, you should be happy that it is Sister here and not Constable Barnes."

"Sorry," Gavin said. For the first time, Sister Agatha felt sorry for him. "I was here at the rectory that night."

"Is there any way that you can prove it?" Sister Agatha asked.

"I was on my laptop."

"Talking with someone?"

"No."

"What were you doing?" Father Selwyn said.

"I was on NetBet. Playing Zeus III."

Gavin's voice was so quiet Sister had to lean forward. "You were what?"

"Zeus III. It's a gaming site. Like an online casino."

Father Selwyn blew out his breath. "*Holy Mother.* With what money? I thought you were tapped out."

Sister Agatha watched as Gavin tossed his phone down and buried his head in his hands, long slender fingers entwined through his oily hair. Sister noticed that his fingernails were broken and dirty. "I had a credit card."

"Your card?"

Gavin didn't move or speak.

"Tell me that you didn't steal the church credit card." Father Selwyn leaned forward, staring at Gavin.

The sobs that choked out of Gavin nearly broke Sister Agatha's heart. "I took the one in the vestry. You know, the one for candles and shit. No one ever uses it. I'll pay it off as soon as I hit a lucky streak."

"Mam sanctaidd fair." *Holy Mother of God.* Father Selwyn pulled his chair up so that it was only inches from the sobbing young man. He took both of Gavin's hands and held them tight. Sister Agatha sat without moving, barely breathing. She began to pray silently. After a few moments, Father Selwyn stood and made Gavin stand with him. He pulled him into his arms and held him as the boy sobbed. He looked over Gavin's shoulder. "Let's check his computer and his phone and see if you can figure out where he was every minute up to Jacob's death."

TWENTY-NINE

"NetBet has a good system, I must say, if you want to track someone's gaming," Sister Agatha said. She took a seat at Father Selwyn's desk and clicked through her phone. Sister Agatha had gone to the Abbey for evening prayer and then returned. Reverend Mother had given her the keys to the minivan, and she stepped into the sanctuary just as Father Selwyn finished the Evensong service at St. Anselm's. In the meantime, she had downloaded the NetBet app and added her credit card. She was a little stunned at how easy it was to use one's phone to gamble. Father Selwyn stood staring out the window. Gavin's parents had arrived unexpectedly — a day early — and gathered up their son and left for the train station.

"It looks like he only stopped when he maxed out the church credit card, and he didn't have any money left. I just called the company. I can't believe I let that card sit in an unlocked drawer in the vestry. It was only used occasionally by the Chancel Arts Committee." Father Selwyn shook his head. "I'll have to answer to the parish council on that one. Who knew my star deacon would steal from the church office?"

She and Father Selwyn sat looking at each other. They sat in silence as the bell in the clock tower chimed. "I have Reverend Mother's phone." Sister Agatha took Reverend Mother's cell phone out of her pocket and read aloud.

> Jacob, thermostat malfunctioning. Thought you fixed it. Aging room near 100 degrees. All the cheese will be ruined. Pls come.

"That text was sent from Reverend Mother's phone? But how do you know Gavin sent it?"

"I don't know for sure, but I think he stole the phone. Her phone disappeared the day that the confirmands were at the Abbey. With Gavin. We've all been looking for it ever since. She didn't have the phone the night of Jacob's death. But I think Gavin did." The two friends sat in silence for a few minutes. "I need to question him."

"Too late. His parents came and took him.

I tried to get them to stay, but they were determined to get on the six twenty to Manchester." Father Selwyn opened his bottle of Penderyn malt and poured each of them a tumbler full. "I should be calling the constable, shouldn't I? It's just that I can't imagine why Gavin would kill Jacob."

"What if Jacob had some sort of information on Gavin — that Gavin didn't want him to know?"

"That seems like a stretch. Although, I must say, Gavin is in a desperate place in terms of addiction. And addiction can drive good people to terrible things."

"I think Gavin stole the silver set, and Jacob saw him. And he stole it to sell to pay off the loans." She watched as Father Selwyn blew out a long breath and closed his eyes. He leaned against the back of the sofa. Sitting up suddenly, he looked at her. "Dear God. You're right."

Sister Agatha didn't say anything. Everything was falling into place, but it wasn't the satisfied feeling she had thought she would have — that all the detectives in her favorite books had when they figured out the murderer. All she felt was sad. Sad for Gavin and his parents. Sad for Jacob and Alice and Michael. Sad for Father Selwyn.

There was one last thing she needed to check. "Do you mind if I search his room?"

Gavin's room was a disaster of books, electronic devices, and dirty clothes. His parents had wanted him out of Pryderi as fast as possible and had told Father Selwyn they would come back to get the rest of his stuff in a few days. The black toolbox sat in the corner, a pair of jeans tossed over it. Father Selwyn kicked the jeans off, picked the toolbox up, and placed it on the top of Gavin's desk. Then he stopped and looked at Sister Agatha. "Honestly, Sister. I really don't want to know." He watched while she opened it. The eight-piece spanner set was on top in a clear plastic carrier. Each individual spanner sitting in its appropriate slot. The slots for the two largest spanners were empty. It was the final piece of the puzzle. Taking out her cell phone, she took a quick photo.

Father Selwyn hit his brakes, skidding to a stop at a crosswalk. Sister Agatha clutched the dashboard. "That text was sent at four thirteen Monday morning. I think Gavin sent the text and then threw the phone in a ditch. He had no idea Sister Matilda would be classifying the plants."

"Classifying plants?" He turned and looked at her, eyebrows raised.

"Eyes on the road, Father. I'll explain later."

"Are you saying that you think he loosened the bolts of the shelves, lured Jacob in, and then what?" Father Selwyn skidded to a stop at a red light.

"I don't know exactly, but I'm guessing he hid at the open window and then, when Jacob was standing with his back to the shelves — probably looking at the thermostat — shoved the shelving unit down on him. He stashed the silver and the tools in the canning cupboard, thinking no one would ever look in there, and he could come back later. He probably started for home when he realized he still had the phone in his hand. So, it went out the window."

"What about Jacob's phone?"

"I don't know. Maybe he kept it or forgot to toss it."

"He said he was gambling all night."

"He could have taken a break — while still signed into the site — for forty minutes. Just long enough to commit murder." Sister Agatha grabbed the dash as Father Selwyn turned sharply and screeched into a parking lot of the train station.

"Five minutes to spare," he said, unbuckling his seat belt and throwing open the door.

They ran inside and stopped short. The place was empty except for a middle-aged couple standing in the center of the small lobby. The woman was openly weeping, and the man stood motionless with his arms at his sides, looking as lost as anyone Sister Agatha had ever seen. "Father," he said. "You're here. I just called you. Your secretary said he didn't know where you were."

"We need Gavin," Father Selwyn said, looking around.

"He's gone."

"What do you mean, *gone*?"

"He excused himself to the men's room. And when he didn't come out, I went back. He must have climbed out the window." The man took a deep breath. "And Father," he said. "I believe Gavin's stolen my wallet."

Constable Barnes closed his notebook and looked hard at Sister Agatha. "That's a lot of new evidence to be keeping to yourself." Sister Agatha, Father Selwyn, and Gavin's parents sat crowded in the small office off the waiting room of the train station.

"I realize that, but it all came to light in the last few hours, Constable. Although, if you will recall, I have always said there was a bit more to this case than a tragic accident."

The constable took in a deep breath and leaned forward, elbows on the desk. "All right then. We've got two officers searching the rectory; I have an officer here at the train station. The boy is on foot and has limited funds." It turned out that Gavin's dad had had less than a tenner in his wallet and the one credit card he owned was in his wife's purse. For emergencies, she had said. *If only their sense of caution had worn off on their son.* "I don't think he's going far. If anyone sees him or if he makes contact, call the station immediately." The constable leaned back. "I say that we sit tight and see what unfolds." He turned to Gavin's parents and said in a kind voice, "I know you're worried about your boy. I assure you we will do everything we can to see that he is safe. In the meantime, I will ask that you not leave the village."

"They're staying with me at the Rectory," Father Selwyn said, turning to Gavin's parents. "You'll be comfortable there and on hand when we find Gavin."

"Is my son considered a . . . a fugitive?" Gavin's mother sounded as if she could barely say the words.

"No, madam. Not a fugitive." The constable shot a glance at Sister Agatha. "That would only be if he had been arrested."

"But you're going to arrest him, aren't you?" The pain in Mrs. Yarborough's voice was almost more than Sister Agatha could bear. She reached over and took her hand.

The constable hesitated just a moment too long to sound convincing. "No," he said. "Well, to put it better, young Gavin is only a suspect in a questionable death, and we want to bring him in for questioning. There is no reason to think — quite yet — that we will need to arrest him."

"But you'll be careful with him, won't you, officer? When you find him?" She looked from the constable to Father Selwyn. "He's a good boy. He really is. Isn't he, Father?"

Father Selwyn smiled at her. "Indeed," he said. "Indeed, he is." But Father Selwyn's strained voice gave him away. No one was sure anymore about Gavin.

"Sister, did you see this?" Reverend Mother said. She slid a newspaper clipping across the kitchen table to Sister Agatha as she sat down with her tea. Sister Agatha had just finished filling in Reverend Mother on the events of the evening, the missing cell phone, and the message. It had been a long, grueling day, yet she was wide awake, pent up with competing emotions. The only light still on at the Abbey was in the kitchen, where she was comforted to see Reverend Mother sitting at the farmhouse table — a mountain of insurance documents, last week's *Church Times,* and a printout of *Your Guide to College Basketball* spread in front of her. A cup of Glengettie steamed next to her, and the kettle was on. It looked as if she was settling in for a long night.

Sister Agatha picked up the newspaper clipping and squinted at it. She felt almost too tired to read.

"It's from last week's *Parish Press.* I just saw it."

Sister Agatha read aloud:

> The Rt. Reverend Suzanne Bainton, Bishop of St. Asaph, officiated at the welcoming ceremony for the new vicar for Llanasa and Ffynnongroyw, near Holywell in Flintshire. Reverend Gwyneth Winpoole was installed as vicar during evening worship in Ffynnongroyw on August 30th led by the Bishop of St. Asaph, the Rt. Reverend Suzanne Bainton. The festivities were part of an all-weekend retreat led by Reverend Suzanne Bainton at the Flintshire Retreat Center. The retreat con-

cluded with a spirit-filled liturgy of welcome to the new vicar during early mass the next morning.

Sister Agatha looked up. "What day was this?" she said, flipping the page over and then back again.

"Sunday, August thirty-first. The photo was taken the evening before Jacob died."

"So, if the retreat that the bishop attended had a 'spirit-filled' service Monday morning, then the bishop was in Flintshire when Jacob died." Sister Agatha sat heavily into a chair. Bishop Suzanne Bainton was off the suspect list.

"Look a little more closely at the photo."

Sister Agatha stared at the photo. *Halwyn Griffiths.* Photographed at the new-vicar reception. Sister Agatha shook her head. "Flintshire is seventy-five miles north of Pryderi. It's a perfect alibi for him. Almost too perfect. Why would a contractor be at a retreat led by the bishop?"

"No idea," Reverend Mother said, pouring another cup of tea. "But unless the two of them can teleport, neither one killed Jacob."

Thirty

Sister Agatha listened as the bell in the village clock tower chimed twelve times. Midnight. Sitting up, she turned on the light next to her bed and looked at the orchid-blue notebook sitting on the bedside table. Beautiful when she had first ordered it from Smythson's in London, the exquisite and expensive notebook was now a bit worse for wear, its cover creased and corners bent from being stashed in her apron pocket or tossed across the table in her booth at The Buttered Crust or crammed into the hymn rack in her pew in the chapel. Cup rings stained many of its cream-colored pages, and dirt smudged its gilt edges from its being dropped in Sister Matilda's herb garden and not found until the next day.

The title, written in all caps with a black Sharpie on the front cover, however, was as clear as ever. *MURDER.* It stared up at her.

She hated to admit it, but the evidence

against Gavin was not as solid as she would want — or as solid as Inspector Rupert McFarland would want. And, with the newspaper photo, she had nothing on Halwyn Griffiths or the bishop. Opening her notebook and flipping through the familiar pages, she checked things off as she read. The spanners and crowbar left in the kitchen were suspicious but not definitively linked to Gavin. Two spanners were indeed missing from Gavin's toolbox, but who could say they were the same ones found stashed in the canning cupboard or the ones that must have been used to loosen the bolts of the shelving unit in the aging room?

She sat back, leaning against the headboard of her bed, and looked out the window. The simple white curtains fluttered in the slight breeze, and the night was dark as pitch. She wondered where Gavin was. Had he found shelter? Was he safe? She shook her head and said a quick prayer.

She turned back to the notebook. Yes, Gavin could have stolen the silver set to sell to pay off his debt, but it had turned up at the Abbey, not a pawn shop. The constable had dusted the communion set for fingerprints, and Gavin's prints were all over it; but then so were Father Selwyn's and Bevan's.

She sighed. She wished she had grabbed a few of those gingersnaps she had seen in the kitchen. She and Reverend Mother had sat talking for an hour or so and then turned off the lights and gone to their rooms, stopping in the chapel for a moment of prayer for Gavin and his parents. She turned back to her notebook again.

There was the text message on Reverend Mother's phone that had been sent to Jacob — sent less than an hour before the murder and two days *after* her phone had gone missing, which meant that Reverend Mother couldn't have sent it. This was the text that had lured Jacob to his death. But who had had the phone? Gavin? It had to have been Gavin. Who else? She could imagine Jacob reading the message, biking to the Abbey, going at a run into the aging room, then standing with his back to the wall checking the thermostat. As he stood there, someone outside and next to the open window had reached in and shoved the shelving unit down. Whoever had stolen the phone was intimately connected to Jacob's death. But who? And why? She sighed in exasperation. Not a single piece of hard evidence connected Gavin to the phone. Or anyone else. If only she could find Jacob's cell phone.

Standing up, she snapped the book shut

and tossed it onto the bed. Jacob's cell phone was crucial. Gavin knew that the cell phone could incriminate him, and he would therefore make certain to dispose of it — like most people, he probably didn't realize that anything on a digital device could easily be traced with a proper search warrant. So, if Gavin thought getting rid of the phone would get rid of the evidence, then why hadn't he tossed the stolen phone with Reverend Mother's phone? Or at least hidden it with the tools and silver? Of course, he could have thrown it in a dumpster, but somehow Sister Agatha didn't think so. Dumpsters were easily searched. As Inspector Rupert McFarland was always saying, criminals never realized the difficulty in disposing of physical evidence until it was too late.

She stared out the window. Jacob's ring of keys had also gone missing. Whoever had killed Jacob must have grabbed his phone when they took the sexton's keys. She retraced the whole event in her head as she imagined it: Gavin driving into the Abbey in the early hours of the morning while everyone still slept. Slipping into the aging room, loosening the bolts of the heavy shelving unit. When all was ready, he texted Jacob on Reverend Mother's stolen phone, making Jacob think there was an emergency in the aging room. She pictured Gavin hiding in the lilac bushes outside the window — a window that he had eased open. Waiting until Jacob went into the room, and then pushing, with all his strength, the heavy shelves that stood up against the windows. Then he ran into the aging room and grabbed Jacob's cell phone and keys. Realizing that he needed to hide all the incriminating evidence, he used Jacob's keys to get into the kitchen, where he stashed the communion set, crowbar, and spanner. Too farfetched? Maybe. *Maybe not.*

Sister Agatha paced the small room. Gavin had known that he couldn't be found with the spanner or crowbar in his car, so he hid them in the back of an unused cupboard in the kitchen and, at the same time, hid the silver. In her mind's eye, she saw Gavin standing at the heavy outside door of the kitchen. He had in his hands the silver chalice, the paten, the ciborium, the crowbar, the spanner, two cell phones, and Jacob's keys. He had to then fit the key into the lock and open the kitchen door. The communion set and tools had made it into the cupboard, and one cell phone, Reverend Mother's, had gone into the ditch.

Where was the other phone and where

were the keys? She closed her eyes and saw Gavin clutching all these items, fumbling with the key. She imagined the key sticking, as did all the keys in the old kitchen door. He finally got the lock to turn; the heavy door creaked open. Hands and arms full, he leaned a shoulder into it. One foot stuck in to hold the door open, he pushed and turned around at the same time. As he backed in, the door shut behind him.

A bit of moonlight broke through the clouds and illuminated the edge of the crucifix over Sister Agatha's dressing table. On the same wall was her autographed photo of Louise Penny that a friend had sent her from a mystery writers convention in Quebec. And next to Louise Penny was Sister Agatha's diploma from St. David's: Master of Fine Arts in Creative Writing. *A lot of good it's doing me.* She thought of her mystery novel sitting lifeless in the drawer, and now there was a real murder mystery — coming to life before her very eyes.

She went over it again: Gavin clutching the silver chalice, the paten, the ciborium, the crowbar, the spanner, two cell phones, a set of keys. *He fumbles with the keys, pushes against the heavy the kitchen door, and . . .* She slipped the notebook into her apron pocket, grabbed a flashlight, and, giving a nod to Louise, shut the door behind her. After going down two flights of stairs and into the kitchen, she stopped to grab an empty plastic bag, a quick sip of cold tea, and a gingersnap.

Then, heading out the side door of the kitchen — the same door that Gavin would have used — she crouched down and shone the flashlight under the rhododendron bush next to the door. One zucchini, a ball of yarn — and a cell phone. Getting down on her hands and knees, she nudged the cell phone into the plastic bag. She didn't care so much about the keys. Perhaps they had been tossed into the ditch as well and would never be found. Right now she needed to find a power cord and plug in the cell phone. Grunting a little as she stood up, she brushed off her habit. Climbing under a rhododendron bush just wasn't as easy as it used to be. Using her flashlight, she did a quick examination of the phone without removing it from the bag. She smiled. Progress. *Finally.*

"That's mine. Give it."

THIRTY-ONE

Sister Agatha jumped back, her heart hammering in her chest. Halwyn Griffiths looked as calm and put together as he had in the photograph with the bishop. "Good heavens, you scared me. What are you doing here?" In answer, he stepped around her and pushed a gun into the back of her neck. At the same moment, he jerked the bag out of her hand. "We're taking a walk." He gave her a painful shove with the gun.

She twisted to the side and planted her feet in the gravel. "Walk where?" The Abbey was silent. Where was that police cruiser that was supposed to be sitting and watching for Gavin? Or Reverend Mother and her infernal basketball?

"Move," he said, pushing her forward again.

"What are you doing here?" Stalling for time was something detectives in books always did. Her mind raced. Didn't Kinsey

Millhone generally talk a blue streak when she was grabbed by the bad guy? And what about Stephanie Plum? She was always rattling on. As far as she could remember, Inspector Rupert McFarland had never given any advice on what to do in the event of a gun in one's back.

Halwyn pushed her toward the cheese barn, poking the end of the gun into her shoulder. "Stop talking."

"Seriously, I need to know where we're going." She walked a few steps and planted her feet again.

"Do you always keep talking when you're told to shut up?"

"Having a gun pointed at me makes me want to talk."

"Jesus, you're annoying." This time Halwyn shoved her hard enough that she fell forward and was forced to take a step just to keep from hitting the ground. She took several steps forward and then stopped again, crunching her heels into the gravel. Halwyn shoved her again, and this time she walked about ten feet before halting in the grass in front of the herb garden.

"Do you like small spaces, Sister?"

"Not really, no." Would she die like Jacob? She twisted around and looked him in the eye, getting a terrible jab in her side with the gun. "You killed Jacob, didn't you?"

"No, I did not kill Jacob. Are you seriously writing a murder mystery? Because your detective skills are totally lacking." Holding the gun with one hand, he grabbed her elbow and, wrenching her shoulder, yanked her forward. They stumbled across Sister Gwenydd's rows of basil and oregano and onto the lane that led to the orchard. Sister Agatha noticed that clouds had covered the moon. *You could barely see the gun in front of your face.* At least that's what Stephanie Plum would have said. She whispered a quick prayer.

"You know that old stone shed your moth-eaten pony is so fond of? The one where Gavin put him right before he set the cheese barn on fire?"

"What do you mean?" Sister Agatha had a horrible thought. "What have you done with Gavin?"

He gave a harsh laugh. "Shut up and keep walking. You thought you were so smart, Sister. The big detective." Halwyn's arm dropped, and he held the gun loosely in one hand.

Sister Agatha wondered if his arm was getting tired. Most criminals didn't realize how heavy guns were. Rookie mistake on Halwyn's part, she thought.

"You figured all sorts of people were involved in the downfall of your little Abbey, and all of it had to do with the murder of that sexton. Did you ever think to look right under your nose?" Halwyn raised the gun up to her head again. "Your little church nerd did it."

"So Gavin did kill Jacob?" Sister Agatha said. Despite the gun barrel pressing painfully into the side of her head and her wrenched shoulder, her real pain was the realization that Gavin had truly committed murder. *Gavin.* A murder in cold blood. She felt sick. Stumbling, she fell and went down onto one knee.

Halwyn jerked her up, this time jabbing the gun barrel between her shoulders. "With all your detective work, you actually missed the fact that it was Gavin the whole time?" Halwyn snorted.

"I admit, all the evidence leads to Gavin — the stolen silver set, the spanner, the cell phone. All the facts make you think it was Gavin. It's just that he was . . ." She felt both sick that it was Gavin and a little defensive about her detective skills.

"That he was one of you? One of you church geeks? I haven't noticed that going to church has ever kept anyone on the straight and narrow. Not when it really mattered, anyway." Halwyn gave the gun a fresh shove. "Of course, there's the fact that Gavin seems like he'd pee his pants if he had to kill a butterfly." He stopped and looked around, then shoved Sister Agatha onto a dirt path that led through the meadow. "So I can see why Gavin wasn't your first choice. Jacob saw Gavin steal those silver pieces, and Gavin needed him to be quiet about it. But, like you, Jacob just kept talking. And now, well, now he's dead."

Halwyn stopped and looked at Sister Agatha, moving the gun up against her temple. He grinned. "You need to go back to mystery-writer school or whatever you call it." He stopped again and looked around. "I hired Gavin to sabotage the Abbey. Mostly to rattle you nuns. Gavin knew the Abbey grounds and wouldn't be suspected if he was found hanging around."

"Hired him?"

"Well, pressed him into service." Halwyn grinned again. A sick grin. It gave Sister Agatha a chill. "You see, I met up with Gavin at the payday loan office when he first had trouble making his payment. I own it."

"You're kidding. You own that awful place? It should be shut down. It's horrible."

"Horrible? It's perfectly legal and serves a

population in this community. Just as you nuns help the poor, so do I." He turned and looked back toward the lane. "I didn't lure Gavin into payday loans. He came of his own choosing. But when I saw that my new client was an upstanding member of Saint Anselm and was in a bit of gambling trouble, I decided to put him to work. I dressed him up as your Reverend Mother and made him steal those documents from that ridiculous cheese competition. I held a gun to his head while he used his sweet young voice to cancel your wonderful table at the festival. I taught him how to set fire to a building so that even the fire chief couldn't tell it was arson — of course, he screwed that up, too. Why do you think that pony of yours was carefully moved out of the barn the night it burned? He has a tender heart, our Gavin." He shoved her forward. "Keep walking."

"You threatened him?" Sister felt sick thinking of Gavin in the clutches of this hideous man. She stumbled forward and could see the shadows of the apple shed ahead. It lay just behind the orchard. The night was too dark to make out the rows of gnarled trees already laden with Cadwaladr apples.

"I simply let him know that if he didn't work for me, I would turn him in to the priest for murder. Yeah — he told me about killing Jacob and the loan shark. In a total crybaby fit. Some guys just can't handle a little torture."

Sister Agatha felt sick. "You tortured him?"

"Oh, please. I pulled his hair. People hate that. Threatened to kill his mother. Little stuff. Nothing big." Halwyn shook his head. "Bawled like a girl. I guess it's hard to become a priest in the Church in Wales if you're serving time in Her Majesty's prison."

The apple shed, a small building made of red sandstone, was only a few yards away. Sister Agatha could see a sliver of light under the door. It stayed cool in the summer, so they kept the door open for Bartimaeus on hot days. Sister Agatha hoped he wasn't in the apple shed tonight. A cheerful nicker from inside told her he was. "Why did you want the Abbey's reputation ruined? What did we ever do to you?"

"I wanted to buy it. Even you figured that out."

"And you wanted to buy it at the cheapest price you could and turn it into a spa?"

"I was all set to buy it from the diocese when your bishop started to drag her feet. I don't know why exactly, but something made her think your ridiculous girls' club was worth saving."

Worth saving? That was news to Sister Agatha. But then Halwyn Griffiths wasn't exactly a trustworthy source of news. "So, you sabotaged our cheese sales, burned down the barn, and undermined our belief in Reverend Mother just so you could buy us out?" Sister Agatha was incredulous. "How could you be so evil?"

"Oh, for Christ's sake, Sister. Don't be dramatic. Consider it encouragement to sell. And I had Gavin doing all the dirty work for me. I didn't set the barn on fire. I didn't steal anything. I didn't defame the dear Reverend Mother. Your boy Gavin did. I was in London conducting business."

He kicked open the door and shoved her in. A lantern swung from the single rafter, and in its jagged shadows, she saw Gavin, tied and gagged, sitting on the floor, against a bale of straw. She rushed to him and began to work the gag out of his mouth.

Halwyn strode across the shed in three steps and grabbed Sister Agatha's arm — but not before she had gotten the handkerchief off Gavin's mouth. It had cut into his bruised skin and swollen lips. "Are you all right, Gavin?" she said as Halwyn yanked her to her feet.

"I'm OK," he said, coughing. "Do what he says, Sister. He's not a nice guy."

Sister Agatha couldn't help but think that Gavin wasn't such a nice guy either.

Halwyn shoved her down into the bales of hay and, stepping back, pointed the gun at her. "Stop talking, both of you."

"Whatever you plan to do with us, could you at least turn Bartimaeus out into the pasture? He's old and blind and doesn't deserve any of this." Sister Agatha was amazed at how calm her voice sounded. Bartimaeus stood watching them. Sister Agatha noticed that he didn't look particularly stressed. In fact, he was munching an apple.

"What part of 'Stop talking' don't you understand?" Halwyn walked over to the door and pulled it completely shut so that no light leaked out, although Sister Agatha knew it was hopeless that anyone at the Abbey could even see the stone shed. It sat below a dip in the hill and was several yards off the lane. And, she suddenly realized, the shed was probably soundproof.

"What are you going to do? Kill us and hide the bodies?" Gavin said.

"Good idea, choir boy," he snarled, spinning the cylinder of the gun and then pointing it again at Sister Agatha.

"You don't want to do that," she said. "A double murder. You'll never get away with it."

"Really? Because Gavin here got away with murder."

Gavin turned to Sister Agatha. "I'm sorry, Sister. I am so sorry. Jacob saw me steal the communion set. He was going to turn me in." Gavin's face contorted. "Then I panicked and . . ." Gavin nodded toward Halwyn. "He figured it out and . . . and . . . I'm so sorry, Sister. I can't even tell you. And tell Sister Gwenydd I'm sorry I didn't give her the silver cross back. It was in his car, by the way." Gavin shot his eyes at Halwyn. "I found it. I should have come clean then. I couldn't."

"I know. But you can confess your sin, ask forgiveness . . ." Sister Agatha's voice trailed off. The image of Jacob's mother crying at the funeral came back to her. Then the image of Gavin's devastated parents at the train station. They were losing a son as well. The immense weight of sadness pressed down on Sister Agatha, almost making her forget that a nine-millimeter was pointed at her head. She looked into Gavin's eyes. "God forgives everything," she said in the most confident voice she could. Gavin nodded. She took his hand and squeezed it, and when he pulled away, she let him go.

Halwyn snorted. "You religious types just don't live in the real world, do you? You're all the same. Except that sweet little number in the black dress that calls herself a nun. Not sure just how religious she is."

Sister Agatha would have been furious at anyone talking that way about Sister Gwenydd, but at that moment, her claustrophobia was setting in — the three of them plus Bartimaeus made for a tight fit. She thought Halwyn must have felt the same, because he gave Bartimaeus a slap on the rump and tried to push him to the side. To the pony's credit, he refused to budge.

"Jesus," he said. "Why do you keep this candidate for the glue factory around?"

"Careful where you step," Sister Agatha said.

"What?" He lifted one foot up and then the other, examining his black loafers. She took a furtive glance at the door. Halwyn raised his gun. "Like I said before, Sister, do you like small spaces?"

"No. Why?"

"Well, once I kill you two, I plan to stuff your bodies into that old cistern at the end of the meadow. By the time they find you, all the evidence will have drained away. Literally."

Sister Agatha realized that she had started to shiver. *Dead* was bad enough, but the thought of being shoved into the underground water tank gave her the willies the way a bullet to the head just didn't. Bartimaeus whinnied. He was either getting anxious or he wanted another apple.

"When the sisters of Gwenafwy open the paper tomorrow morning, they will see my picture at the National Museum in Liverpool where I was a guest speaker." For the first time, she noticed that Halwyn was wearing a tuxedo, complete with cummerbund and tie. "I have friends who will vouch for my whereabouts."

"The least you can do is turn the pony out," Sister Agatha said. "Scaring us is one thing, but scaring a defenseless and blind Shetland pony is another."

"Why? So he can run back to the Abbey and alert the nuns? I don't think so." Halwyn opened the door a crack and looked out. Satisfied, he pulled it shut.

"I don't think Bartimaeus is going to relay a message of distress. Who do you think he is, Lassie?" Sister Agatha said. She thought maybe she could distract Halwyn or at least keep talking and then maybe come up with a plan of escape. *What would Stephanie Plum do? Jessica Fletcher? Adam Dagliesh? Ar-*

mand Gamache? None of them came to her rescue. Her mind was a blank.

"I don't care two hoots about the stupid animal," Halwyn said. "Why don't you pray, Sister? Isn't that your fallback? When all else fails?"

"I know you don't want to kill us, Halwyn. Murder is not what you do. You build things. You're an artist. At heart, anyway."

He raised the gun again and pointed it directly at her.

"Put the gun down."

He took a step forward, moving the gun closer to her face.

"Seriously. You do not want to do this."

She heard the click of the hammer as Halwyn cocked the gun. She began to whisper the last words that she had heard at evening prayer that night.

Before the ending of the day,
Creator of the world we pray,
That with thy wonted favor thou
Wouldst be our guard and keeper now.

The sound of the gunshot drowned out Gavin's scream and the pony's terrified squeal.

Thirty-Two

"We've always defended Bartimaeus, telling everyone that he is perfectly friendly and never kicks, but the truth is, he really can kick. Knocked Halwyn Griffiths right off his feet." Sister Agatha shifted the ice pack from the side of her head to her shoulder. "He dropped the gun, and it went off. Fortunately, shooting nothing but that old lantern." She took a long sip of tea. "We've always said no to sugar cubes for Bartimaeus, but I think the time has come." Sister Agatha leaned back on the couch in Reverend Mother's office and looked at the faces of her good friends: Reverend Mother and Father Selwyn, Sister Callwen and Sister Gwenydd, Sister Harriet, Sister Winifred, Sister Matilda. "Good heavens, you people are like sheep caught in the headlights. I'm perfectly fine. Not dead at all."

"I should have known Halwyn Griffiths

was behind all this," Sister Harriet said. "I've never liked the look of that man." She turned to Sister Agatha. "So, Gavin was not only a murderer, but Griffith's henchman — murdering our Jacob, setting fire to the barn, impersonating Reverend Mother, sabotaging the Cheese Festival?"

"I wouldn't call him a henchman as much as a frightened flunky. Halwyn kept him terrified the whole time. Especially after he found out Gavin had killed Jacob," Sister Agatha said.

"Gavin murdered Jacob," Father Selwyn said, shaking his head. "I'm at a loss for words." Gavin's stricken parents had followed the constable to the hospital, and Father Selwyn had promised them that he would be at their son's hearing the next morning.

"Good people can do very bad things. If they are fearful enough," Sister Gwenydd said. "I can imagine that Gavin panicked." The room was silent for a moment, each person remembering that Sister Gwenydd had spent several months thinking she had killed someone and not coming forward about it.

"Gavin seemed like a good person. To the outside observer," Sister Winifred said, breaking the silence and taking Sister Gwenydd's hand in hers. "A bit weak though, I always thought, for a Welshman."

Sister Harriet let out a snort. "Gavin may be a good person gone wrong. Terribly wrong. But Halwyn Griffiths is pure evil. Through and through. To ruin the reputation of the Abbey so it could be sold at the lowest price." She picked up her sketch pad and slashed her charcoal pencil across the page. She flipped the pad around — a very good likeness of Halwyn Griffiths. Wearing horns and waving a pitchfork.

"Sisters, really," Reverend Mother said. "We should be praying for his soul right now, which could be in mortal danger. A pony kick like that could be fatal."

"I don't think you need to worry about Halwyn's soul," Father Selwyn said, glancing at his phone. "Dr. Beese just texted that he is coming out of his coma and talking. He should make a full recovery."

"And live to stand trial!" Sister Callwen said. All eyes turned to her. She had been noticeably quiet, replacing the ice pack twice for Sister Agatha and not leaving her side. "I just hope he doesn't just walk away from this."

"He won't, I assure you," Father Selwyn said. "And I intend to see Gavin through it as well." Father Selwyn sighed. "Even though it will mean visiting him in prison."

The room fell silent again; the only sound was the bell in the village clock tower as it chimed five times. It was five in the morning, and they all felt as if they might never sleep again. After a moment, Sister Agatha opened her notebook and, retrieving a Sharpie from her apron pocket, began making notes.

"You're kidding me," Sister Callwen said, turning to her. "You haven't had enough of murder? You need to keep going with that detective obsession of yours?"

"Just a few loose ends to tie up," Sister Agatha said. She put the notebook down. "Although I must say, I'm not bouncing back like Stephanie Plum, which is a disappointment. She figures out the bad guy, gets shot, her car blows up, and then the next thing you know, she's making out with her boyfriend. I feel more like lying down. Alone."

"Sister. Honestly." Father Selwyn shook his head.

"I do wish you would let us take you to hospital. I don't like the look of that shoulder or the cut on your head." Sister Callwen poured more tea into Sister Agatha's cup.

"Holy Mary," Father Selwyn said, rising

from his chair. "This is not a moment for tea. Haven't you anything stronger, Reverend Mother?" He began to open cabinet doors.

"Top desk drawer," she said, not taking her eyes off Sister Agatha, who sat, seemingly perfectly relaxed, on the sofa, once again writing furiously.

"Nice," he said, opening the drawer and lifting out a bottle. Then he let out a low whistle. "I apologize, Reverend Mother. I had you pegged as a Welsh ale woman. And instead, my favorite — Penderyn single-malt whiskey."

"A last year's Christmas gift from The Rogue Creamery," she said. "I never actually drink it."

"Really? Because it's been opened. And I've never known a bottle in a top desk drawer that went totally neglected."

"Well, maybe a little now and then," she said. "I will remind you that our Lord drank wine. And I've always thought he would have liked Penderyn single-malt."

Father Selwyn located a stack of paper cups in the bottom of a filing cabinet and, filling each one, handed them around solemnly, as if it were the Eucharist. Raising his own paper cup, he said in a clear voice, "Sister Agatha, let us drink to your health.

And, may I say, to your ability to live nine lives." Taking a sip, he closed his eyes. "And to the boys in Penderyn, who know what they are about. Iechyd da!" *Good health.*

"Iechyd da!" the nuns responded.

The rising sun broke across the horizon, and a beam of light hit the stained-glass window. In the midst of the laughter and talking that had begun, Reverend Mother's phone buzzed. Picking it up, she read the text, then looked up, her face ashen. The room fell silent; the laughter broke off. "From the bishop," she said. "Coming here. This evening. She wants to meet with the entire Abbey."

"Why?" Sister Harriet asked.

Reverend Mother stared down at the phone, not speaking.

"You don't think she is coming to . . . ?" Sister Gwenydd couldn't bring herself to say it.

"Close us down?" Sister Agatha said, sitting up, the ice pack sliding off her shoulder onto the couch. "But not now! After all this?"

Reverend Mother laid the phone on the coffee table next to the bottle of whiskey. "I believe that is indeed why she's coming. To close the Abbey. It may very well be that HG Construction is no longer in operation.

But that doesn't change the fact that the diocese wanted to close us." She looked directly at Father Selwyn. "It's over, isn't it?"

"It's never over," he said quietly. "Until the last prayer is said, the last hymn is sung, and the last bit of love given." He leaned forward and poured more whiskey into her paper cup.

Thirty-Three

Sister Callwen was not in her usual pew. Reverend Mother had wanted to talk with her sisters alone before the bishop arrived, and she had asked that they gather in the chapel. She watched as each woman knelt and then slid into a pew. Several held hands; a few wept. One or two looked angry. They were all there. Except Sister Callwen.

Reverend Mother stood back in the darkness of the doorway behind the pulpit that led into the vestry — a small room where the nuns kept the altar cloths, vestments, communion trays, silk flowers, and candles. Reverend Mother had always liked the vestry with its smell of incense and candle wax. She breathed deeply, closing her eyes for a moment, and then opening them, looking out on the pews. She could see the sisters of Gwenafwy, but they couldn't see her. Truthfully, she had never felt more like hiding. The community was reeling from the news this morning that Halwyn Griffiths had masterminded all the strange events at the Abbey, and that Gavin, everyone's favorite young deacon, had killed Jacob. It all felt like too much to take in, and now the bishop was about to arrive — most likely with the news that Gwenafwy Abbey was to close forever.

She looked out at the women she had lived and worked and prayed with day in and day out for all these many years. She wanted to hold this moment and memorize it, inscribe it on her heart and in her head. Memorize forever exactly where each nun sat in her favorite pew, memorize forever how the light filtered in through the west window and warmed the flagstones. She knew she needed to step up to the pulpit, to come out of the shadows and speak to her sisters, but she couldn't seem to move. But she had to. Finally, taking a deep breath, she forced herself to leave the darkened vestry and step into the pulpit. Looking out and about to speak, she saw the door at the back of the chapel open. Suzanne Bainton slipped in and, after a moment's hesitation, took a seat in the back pew. "Come forward, Bishop," Reverend Mother said. "I didn't expect you for another hour. I had hoped to talk with my sisters first, but perhaps it is best that you are here from the start."

A decided murmur arose as the bishop walked forward and sat in the front. Reverend Mother was certain Sister Agatha uttered something that included the words "snake in the grass." Taking a deep breath, Reverend Mother began. "As you all know, we have been tasked with increasing our membership, stabilizing our finances, and bringing our mission to the world into a more . . . contemporary realm." This time, Sister Agatha was clearly heard making a snorting noise.

"Yes, Sister Agatha, I know." Reverend Mother looked at her old friend and felt tears in the corners of her eyes. She had spent the afternoon walking the meadows outside the Abbey, praying that she could somehow ease them all through this final crisis. "We have done our best, with the help of God, to turn things around here. But it just wasn't enough. The death of Jacob, the barn roof catching fire, the loss of cheese sales. It was all too much, my dear sisters."

She took a breath and, willing herself not to cry, looked around again for Sister Callwen. As one of her senior nuns and her good friend, Sister Callwen had been her port in every storm. Reverend Mother fought the growing realization that Sister Callwen might have given up on the Abbey. There had been her strange behavior — disappearing from meetings, going off alone with her iPad — and her lack of enthusiasm right from the start about anything the nuns tried to do to save things, to turn things around. Had Sister Callwen moved on already, planning the next abbey she would live in, the next big thing in her life?

Wounded by her friend's absence, Reverend Mother could barely speak. "Sisters," she began again, struggling to say the words. "We do not know where God is leading us next. We do know that God has a plan and that He has never abandoned us, nor will He." The heaviness in the room was overwhelming — the quiet sobs of Sister Matilda in the back, the resigned look on Sister Harriet's face. Perhaps the saddest countenance in the room was Sister Gwenydd's. New to thinking she had her life back, she was now losing almost the only family she had ever known. "Sisters, we have given it all. Now it is time to say . . ."

Reverend Mother could not bring herself to say it. To say that the Abbey was to be closed, that it was no longer the vibrant community of faith it had been for decades? And worse, that it had closed on her watch? She tried to speak, but her throat was too tight, and the tears that she had willed back were about to pour forth.

The back door to the chapel opened. Sister Callwen stepped in, her iPad open in front of her. She appeared to be Skyping. The entire community followed Reverend Mother's gaze and watched as Sister Callwen, still focused on the screen of the iPad, walked to the front of the chapel. As she walked, they could see a face on the screen, and it was talking.

Sister Callwen and Reverend Mother looked at each other. It was a look that passed through decades of understanding. "Please," Reverend Mother said, moving away from the pulpit. Sister Callwen stepped up and, placing her iPad on top, turned it around so that it faced the pews. "First,' " she said, looking out at her sisters. "I must apologize to Reverend Mother for not telling her all about this right away." Sister Callwen looked at Reverend Mother for a long moment. Reverend Mother held her gaze and then nodded. "OK, then," Sister Callwen said. "Let me introduce all of you to Sister Bernice Bolton, prioress of the Order of Saint Helena in Los Angeles. You know, the United States."

In a daze, the nuns leaned forward and stared at the screen. "Sister Bolton," Sister

Callwen said. "Meet the sisters of Gwenafwy Abbey."

Thirty-Four

"And so, that settles it," Reverend Mother said. None of the nuns had gone to bed after the Skype meeting with Prioress Bolton; instead, they had gathered in the Abbey kitchen, drinking tea, which they soon traded out for celebratory glasses of wine. At midnight, Sister Gwenydd had started cooking, and as the bell in the village clock tower chimed three times, the sisters had sat down to a meal of lamb stew — without sage — followed by a warm *bara brith* straight from the oven.

Ten nuns from the Order of St. Helena in Los Angeles were coming to Gwenafwy Abbey. These young women desired a more traditional approach to a religious order than they had found at their own convent — they wanted to wear habits, participate in the celebration of Hours, serve the poor. They had learned about Gwenafwy Abbey while ordering cheese online. And the Welsh

Abbey seemed to have the lifestyle and commitment they longed for. The nuns had called the Abbey office, and Sister Callwen had just happened to be the one to pick up the phone. This began a long process of discernment, which had ended in last night's Skype.

Sister Callwen apologized all around that she had kept the meetings with the American convent secret, but she hadn't wanted to raise false hopes. It wasn't until the very last day, when all the final agreements had been decided upon, that she had felt she could let her sisters in on her endeavors.

But the biggest surprise of the evening had come when the bishop had stepped up to the pulpit after all the sisters had had a chance to Skype with the American nuns. She welcomed the new sisters to the Church in Wales and then turned to the sisters of Gwenafwy. Like the rest of the Abbey, Sister Agatha sat on the edge of her pew. How would Suzanne Bainton ever manage to clear her name and regain the trust of the Abbey? She did it the only possible way — at least to Sister Agatha's way of thinking. *The Right Reverend Suzanne Bainton admitted she had been wrong.* And asked forgiveness. Which was exactly what Inspector Rupert McFarland would have done, Sister

Agatha thought. As he had once said in his podcast "Foibles and Failures: No Detective Is Perfect," "The good detective is always ready to say when he or she is wrong. There is nothing learned or gained by imagining that you are perfect." The bishop had also explained that she had had no knowledge of Halwyn's involvement in Jacob's murder. Sister Agatha believed her. The bishop might be a bit too interested in appearances and money, but that didn't make her an accomplice to murder.

Sister Agatha locked eyes with Sister Callwen, and they smiled at each other. All of Sister Callwen's secret meetings and cryptic phone calls had been related to getting the new nuns to the Abbey. Sister Agatha wished Sister Callwen had seen her way to bringing her up to speed, but she hadn't, and that was OK. Sometimes you just had to let people be who they were.

"You know," Reverend Mother had said to the iPad screen when she got her own chance to Skype with the sisters in Los Angeles, "Gwenafwy may be an active abbey in need of new and young nuns, but we are very nearly at the breaking point — financially, that is. We want you, but you may not want us." Then the biggest news of all had been revealed. Sister Callwen explained that not only were ten young nuns coming from America, but they were bringing their funding with them. In other words, their convent was sending them with seed money — a substantial endowment that would be invested and given to Gwenafwy over the next ten years.

"A convent saved," Sister Agatha said, finishing off the last bit of lamb stew. Her eyes strayed to the center of the table, where she had tossed her orchid-blue slimline notebook and Sharpie. "And a murder solved!"

ACKNOWLEDGMENTS

I would like to thank my agent, Stephany Evans, who called me at 4:20 on the afternoon of Maundy Thursday to tell me she had finished reading my manuscript and wanted to be my agent — making it the best Holy Week I had ever known.

Many thanks to my publisher, Crooked Lane Books, for sending me such awesome editors, for caring so much for the quality of the finished product, and most of all, for their enthusiasm for Sister Agatha and all her friends. To my editor, Anne Brewer, for her painstaking and astute edits — all of which helped me to make this the book I aspired to write. To the copyeditor I know only as ***rsbk***, which I am pretty sure stands for something like Really-Smart-Brilliant-all Knowledgeable because her attention to detail was both sensitive and relentless. To Jenny Chen, editorial assistant, for her prompt and cheerful response to all my questions. And to Teresa Fasolino, whose compelling cover art captured so perfectly the world of Gwenafwy Abbey.

I would like to express my gratitude to the Collegeville Institute and to the Lilly Endowment for their financial support of the Collegeville writing programs and to the Massachusetts Conference of the United Church of Christ for the encouragement it offers to members of the clergy to attend Collegeville. I especially want to thank all the writing coaches who make Collegeville so amazing: Mary Nilsen, for teaching me the power of a good verb as well as talking to me as if I were a real writer and helping me to become one; Michael McGregor, for his insightful coaching and spot-on suggestions; Maren Tirabassi, for her shrewd editing and timely encouragement, such as when she said to me, "So? Where is it?"

I would like to express my gratitude to my friend Larry Spongberg for his help in shaping Sister Agatha into a believable Abbey librarian. To Robyn Thomas, for all things artistic, and to Chris Isherwood, for many things Welsh and to whom the village of Pryderi owes its name.

Thanks also to Jerry Goddard, a good friend in writing and in life.

To Dr. Anne Nafziger, for her expert

advice concerning how a corpse might look, how a heart attack happens, and which poison might kill the most efficiently. And, more than anything, for her nearly daily inquiry in my morning email: "How is the writing going?"

Endless thanks to Barbara Melosh, my talented work-ethic-that-never-quits Lutheran writing partner and colleague in ministry. Our Monday afternoon writing exchanges moved this book forward, kept me energized, and made me a better writer — dangling participles and all.

To Jane Gardner, a gifted writer and true friend, who was there from the very first sentence to the day I called her shrieking that I had an agent. Always at the ready with encouragement, kudos, commiseration, and undying interest, Jane is the friend that everyone needs to bring a first novel to completion. Actually, she is the friend that everyone just needs.

And to my husband, Don, who inspired me, brought me coffee, explored Wales with me, and never once stopped believing in me as a writer.

ABOUT THE AUTHOR

Jane Willan wants to live in a world where everyone has time to read their favorite books, drink good coffee and walk their dog on the beach, but until that can happen, she enjoys life as a pastor and writer. When she's not working on a sermon, or hiking with her husband, Don, you can find her re-reading Jane Eyre, binge-watching Downton Abbey and trying out new ways to avoid exercise. This is her first Sister Agatha and Father Selwyn mystery.

The employees of Thorndike Press hope you have enjoyed this Large Print book. All our Thorndike, Wheeler, and Kennebec Large Print titles are designed for easy reading, and all our books are made to last. Other Thorndike Press Large Print books are available at your library, through selected bookstores, or directly from us.

For information about titles, please call:
(800) 223-1244

or visit our website at:
gale.com/thorndike

To share your comments, please write:

Publisher
Thorndike Press
10 Water St., Suite 310
Waterville, ME 04901